# The Angry Puppet Syndrome

# The Angry Puppet Syndrome

John Menkes

Demos

Demos Medical Publishing, Inc., 386 Park Avenue South, New York, New York 10016

**Library of Congress Cataloging-in-Publication Data**

Menkes, John H., 1928–
    The angry puppet syndrome / John H. Menkes.
      p.  cm.
    ISBN 1–888799–27–7
    I. Title.
    PS3563.E527A8   1999
    813′.54—dc21                 99–23055
                                   CIP

**Made in Canada**

# To My Dearest Friend

# Acknowledgments

Sincere thanks for assisting me with the final form of this book go to Dr. Allan J. Tobin and Ms. Margaret Power. Dr. Tobin is Professor of Biology at the University of California at Los Angeles and Head of the UCLA Brain Research Institute. He is one of the world's outstanding neurobiologists. Ms. Power is a prominent Chicago attorney and a member of the law firm of Corboy and Demetrio. Neither Allan nor Margaret is responsible for the plot of the book but made certain that I avoided some of the more obvious inaccuracies.

My thanks also go to Ms. Barbara Loe Fisher, who encouraged me at all stages of my work on this novel.

*Syndrome: A concurrence of several symptoms in a disease*

O.E.D.

# PROLOGUE
# CASE 1
# A.B.

$\mathbf{A}$s Sue Barton was driving home from the January meeting of her book club, she realized that there was something seriously wrong with her husband. This was not another of the many mild depressions and neuroses through which she had nursed him in the course of their twenty-eight years of marriage. This was quite a different matter, something unfamiliar and frightening.

She stopped at a light and looked at her hands as they curled around the wheel: nicely shaped, well-manicured with clear nail polish, and with none of the blemishes that one might expect on a 51-year-old woman. She used to tell her friends that she knew her husband like the back of her hand. That was no longer true; in the course of the last two to three months he had become a stranger to her, and it was high time she found out what was going on with him. She glanced at herself in the rear view mirror, adjusted her sunglasses, and when the light changed made a left turn and drove into the hills.

That evening when Arnold came home from his office, Sue had everything ready for him in the garden: shrimp cocktails, crackers, and a chilled bottle of white wine.

"Let's talk," she said, and steered him to a wicker chair. He smiled and sat down.

There is something wrong with his smile, Sue thought. It had a darkness to it that concerned her; it seemed to be directed inward and downward like the glimmering surface of a deep well. All at once she recalled a recent photo in the newspaper. It was that of a serial killer being arraigned in court. Flanked by sheriff and deputies, the man was smiling. The same smile: weak, yet sinister. She shook off her thought: all nonsense. Aside from Arnold's recurrent depressions, they had managed to have a good marriage. Their daughter was in New York in the advertising business, a son in Saudi Arabia working with an oil company. By dint of hard work and a good head, Arnold had climbed the corporate ladder, and last October had been appointed Managing Director at South West General Electric. It was a much sought after position and gave him a seat on the Board of Trustees. He had been depressed after the promotion came through. Not much of a depression, just a letdown. That is how Dr. Beringer had explained it to them when they had gone to see him.

"You won't let yourself enjoy your success. You are afraid of being envied."

Sue had agreed with him. Most people were envious of them. But now?

"So, how was your day?" Her voice was controlled, and she managed to hide her concern. He shrugged and returned her smile.

"Tell me, Arnie, is something bothering you?"

"Of course not."

"Are you sure?" It was growing dark. A faint wind blew through the hydrangeas and ruffled her hair. She retrieved a few strands and tucked them behind her ears.

"What are you doing with your hands?" His voice was sudden and harsh and hissed like gas escaping under pressure. It was as if a different man sat in the wicker chair across from her.

"Can't you tell? I was adjusting my hair."

"Are you sure?"

"Of course I am. Would you like some shrimp?"

He nodded and took the plate. His hand stopped in midair, and he looked at the shrimp and the pad of red sauce as if he had difficulty comprehending them.

"I worry about you," Sue said.

"You worry about me?" The harsh voice again, unexpectedly belligerent, then the smile. "I can't imagine why. I have never felt better."

"I would like you to go back to Dr. Beringer."

"I don't see the slightest reason why I should take off work to see a psychiatrist."

"Please."

"You know what it would do to my career if anyone finds out."

"No one is going to find out."

"I am not going."

"Please. I am asking you."

"I don't care to."

"Why not? You went to see him in October when you were depressed."

"I was not depressed; I simply felt a letdown after I got my promotion. And I am not depressed right now."

That was true. If he had been, Sue would have known and would not have been quite as concerned.

"I'll come with you."

Arnold took a shrimp, dipped it into the sauce, and, with his mouth full, nodded.

"All right. If that's what you want from me." A sudden about-face was quite unlike him. Arnold had never been the kind of man who was easily persuaded. A stubborn Irishman, that was how Sue's family had labeled him. He swallowed three more shrimp in an automatic manner and washed them down with a bit of wine. He had never been much of a drinker.

"Why don't you have the last two?" She refilled her husband's plate and with a spoon added a fresh dollop of cocktail sauce.

"I don't want any more."

"Come on . . . we can sit here and watch it get dark. It's such a lovely time of day."

"Lovely! What a petty, stupid thing to say!"

"What do you mean?"

"You know goddamned well what I mean."

"Please, Arnold!"

"Don't 'please Arnold' me. I can't stand your shit." He jumped up and with an explosive movement picked up the small table and threw it at his wife. Plates shattered and the cocktail sauce splattered over Sue's gray slacks and ran down the legs like freshly shed blood. Arnold hurled a curse at her and after an instant of hesitation ran into the house.

Sue remained seated, stunned and petrified. Slowly she pushed back the wicker chair, got up, and gathered most of the broken glass. When she came back into the house she found Arnold in front of the TV watching the six o'clock news and smiling. His face seemed contorted.

"What happened?" she asked.

"Who knows? I suppose something just came over me."

"What was it? Tell me."

"Forget it."

"I can't. We can't live like this. It's too scary."

Arnold shrugged and using the clicker turned up the volume of the TV. Sue sat down. In the morning she would call Dr. Beringer for an appointment. She did not know how best to describe her husband's behavior. All she knew was that she was unhappy and terribly worried.

\* \* \* \* \*

"**A**NY calls?"

It was ten-fifteen on a Tuesday morning in February. Dan Lerner was not the early type, the kind who arrives at the office by seven-thirty in order to catch up with the paperwork of the night before, who has a couple of letters ready for his secretary to type on the word processor by the time she arrives, and who still has ten to fifteen minutes to spare for a few phone calls to the East Coast. That was not how he operated. He generally came in between ten and eleven and stayed late: until seven or eight, or even nine at night. He claimed he was unable to function in the morning and that his brain did not start to churn over until two or three in the afternoon. At least that is how he explained it to anyone who might have called him from the East Coast and complained about not getting him before lunch, East Coast time.

That Tuesday morning Brenda handed him some messages. Nothing important, at least that is how she saw it.

"Dr. Brennan called." she said, as her boss glanced through the message slips. "He wants to see you in his office after Grand Rounds."

"Did he say what it was about?"

"No. Actually, it was Tara, his administrative assistant, who called, so I never got to talk to him."

Dan went into the inner office, closed the door, and sat down facing the windows that overlooked the Barrows Botanical Gardens. An overcast morning; in an hour or so the sun would break through to uncover another inevitably sun-drenched day. He spread out the four message slips to the left of the telephone like a hand of cards and sorted them into calls that were positive—like the one from his old friend Peter in Boston—those that were neutral, and the negative one from Brennan.

A tickle started in his nose; a barrage of sneezes quickly followed it. His nasal allergy had returned: a sure sign that spring was here.

Dan pulled out his handkerchief and got himself into the proper frame of mind to deal with the negative call. That's the type of person he was. He preferred to deal first with unpleasant events; once they were out of the way, he could set them aside and forget them.

This was how it had been during his three years in the Peace Corps. He would start the morning by having his talk with the head nurse, a narrow-faced, gaunt discontent who irritated him by announcing at frequent intervals that he had saved enough money to leave the bush for the city. Life was exciting there, he would say, gesticulating to make his point: there were fast cars, soccer games, and a real dance club, with many women, flashing lights, and a disc jockey. Dan suppressed his inclination to tell the man to fuck off; instead he assured him that he respected his abilities and that not only the clinic, but also he, Dr. Dan Lerner, personally, needed his presence. After the head nurse had accepted Dan's banknote with a shake of his head and a glum pout, much like the expression deployed by the Indian merchant who ran the all-purpose village store and whose exorbitant prices had constantly to be bargained down to realistic levels, Dan was able to turn to other more positive matters. That was when he would set out on ward rounds and a morning during which he enjoyed the reverence offered to the great white magic doctor who was able to save a life when no one else could.

In many ways, the three years in the bush had been wonderful. To be sure, days were long and exhausting, but when by nightfall Dan took himself to the canteen and reflected on his life over goat meat and beans, washed down with a couple bottles of tepid beer, he felt that he would not want to do anything else. As torrents of rain beat down on the corrugated roof and lights flickered, Dan concluded he could not have done any better with himself. Whatever its drawbacks, life was superb and exciting, and with time his miserable marriage to Judith had become like the memory of a debilitating illness from which he now considered himself fully recovered.

Then after three years, the money that up to then had trickled in from Scandinavia to support the clinic ran dry and Dan was forced to return to civilization and the West Coast. There a unique job opportunity awaited him at his old medical school. The way Gordon Fowler had arranged it, Dan was to divide his time between international medicine and neurology. However, these arrangements fell apart when Fowler was swept away by an avalanche while skiing in the Chilean Alps, and Dan had to content himself with an untenured position in the neurology department. Like other members of the department, he was strongly encouraged to set up a research project and obtain outside grant money to support himself, the project, and indirectly the department as well.

Dan looked at the slip that Brenda had handed him and buzzed the Chairman's office.

"D'you know what it's about?" he asked Tara when she got on the line.

"Dr. Brennan said it had something to do with your grant from the National Institutes of Health, the NIH. The pink review forms came in last Friday and he wants to discuss them with you." Her English accent had remained impeccable despite five years in California. "But he won't be back from the Dean's office until after Grand Rounds."

"I guess I'll see him there." Dan said and hung up.

He next turned to the neutral calls. The first was to Bill Light from Santa Monica. The message slip read: "Wants to refer a patient to you." And that is exactly what Bill had in mind.

"Could you see this man for me?" he started out. "I can't figure him out to save my life, and I am sure he is right up your alley. He is in his early fifties, and I think he's suffering from some kind of dementia. The story, as far as I can get it from his wife, is that he was his usual self until about four, five months ago. That's when he started to have a change in personality: he's become irritable, the slightest thing sets him off. But that's not quite the right description. His wife says he's turned into something like an angry puppet."

"An angry puppet? What d'you mean?"

"That's the phrase she used. The way he looks to me, he's angry, all right. But in a strange, almost scary way."

"I don't understand."

"You will when you see him."

"What does he think is wrong with him?"

"Nothing. He insists that he is fine. But I suspect that deep-down he senses something's wrong and he is worried."

"You've done a CAT scan?"

"Wouldn't have phoned you if I hadn't. It's negative, as was his MRI, and his EEG. First, I thought he might have some kind of new-onset epilepsy."

"Epilepsy? He's never had any frank seizures, has he?"

"Not that we know of. I also thought of multiple sclerosis."

"By the way, you did test him for AIDS?"

"As a matter of fact, I did. It's negative."

"Why don't I see him then. Have his wife phone Brenda and set up an appointment."

"Look, I hate to be a pest, but your secretary already told me your first opening is not until the middle of next month. I don't think the family will want to wait around that long. Can't you see him any earlier?"

As it turned out there was a cancellation in clinic that after-noon and Dan promised that he personally would see the man. Not just have a resident work him up, the way it was usually done at the University with outside referrals.

"Can you give me a call when you've had a look at him?"

"Sure will. Doubt that I'll come up with anything."

"Doesn't matter. At least the family will be satisfied that he's been to the ivory tower."

By the time Dan had finished with the rest of the phone calls, he was, as usual, late for Grand Rounds. That morning they were presenting a case of Shy-Drager syndrome, a condition in which there is a progressive deterioration of the various involuntary, automatic functions. It was the sort of once-in-a-lifetime patient who has medical students bubbling for days on end. Dan sat in the last row of the auditorium, listening and at the same time thinking about his NIH grant. Jack Brennan, in his sparkling white Grand Rounds coat, reflex hammer protruding from the side pocket, sat in the front row, flanked by Nick Brindle and Colin Pearson. After the chief resident had presented the clinical history and had demonstrated the important aspects of the patient's neurologic examination, Jack got up. Tall, with steel-blue eyes and perfectly parted, prematurely gray hair, he made an impressive figure. Without doubt, the Selection Committee had made a wise choice when the year before they had brought him out from Tufts Medical School in Boston to replace Gordon Fowler as chair of the University's neurology department with a mission to lead it into the new century. During his tenure as head of the small neurology department at Tufts, Jack had not only proven himself as an able administrator, but what was far more important in the current academic climate of fiscal restrictions, he had been able to attract a large amount of grant support, which he had used to modernize the facilities of the department and bring in a number of young and extremely capable physicians.

Jack turned to the patient. "Do you ever get lightheaded?" he asked. A thin-lipped automatic smile asserted itself over the lower part of Jack's face, leaving his eyes unmoved.

The patient, a Mexican immigrant, did not understand. The chief resident quickly interposed.

"Mr. Zuniga does not speak English. However, we did pose that same question of him through an interpreter. And the answer we got is that he does get lightheaded when he stands up for more than a few minutes."

Jack wheeled to face the audience.

"I don't need to tell anyone in this auditorium as to the importance of questioning patients with Shy-Drager syndrome about lightheadedness." He took a small nickel-plated pointer from the breast pocket of his white coat, briefly extended it to about ten inches, and then with a quick movement of both hands returned it to its original size.

The patient stared in front of him, holding fast to the arms of his wheelchair. Dan wondered whether Mr. Zuniga was aware of his role as an interesting but essentially inanimate object, akin to one of the uniquely marked sand dollars uncovered by the receding tide. Like the sand dollar, he was about to be examined and felt, turned from side to side, and passed from one person to the next, not because of any caring, but merely on account of the singular markings on its shell. Jack embarked on a brief clinical commentary.

"We must not forget that many patients with Shy-Drager syndrome will experience episodes of blurred vision. In the cases I have seen, this starts peripherally and encroaches on central vision just before the patient loses consciousness. And, of course, laryngeal stridor, a high-pitched noisy breathing. There have been several recent cases that have presented in that manner."

In the last few rows of the auditorium some of the medical students assigned to the neurology service were taking copious case notes. Others were dozing, heads in the crooks of their arms. Andy Walker, the last of the old-time university-based clinicians, sat among them. He appeared alert and interested.

Jack turned to Colin Pearson.

"Did we get a PET scan?"

For an instant, Colin was taken aback. Although he was the local expert on positron emission tomography, familiarly known as a PET scan, the newest tool used to examine the anatomy of brain metabolism, he had not scheduled Mr. Zuniga for this extremely expensive and time-consuming study.

"We don't have him on our books," he said. This was understandable, as far as Colin was concerned. His research interests dealt with the PET scan in Alzheimer's disease, so that there was no reason for him to become involved with this particular patient.

Feeling the expectant eyes of his chairman, Colin did an instant about-face. "A PET scan would indeed be very interesting," he said quickly but without committing himself to doing the study. "As it happens, the group in Vancouver have already published their findings on a series of patients with Shy-Drager syndrome."

From the way Colin hesitated, Dan could tell that he was attempting to recall what their findings had been. It would never do to have them wrong. A resident or, even worse, a medical student might have read the paper and would not hesitate to correct him. Fortunately, the answer came to him.

"They found what everyone would have expected: a disorder in the nigrostriatal dopaminergic pathway."

The medical students scribbled furiously; one of them was about to raise his hand to ask where and what the nigrostriatal dopaminergic pathway was all about, but changed his mind; better to look it up in the library than to appear ignorant.

Before too long Mr. Zuniga was wheeled out of the auditorium. This was the cue for Marty DiChiro to get up in front of the audience. Marty was the most prominent new addition to the department, having been brought out from Chicago by Jack on the basis of what Jack termed his "groundbreaking work" that dealt with the role of neurotransmitters in the function of the monkey hypothalamus, an area of brain closely related to the pituitary gland and deeply involved in controlling and altering behavior.

Even though Dan never considered the work that Marty had done to be totally original, he knew that he had managed to use the results, some published, some as yet unpublished, to arouse the interest of the Wallace Foundation, a charitable organization founded by E.B. Wallace, a man who had made his fortune by selling spare auto parts for less than his competitors. Franky Wallace, E.B.'s youngest son, was serving time in the Indiana State Penitentiary for aggravated assault and battery on his college roommate. The young man had always suffered from a short temper and a tendency to violence; a few years before his conviction his father had taken him to the Mayo Clinic for a thorough evaluation. The diagnosis had been "episodic discontrol." That is where the hypothalamus came in. The doctors at the Mayo Clinic assured E.B. that episodic discontrol had nothing to do with the boy's upbringing, but was a disorder of the hypothalamus. The old man was relieved. A week later he launched the Foundation and dedicated it to the support of research relating to diseases of the hypothalamus and the chemicals, some known, but most unknown, that made his son the way he was.

Marty got in touch with E.B. and before long got the old man to furnish him with funds to establish the Hypothalamic Research

Center. With a multimillion dollar, five-year grant from the Wallace Foundation as part of his résumé, he was the obvious person to be appointed director of the laboratory.

Despite an outpouring of publications from Marty and his collaborators, the breakthrough, when it came, was not the one that E.B. had hoped for. Rather it took the form of an offer from Jack Brennan that Marty could not refuse. He packed up the other six members of the DiChiro family, their various personal belongings, laboratory equipment, technicians, and the grant from the E.B. Wallace Foundation and moved out West, the star of Jack's Recruitment for Excellence program.

Now at Tuesday morning Grand Rounds Marty came up to the podium. Although nearly bald with a slight, unimposing figure, the intensity and range of feeling in his voice conveyed an absolute assurance. The lights went out and he showed his first slide, the anatomy of the sympathetic and parasympathetic nervous system. Dan had already seen it; in fact, he had the distinct impression that he had heard Marty's talk on at least one other occasion.

His mind reverted to the grant application, which he had sent to the NIH, "Neurotrophic Molecules in the Pathogenesis of Alzheimer's Disease."

"Can you explain to me what you are doing?" Maureen had asked him a few nights ago. She sat next to him as he was correcting the first draft of his application.

"Are you really interested?"

"I wouldn't ask you if I weren't."

Judith had never asked him about his work. Not that she found it uninteresting, but she was always intimidated by matters that she could not readily comprehend.

"All right then, I'll go slowly."

"Don't worry, I'm pretty smart. At least that's what Tom tells me, and over the years he has seen a lot of lawyers come and go through his office."

"You see, what I want to do is look into what causes Alzheimer's disease."

"Right. That's a big problem, isn't it?"

"It certainly is. Now there are a number of chemicals in the brain—some fifty of them or maybe even a hundred—that stimulate the growth of nerve cells and keep them from dying off before their time has come. I want to see if one or more of these chemicals are missing or defective in the brains of people who come down with Alzheimer's disease."

"And if they are?"

"Then we might be able to provide them and prevent the illness from progressing."

"Sounds pretty good to me."

It was pretty good, but the first time he had sent off his proposal, it had returned to him: approved but not funded, the epitaph for unsuccessful applications. He now had two months in which to rewrite and resubmit it in the hope of obtaining a higher score. Only those grants with the top priority scores were funded by the National Institutes of Health. In the meantime, Dan would need interim funding for Donna, his technician. Not to mention a fair bit of money for laboratory supplies. The $5000 he had managed to get from the Bay Area Alzheimer Group would not be enough to tide him over for more than a month or two.

After Grand Rounds a group of doctors stood outside the auditorium.

"Hey, Bill! How's it going?"

"Can't complain. What about you?"

"No problems on my end."

Jack was involved with Colin Pearson. Dan waited for Jack, intending to walk back with him to the chairman's office. He managed to overhear snatches of their interchange.

"We've got to talk." Jack said. "I just got word from the dean. He can't free up any funds to develop the B Floor."

Even though Colin's face, handsomely framed by a dark, well-trimmed beard, did not show any emotion, Dan knew he was taken aback by the news.

"So what happens to my PET scanner?" he heard Colin ask.

"We will just have to mark time until we get some other source of funding. Don't worry, I'm working on it."

For the past couple of years Colin had to use his own grants to provide salary support for two technicians who did not work for him but for the radiology department. It was a rental payment of sorts.

"They would never have gotten a second scanner if it hadn't been for my grant," he would grumble at the departmental meetings.

At such times Jack would make sympathetic noises, but short of a confrontation between the two departments, there was no way Colin could avoid paying rent for the space that the scanner occupied in the radiology department.

Jack saw Dan waiting a couple of steps away and cut short the conversation.

"Let's go over everything later this afternoon," he said. As Colin moved away, Jack turned to Dan. "You and I have a lot to talk about," he said, giving him a condescending pat on the shoulder.

Jack's office was dominated by a red and purple painting of his own making. Entitled "One for All and All for One," it was an oppressively garish abstraction of neuronal synapses. Even though it had recently been shown in a gallery owned by the wife of one of Jack's multiple sclerosis patients, it had attracted neither a buyer nor a single kind critical review. As Dan sat across from Jack, he became sidetracked by the material piled up on the desk: files, unsigned letters, architectural plans. He could make out the caption for the plans: "B floor renovation."

"What are we going to do about your NIH grant?" Jack asked, looking playfully serious.

"I've already started to rewrite it."

"Will you be able to get it back to them by May?"

"No reason why not."

"That means January funding—if it is funded." An ominous pause ensued. Jack flicked through his files and came up with a copy of the pink sheets, the criticisms of Dan's unsuccessful grant application prepared by the panel of scientists who acted as consultants to the National Institutes of Health. He gave it a quick glance. Obviously he had already read it.

"Neurotrophic Molecules in the Pathogenesis of Alzheimer's Disease." He paused: a pause to allow Dan to reflect on the inadequacy of his application.

"Shall we be honest with one another?" Jack smiled: two rows of perfect, brilliant white teeth. There was another pause. Dan nodded. Jack picked up the pink sheet and gave it a quick wave. "This won't be funded. Not in the current climate." He leaned back in his chair and stroked the back of his head with the right hand. "D'you have any other grants pending?" He pulled out his pointer.

"Not at this point."

"I didn't think so." Another pause. Time for the pointer to return to its pocket. "In my opinion the time has come for you to consider changing to doing straight clinical work. That way, we won't have to worry about finding money to keep your lab going."

The intercom buzzed. Jack picked up the phone and listened.

"Put him on." After a moment. "Say, Marty, you did a great job. Very scholarly. So what's on your mind?" He listened for a few moments. "Look, this is nothing to panic about." A cloud came over his face and he gave Dan a quick glance. "I understand. Yes, naturally." Another pause. "Why don't you come by this afternoon. Make it at five. I should be free by then."

He hung up and returned to Dan.

"There is nothing wrong with doing clinical work. I have been told that you have considerable excellence in taking care of patients, and I think that's where your heart really lies." He picked up the pink sheet and, with an offhand gesture, tossed it on the pile of correspondence.

"Think about it." He gave Dan an intense look. "And keep the whole picture in mind. You know the mission of the department and what our priorities are—not only in terms of research but also our role in the community. After all, that Peace Corps experience of yours should have taught you the value of community work."

Without a change in expression, he glanced at his watch. Dan knew this to be a sign that the meeting with the department chairman was over.

\* \* \*

Dan arrived in clinic twenty minutes late.

"There's a Mr. Arnold Barton waiting for you," the clinic secretary told him. "His wife said they had an appointment, but we don't have him down on our list."

Dan saw Mr. Barton as he sat in the waiting room, a middle-aged man in a navy blue three-piece suit, clearly too dressed up for a visit to his doctor. He had seen this sign before. It usually indicated that the patient wanted to assert his status to himself and to the doctor. Sue Barton was there as well. Black blouse, black slacks, black shoes and socks, costume jewelry bracelet and necklace. Fingers curved, her hand rested lightly on her husband's shoulder. At the outset, Dan was struck by the lack of expression in Mr. Barton's face. An unwarranted calm, a placidity out of place in a doctor's office.

Sue got up as the doctor came in.

"May I speak to you for a few minutes? Alone."

Dan led her into the first available room. It was furnished like all the other rooms in the neurology clinic: a standard desk, an examining table, and an ophthalmoscope affixed to the soothing pastel yellow wall.

"Arnold is going to deny all of this," she started out, "but I know that he is not the same any more. He is different from the way he was a few months ago."

"In what way?"

"I'm not sure."

"Come on, you must have some idea."

"Didn't Dr. Light tell you? It's like he doesn't care about anything anymore. He sits in front of the TV with a constant meaningless smile on his face, as if he were happy with whatever he is watching. Then suddenly, out of nowhere, he has one of his outbursts."

"An outburst?"

"That's right. One minute he'll be smiling, then all at once he blows up. Without any provocation."

"You've been to a psychiatrist?"

"That's where we started out. I told Arnold we had to see someone. I couldn't take him anymore, the way he was. So we went to see Dr. Beringer, first the two of us and then Arnold by himself. For a month. That's who referred us to Dr. Light. He told me that there must be something wrong with Arnold's brain. That some of his brain centers were not functioning normally. That's why we had all these tests done. Arnold didn't want to go through with them, but I insisted, and now we are here."

Dan asked a few more questions. No, there was nothing wrong with her husband's memory, and he had never physically attacked her, although she was afraid that some day he might. The outbursts were brief, usually no longer than five minutes, and Arnold said that he remembered everything that happened during them. No, she did not recall how it all started except that he had been a bit depressed since October and he did have the flu a couple of weeks before.

"As long as I have known him, Arnie's had his depressions. They come and they go. I've stopped worrying about them."

It was time for Dan to see Mr. Barton, who insisted there was nothing wrong with him and thought he was working just as effectively as before. When Dan pressed him, he admitted that he had not been getting along too well with his staff, and that, in fact, last week he blew up at the C.E.O. While his wife shook her head in contradiction, he assured Dan that the confrontation had not been his fault.

"I can't take that man any more. I might have, a couple of years ago, but not now. It's like he makes me lose my cool."

"How long have you been married?"

"Twenty-eight years," Arnold replied, flatly. A figure extracted from rote memory.

"Twenty-eight years."

Dan did an extensive neurologic examination, knowing full well, even before he got started, that he would not find anything abnormal. Bill Light was much too careful a neurologist to have missed anything.

"You look fine to me," he told Mr. Barton when he was done.

"I thought you'd say that. Now will you please tell that to my wife so she'll stop bugging me."

"But there is something wrong with you," Sue said. "You even said so the other night."

"Didn't you just hear the doctor say there is nothing wrong with me?"

"He didn't want to upset you."

"Upset me? Boy, are you controlling."

"For God's sakes! When have I ever been controlling? You don't know what you're talking about."

Mr. Barton stared at his wife. One shoe was on his foot and laced, the other was still in his hand. Suddenly he threw down the shoe and jumped up.

"You bitch! You lousy bitch!" he shouted. His eyes became drunken and unfocused, and slowly, as if pulled by invisible wires, he picked up the chair on which he had been sitting and crashed it down on the floor in front of his wife. As she screamed and jumped aside, he ripped the coat hanger from where it had been screwed to the back of the office door. Coat hanger raised over his head, he moved toward his wife. Dan interposed himself to ward off the blow, but the blow never came; instead Mr. Barton's hand became fixed over Dan's head. Abruptly and with a strange, jerky movement, he threw down the coat hanger.

"Bastards! Fucking bastards!" There was saliva on his lower lip.

Dan was startled, not only by Mr. Barton's sudden explosion, but even more so by the bizarre, automated movements and his grotesque mechanical voice. Pale and perspiring, the man extended his trembling hands, looked at them, and shook his head from side to side. His index finger oozed blood from where he had pulled off a corner of his nail. Ignoring his injury, he replaced the chair and sat down to put on the other shoe. By the time her husband was fully dressed, Sue had recovered her composure.

"Now you know what his outbursts are like," she said.

"I am sorry, Sue," Mr. Barton said, placing his hand on her arm. "I don't know what set me off." Then, as if trying to explain himself to Dan, "You should know that I've been under a lot of stress. We've been expanding our services into Arizona and New Mexico. It's been absolutely hectic."

A few minutes later, while her husband was sitting in the clinic office, signing insurance forms, Sue sought out Dan.

"What do you think?" she asked.

"I don't know . . . it is strange."

"Yes. But that's not much help to us, is it?"

"I suppose not."

"I don't know what to do. We've had our ups and downs all the years we've been married: good times and disappointments. I guess every couple has. But now everything is different. What seemed important before no longer matters. It's like Arnold's illness is everywhere, waiting to catch me unawares. It keeps me awake at night. I go to the market, I take care of the house, and I work at the university credit union as if nothing has happened. But that's not the way it really is. I feel like I'm starting a new chapter in my life and I don't know how it's going to end." She waited for Dan to respond.

"I don't know what's going on with him," he said. "That's the long and short of it." He felt that he could only offer her honesty. Not a good feeling, being helpless like that.

"You're not much help to us."

"I wish I could do more for him. I'll tell you what: I'll do some reading in the library. If I come up with anything, I'll give you a call."

After the Bartons had left, Dan reflected on what he had just seen. It had hardly been an epileptic attack, for not only had it been triggered by a husband and wife argument, but also there had been neither loss of awareness nor any depression following the attack. Episodic discontrol seemed to be the best diagnosis. But why would that condition appear in a man who for over forty years had led an unremarkable, exemplary life? Perhaps the flu that had preceded the first attack had something to do with it.

Later that day, on the phone with Bill Light, he didn't have much more to say. "One might label him as suffering from episodic discontrol, but that doesn't tell us anything." Dan suggested a trial of anticonvulsants, but he knew full well that they wouldn't work. Not unless they had some sort of placebo effect.

* * *

That night Dan returned to the library and picked up a review on episodic discontrol. How common was it for an infection to precede the onset of the syndrome? The review did not mention infection; rather it pointed to head trauma as initiating factor. He had asked Mrs. Barton whether her husband had suffered any head trauma prior to the onset of his symptoms. She assured him there had been none. The review, however, referred to an older paper entitled "Risk factors in episodic discontrol: a case-control study," which had been published in the 1980 volume of the *Archives of Neurology and Psychiatry.*

Deciding that he should read that paper, Dan climbed three flights to the section of the stacks where the bound journals were kept. The complete set of the *Archives* was there. Complete except for the 1980 issue.

Muttering a curse, he looked around the shelves. The volume had not been misplaced. Probably checked out. That was exactly what the librarian confirmed after she had looked through the computer files. Dan was about to give up on his search when he remembered that the neurology departmental library adjoining the chairman's office had a fairly complete set of the *Archives*.

A few minutes later he let himself into the library with his pass card. It was past seven and the place was dark. He switched on the lights and looked through the shelves. The 1980 volume was there all right, and with a sigh of relief he sank into an armchair and started to read the paper.

"If the records are examined for major infections that took place less than three years prior to the onset of episodic discontrol, then 12 cases had suffered an infection and 35 had not. Seven controls had suffered an infection and 78 had not ($p < 0.01$)."

Unused to statistical papers, he reread the paragraph, jotting down the numbers on a slip of paper.

"I don't want this to come out! Understand?" Jack's voice came through the wall from the chairman's office next door. The response was inaudible.

"Marty, you are being too simplistic about the whole matter. You have put in two years' work, first in Chicago and now here. You just can't throw everything over."

Another inaudible response.

"Never mind that. It's probably coincidence anyway." Jack's voice moved closer. Dan suspected that he was pacing up and down in his office, close to the library partition.

"How about some coffee?"

"Sure. Why not?" It was Marty DiChiro. He must have gotten up and helped himself to coffee.

"So what kind of grant do you have from them?"

"Five hundred and seventy-five thousand over the next five years."

"And what do you think will happen to that grant if you call them and tell them?"

A pause.

"Exactly. So let's sit down, and I'll tell you how we're going to manage this."

There was some shuffling of chairs, and both voices became inaudible. Dan returned to the paper. Much later he wished that he hadn't.

"Similarly, for events that occurred less than or equal to two years prior to the onset of episodic discontrol. . . ."

He no longer could manage the complexities of the paper. Instead he tried to remember which one of Marty's research projects they were talking about. Someone, Dan had forgotten who, had mentioned to him that there had been an outpatient conference a month or so earlier in which Marty's work had been discussed. It had probably been one of those many conferences Dan had not bothered to attend. A schedule of the outpatient conferences was tacked on the bulletin board of the library. He got up and looked at it. January 5, the first conference of the new year.

"Synthetic human placental lactogen in male impotence: a preliminary study." The conference had been given by Philip Gregson, neurourologist at the University Hospital. The other conferences had even less bearing on what Marty could be working on. Obviously Dan's memory had been playing tricks on him. Then he remembered: he had attended that neurourology conference and at that time Marty did make some comment. For the life of him, Dan was unable to remember what it was.

It was getting late and he was hungry. Even though he had become quite skilled at cooking since he had left the Peace Corps, he was in no mood to go home, turn on the stereo, open a bottle of wine, and cook his own dinner. There was too much on his mind. Should he rewrite his grant and resubmit it, hoping for the best, or take Jack's advice and change over to clinical practice? And then there was Mr. Barton and his episodic discontrol. Dan wished he had someone to talk to about that as well.

He returned to his office and dialed Maureen's number. She was not home and she did not have an answering machine. Next Dan tried David Schaffer.

"David?"

"Yes."

"Have you had dinner?"

"Not yet."

"Good. Let's get together then."

\* \* \*

The two of them met at La Torta Calda. Although David was bright and erudite, he was content with running the neurologic outpatient service at the Veterans' Hospital. He was a gentle man who walked with his head and trunk bent slightly forward, as if he wanted to protect himself from the onslaught of the world. Life had not been good to him. Liza, his wife, whom he adored, had been in and out of the Westridge Hospital for the past five years. Although David never said so, word at the university had it that she was a chronic schizophrenic. They had no children, which was just as well. A year ago, after her discharge from Westridge, Liza went to a gypsy fortuneteller who told her that she would give birth to three children—all boys. That night while David was at the hospital, Liza slashed pillows and bed linen and disappeared from the house. Two days later she was picked up by the police at the Staunton Park Observatory, where she had created a disturbance by insisting, against all assurances to the contrary, that the planet Earth had three moons rather than one and that the other two moons had been converted into secret space stations.

Now David was sitting across from Dan at La Torta Calda. The topic was episodic discontrol. Dan had just told him about Mr. Barton.

"Although most people consider it to be a disorder in the function of the temporal lobe, I totally disagree." David leaned back and presented his reasons. They were so precise and so elegantly thought out that Dan could readily imagine himself at the plenary session of the American Academy of Neurology rather than in a small Italian restaurant.

When he had finished, David refilled his glass and Dan's. The Chianti was good, but as always it contained more tannin than was to Dan's liking. A thought flashed through Dan's mind.

"Do you have any idea what kind of grant support Marty DiChiro is getting?"

David reflected. "The Wallace Foundation. . . ." He paused.

"I know about that. Anything else?"

"Beats me. That man runs a big operation, with a bunch of Ph.D. post-docs. He probably has half a dozen other grants. Why d'you ask?"

"Just curious." For a moment Dan considered relating the conversation he had overheard in the departmental library. But then he realized it was not a real conversation, but only bits and snatches of one. So it was better to keep quiet.

The restaurant, which had not been particularly busy even when the two men arrived, was empty by then and the posters of Florence, Tuscany, and Lake Como had acquired a smudged, dilapidated look. Dan finished the Chianti.

"Are you seeing anyone?" David asked while they were waiting for the check.

"Yes."

"Good." Then out of nowhere he added. "It has always been a puzzle to me why one couple stays together, even though by rights, personalities, and events should have annihilated whatever attachment they ever had for each other. And then, just as inexplicably, another couple who appear perfectly suited to each other break up without any apparent cause."

Dan thought of Judith and himself. Why had their marriage fallen apart?

"Did you ever meet Judith?"

"Of course I did. I was out to your house when you two were still together."

"What did you think of her?"

"I can just barely picture her face. She had sad eyes. Like those of a neglected, angry little girl."

Dan nodded.

"I find it interesting," David said, "that after all these years you want to know my opinion of her. You are still involved?"

"I suppose I am. The Peace Corps did nothing to get her out of my system."

David's mouth moved into a smile. "Guilt?"

"Probably."

Both men lapsed into silence. David lifted his wineglass, and, as if an afterthought, put it down.

"Whatever happens with Lisa," he said, "I still wouldn't want to be with another woman. Do you think love is just one form of loyalty?"

"For some, perhaps. For others, it is a compulsion."

"What was it for you? With Judith, I mean."

"In the beginning I was excited to have found a woman with whom I could share my life. After a year or so she became more and more predictable and she held no more mysteries for me. When that happened all the excitement drained out of our marriage. That is when I began to distance myself from her. On her part, she grew more dependent and possessive of me. I felt I had become responsible for all her joy and misery. For a time I entertained myself by fantasizing that she was conducting an affair while I was at the hospital."

"Did she?"

"Almost certainly not."

"Haven't you ever noticed that a great passion does not last; it consumes itself."

"I suppose you are right."

David reflected. "I have read that one or the other partner has to be miserable in order for love to persist with its initial intensity."

Dan was certain that David was thinking of his own years with Lisa. "I have started to pray for her," David said and closed his eyes. "I have tried everything: psychotherapy, ECT, electric shock, so why not prayer? I want to have the assurance that I haven't left a stone unturned. I miss her. When I come home at night, I still expect to see her sitting in the den under a cone of light, reading. Some days I think it will never happen."

"What do you mean?"

"That we will live together again, side by side, and watch the years go by, as one would watch the turning of foliage. With contentment and resignation."

The check arrived. The two men split the bill and left the table.

"I'm going to send you a couple of reviews on episodic discontrol," David said as they were waiting for their cars to be brought around.

"Good. I'd like to learn more about it. You know, that man really puzzled me. There seemed to be so much anger in him, and what was worse. . . ." Dan broke off. He was trying to get a grasp of the feeling he experienced when he saw Mr. Barton's fist raised over his head. "I knew there was no way I could reason with him. That if he was programmed to do violence on me or his wife, it would happen, regardless of what I said or did."

"Like a robot?"

"Somewhat. His wife says he has become like a puppet. An angry puppet."

* * *

Earlier that afternoon Arla Barton flew in from New York to see her parents. As the three of them had dinner Arla kept up a constant chatter about the latest Madison Avenue gossip. Her father listened with a fixed smile, and before Sue brought around the coffee, he disappeared into the study and turned on the TV.

"I can see why you are worried about Dad. What's going on with him?"

"No one really knows. This afternoon I took him over to the University Hospital. We saw this doctor who is supposed to be an expert on Alzheimer's disease. He said Dad doesn't have Alzheimer's disease, but I already knew that. It's so frustrating."

"Maybe you should bring him back to New York. I can call around and see if there is anyone who specializes in his kind of illness. Except I don't know how to describe it."

"I don't either. Sometimes I think there is a motor inside him that dictates what he says and does. I wish Eric were here. I've talked to him on the phone, but how can he help? He is so far away. He hasn't seen Dad for over four months."

Sue looked at her daughter, who was drawing circles on the tablecloth with the handle of her spoon. The girl looked tired. She had had a long flight, with the plane having to sit on the runway for over an hour before it was cleared by flight control.

"I feel so helpless . . . so utterly helpless," Sue said. "I never know when he is going to blow up."

Arla got up and put her arm around her mother.

"Please don't cry," she said, and kissed the top of her head.

"It's like there is a dark force crushing the two of us, something I can't understand, and I don't know how to fight."

"I'll help you, Mom. I promise I will."

But as she said it, Arla knew that in two days she would be free to escape from her parents, to fly back to her own world, her work, and her friends.

\* \* \*

No sooner had Dan returned to his apartment from his dinner with David than the phone rang. It was Maureen.

"I called you earlier," she said. "You must have been out."

"I had dinner with David. I tried to reach you but you weren't home."

"I was working on a new case. Just came into our office. I don't know whether we should take it or not."

"What's it about?"

"I'd rather not discuss it on the phone. But I do want your advice."

"What about dinner tomorrow night?"

"I'd love it. Could we make it at La Toque? It's quiet there and we can talk." She sensed Dan's lack of enthusiasm. "I know it's expensive. I'll get Cosgrove and Costello to pick up the bill."

"I miss seeing you. It's been over a week."

"Same here. I don't know which one of us works harder."

The following night they met for dinner at La Toque. It was a dark place; quiet enough so they could talk. Dan was late and Maureen was waiting for him at the bar. As was always the case when he had not seen her for some time, he was surprised by her compact form outlined by the lights above the bar. Such energy and vitality in such a small body. She looked stunning in a gray tailored jacket with broad lapels and a matching skirt, an outfit that enhanced her fair skin, green eyes, and auburn hair.

"Sorry I'm late," he said as he sat down next to her. "Judith called just as I was about to leave. She wouldn't let me get off the phone."

"What did she want this time?"

"She was upset by a letter addressed to me that had come to the house."

"So what's wrong with that?"

"It was from the Ojai Inn confirming our reservations. She had a fit about it because I had made them in the name of Dr. and Mrs."

"She opened your letter? That bitch!"

Regardless of what had happened between Judith and himself, Dan did not like to hear Maureen, who had seen her briefly on one occasion, call her a bitch. He never considered Judith to be a bitch; the worst he could say about her was that she stifled him.

"So when are you going to file for divorce?" Maureen asked after they were seated at their table.

"I don't know. In fact, I don't even know whether I want a divorce."

"Sooner or later you will have come to some decision. It boils down to your making up your mind as to what you want."

"I know what I want. I want to feel the way I did when I was working in the bush—to wake up in the morning excited by what I am doing and by the kind of life I am living."

Is that why he had left Judith, because she kept him from leading a more exciting life?

"You are being self-destructive," Andy Walker had told Dan. The two men were attending the Academy meetings in Detroit. It was late and they were sitting at the bar over nightcaps. Dan had told the old clinician that he had decided to leave Judith.

"Judith is as good a woman as you will ever find," Andy had said. "Of course she has her faults, but then who doesn't? The way I see her, she is rich, smart, interesting, and she certainly knows how to dress. You won't find anybody better."

Dan had attempted to explain to Andy why he wanted to get out of the marriage but what he said made no sense. Since then he had spent three years in the Peace Corps trying to sort himself out, and he still was no wiser.

"I really don't know why I left her," he said to Maureen. "Perhaps I was being self-destructive."

Maureen shook her head. "I don't believe that for one minute. You insist on blaming yourself for something that was not your fault."

Her critical tone made him recoil. He picked up the menu and looked at the list of entrées.

"Please don't hide from me."

Maureen leaned forward and extended her arms toward him, palms up. He put down the menu and took her hands. They were shapely and expressed an innate dignity. As always, their roughness came unexpectedly; they were more like the hands of a farmer's wife than those of a successful Los Angeles attorney.

"You must forgive me," she said. "Sometimes I get too impatient with you." The spotlight that was trained on a Toulouse-Lautrec poster illuminated the side of her face—soft, with prominent cheekbones. Over the last few months Maureen had become dear to him.

Sometime later that evening Maureen put down her knife and fork. "As I said to you on the phone, I need you to help me decide on a case that's come across my desk. I think Cosgrove knows it's a weird one. That's why he is trying to dump it on me. My inclination is to tell the man to go to hell, but before I do, I want your opinion."

Dan refilled Maureen's glass and became attentive.

"Saul Marcus is the man's name and there is no doubt he is strange. He wants to sue his internist for screwing up his head."

"He does sound weird."

Maureen ignored the interjection. She adjusted a wayward lock of hair with two fingers of her left hand and started out on her story.

"According to what Mr. Marcus tells me, he has been depressed for years. He was married for a few years, but then his wife left him for one reason or another and took their kids with her. That upset him considerably. On top of it he didn't get the promotion he had been expecting, and there were a few other things that went wrong in his life. I have to tell you the man goes off on tangents. I must have taken at least six pages of notes. In any case, some five months ago he went to see this Dr. Frank Ferdinand, and ever since then he says his head is screwed up. He can't think for himself and he says it feels as if outside forces are compelling him to get angry at everything and everybody."

"Sounds like he should see a psychiatrist, not an attorney."

"He's been to a psychiatrist. In fact, he has been to three psychiatrists, including Allen Beringer, who, I understand, knows his business. That's what he tells me. I'm going to check all that out, of course."

"So what did the psychiatrists come up with?"

"Not much. His story is that everybody had a different diagnosis and all of them wanted to put him on tranquilizers. But he insists he was fine, just upset and a bit depressed before he went to see Dr. Ferdinand. And that's why he wants us to sue him."

"I don't think you should take the case."

"Right. I still would like you to see him and tell me what you think. And send your bill to Cosgrove and Costello. I'll make sure they pay it."

Dessert arrived and for a time they talked about other matters. Maureen was scheduled for a deposition in Seattle the following Monday morning, which meant they might have to cancel their weekend in Ojai. She was trying to get someone else in the firm to cover the deposition but so far had not been successful.

"Jack Brennan is such an asshole." Dan said, totally out of the blue. Maureen looked puzzled, so Dan told her about his meeting with Jack.

"You've got to explain something to me." Maureen said. "What's wrong with your changing over to the clinical work?"

"A lot. For one, I would have to give up my lab."

"So. Ever since I met you, you've been bitching about your research, telling me it's not going anywhere."

"That's true. I am not made for that kind of work."

"I don't blame you. I don't know how you guys do it. You must enjoy constant frustration."

"That's only part of it. When I first got started, I thought that in order for someone to succeed in research he had to be creative. Now I know better. It's mainly a matter of politics. If you kiss up to the right people you can get grants, and with enough grants in your pocket you can hire enough technicians and post-docs and publish enough papers to delight your chairman's heart. That's when the promotions and all the perks start to come your way. The days are gone when a scientist could work in a cluttered little lab, content with a meager salary, not talking to anybody or seeing a soul for days on end, all the time pursuing some hare-brained idea."

Maureen nodded and emptied her glass. As the candlelight lit the remnants of wine, Dan suddenly realized that he had deceived himself. Success had failed to come his way not because of politics, but because he had never been committed to his work. In the beginning, when he had set up his laboratory, he had been excited about the proposed project. His head was filled with ideas and he was certain that sooner or later he would clarify the complex functions of the various chemicals that stimulate the growth of nerve cells, the neurotrophins, and discover how their disordered metabolism led to some of the major diseases that affect the brain.

The months passed and nothing significant happened. To be sure, he published a few papers here and there. There was an occasional presentation at a neuroscience meeting, a ten-minute talk attended by half a dozen people, mostly graduate students, and gradually, without Dan's becoming fully aware of it, his enthusiasm evaporated. Was that what had happened to his marriage—a waning enthusiasm replaced by a sense of constriction until there was nothing left but regrets?

How was he to convey all this to Maureen? He took her hand. A long silence precluded the fatal disclosure.

"My apartment or yours?" Maureen asked. Her question came as a relief.

"Yours."

Maureen's apartment was on Rossmore. It dated back to the twenties, a time when Hollywood was self-consciously flamboyant, and she had taken advantage of the tall windows and high ceilings to fill the space with Victorian furniture. The living room was dominated by a marble fireplace with a pair of lion-shaped iron fire dogs and a small but reputedly genuine Bonnard that hung over it, a painting she had found in an antique store behind a stack of prints. In the bedroom there was a four-poster iron and brass bed, a brass lamp with a green glass shade, and a Victorian English oak wardrobe whose drawers had an irritating habit of getting stuck.

Maureen brought an earthy roughness to lovemaking.

"It's fun and it's free," she would tell Dan. "What more can one ask for?"

A contrast to Judith, who would make him feel as if her body were a gift to him, to be presented or withheld according to her discretion.

\* \* \*

When Dan arrived at the office Friday morning, he had a message to see Dr. Brennan ASAP. It was another overcast day and even before getting that message his nasal allergy was as bad as it ever got.

A few minutes later, handkerchief in hand, Dan sat across from Jack and his red and purple abstraction of neuronal synapses.

"I really hate my job," Jack started out. Dan nodded sympathetically and desisted from making an offer to take it from his hands.

"A department is like a family. We have a program and all of us have to pitch in to make it succeed. You agree?"

"Of course."

"The other day I had a talk with Marty, and it looks as if he will need your help. You see he has gotten himself way over his head with his research. He has these two new post-docs from Japan working for him. I'm sure you've met them." He hesitated and glanced at a paper on his desk. "Kyoshi and Takafumi."

A good chess player can see five moves ahead. But even a beginner could tell what was coming. And it came.

"You will understand that I am reluctant to reassign your space. But Marty has a productive research program and we don't want to obstruct it. Now then, as of the first of the month you won't have any funding for your lab tech."

"Actually I do."

"Oh, yes. Your Alzheimer grant. But that takes care of only 25 percent of her salary."

He was correct on all accounts. Jack was a man who did not neglect details.

"I'll get Marty to take over her support so she won't be out of a job. And I will see to it that you are switched over to clinical work by the first of March. What we'll do is get you to run Marty's Monday clinic up at Las Virgenes Hospital. That'll keep him from bitching to me that he doesn't have time to concentrate on writing his Program Project Grant. How does that sound?" He protruded his lower lip and jaw.

It didn't sound good to Dan. Las Virgenes Hospital was a forty-mile drive and the clinic started at eight in the morning. Jack picked up on Dan's hesitation.

"I know that clinic is a bit of a chore, but they do refer a lot of good cases to us—solid, hard-core neurology. In a way, it'll remind you of your years out in the bush. And another thing—the hospital is paying a third of Marty's salary."

"I thought he was getting funded by the Wallace Foundation."

"He is, but we are setting aside some of the Wallace money to do up the B floor. We need to bring our PET scanner back from radiology and set up a functional MR imaging unit. Those are my two top priorities for the department."

"But wouldn't Las Virgenes Hospital want Marty to run the clinic? After all, they're putting up his salary, not mine."

"The way I have arranged it, you're Marty's temporary replacement."

"Temporary?"

"That's what I told them. I'm sure they'll be happy to have you in place of Marty. If things don't work out, we'll review our affiliation in a year or so. Remember, there is nothing more important than all of us pitching in. D'you know what I entitled this painting of mine?" He pointed to the red and purple eyesore. "'One for All and All for One.' That's what makes a good team player. Right?"

He got up and extended his hand: end of interview.

Dan didn't have the heart to go up to his lab and tell Donna that as of March 1 she would have the choice of being out of a job or working for Marty DiChiro. Instead he went to the cafeteria and got himself a cup of coffee.

As he sat over coffee and reflected on his options, his beeper went off.

Brenda was on the line. She sounded upset.

"I've got Mrs. Barton on the other phone. Mr. Barton tried to kill her and then stabbed himself with a pair of garden shears."

Concerns about his laboratory and the early morning clinic at Las Virgenes disappeared.

"Tell her I'll call her right back."

When Dan got to his office and called Mrs. Barton, the answering machine was on. He left his name.

"Did she say what happened?" he asked Brenda.

"Not really. She just sounded upset. Apparently Mr. Barton went after her and she had to lock herself in the bathroom. When she came out, he was lying on the floor in a pool of blood. She called 911 and then called you."

"I don't get it," he said and went back into his office.

Two minutes later the phone rang. It was the emergency room at St. Joseph's. Mr. Barton had died in the ambulance on the way to the hospital. Sue Barton was all right except for a few cuts on her arms and thighs and, of course, the shock of the experience. Did the doctor have any light to shed on the suicide? Dan told them what he knew and asked Brenda to fax his neurology consult note to the hospital. He then got on the phone to talk to Bill Light.

"Isn't that something?" Bill said, after he had heard the story. Dan agreed. But when he got off the phone he wondered whether there was anything he could have done differently.

\* \* \*

Mr. Saul Marcus was the last patient for the Friday afternoon clinic.

He was a balding man in his late forties, with stooped shoulders and a persistent, apologetic cough that came close to being a tic.

"I don't know why Miss Durrell had me come to see you. The last thing in the world I need is a neurologist. Certainly not someone who works on Alzheimer's disease. Is that what Miss Durrell thinks is wrong with me?"

"Of course not. But you told her that you had been to three psychiatrists and that they couldn't help you."

"They sure took my money, though. Frankly I don't think they liked it when I told them that I haven't been able to think right ever since I went to see that Dr. Ferdinand."

"I don't understand. Can you explain that a bit more?"

"Sure. It's like there are times when something takes over in my head and before I know it, I go out of control."

"Miss Durrell said you went to see Dr. Beringer. What did he say was going on with you?

"Him? He said nothing. He just sat there with his hands folded over his belly and listened. I never got one word out of him."

Over the next half-hour Dan obtained a detailed medical history from Mr. Marcus. He had been depressed for years but did not think what was going on with him right now was a depression. It was something strange and different. On several occasions he said it outright: he felt as if he had lost control over himself and that scared him. At Dan's request he got up to go to the examining room. As he did so, he stubbed his foot against the leg of the desk. He winced. An instant later his face froze and his eyes became drunken and unfocused.

"I'll get you for this!" he yelled at Dan. Before Dan had a chance to respond, he picked up a glass paperweight and threw it at his head. Dan ducked; the weight crashed against the wall and knocked down a landscape print.

"You asshole!" Mr. Marcus shouted. Fists raised, he charged around the desk. Dan managed to block his way with a chair; that gave him enough time to run out of the office and call for Security. Fortunately, Mr. Marcus did not pursue him.

When Security arrived a short time later, they found Mr. Marcus sitting in a chair, staring at the sole of his shoe. The shattered glass, the disarray on the desk, and the fact that beads of perspiration glistened on the man's face and forehead provided tangible evidence of what had just occurred.

"Are you all right?" Mr. Marcus asked Dan when he returned. He had resumed his former apologetic appearance and his nervous cough was back.

"I'm okay." Actually Dan was a bit shaky and there was a ground glass feeling in the pit of his stomach.

"Sorry about all this. But at least you've had a chance to see what I have to contend with. You have no idea how terrible it is. When this thing comes over me, I can't control it. I simply disintegrate. It's not only emotionally horrible, it's physically painful and debilitating."

Dan picked up remnants of the landscape print, put it on the desk, and threw some of the larger pieces of shattered glass into the wastebasket.

"Would you mind if I talked to Dr. Beringer?" he asked.

"Be my guest."

Dan then went through the formality of a neurologic examination, which, as he had expected, was entirely normal.

When Mr. Marcus left, Dan picked up the phone and dialed Dr. Beringer. He was lucky to find him between therapy sessions.

"This is Dr. Lerner. I am a neurologist at the university, and I have just finished seeing a Mr. Marcus. Saul Marcus. He told me he had been to see you a month or so ago."

There was a moment's hesitation. Dan suspected that Beringer was either trying to remember the patient's name or was undecided whether to talk to Dan over the telephone. "That's right, he did see me," he finally said. "He related quite an unusual story. It did not seem to be too coherent. In fact, he told me he feels . . . possessed." He was being careful with his words. "I saw him as an . . . an angry man with outbursts that he cannot control. I couldn't come up with a better diagnosis, but I certainly didn't accept what he told me about all this having started after he had seen Frank Ferdinand."

"Have you ever seen anybody like him?"

"Not really."

"Do you remember Mr. Arnold Barton? He sort of reminds me of him."

Beringer thought for a few moments. "Barton. Yes, of course, I do recall him. You are right. There are certain similarities between the two men."

"Except that Mr. Barton is dead. He killed himself with a pair of garden shears. This morning."

"Killed himself! Good God!" There was a long pause on the other end of the phone, as if Beringer regretted having momentarily lost his cool. "That man never once gave me the slightest indication that he was suicidal." He sounded as if he were accusing his patient of deception. Dan agreed, and before hanging up promised to keep Beringer in touch with any new developments.

\* \* \*

That evening Dan had dinner at Maureen's apartment. Her presentation of steak Diane left little to be desired. The setting featured an eighteenth century oak dining room table, a damask tablecloth, a pair of silver candlesticks, and Royal Minton dinnerware with an exquisite pattern depicting spring flowers entwined with ivy. Maureen had put on a long black hostess gown with a plunging neckline. She looked terrific, and Dan told her so.

"Thanks," she said simply and started to busy herself in the kitchen.

They had a lot to talk about. Of course, there was Mr. Marcus and how similar his behavior was to that of the late Mr. Barton.

"Wow! Isn't that something," Maureen mused. "I am not sure what to make of it. Right now, though, I will vote for a coincidence. What do you think?"

"I am not sure. I wish I could talk to this Dr. Ferdinand."

"That won't be easy. He knows that Marcus is suing him and he certainly is not going to speak to a voice over the telephone, even if you tell them who you are."

"Maybe I can talk with his lawyers."

"You are going to get even less from them. The best thing is that I subpoena Marcus's records and have you go over them. In the meantime, why don't you get Mr. Barton's records and see whether there is some sort of common denominator."

With a quick movement, Maureen got up from the table.

"I almost forgot. Larry gave this to me. You might be interested in it. He found it among a bunch of in-house documents that he obtained from Marat International. I think I told you he has been working on a products liability case against them. Apparently they've known for years that their Breathelite inhaler was defective and didn't do a thing about it."

She handed him a copy of a letter on Marat stationery. It was an in-house memo directed to Melvin Walton, Vice President of Consumer Relations, and signed by Dr. Albert Lessing, Medical Director. She put on her reading glasses and moved her chair closer to Dan in order to read over his shoulder.

"Dear Walt: As I told you last week, the neurologists at Southwestern University are quite anxious to proceed with developing their PET scan unit. I am of the opinion that we should help them in a substantial manner. Since I am scheduled to be on the West Coast at the end of next month, I intend to use the occasion to meet with Jack Brennan, their chairman. I am certain he will press me for some sort of commitment. Do you think you can get me an answer by then? I can assure you they are doing outstanding work in facilitating our final approval for MI-37801."

Dan handed the sheet back to Maureen.

"Interesting."

"Right," she said and folded up her glasses. "Do you know anything about MI-37801? What kind of drug it might be?"

"I don't recognize it from their in-house number. But I do know that ever since Jack came out West he has been looking for money to develop an imaging center on the B floor."

"Larry says that Marat has quite a few medical schools in its pocket. Lots of the big name schools are hard up these days and they can be bought cheap."

"What do they have to do for them in return?"

"Evaluate new drugs as they come off the pipeline. That's what happened with the asthma inhaler. One of their grantees wrote a paper in which he said that it was 90 percent effective in breaking up severe attacks of asthma, when it turned out it was no better than placebo."

"Who was that?"

"I don't remember his name, but Larry would know. Some professor at a New England medical school. In any case, the study that touted its effectiveness got published and was immediately picked up by the *Wall Street Journal*. It wasn't until Larry found a few people who got in serious trouble when they used the Breathelite inhaler that he started to look around and found a few papers showing that the inhaler didn't deliver adequate blood levels of theophylline, the active agent. One was from Europe and the other one came out of North Carolina. Neither of the papers had been published in American journals."

"How come?"

"I guess no American medical journal would want to ruin the reputation of Marat International." After a moment, she added, "I haven't told you but I managed to get Bill Cowen to cover my deposition next Monday."

"Great! That means we will have three days at Ojai."

"Right." And they started to plan what to take along. It was getting late. She poured a couple of brandies and Dan stayed over for the night.

* * *

When he got back to his apartment the following morning, a call from Peter awaited him. It was Saturday. Dan generally spent the morning in the lab to go over the week's data. This morning, however, he did not have the heart to sit down with Donna. Instead he called her and told her not to bother coming in. He then phoned Peter.

"How are things in Boston?"

"It's freezing cold. I'm sitting in my office wearing a sweater and a jacket."

"It was 74 in L.A. yesterday."

"Don't rub it in. Anyway, I called you last night because I need to pick your brain. I saw two patients, a man and a woman, whom I couldn't make any sense of. What's even stranger, the other day I talked to John Rose over at Tufts, and he has been following a man just like them. If I had to pin a diagnosis on them, I would call it episodic discontrol."

"Episodic discontrol!" The words made Dan take notice.

"For lack of a better term. Actually, there are several features that argue against the diagnosis. For one, all of them are middle-aged people without any previous psychiatric history, except possibly a mild, partly situational depression."

As he went on, Dan thought he heard a summary of the behavior of Mr. Barnes and Mr. Marcus. Finally he could no longer restrain himself.

"Would you believe it: I have two such cases. Actually, only one. The other one just killed himself."

"One of mine nearly did. She got so pissed off waiting at a stoplight that she drove right through it, totaling her car and that of another driver."

"What do you think this is all about?"

"I don't have the faintest idea."

"We should bring one of these people into the hospital and do a complete work-up."

"It won't show anything. Mr. Barton, he's the man who killed himself, had every conceivable test done on him. They were all normal. But I'll tell you what I am doing. I am getting the medical records on both my cases and I'll go through them to see if I can find anything to explain their behavior. By the way, I've thought of a good name for this disorder—the Angry Puppet Syndrome."

"The Angry Puppet Syndrome. I like that. I understand there is something mechanical about their outbursts."

"The way I see it, they act out the anger that's in all of us and that we are normally able to repress. Remember what Thoreau said: 'The multitude of men lead lives of quiet desperation.' For these people the reins that hold in this desperation snap, and off they go."

"Thank God we've only got four cases. We'd really be in trouble if we had an epidemic of them."

That evening Dan and Maureen went to the Music Center. It was an all Brahms program and with Esa-Pekka Salonen directing, the sounds were burnished in chestnut and gold.

As they were driving back to Dan's apartment, he told her about Peter's call.

"We should have most of Mr. Marcus's records by the end of next week. But I won't give them to you until after we come back from Ojai."

"Afraid they'll distract me?"

"Right."

\* \* \*

The week went by quickly and before long it was Friday afternoon, time for them to drive up to Ojai. Just before Dan left his apartment to pick up Maureen the phone rang. It was Judith.

"Dan. When are you coming home?" Her voice was tearful and unreal and he was sorry he had picked up the phone.

"I am home. In my apartment on Doheny."

"You know what I mean—home to me."

"This is no time to talk about it."

"Yes it is. Kim called me last night. She is still unable to reconcile herself. . . ."

"Of course she is. . . ."

"That's what she tells you. It's her brave front. I have been thinking about us. A lot. I know you don't really want to get a divorce. Neither do I. What we ought to do is start all over again. With a fresh mind and our hearts full of love for each other."

"Oh, come on, Judith! That's all water under the bridge."

"I promise to forgive you. Really I do."

There was a bit more about starting over and being forgiven before Dan managed to get off the phone. He congratulated himself that for his part he had been able to keep the conversation on a superficial level. But then, during the years they had lived together, all their conversations had been on a superficial level. It was as if neither wanted to appear truthful and vulnerable. The suitcase lay open on the bed. His relationship with Maureen was easier. They both held back, each for their own reasons; as a result, they avoided that degree of closeness where absence of honesty becomes like a weight that drowns a long-distance swimmer. He zipped up the overnighter and, muttering a curse—God knows where it came from—took his garment bag from the closet. He tossed both suitcase and garment bag into the car and drove to Maureen's apartment. By the time he arrived, he already felt a bit better, and Maureen's hug when she opened the door freed him completely from the weight of his brooding. She set out three days of food for Max, her Siamese cat, and a few minutes later they were off for Ojai.

As it turned out, their weekend was as close to perfect as two imperfect humans could achieve. The sky was lavender from morning to night and a sensual aroma of eucalyptus and laurel surrounded their cottage. To top it off, Dan's nasal allergy disappeared as if by magic. As they were driving back to L.A., Maureen reached into her bag and handed him a file.

"Here it is, like I promised you, the medical records of Mr. Marcus."

"Thanks. I intend to go over them tomorrow night."

\* \* \*

It turned out otherwise. The Monday morning drive out to Las Virgenes took two and a half hours because of freeway construction and he was an hour late getting to the hospital. A dozen patients, all of them Spanish-speaking, were waiting for him and he had to work through lunch hour. Sometime during the afternoon a nurse came into his office.

"Dr. Santos-Alvarez wants to have a few words with you."

Dan didn't know who Dr. Santos-Alvarez was, but the awe in her voice augured that he was someone important. And important he did appear. He was over six feet tall, with a heavy frame and carefully parted black hair. He wore a starched, immaculate white coat, and a shiny, unused stethoscope protruded from the side pocket. All in all, he was a superb specimen of a hospital administrator. Dr. Santos-Alvarez extended his hand.

"Good to have you on board, Dan. I hope we aren't overloading you."

"It's been pretty hectic today but I'm managing."

"Jack was certain you would. We are glad to have someone as competent as you to fill in for Marty." He paused. Dan nodded in agreement, resisting the urge to ask him whether he had played college football. "Let me know if there is anything I can do for you," Dr. Santos-Alvarez said and patted him on the shoulder.

Dan assured him he would. The magnificent white figure moved down the corridor nodding to a row of hunched-up patients who sat motionless as they waited for their doctor.

Dan did not get home until seven and by then he was in no mood to look at Mr. Marcus's records. Instead he prepared cold cuts and washed them down with a few glasses of single malt scotch. It was not one of his most inspired meals.

\* \* \*

Marty DiChiro called bright and early the next morning.

"Say, Dan, if you've got a few minutes, come by my office. We've got to talk."

Dan arrived there an hour later and sat down with his back against a bookcase crammed with bound and unbound journals. Marty backed up the computer file he had been working on and swung his chair around.

"I guess Jack told you that a couple of my post-docs will be moving into your lab. I hate to screw up your research but I understand you haven't been able to get funding for it anyway."

"My grant was approved but I just missed the cutoff."

"I know, it's getting tougher and tougher every year." He paused—a moment of silent sympathy. This gave Dan time to look at the large silver-framed family portrait on Marty's desk: Marty with his hand on the shoulder of a fair-haired woman seated with trunk erect; two teen-aged boys on either side of her, three children sitting cross-legged at her feet. All of them smiling for the camera, smiling in anticipation of a contented and harmonious future. All except the youngest, a scowling boy with tousled hair and a resolutely sour expression. Dan wondered what his future would be. A perpetual rebel? Drugs? Perhaps a belated resignation to convention?

The phone rang. Marty picked it up.

"Dr. DiChiro." Then, "Just a minute." He rotated his chair and, bending down, pulled open the bottom drawer of a black steel file cabinet. He took out a folder and, using his foot, pushed the drawer shut. Dan had enough time to see the label on the drawer: Dulcian. For a moment he wondered what kind of work Marty was doing with Dulcian, and how that could relate to hypothalamic function. With his hand over the receiver, Marty motioned to him. "I'll see you at Grand Rounds," he said.

It was the signal for Dan to leave the office.

"Take care," was Marty's parting remark.

"You too."

\* \* \*

That night Dan started to go over the medical records of Mr. Marcus. Cosgrove and Costello had been thorough and there were three inches of records, going back to a 1975 admission to Fairview

Hospital for repair of an inguinal hernia. He thumbed through the admission examination, looking for an evaluation of mental status. Not much help. All it said next to it was "nl," which meant "normal." From that he surmised that in 1975 Mr. Marcus was neither suicidal nor wildly combative. Surgeons are action-oriented and tend not to contemplate their patients' psyches. Following his surgery Mr. Marcus had seen an internist off and on, and there was another hospital admission in 1985 to Mt. Sinai Hospital for infectious hepatitis. Cosgrove and Costello had provided him with everything that pertained to that admission, including nursing notes, intake and output records, and all laboratory tests. Because Mt. Sinai was a university-affiliated hospital, there was an extensive fourth-year medical student's note that included a psychiatric history.

"Patient has been subject to depressions for the last five years. He states that their onset was related to his divorce and to the fact that his wife was claiming alimony at a time when he was out of a job. He has not been treated and has not sought psychiatric help."

Nothing about outbursts of anger or episodic discontrol. Would a fourth-year medical student know anything about episodic discontrol?

Finally, he came to Dr. Ferdinand's office records. The handwriting was almost illegible and he had to guess at every other word. What he could make out indicated that Mr. Marcus had started to see the doctor about a year ago. His first visit to him was on March 29 because of ringing in his ears. For this he received Dramamine, Benadryl, and Phenergan. It was clear to Dan that Dr. Ferdinand was anything but timid in his use of medications. When Mr. Marcus returned on April 5, there was no improvement. Dr. Ferdinand added erythromycin to the regimen. The note stated. "Rtn 1 wk. If no imprvmt, cons ENT conslt."

"Return in one week," Dan mumbled to himself, as he deciphered Dr. Ferdinand's hieroglyphics. "If no improvement, consider ear, nose, and throat consultation."

The records indicated that a week later the ringing had stopped, and there was only a note for "Re-ck 1 mo." Dan could find no indication that Mr. Marcus kept that appointment, and the next office visit was not until October of the same year. Once again Dr. Ferdinand's note was laconic. "Depressed for years. Saw psychiatrist last month. N.I." It took some time before Dan realized that N.I. stood for No Improvement. If Dr. Ferdinand's note was brief, his treatment regimen was not. "Try Lithium (300 mg bid), Xanax (0.25 mg bid), and Dulcian (5 mg tid). Ret. 2 wks."

Mr. Marcus did return in two weeks. "No better" the note read, then added "Consider 2nd psych opinion." And that was the end of Dr. Ferdinand's office notes. Dan looked for the notes of Mr. Marcus's three psychiatrists, but they were not in the pile. He phoned Maureen. She was still in her office.

"I've just gone over Mr. Marcus's medical records."

"Find anything?"

"Not much. You weren't able to get any of the psychiatric records?"

"No. They're privileged information. I'd have to file the suit and then go to court to obtain them. So what do you think?"

"I think that Dr. Ferdinand keeps inadequate medical records and that he prescribes a lot of drugs."

"So, could this be a drug reaction?"

"I doubt it. According to what Mr. Marcus told me, he is on no medications right now, and any drug reaction would have worn off by now."

"Right. Do you think we should take this case?"

"Oh, come on, Maureen. How should I know? I'm not a lawyer. I can only tell you that I saw nothing Dr. Ferdinand did that could have brought on Mr. Marcus's condition."

"Thanks. That's all I need to know."

"Great . . . when do we see each other?"

"Depends. I'll be in Oakland tomorrow night and all day Thursday but I should be back by Thursday night."

"Let's have dinner Friday night then. Somewhere real casual."

"Fine with me."

Two days later Mr. Barton's medical records arrived in Dan's office. Even though they were quite scanty, he took them home to go over them without being disturbed.

That was not to be. No sooner had he started to go look at the internist's notes than the phone rang. It was Judith.

"What are you doing?" She sounded not only firm and determined, but also a trifle drunk.

"What do you mean what am I doing? I am working."

"Is she with you?" Judith always referred to Maureen as "she."

"No."

"I have to talk to you. Right now."

"I am working."

"I don't believe you. I think she is at your apartment."

"I am working and I am not in the mood to talk to you tonight. So please don't call again. D'you understand?"

"Don't think you can just hang up on me. . . ."

"I certainly can." And he did, and felt proud of his determination.

Determination or no determination, by the time he returned to Mr. Barton's records he no longer was able to concentrate on them. He leafed through the few pages of notes written by Dr. Maxwell, the internist whom Mr. Barton consulted in October because he had been depressed and couldn't shake a cold. Dr. Maxwell must have decided that he could treat what looked like a simple depression. "Rx: Dulcian. Start at 5 mg/day, then in one week increase to 5 mg bid. Return in two weeks."

The follow-up note indicated that there had been no improvement. Dr. Maxwell stopped the medication and informed Mr. Barton that he and Mrs. Barton might consider seeing a psychiatric social worker.

Dan was about to turn the page when it came to him in a flash—both Mr. Barton and Mr. Marcus had been on Dulcian. So what? he asked himself. Pure coincidence. Dulcian was a new antidepressant and a number of physicians were using it for their mildly depressed patients.

He went on with Dr. Maxwell's records. Mr. Barton returned to him in early December. By then it was evident that his behavior had changed. "Outbursts of unprovoked anger," Dr. Maxwell's note read. "Often gets violent. Wife very concerned. "Could we be dealing with a form of dementia?" Dr. Maxwell wrote under Impression. "To Allen Beringer and Bill Light for evaluation."

Dan knew the rest of the story.

That night he could not sleep. On the one hand, he had found the common denominator he was looking for; on the other hand, it was totally implausible to him that a reaction to Dulcian was the cause of what he now called the Angry Puppet

Syndrome. Again and again he reached the same impasse. His nasal allergy began to make itself known. Finally he got up, put a box of tissues on the bedside table, and started to read, not a medical book, but something less demanding—one of the murder mysteries he kept at his bedside. A page or two later he put down the paperback.

The first and most likely possibility was that he was dealing with a coincidence. The second possibility was that he had encountered a new and previously unrecognized reaction to Dulcian. It would have to be an irreversible reaction. The Angry Puppet Syndrome would have to represent an irreversible change in one important aspect of brain function, something like a dementia that affects only a portion of a person's intelligence. He had never before heard of such a condition.

At four in the morning he phoned Peter. It was seven in the morning in Boston and he was having coffee.

"Dan! Where on earth are you?"

"In Los Angeles."

"What are you doing up at four in the morning?"

"I couldn't sleep. I was thinking about the Angry Puppet Syndrome. Both of my patients had been on Dulcian."

"Dulcian." There was a pause. "A lot of people are taking Dulcian these days. It's become fashionable. I read somewhere that its sales are enormous—five billion dollars a year within three years."

"I've also heard that. You told me you had three patients in Boston. Can you find out whether any of them had been on Dulcian at one time or another?"

"No problem. I'll make it my first priority when I get to the office."

He did. Feeling jet-lagged and with a cup of black coffee next to the wash basin, Dan was in the process of shaving when the phone rang.

"Would you believe it! Both of my patients have been on Dulcian," Peter said. "One of them for a month or so, the other for just a week. That's Mrs. Dunmore, the woman who smashed up her car. She developed a rash, or some sort of reaction, and her doctor took her off it."

"What about John Rose's woman?"

"I don't want to call him. Not yet. This looks like an interesting paper for the two of us, and if we include his case, he'll want to have his name on it."

"You are right, he would. So what do you think?"

"I think we either have the most amazing set of coincidences or we have a new and horrible type of drug reaction."

"You know what Sherlock Holmes said: 'When you have eliminated the impossible, whatever remains, however improbable, must be the truth.'"

They agreed to combine their cases and write them up as quickly as possible. The title of the paper would be: "The Angry Puppet Syndrome: An Unusual Adverse Response to Dulcian." Dan would call Marat International, tell them about the patients, and tell them that he suspected Dulcian to be somehow involved in this bizarre dementia.

After he hung up Dan realized that in the last few days his personal clock had been turned back. He was once more excited and enthusiastic about his work, feelings he had not experienced since the days when he had worked in the bush and saved children from dying of meningitis.

After lunch Dan looked up Dulcian in the *Physician's Desk Reference*. The PDR, as it is commonly called, is a hefty book that lists all proprietary drugs, their toxicities, and every conceivable adverse reaction, as reported by the drug companies. Adverse reactions to Dulcian were relatively sparse: rashes, a few cases of transient and reversible bone marrow depression, and as far as central nervous system reactions were concerned, the book listed only depression, drowsiness, and headache. All were so nonspecific that they could well have been placebo effects, that is to say the same effect could have been produced by a pill that contained nothing but sugar. When Dulcian was given in toxic amounts, patients developed abnormalities in liver function, vomiting, and double vision. All in all, it looked as if Dulcian was as harmless as any other antidepressant. With that information in hand, Dan called Marat International and asked to speak to Dr. Albert Lessing, their medical director.

"Who is this?" his secretary asked. Dan gave her his name. The pause of nonrecognition was an indication that Dr. Lessing was in his office, available to some people but not to others.

"Dr. Lessing is in a meeting this afternoon. Can he call you back Friday?"

"Certainly. Tell him I want to report a new adverse reaction to Dulcian."

She agreed to leave the message and took down Dan's number.

As his secretary promised, Dr. Lessing returned the call on Friday morning.

"I have a message that you called about an adverse response to MI-37801."

"MI-37801?"

"Dulcian."

"I did call. Dr. Peter Carter and I have four patients who have been on Dulcian and who have developed a very circumscribed form of dementia. Very much like episodic discontrol. One of my patients committed suicide during such an episode, and one of Dr. Carter's patients smashed up her car and wound up in the hospital."

"I see. Can you tell me a bit more about this reaction?"

Dan gave him a capsule history of his two cases.

"And Dr. Carter thinks he has two more cases like yours?"

"That's right. Both of them are from the Boston area."

"I see. Any others you might have heard about?"

"There is supposed to be one other woman in Boston."

"Also in Boston?"

"Dr. John Rose at Tufts is following her."

"Have you talked to him?"

"Not yet."

"And you do not know of any similar cases from any other part of the country?"

"No."

"Well, Dr. Lerner. Wouldn't you agree that this is a trifle strange? You have found two cases in Los Angeles and two cases in Boston, but not a single case from anywhere else in the country. Don't you think this speaks clearly for a coincidental connection? Remember, post hoc does not denote propter hoc."

"Of course it doesn't."

"Good. I'll tell you what we will do for you. We will send a memo to our field representatives and tell them to be on the lookout for the reaction you think you have encountered. We shall soon know whether any other case turns up. At this point in time I am willing to wager that there won't be any."

"So what do you think we are seeing?"

"That, Dr. Lerner, is your problem, not mine. We'll get in touch. That is, if there is anything to get in touch about."

After he had hung up, Dan phoned Peter.

"I talked to Lessing. He says that Marat has never heard of such a reaction to Dulcian and that it's all coincidence. What do you think?"

"He could be right."

"I don't think so. That's why we must go ahead and write up our four cases. Once the paper is published, we'll soon know whether there are any others out there."

Maureen and Dan had planned to have dinner that night. She was to come by his apartment after work and they would go to a small Italian restaurant a few blocks away. As it turned out, she phoned to say she would be quite late. The office was having a reorganizational meeting with Mike Cosgrove and Tom Costello, and would Dan mind having dinner on his own?

"Of course I would mind, but it doesn't look as if I have a choice. What about you?"

"I can skip dinner. It's good for my figure. Why don't I come by when I am done and we can have some wine."

"I'll pick up dessert for us. And you'll stay over."

"Right. If that's what you like."

"I sure would."

That night, over a good California Cabernet, sliced pears, and petit fours, Dan told Maureen about his four cases and his conversation with Arthur Lessing.

"Lessing is a liar," she said.

"What makes you say that?"

"Because he has lied before. Larry took his deposition in the Breathelite inhaler case last month, and that man is unbelievable. He told Larry under oath that the clinical studies run by Marat showed that their inhaler preparations give adequate blood theophylline levels."

"They don't?"

"They're a joke. They submitted 85 cases to the U.S. Food and Drug Administration, the FDA. Only a handful had concurrent blood levels. And most of these levels were subtherapeutic. Far too low to control even the mildest attack of asthma."

"How did all that get past the FDA?"

"Don't ask me. If I had to guess, I would say that Marat had one of the principal reviewers in their pocket."

"Do you think so?"

"It's being done all the time. When a drug house is as big as Marat International, they have the power to manipulate the FDA." She got up, took off her jacket, and kicked off her shoes. Seating herself on the couch, she tucked in her legs and leaned back.

"I'm worried about Tom. I think he's losing it."

"What makes you say that?"

"He sat in on our meeting, stared at the books, and never said one word. Larry thinks he is depressed, or maybe he's got Alzheimer's disease."

"How old is he?"

"Sixty-four. I've told you he was the one who took me into the firm. He's always had respect for me, gave me support when people were picking on me; it didn't matter to him that I was a woman. I tried to talk to him after the meeting, but he just looked through me, as if he were in another world. I think I'll go see him and get his opinion on Mr. Marcus. Maybe that'll make him come around."

The phone rang. At ten-thirty at night Dan was sure it was the hospital. It turned out to be Judith with a few drinks inside her.

"Dan."

"What do you want?"

"Are you alone?" When he didn't answer immediately, she asked, "Is she there?"

"That's none of your business."

"Just tell me: yes or no. Is she there?"

"I told you it's none of your business." And he hung up.

"Who was that?" Maureen asked when he returned to the dining room.

"Who do you think?"

"Judith. She's checking up on you. I suppose she wanted to know if I was here."

"She did."

"And you told her."

"I didn't."

"Right now I don't give a damn whether you did or didn't. I am going home. You can call me whenever she gives you permission."

She put on her jacket and shoes, picked up her briefcase, and stormed out of the apartment.

\* \* \*

When Dan phoned her at the office the following morning, she had cooled down.

"Just explain one thing to me: what makes you put up with her? Why can't you simply tell her to fuck off?"

"What would that solve?"

"I wish to God she at least would find herself another man."

"So do I."

"The trouble is she doesn't want another man. She prefers to keep her grip on you."

Dan tried to conjure up an image of Judith in bed with another man. It was easy enough to see Judith in bed—pale skin, hazel eyes, full breasts, and wide hips, but the picture of the other man would not come. Instead he saw himself in bed with Maureen, as reflected from the mirror in the partly open door of the oak wardrobe in her bedroom. He told that to Maureen. She laughed.

"I didn't know you went in for that sort of thing. Maybe I should get a mirror for the ceiling as well. Or would that be too obvious?"

Dan thought it might be.

"What I never got around to telling you last night. . . ."

"You were too mad at me."

"Right. What I want to tell you this morning, though, is that you and I should meet with Mr. Marcus. If Lessing is the liar I think he is, he knows more about adverse reactions to Dulcian than he lets on. I want to get Mr. Marcus's permission to file a products liability suit against Marat International."

"How can you? We have no evidence whatever that the Angry Puppet Syndrome has anything to do with Dulcian."

"Now wait a minute. You've told me you have four cases of your syndrome and all of them have been given Dulcian. . . ."

"Have been exposed to Dulcian," Dan interrupted. "That's the proper term." He heard himself sound pedantic and hated himself for it.

"All right. Exposed to Dulcian. So what do you think the likelihood is that you are dealing with a coincidence?"

Dan did some quick mental calculations. Although he was not good with statistics, he could see that if 0.1 percent of the U.S. population had been exposed to Dulcian at one time or another—a more than generous estimate—then the likelihood that they were dealing with a coincidence was 1 in 1000 to the fourth power, which was 1 in 1 followed by 12 zeros. If the fraction of people exposed to Dulcian was as high as 1 percent, an implausibly high assumption, the likelihood of a coincidence was 1 in 1 followed by 8 zeros. Both figures were astronomically small ratios. Dan gave these values to Maureen.

"Great," she said.

"Are you sure?"

"What kind of odds do you think I need to file a suit? I've got all weekend to get the papers together. Monday morning I'll get Charlotte to go downtown and file it in court."

"I won't see you then?"

"I don't think so, even if I can get Larry to help me, which, knowing Larry, is a big if."

It was a working weekend for the two of them. Dan worked on the first draft of his paper, and Maureen worked on getting the suit filed. At two o'clock Sunday afternoon she phoned.

"I just talked to Mr. Marcus. I'm having him come by my office in an hour. Can you be there?"

An hour later the security guard let Dan into the building. Cosgrove and Costello was on the top floor of the West-Wilshire Center. It was a clear, smog-free afternoon and the view from Maureen's office extended over the entire Los Angeles basin from the Hollywood Hills to the Marina. The sunlight was reflected from the glass of her University of Michigan Law School diploma and bounced off the glass doors of her bookcases. Dan moved a couple of cartons filled with files from the sofa to the floor and sat down.

"What a view you've got!"

"I should take you to see Mike's office. He's got the corner office. It's unbelievable."

"Mr. Marcus is late."

"I told security he would be coming. So he shouldn't have any problem downstairs."

"By the way, what do you need me here for?"

"To be on the safe side. If something triggers that man off and he gets violent, I'd hate to be alone with him."

"Makes sense."

They started to make small talk. Maureen was wearing a white blouse and a fitted black velvet jacket that Dan had never seen on her before. The broad white collar resting against the black shoulders made her appear demure—a look that was totally out of place in Beverly Hills. Dan commented on how well the jacket suited her.

"Nordstrom. They had it on sale. Marked down by two-thirds. I guess no one wanted it."

"Judith never buys anything that is on sale. She says it lowers her standards."

"How much are you giving her each month?"

"Too much. She doesn't need my money."

"I can imagine. You're much too easy on her. You should tell her to get a job rather than drive around Beverly Hills in her silver Rolls Royce. It would do her a lot of good."

More small talk. Mr. Marcus was already twenty minutes late.

"Larry was in here earlier today, complaining to me because our weekend secretary hadn't come in. He's sorting out a stack of new in-house documents that he just obtained from Marat. You and I should go through them after he is done. We might find something that pertains to Dulcian."

Maureen looked at her watch. "I think I'll give Mr. Marcus a call and see what's keeping him."

She dialed a number. There was no answer.

A few minutes later Dan's beeper went off. It was the answering service. A Sergeant Dobson from the West Hollywood Police Station. Dan returned his call.

"This is Dr. Lerner. I understand you are trying to reach me."

"I certainly am. Do you know a Saul Marcus?"

"Marcus. Of course. He came to see me a few days ago. What's happened?"

"To make a long story short, Mr. Marcus is dead."

"Dead!" On the other side of the desk Maureen put down her pen and looked wide-eyed.

"That's right."

"What happened?"

"He put a bullet through his head."

"For heaven's sake!"

"Anything you can add to this? Like a preexisting psychiatric illness?"

"In a way, yes."

"I thought as much. Do you mind if I come by your office tomorrow morning and get some more information?"

"Of course not. Except that I'll be at Las Virgenes Hospital much of the day."

"No problem. I'll have a squad car drive me up there."

"Did you hear that?" Dan asked Maureen after he had hung up. She shook her head.

"What happened?"

"I don't know. All I know is that Marcus put a bullet through his head. I'll find out more tomorrow."

There was a minute of silence. Somewhere in the office a refrigerator started to hum. The neon lights in the copy room buzzed like trapped flies.

"There is no use in your filing the suit then, is there?"

"No. It'll be practically impossible for me to find his ex and kids and have them file for wrongful death. The only thing that I could do is to get one of the remaining patients to file a suit." She stood up. Wrapped in thought, she leafed through the documents on her desk. She picked them up, tapped them into order, and placed them into a folder. Her hands looked efficient and business-like, not one wasted motion.

"Let's go," she said.

As they got out of the elevator, she said, "I'll fly out to Boston tomorrow morning. Can you call your friend Peter and let him know I'll want to meet with him?"

Although Maureen appeared composed, she was too upset for dinner.

"I still have to talk with Mark Lynch and see if he can help me file the case in Massachusetts. After that I'll have a whiskey and read the Sunday *New York Times*. And then I'll do my packing."

"How long will you be gone?"

"Three, four days. Let's hope I won't be too late. That syndrome of yours seems to have a significant mortality."

\* \* \*

In view of the daily stream of drunks, drug addicts, and shooting victims, a squad car pulling up in front of the clinic building at Las Virgenes Hospital arouses little attention. So when Sergeant Dobson appeared in the waiting room of the neurology clinic and asked for Dr. Lerner, the secretary simply directed him to the doctor's cubicle. As luck had it, Dan was between patients.

"Fill me in on what happened," Dan said.

It had all started when Mr. Marcus was about to go to the supermarket for the Sunday *Times*. As he went to his car, which had been parked overnight in front of the apartment house, the dog belonging to the man across the street ran up to him and barked. A neighbor, who at the time was watering his plants, saw the whole episode. He told Dobson he was certain that the dog did not actually attack Mr. Marcus and that Mr. Marcus blew his top without any other obvious provocation. In a matter of moments he had opened the glove compartment of his car, taken out a gun, and fired three shots at the dog, two of which struck the animal in the chest and killed it instantly. When its owner came out of the house and screamed, Mr. Marcus fired two shots in his direction. One went through the window of the apartment house; the other entered the man's thigh, barely missing a major artery. After all that Mr. Marcus returned to his apartment, locked himself in the bathroom, and put the remaining bullet through his head.

"He must have been an angry man," Sergeant Dobson concluded with considerable perspicuity.

"Not always." Dan provided the sergeant with a capsule history.

"That is weird. Like nothing I've ever heard."

Dan agreed. Sergeant Dobson pocketed his note pad, shook hands with the doctor, and strode away. Before Dan had time to reflect on the events, his next patient had checked in and was ready to see him.

\* \* \*

With Maureen out of town, Dan's evenings were free and in a few days he completed the first draft of his paper. He called Peter and told him he would fax a copy for him to work on.

"Who is this Maureen Durrell?" he asked.

"An attorney I have been working with."

"She came by to talk to me. Quite a neat looking lady. A bit aggressive, but I suppose you have to be in her line of work. She thinks you are the greatest."

"Does she, now?"

Peter was not taken in by Dan's off-hand response. "Anything going on between the two of you?"

Dan was straight with Peter. He always was. When Judith and Dan had separated. Peter was one of the first to hear about it.

"She's a lovely lady. I wish I had her here in Boston."

"You don't need her. You have Jackie."

"Of course. But with Jackie one longs for a bit of variety."

Jackie was a stunning redhead fifteen years younger than Peter. Intelligence was not her strong suit.

\* \* \*

That evening Dan made considerable progress on the second draft of the paper, and by the end of the week he and Peter had a concise manuscript of some six double-spaced pages and about a dozen references.

This would be an important piece of work; far more important than the work he did on the role of neurotrophic factors in Alzheimer's disease.

"We should develop a hypothesis as to why Dulcian induces this condition," Peter said. "I for one would like to suggest that the drug induces an irreversible increase in excitability of a circuit in that portion of the brain which we share with even the simplest vertebrates and which translates an inner feeling of anger into a physical stereotypic response."

"You know much more about this than I do."

"I probably do."

\* \* \*

Maureen called from Boston that evening. Dan was at his desk checking the citations.

"I hear that you and Peter Carter have written your paper."

"Pretty much so."

"Good. Now will you please explain to me how Dulcian acts on the brain."

"Do you have a few minutes?"

"I wouldn't have phoned you if I didn't."

So Dan explained Peter's hypothesis to her, namely, that Dulcian caused a set of nerve cells in the brain to go into high gear and speed up permanently. Because these particular nerve cells were located in a primordial part of the brain that deals with the arousal and feeling of anger, and acts on it, it would result in unpredictable outbursts of violence in response to what normally were trivial frustrations.

"He thinks that Dulcian switches on a primitive defensive rage behavior over which the higher brain centers have no control whatever."

"And this never wears off?"

"Apparently not. The drug probably is attached irreversibly to the nerve cells in this primordial circuit."

"That's an interesting hypothesis, but of course there is no way you two can prove it."

"Not right now. Peter has some ideas about that, but first we need to find some more patients."

"And why do you think that Dulcian only does this to a few selected people?"

"I wish I knew. It puzzles me."

"Sorry I can't help you."

"There's a man in our department who specializes in this area of the brain. I don't know if I've mentioned him to you: Marty DiChiro. He runs the Wallace Research Laboratory."

"DiChiro. Isn't he the one who took over your technician?"

That's right. Peter calls him a vulture. I consider him a political animal. But he also is very bright. I intend to talk to him and see if I can pick his brain."

"Don't let him find out why you're interested."

Dan assured Maureen he would not.

Friday afternoon, after having seen his last clinic patient, Dan set out to contact Marty. First he went to his old laboratory. Donna was there. She was pipetting buffers into a series of plastic micro-tubes. She smiled when he sat down on the stool next to her.

"How are things?" he asked.

"Coping." She removed the pipette tip and pulled off her plastic gloves, throwing them into the metal can by her feet.

"Want some coffee?"

"Why not?"

"No cream or sugar, right?"

"That, at least, hasn't changed."

A poster of Notre Dame hung on the wall behind Donna's lab bench. Dan had mounted it when he had first moved into the lab. Whenever he looked at the poster, he could imagine a throng of ragged and impoverished medieval peasants crowding into the cathedral on feast days. Religion provided hope for them, the promise of eternal life.

Donna glanced around the lab. They were alone.

"One of my problems is that I can't make out Dr. Kyoshi's English," she said. "He carries this dictionary with him, and whenever I can't understand him, he tells me to wait and then points to the word he wants. That man lives in the lab. He is here in the morning when I arrive, and he is still here when I go home at night."

"Where is he right now?"

"He just left. Probably went to see Dr. DiChiro."

"Do you think you can come in next weekend and help me finish the last run of slides?"

"I'll try. If Kyoshi objects, I'll act as if I don't understand him."

Dan finished the coffee and put the dirty cup into the sink.

"You haven't seen Dr. DiChiro?"

"Not today. The other techs tell me he hardly ever comes around in the afternoon."

As it turned out, Marty wasn't in his office either. His secretary thought he had gone to see the chairman. She had no idea when he would be back. The door to Marty's office was open and from where Dan stood he could see the silver-framed family photo of the smiling winners. The concept of quiet desperation was unknown to any of them, except possibly to that scowling little brat in the front row.

He had just returned to his office when Marty's secretary phoned to tell Dan that her boss could see him Monday morning at eight. Suppressing a natural reluctance to agree to a meeting at such an ungodly hour, he told her that he would be there.

He spent Saturday afternoon in the library verifying the references for his paper and reading up on what was known about episodic discontrol and its relationship to the primordial circuit that arouses and controls anger and rage. He even found one of Marty's papers: "Role of NMDA receptors in hypothalamic facilitation of feline defensive rage."

It was a complicated paper. It showed that it was possible to induce an outburst of intense rage in a cat by applying NMDA, one of the many chemical messengers by which nerve cells talk to each other, to the surface of nerve cells in the hypothalamus, a portion of the brain that is an important link in the primordial rage circuit.

After Dan had finished reading the paper and had gone over the various graphs and tables, he was not sure whether he had understood any of it.

Later that day when Dan got back to the apartment and turned on his answering machine, he heard Maureen's voice. She was back in town and would love to see him. He returned her call and they made arrangements to have dinner at her apartment.

"I hope you won't mind. It'll be take-out food."

"Pizza?"

"Don't be silly! I can do better than that. I'll stop off at Michel-Francois to get some paté and a casserole of chicken chausseur. Doesn't that sound good?"

"It does. I'll bring some wine."

"If that's what you want. See you at eight."

Over dinner Dan found out that while in Boston Maureen had met with Mrs. Dunmore, and that with Mark Lynch as co-counsel, Mrs. Dunmore had filed a suit against Marat International under the Massachusetts Products Liability Act.

"What if she kills herself?"

"We took care of that contingency. We have named Shawmut National Bank as co-litigant and guardian for her estate, which will be in the name of her two minor sons."

"Now what?"

"We'll see what the defendants' response will be. I can't wait to depose Lessing and find out what his experience has been with adverse reactions to Dulcian."

"What if he tells you just what is listed in the package insert and in the PDR?"

"We will do what Larry did. Before we depose him we will get Marat to turn over the in-house documents on Dulcian."

"They won't agree to it."

"You mean they will claim the documents are protected by privilege?"

"Is that how you term it?"

"Yes. They'll probably have to come up with them, though. If they object, which I am sure they will, I'll file a motion to compel their production. I bet the court will go along with me."

Even though they had finished the bottle of zinfandel Dan had brought and quite a bit more of Maureen's cognac, neither of them had a hangover and Sunday morning was as pleasant and casual as could be with them drinking coffee, making love, and reading the *New York Times*, which took care of any other activities for the remainder of the day.

\* \* \*

Although not fully awake, Dan managed to be in Marty's office Monday morning at eight.

"Come and sit down, and tell me what's on your mind." Marty sounded bright and energetic, as if he had gotten up three hours earlier for a few miles of cross-country jogging. "I hear that things are working out pretty well between you and Kyoshi as far as the technician is concerned."

"She manages to come in a for a couple of hours each weekend. She should have finished her work for me by the end of next month."

"Super." He was waiting for Dan to get started.

"What do you know about neuronal receptors in the hypothalamus?" Dan asked. Marty gave a soft laugh and moved his ball-point pen back and forth across the desk. Dan avoided looking at the All-American family.

"What type of receptor are you interested in?"

"The NMDA receptors."

Marty looked at him as if he were a hopeless idiot. Everyone was supposed to know that there were several completely distinct types of NMDA receptors in the brain. It was no longer fashionable in scientific circles to lump them together.

"You mean the NMDA receptors in the dorso-median hypothalamus? That's Shakar's work. He has a couple of recent papers that you might want to look up. He is one of the major players in this field."

Dan made a few notes.

"By the way, why do you want to know?" Marty asked. Dan had his story ready.

"This is what it's about. I volunteered to give a talk to the people at Las Virgenes, and I thought I would tell them about the neurology of emotions. It seemed to me that this kind of topic would keep them from falling asleep."

"How come they have you giving talks? They never asked me."

"It's a new idea that Santos-Alvarez has come up with. Something he calls interactive learning. "

"Interactive learning. A great title."

"There will be lectures by doctors, nurses, physiotherapists, social workers, and even by some of the nonmedical employees. The clinic clerk is going to give an hour's talk on commuting between East L.A. and Las Virgenes."

"And you are going to talk on what?" He obviously had not been listening.

"The neurology of emotions."

"So how can I help you?"

"I would like you to steer me to some key papers, preferably reviews, on how drugs can affect emotions." The file drawer labeled Dulcian stared Dan in the face. He pointed to it. "Like Dulcian. How does that work as an antidepressant? I imagine you're doing a lot of work on that."

"Oh, Dulcian." Marty made a deprecatory movement. "Not really. I'm doing some exploratory work on its effect on impotence. Nothing very exciting."

The conversation Dan had overheard in the library concerned a drug house grant of $575,000 over the next five years. Hardly the amount anyone would receive for some exploratory work on the effect of Dulcian on impotence. Even though in the course of the neurourology conference Marty had said something to the effect that the positive effect of Dulcian on impotence could open up a whole new market for the drug.

"I hope Marat is funding you," Dan said.

"Actually they are not. Jack gets a bit from them. Not enough to make any difference to his budget." All at once he became abrupt. "Now look. Why don't I give you a couple of references to get you started? When did you say you are giving your talk?"

"I am not sure yet. Sometime next month."

Marty pulled over a pad and started to write down names. He tore off the sheet and handed it to Dan.

"That should do it. Just do a computer search on any of them and that'll get you started."

When Dan returned to his office he realized that he had not learned much from his talk with Marty, except that Marty wasn't being straight with him with respect to the funding he was receiving from Marat International. There was always a possibility that he was getting the $575,000 from some other drug house. Which firm and for what work was still a mystery.

Maureen did not think it would remain a mystery for too long. "If Marty or Jack is receiving a grant from Marat, the amount and what it's for should be in the company's records. We'll wait and see what turns up next."

* * *

As far as Dan was concerned what turned up next was a visit from Marat's Regional Sales Representative. Frank Duffy was a man in his late twenties, tall and already a trifle on the heavy side, with an ingratiating smile and an easy manner. He loved to chat whenever he came by Dan's office and in the course of past visits Dan had learned a lot about him. His father had died during Frank's senior year in college and the young man had to take a job right after graduation. For the last year or so he and his girlfriend had been living together, trying to save enough money for him to attend medical school, which he hoped to do before another three or four years. Dan had encouraged him, told him that he would make a great doctor, and promised to write the necessary recommendations when the time came.

"So what's new?" Dan asked when Frank appeared in his office carrying a heavy black sample case.

"We've just come out with Luperdol. It's the best antacid on the market. No adverse reactions and it really is well tolerated by patients. And then we have Migrinal, which is a great drug for migraine. It doesn't have the high incidence of recurring headaches that sumatriptan has, and it can be given both by injection and orally. Why don't I leave you some samples for your patients? And, of course, we think that with Dulcian we have the best antidepressant there is. It is prompt-acting and patients only require one to two doses a day."

"Any adverse reactions to Dulcian?"

"Nothing of any importance. You've seen the package insert, haven't you?"

"Yes. Anything you've heard of that isn't in the insert?"

From the look that Frank gave him, Dan could tell there was something he was keeping to himself.

"May I sit down?"

"Of course." He sat down and placed the sample case between his legs.

"A funny thing has come up that I might as well tell you about. A doctor up in Modesto told me about a woman he had put on Dulcian, and after a few weeks or so her personality changed. She started to have outbursts of temper like nothing else. So he stopped the medication."

"What happened to the woman?"

"I don't know. I haven't been up there for quite some time. She wasn't the only one, though. There also was a man in Carpenteria who did something quite similar. His doctor phoned me and asked whether he should take him off Dulcian. I told him I didn't know but that I would talk to our medical director."

"Did you?"

"I sure did. Dr. Lessing said for us to be on the safe side and have the doctor stop the Dulcian. So that's what I told him."

"I know of five other cases like that."

"No kidding?"

"Do I sound like it? I have seen two, and there are three more in Boston. The two in L.A. are dead."

Frank fixed his eyes on Dan and nodded. Bending down, he opened his sample case and took out a pad. He scribbled a note to himself. "I'm going to call these doctors tonight and find out what happened. Isn't that what you want me to do?"

"Yes. And call me back as soon as you have any information."

"I think I'll also phone Dr. Lessing and tell him about your cases."

"Don't bother. I already did. Are you going over to see Dr. DiChiro?"

"I was planning to. Why do you ask?"

"Not a word to him about our conversation. Please. Not until I give you the okay. D'you understand?"

Frank Duffy promised not to say a word. He picked up his sample case.

"Isn't that something?" he said as he was about to leave. "And I thought we had a real winner."

\* \* \*

Frank was as good as his word. Friday afternoon, while Dan was in clinic, he phoned.

"You won't believe this. They're both dead."

"Both?"

"Both the woman in Modesto and the man up in Carpenteria. The woman—she was working for an insurance company—she jumped out of the window of her office building, and the man picked up a gun and killed his wife, his two children, and himself. And this morning I got a call from a doctor in Fresno. He has a man who was on Dulcian and has developed what he says are horrible mood swings. Do you have any idea what's going on?"

"Not really. By the way, did you get a memo from Dr. Lessing about these reactions?"

"No. Should I have?"

"Maybe you will before too long. When you do, give him a follow-up on your cases."

After Dan finished clinic, he phoned Maureen's office. Her secretary told him she was not at her desk and that she was not expected in until Monday morning. He left his name and then called her apartment. She was not home and there was no answering machine.

Dan finally reached her at nine.

"Where have you been? I was getting worried."

"Having a few drinks at the Peninsula Hotel." She sounded peculiar.

"What's wrong?"

"I feel shitty, Dan. Absolutely shitty."

"Tell me."

"I don't feel like talking. I just feel like going to bed and sleeping."

"Would you like me to come over?"

"No, thanks. I just want to be by myself."

"What happened?"

"Didn't you hear me? I don't want to talk about it. I'll call you in the morning."

"Promise?"

"Yes. Good night and thanks for worrying about me."

Next morning when Maureen called, the explanation for her behavior became clear. She had gone to see Tom Costello with the Marcus and Dunmore files in order to get his opinion on how to proceed with the cases. The moment she came in, she knew Tom was acting strangely. At first she thought he was drunk, but that wasn't it. Before too long he brought up her Christmas bonus and what a valuable member of the firm she had been, all the time staring at her bosom. She tried to stay cool, but he would have none of it.

"He made a serious pass at me. He is sixty-four years old, with a thirty-five-year-old wife, and that jerk makes a pass at me."

"What did he do?"

"Oh, come on! Use your imagination. He locked the door of his office, and I was begging him to unlock it."

"You got away?"

"Not before he made me take off my blouse and bra. I tell you if I hadn't done that, that man would have raped me. What do you think I should do?"

"Why don't I come by and we can talk about it."

"Okay. I'll make some coffee. I haven't had anything to eat since yesterday morning."

"I have some Danish. I'll bring it over."

Dan was to meet with Donna and go over their new data. He phoned her and told her to try to put in a few hours without him and that, Kyoshi and Las Virgenes willing, they'd get together Monday night.

Over coffee and Danish he tried to console Maureen.

"It is so degrading, so utterly degrading," she repeated over and over again. "He had always been so supportive of me. He was the dad I never had."

Maureen looked into her coffee cup. The Danish remained suspended over the plate. "My father never thought I would amount to anything. As far as he was concerned, I should have gotten married and had children. Never put out a penny to help me through law school. Never was there for me. Even when I was little I tried to make up to him; I'd do my best, be cute, say smart things, but he would push me away, shut me out. I'd climb the stairs to my room and immerse myself in a book. No way was I going to cry, even though, God knows, I felt like it most of the time." She took a bite of her Danish. "I loved Tom. He respected me, thought I was great, but now. . . ." Although she tried to hide it, Dan could tell that she was fighting back her tears.

"I don't know what to do," she said. "How can I go on working with a man like that around me? And if I quit, I've lost all my seniority. It's more than I can stand. That jerk! Why did he have to do such a thing to me?"

"Can you talk to Cosgrove?"

"That wouldn't do any good. Mike isn't interested in such things. He'd class them under the heading of office gossip."

After more coffee and Danish, they decided that the best thing would be if Maureen were to go back to the office and try to act as if nothing had happened. Dan was pained to see her in such distress. He felt the only way he could help was to sit with her in the kitchen, cut thin slices of Danish pastry, and refill her coffee cup.

"Life's a bitch," Maureen finally said, "a lousy bitch."

Dan agreed, but from the banality of her remark he could sense how upset she was.

\* \* \*

The following day they took a ride to Malibu and walked along the beach. Being March, the sky was overcast and it was still chilly and they were spared the usual Sunday crowds. Maureen was subdued and hardly talked all day. They had an early dinner at Bernie's on the Beach and he drove her back to her apartment.

"You won't mind, will you," she said. "I'd rather not have you stay over tonight. I'll get over this soon, I promise."

When Dan got home from Las Virgenes the following evening there was a call from Maureen on the answering machine, asking him to come by.

He washed up, did a quick look through the mail—bills and advertising, as usual—and drove over. Maureen filled two glasses with whiskey.

"I want you to see the note I had waiting for me in my office."

She handed him a folded card with the initials TC enscrolled on the front leaf. "It's from Tom Costello," Maureen said. He opened it.

"Dear Maureen," the note read. "My humblest and most profuse apologies for Friday afternoon. I hope you will try to forgive me. The last few months have been difficult for me. I feel that I am losing control of myself. I intend to do something about it, for it has been destructive to everyone who comes in contact with me—family, associates, and not least of all you, who are one of the most valuable members of our firm. Yours, Tom."

"Did you talk to him?"

She nodded. "He is seeing a shrink."

"That's a start."

"I am so glad you came by on Saturday morning. It made all the difference in the world to me."

"Shall we go out for dinner?"

"Why not? I'm starved."

They had dinner at their favorite Italian place. It had rained a short time before, a brief but heavy downpour. There were huge puddles in front of the restaurant and towels had been laid inside the entrance to prevent the water from seeping under the door. It was the first opportunity Dan had to tell Maureen about the three cases Frank Duffy had encountered. She put down her fork.

"That makes eight cases. This is big," she said. "Much bigger than we realize."

"Where do we go from here?"

"Larry said he's finished looking through the Marat in-house correspondence and we can have it. I'll bring it home and you and I can go over it tomorrow night. By the way, what's happening with your paper?"

"Peter has it, and he is making some final corrections. It should be ready to go out as soon as I get Jack's okay."

"Jack? Why him?"

"Chairman's prerogative. He wants to see every paper before it is sent out for publication."

One of the first communications that Jack sent out to all members of his department once he had been appointed chairman was a memo saying that in order to ensure "the continued high standards of excellence of the department," every publication issued by members of the department would have to be submitted to his office for approval. In most instances this turned out to be a mere formality; occasionally he would make some minor suggestions. In rare instances, such as when a paper happened to deal with cerebral blood flow, his area of expertise, he would add a few, often pertinent comments.

"What journal do you think you will send it to?"

"Peter and I thought it was important enough to send it to the *New England Journal*. It has a worldwide readership and we should find out quite soon how many more cases of our syndrome are out there."

"I wouldn't be surprised if there were quite a lot."

"Are you thinking of a class action suit?"

"I don't know yet. I would want to file it in federal court. But this is something I'll have to talk over with Larry or with someone else in the office." She paused. "Oh, God, I wish I could put a halter on Mike."

"What do you mean?"

"That man is in a dozen different places at the same time. When someone asks him about a case, he tells them to talk to Larry, or Nolan, or whoever."

"So what good is he?"

"He is our rainmaker. He does publicity for the firm. Drums up cases, although God knows we have more than enough."

They got up and started to leave. As she stood behind him she placed her hand on the back of his head, then ran it down to caress his neck.

"Anything else we might do tonight?" she asked. It was a gentle but seductive smile. For an instant Dan saw her as a teenager—pretty but vulnerable, a girl who had learned to ingratiate herself with a smile.

\* \* \*

The final version of the paper arrived by fax from Boston the next morning. Dan went over it once more, then gave it to Brenda to make it look presentable before dropping it off at Jack's office for his approval. That night, after a quick dinner of cold cuts at Maureen's apartment, the two of them pored over the Marat in-house correspondence that Larry had left with her.

The material was in two brown accordion folders. Larry's secretary had arranged it chronologically, with dividers for each year. There was little in those folders that had anything to do with Dulcian. Most of the correspondence dealt with production costs of the Breathelite inhaler, plans for its distribution, and analyses of the substantiating research documents that had been submitted to Washington for final FDA approval. There was one item, however, that aroused their interest. It was a memo from Dr. Lessing to Mr. Nicholas Cusworth, Assistant to the C.E.O., Marat International, written about two years earlier.

"At this point it is necessary that we sit down and discuss the difficulties we have encountered with our Breathelite Inhaler. We have received several reports suggesting that the inhaler is not very effective in terminating severe asthmatic attacks. We must, therefore, rethink our advertising posture so that it is more in line with the new data that we have gathered concerning its effectiveness. In addition, there is another different matter of concern that I would like to bring to your attention."

A handwritten note at the bottom of the memo said: "Okay for Tuesday at 3."

"Do you make anything out of this?" Dan asked.

"No. Do you?"

"It could mean something or nothing."

And they left it at that.

* * *

When Dan arrived at work the following morning, Brenda told him that Jack Brennan's administrative assistant had called. The chairman would like to meet with him at five-thirty. She did not know what it was about.

Dan arrived promptly at five-thirty, trying to look as relaxed as possible. His allergies had resurfaced and he was dabbing his nose with tissues.

"Dr. Brennan still has someone in with him," the administrative assistant said. "Would you mind having a seat?" Dan took the chair offered to him. "May I get you some coffee?" In view of the late hour, he declined and waited. After about ten minutes, Marty came out of Jack's office. Dan gave him his best chock-full of charm smile, but Marty did not respond and walked by as if he did not exist. Dan thought the behavior strange but at that moment attributed it to Marty's preoccupation with other, more important matters. There was a buzz on the intercom.

"Dr. Brennan is ready to see you now," the administrative assistant announced.

When Dan came in, Jack was stony-faced and there were none of his usual light preliminaries. The manuscript was on the desk before him. Dan immediately knew that it had been the subject of discussion with Marty.

"Sit down, and let's talk about this. First of all, who is this Peter Carter?"

"He is Professor of Neurology and Psychology at Boston University."

"In Arnie Feldman's department?"

"Yes." Jack scribbled a note for himself and returned to the manuscript.

"Will you tell me just exactly what you are trying to say in this paper of yours?"

"We are presenting four cases of what we consider to be an unusual adverse reaction to Dulcian."

"You are presenting four patients without any substantial evidence, without any controls, without either physiologic, neurochemical, or pathologic data. You call this science?" He pulled out the pointer and with an abrupt movement placed it diagonally on the desk in front of him.

"They are case reports."

"These are anecdotes. I expect more from you than a paper of this sort, and I will not permit it to come out of my department."

"These are not anecdotes, Jack. These are four well-worked up cases. All of them have been exposed to Dulcian and all of them have the same unique clinical presentation. I don't see any reason why we cannot submit them to a medical journal."

Jack put the pointer back into his breast pocket, pushed back the chair, and gave Dan a vicious look.

"I don't know about this Peter Carter, although I intend to call Arnie and find out more about him. But as far as you are concerned, your posture worries me. It shows a lack of respect for the essentials of science. In fact, I have the distinct impression that you are depressed. Deeply depressed. I have been told that you and your wife have separated. Is that correct?"

"We've been separated for several years."

"I see. I have yet to encounter a person whose scientific career has not been adversely affected by a broken marriage. Have you been drinking?"

"What do you mean by 'drinking'?"

"I mean drinking to the extent that it has interfered with your judgment and has allowed you to write a paper that I would consider fiction rather than science." He paused. "I want to be frank with you. You are courting disaster. I question your integrity and your ethics, and I suspect there is someone in the background who has incited you to write this."

"No one has incited me to write this paper."

"There are quite a few law firms in this city who would come up with a five-figure sum to have a paper such as yours appear from a top-flight university department like mine."

"I am not connected to any law firm."

"That remains to be seen."

Dan thought of Maureen. If it had not been for her, he would never have seen Mr. Marcus. He was determined not to let himself be intimidated.

"Don't you believe in academic freedom? In my right to submit a paper as I see fit?"

"Are you challenging me?" Jack's voice rose and his ears turned red.

"No."

"Good. Because I can handle a challenge from someone like you. Any day." Dan was confronted by the chairman's jaw and lower lip. Before he had an opportunity to reply, Jack picked up the folder containing the manuscript and shook it in Dan's face.

"Now take this and don't even think of doing an end run around me."

"What do you mean?"

"You know full well what I mean—publishing it without my approval."

\* \* \*

That evening, with Maureen sitting on his living room couch, Dan had regained his composure.

"What are you going to do?" she asked.

"Publish my paper."

"And what about Jack?"

"What about him?" He paused for a moment and looked into Maureen's green eyes. "What would you think of me if I were to back down? If I told Jack that I had thought things over and that I'll put away the paper until I get his okay?"

"I would understand."

"Yes, you would. But that is not what I am going to do. You see, when I joined the Peace Corps I did so in order to get away from Judith and regain respect for myself. I wanted to wipe out all the shit that was dumped on me by her and, before she came on the scene, by my family. I succeeded, even though it took three years in the bush, a few bouts of dysentery, and near-death from malaria. By the time I left Africa, leaving behind me a neat, well-run, little dispensary, I knew my presence had made a difference to a small region of that continent. There were people alive down there who wouldn't have been alive if it hadn't been for me. I felt validated, so that I can never again become the pathetic little jerk I was when I married Judith. That's why I am going to go ahead with that paper."

Maureen nodded; her face looked beautiful. "What I don't understand," she said, "is why Jack flew off the handle."

She got up from the couch. Her arms fell down to her sides as she looked around the living room. "I forget where you keep your scotch."

A short time later she leaned against the sideboard, glass in hand.

"Let's reason this through," she started out. "I shall assume that I am a department chair and that one of my people brings me a paper that is horrendously bad. I would tell him that it has no business going out of my department in its present form, and I would hand it back to him with more or less concrete suggestions as to how to improve it. But that's not what happened in your case."

"It certainly did not."

"What happened is that Jack Brennan threatened you, accused you of being a loony, or a drunk, and what have you. There is only one reason for him to do this." Glass in hand, Maureen paced about the living room. With a quick movement she turned and pointed the glass in Dan's direction. "What would that be?"

"I don't know."

"Because Jack Brennan felt threatened by you."

"By me?"

"Not by you, but by something in that paper of yours. I can assure you of one thing—that man will do everything in his power to keep you and Peter from publishing those four cases."

"But why do you think our paper threatened him?"

"Right now I have not the slightest idea, but I'm willing to bet that we'll find out before too long."

\* \* \*

The next morning Dan phoned Peter to let him know of Jack's response to the paper. Peter was out of town until Monday, but his secretary said that he could be reached in case of an emergency. Dan told her it was an emergency of sorts and she promised that he would hear from Dr. Carter within a day or two.

It was not until Friday that Peter called.

"What's up?" he asked.

"A lot." Dan related the events of his meeting with Jack Brennan.

"Your chairman is being difficult, and he is doing it in the most idiotic way. I don't think we should allow him to place road-blocks in the way of our submitting this paper for publication."

"How can we send it out without his approval?"

"Simple. As luck would have it, our department policy is a bit less ridiculous than yours. If it's okay with you, I will submit the paper from here. It will merely be a matter of changing the address to which all correspondence should be directed."

"What do you think Arnie Feldman will say?"

"I don't think he cares. He is so involved in setting up an international congress that he doesn't have time to worry about publications that come out of his department. I'll have my secretary redo the title page and Monday morning I'll send it in to the *New England Journal*."

"Good luck!"

"Let's hope they'll accept it."

"What if they don't?"

"We have several options. We could try a few other journals. Or, better yet, we can send it to the *Journal of Clinical Neuropsychology*. I am on their editorial board, so there shouldn't be any problem with them publishing it. I am not worried about that. What I am worried about is what Jack will do to you when our paper appears in print. That man would not hesitate to destroy your career."

"That's a risk I will have to take." There was a pause on the other end of the line.

"I am impressed with you. Frankly, I didn't think you had it in you."

"We never know until we are put to the test."

"You are so right. Most of us are cowards. Heroes are few and far between and almost all of them need to have their heads examined."

On that note, they terminated their conversation.

\* \* \*

A few days went by. One morning Peter phoned.

"Guess what. The *New England Journal* turned down our paper."

Dan was still at home, sitting over coffee and the morning paper.

"I'm not surprised. What did they say?"

"Nothing. Just that the manuscript in its present form was unsuitable for publication. No explanation or anything."

"The editors don't want to antagonize Marat."

"Precisely. They'd lose a large amount of advertising revenue."

"You said you can get it published in the *Journal of Clinical Neuropsychology*."

"I am sure I can."

"With no questions asked?"

"With no questions asked. I'll send it off this afternoon."

"Do you want to be the senior author?"

"I don't think that's necessary. You did all the work, and there is no reason you shouldn't get the credit."

"Or the fallout."

Peter laughed. "Would you like to guess how long it will be before Jack learns we sent out the paper without his approval?"

"Depends on whether the reviewers get in contact with him. I wouldn't be surprised if he knows a few people on the editorial board of the *New England Journal*."

\* \* \*

Jack did indeed know someone on the editorial board, and two days later Dan received a call from the departmental administrative assistant telling him that the chairman wanted to see him in his office.

When Dan entered, Jack received him with a withering look. Two black furrows formed above his nose.

"There is no room in my department for anyone who refuses to be a team player." Dan was still standing inside the door. "When I say there is no room for you, I mean there is no room for you. I shall see to it that you leave this medical school."

"I have tenure. It came as part of my package deal with Gordon Fowler."

"I am well aware of that. You may not know it, but we have ways to remove tenured faculty." His mouth formed a straight line, lips pressed together. "That's all I have to say."

"A university is not the military—sir," Dan said.

"That is all I have to say!" Jack shouted. This time ears as well as face turned red—an inauspicious end to the interview.

* * *

Later that morning Dan sat in his office, reflecting on the respective fates of Galileo and Giordano Bruno. Both denied the Aristotelian system of the universe, championed by the Church. Galileo recanted and was showered with honors; Bruno did not and was burned as a heretic. At what point does resolve become foolishness, and when does expediency become cowardice? He was still debating these questions when the phone rang. It was Frank Duffy.

"You won't believe this, Dr. Lerner. I've been talking to the doctors in my territory and I have what looks like three more cases of this—what did you call it?"

"The Angry Puppet Syndrome."

"That's right."

"Have you heard from Dr. Lessing?"

"Not yet."

"Why don't you call him again and let him know that there are now at least eleven cases."

Frank promised he would.

* * *

That night Maureen and Dan had dinner at their little Italian restaurant.

"Things are not working out too well for you, are they?" she asked after he had told her about his latest interview with Jack.

"I know."

"Did you expect anything different?"

"In a way, I hoped that he would respect my courage. . . ."

"Your obstinacy. . . ."

Dan accepted the word with a nod. "You think I am insane to insist on getting my paper published?"

"I can't answer that. If you must, you must."

"I want to get to the bottom of all this. And I want you to help me."

"You can count on me. That's for sure."

Dan revolved the spaghetti marinara between fork and spoon and remained silent.

"Or we can look at it in another way," Maureen said. "What's the worst that man can do to you?" She sounded warm and maternal.

"Make me leave the university. I suppose I can always go back to the Peace Corps."

"You're too old for that. Besides, you might catch AIDS or some horrible tropical disease. I think you should open an office and make money. Real money and become rich and distinguished. I'd like that."

"You have a point. As long as I have my medical license, I am in good shape."

"Of course you are. So we have nothing to worry about except what to order for dessert."

Over spumoni Dan told Maureen about the three new cases that Frank had uncovered.

"I want you to get me their names and I will contact them. If they get on board, we will have enough members so that we can maintain a class action. Clearly, they were taking—I am sorry—were exposed to Dulcian, and all of them appear to be affected to the same extent. It's just a question of my deciding who to select as representative."

"How do you do that?"

"I will have to find the person who will most appeal to a jury and whose damages are the clearest to demonstrate. First, however, we are going to ask for a hearing in federal court on a motion for class certification. If the motion is granted, our litigation is appropriate for a class action."

Toward the end of dinner Maureen reverted to office chitchat.

"Would you believe it? Larry tells me that Tom Costello beat up his wife the other night. She phoned him in absolute hysterics. She thinks he has started to drink in secret. Even though he gave it up for good a couple of years ago."

"You know how that is."

"I don't. I still don't think he was drunk when he tried to rape me."

"Are you sure?"

"Pretty much so." She picked up the bottle of wine on the table between them and turned it so that the label carrying the government warning faced her. "Right now I don't even want to finish this bottle."

"There isn't that much left. Half a glass for you and half a glass for me."

A short time later they stood on the sidewalk outside the restaurant and waited for their cars to be brought around. Suddenly a hot desert wind arose and whirled dust and shreds of paper around them. Maureen drew close to Dan and ran her hand over the back of his.

"When do you think we'll be able to live together?" she asked. Despite the headlights of passing cars it was too dark for Dan to make out her expression.

"I don't know."

"We could have such a good time. I bet I'm the only woman who can make you laugh."

Even though she was right about being able to make him laugh, Dan had a sudden sense of constriction. Fortunately, at that moment their cars arrived. "Let's talk about it in the morning," he said and opened the car door.

The feeling of constriction remained within him as he drove away, and it was still there when he arrived at his apartment and poured himself a glass of scotch. All at once he had an unaccountable urge to call Judith. He knew that to do so would be madness, and he could not imagine what brought up that idea.

He sipped the scotch—a smoky taste that instantly evoked a picture of Judith and himself in an open, palm-covered cantina on the beach at Hermosillo watching the sunset. The sea had been high, and the moment was simple and good. Yet he felt constricted by her and had left her. Was that the real reason? "The heart has its reasons which reason knows nothing of." Dan recited the phrase to himself and laughed at the inadequacy of the quotation in answering his question.

\* \* \*

A few days went by without any event of significance; in short, they were days unworthy of being recounted, days that blended into each other without markers, the stuff that makes up most of man's time above ground. Now that Dan had chosen to pursue at all costs the problem of the angry puppets, the unexpected could take form at any time—salt to flavor otherwise uneventful days. And before too long the unexpected did take form.

"Dean Weigel wants to see you as soon as possible." Dan had just arrived at Las Virgenes Hospital and the waiting room was filled with patients for the morning neurology clinic.

"Did you tell him that I have a morning clinic?" he asked the clinic secretary.

"No. I talked to someone named Marcia. All she said is to let you know that the dean wants to see you as soon as possible."

Dan sat down in his cubicle and picked up the phone. For once, he was quickly able to get an outside line.

"This is Dr. Lerner," he said when he was connected to the dean's office. "Someone in your office called me and said the dean wanted to see me as soon as possible."

"Let me check." The female voice got off the phone. After a couple of minutes she returned. "That's right. Can you see the dean at ten forty-five this morning?"

"Impossible. I am running a clinic out here at Las Virgenes and there is no one to cover for me. I'll be stuck all day. Will tomorrow do?"

"Let me check." Again she was gone for a couple of minutes. "The dean will have time to talk to you tomorrow at eight."

"At eight?"

"Would you like to come earlier? The dean gets in at seven. "

"No, no. Eight is fine."

"Then I'll put you down for eight. And the dean would like to see your lab notebooks for last year and the year before."

"What do you mean my lab notebooks?"

"I don't know. That's all it says here. Have Dr. Lerner bring in his lab notebooks for the past two years."

By the time Dan had seen the last patient scheduled for the neurology clinic it was late. Instead of going straight home, he stopped off at his office at the university and picked up the notebooks. There were six bound black books, filled with data, pasted Polaroids, and computer printouts that covered the period when he had generated data for his paper on brain neurotrophic factor 7, also referred to as NT-7. Dan's paper suggested that the same as yet unknown factor that turned off the ability of brain genes to form NT-7 could also be responsible for Alzheimer's disease.

Dan had always considered this paper to be a solid piece of work. He had based his future research project on it, the one that had been approved by the National Institutes of Health but for which he had not been able to receive funding.

He leafed through the books and put them in chronologic order. In those days he had two lab techs working for him, Donna Walters and Bert Crandall. In addition, an Israeli neurologist also had worked in the laboratory.

He took the lab books home. With a shot of scotch in front of him, he thumbed through them once again, unsure what made the dean want to see them.

He picked up the phone and called David Schaffer.

"Are you doing anything for dinner?" There was some hesitation on the other end of the line. "I need to talk to you. Something unusual has come up."

David was a true friend. "I was going to stay home. Do you want to come over?"

"Sure. What's a good time for you?"

"How about nine?"

At nine Dan sat in the living room of David's apartment. It was a combination living-dining room, quite spacious, with a prominent piano, which, judging from the music strewn around it, was in frequent use. Photos of Liza were in abundance. Wedding photos of David and Liza, Liza at the beach playing with her weimaraner and looking perfectly happy, Liza in a sailboat looking preoccupied, and Liza at the foot of the Eiffel Tower looking into a far distance. Dan had brought the lab notebooks with him, together with a reprint of his NT-7 paper. David was serving cappuccino.

"Why do you think the dean wants to see the books?" Dan asked. He placed paper and lab books on the coffee table in front of David. David picked up the reprint and glanced through it.

"Do you think this is an important paper?" he asked. "I don't know that much about molecular biology but from the abstract it sounds potentially important to me."

"I think so." In a few words Dan set out the essence of the paper. David got up and leaned on the piano. With his forefinger he struck a few notes, then using his entire left hand, he played a set of chords: D major, D minor, F major, the augmented seventh of

F major. He returned and sat down. "When did your paper come out?"

"About a year ago."

"Has there been any problem with it?"

"Not that I know of. I got a handful of requests for reprints. Mainly from abroad. But there is something else you should know." While sipping the still hot cappuccino, Dan told David about Jack's response to the Angry Puppet paper. "I have been thinking about that, and the best I can come up with is that there is some connection."

"Could be." David reached for the lab books and turned the pages of one of them. "Who actually did all this work?"

"Bert Crandall. And Yaakov. He was an Israeli neurologist who worked with me for a year. I think you met him at the Christmas party that I gave at the Faculty Club."

"Certainly. A very dramatic man. Spoke more with his hands than with his mouth."

"He did the mRNA isolations. But Bert Crandall did most of the autoradiography and dot blots that I used to measure the concentrations of the mRNA. I don't think you got to know Bert. He was sort of strange. I finally had to let him go."

David sat up straight. "You did? What for?"

"I caught him changing some of the radioactivity counts. He wanted to make them perfect. Which, of course, they never can be."

"Anybody else involved in this work?"

"No. You know I never ran a big operation, even when I had my NIH grant. Not like Marty."

"No. Not like Marty. I suppose if Jack wants to make trouble for you, he might say something to the effect that he suspects some dishonesty with your paper."

"But there wasn't."

"I know. But these days. . . ." David never finished the sentence.

\* \* \*

The following morning Dan was in the dean's office. Postmodern furniture, walls and bookcases in mahogany and cherrywood, and on the walls an assortment of diplomas, awards, and photos of the dean with the Kennedys, Lady Bird Johnson, and, to even things out, a beaming Ronald Reagan. The dean was in his mid fifties. His appearance was athletic and his movements were quick and precise. His face, marked by prominent lips and heavy-lidded eyes, was surprisingly coarse.

"I would like Ariel to sit in on this," he said, after he shook Dan's hand and motioned him to a deep chair. "She is one of my secretaries and I want her to take notes. I hope you won't mind."

"No."

The dean buzzed for Ariel, who entered with a steno pad. An Ariel who was five foot four and over two hundred pounds.

"May I have your notebooks?" Dan handed them to the dean, who turned them over to Ariel. "Please take care of these. I don't want anyone to have access to them at this point."

"What is all this about?" Dan asked.

"I will tell you, but I need to be brief. Yesterday morning I would have had more time. My office has received allegations that the work that you published last year. . . ." The dean opened a folder and looked through it. "Yes. Neurotrophin-7 in cortex from Alzheimer disease patients. A paper that appeared in the *Journal of Molecular Brain Research.* D.L. Lerner and Y. Eilat. Who is Eilat?"

"An Israeli neurologist who worked with me for a year or so."

The dean turned a few pages in the folder and nodded. "He went back to Tel-Aviv University?"

"That's right. He also has an affiliation with the Weizmann Institute."

"Now do you believe that the lab books that you just handed over to me substantiate the data in this paper?"

"Yes. Without doubt."

"You say 'without doubt.' Good. Now let me tell you where we are at this point in time. In view of these allegations, I am forced to appoint an ad hoc committee to go over your paper and also the laboratory data, which, you believe, support the data in your publication. The committee will have to determine whether there have been any irregularities. Or, to be blunt, any scientific fraud."

"May I ask who made these allegations?"

"Unfortunately, you may not. That is, you may ask, but I am not in a position to answer. At least not at this time. Now there is another thing I must ask you to do until this problem has been resolved. I would like you to defer from publishing any of your current work."

"What do you mean?"

"What I mean is that until we clear up whatever questions have been raised concerning the paper by Lerner and Eilat, I am requesting you not to submit any other paper for publication."

"What about papers that are already in press? That is, those that have been accepted for publication."

"I would like you to contact the editorial offices of the various journals and ask to withdraw them."

"Withdraw them?"

"Correct. You will agree with me that no paper is better than a seriously flawed paper."

"What if that is no longer possible?"

"I hope it will be. I think you are aware that your scientific reputation is at stake. We have to do whatever damage control is necessary."

The dean rose and came around to where Dan was sitting. A clear indication that the interview was about to be terminated. "You will receive two copies of a memorandum summarizing this interview in the next day or so. I would like you to read and initial them and return one copy to my office."

* * *

That evening Dan had dinner with Maureen at her apartment. With a bottle of wine to take off the sting of the meeting with the dean, he related its details to Maureen.

"What has happened to that paper of yours?"

"We sent it into the *Journal of Clinical Neuropsychology*. Peter is on their editorial board. He doesn't see anything to prevent it from being published. When the proofs come back, I can add all the new cases."

"Good. And what do you intend to tell the dean?"

"The truth. That Peter is out of the country for a few days, and since he was the one who submitted the paper, he is the only one who has the legal right to withdraw it from publication."

"I bet he won't go for it."

"Why not?"

"He'll find some reason. You better plan on it."

"Perhaps I should see a lawyer."

Maureen smiled. Wrinkling her nose, she blew him a kiss. "You are looking at one right now."

The phone rang and Maureen got up to answer. She was gone a long time.

"You'll never believe this," she said when she came back. From the quiver in her voice, Dan knew she was preparing him for a momentous announcement. "Tom has been getting Dulcian. For nearly two months. He just found out about our litigation and he is certain that the drug explains why he lost control when I was in his office and also why he beat up his wife."

"I wouldn't be surprised."

"Neither would I. He wants to talk to you."

"That's fine with me."

"Good. Why, then, don't you come by the office tomorrow afternoon? Mike will be there, which means Larry will have to set aside whatever plans he has and come, and we'll also have Betty there. She's our new paralegal. We shouldn't make it too late though because I also want to have Mark Lynch on the speaker phone."

* * *

The following afternoon Dan and Maureen were in the conference room at the office of Cosgrove and Costello waiting for Mike. Tom was in an armchair by the window, staring at the Hollywood Hills. His hand was over his mouth, a gesture with which he tried to hide what he must have known to be an inappropriate smile. Larry was at the head of the table. He was in shirtsleeves with crimson suspenders. Nolan and a couple of the other partners had joined them, and in addition to Betty there were several other paralegals.

"This looks like a regular war room," Dan said as Maureen introduced him. For his part, he felt exuberant; he was participating in a well-mounted campaign against Jack and the dean.

When Mike Cosgrove arrived, it was as if a force had entered the room. He was a white-haired man with intense, incredibly blue eyes, meticulously dressed in a double-breasted gray silk suit. Conversation ceased as he strode to the head of the conference table.

"I want to get those bastards," he boomed. "Each and every one of them for doing this to Tom and to God knows how many other men and women. And you," his finger made a circle around the table, "all of you, are going to help me." He sat down on the conference table and swung his legs around with a quick movement that belied his age.

"Let's hear from you first," he said, pointing at Dan. "What can you tell us about this drug? I want a capsule summary."

Dan obliged with just that—the chemical nature of Dulcian, its antidepressant effects, the hypothetical site of action within the brain, and, finally, the unique adverse reaction that some people had shown. When Dan had finished, Mike jumped off the table and paced about. He turned to Maureen as if stung by an insect.

"Now where are we with this case? Right now, I mean."

"First of all, this is going to be both a products liability case and a negligence case. We are saying that the preliminary tests conducted by Marat International were totally inadequate and that furthermore they did not warn people of the danger of this side reaction. "

"Good. I don't think we could ever prove to a jury that Dulcian was inherently dangerous."

"Right. We've filed the case in federal court. They've come back with motions for summary judgment and to dismiss the case."

"On what grounds?"

"That the people who have had the reaction had been seriously disturbed prior to taking Dulcian and that they were prone to violent homicidal outbursts."

"Sons of bitches!"

"In fact, they consider our complaint as libelous pleading."

"Who's the judge?"

"Armand Watson."

"A good man. I still think we should see if he ever had any connections with Marat International."

"Can't do any harm."

"The court has Dr. Lerner's paper?"

"In manuscript form."

"And they are aware of his credentials and those of the other doctor? What's his name?"

"Carter. We have provided both to the court."

"In the meantime, I am going to see if we can't get any more information via the back door. There are a couple of people in New Jersey I might be able to tap. And you, Maureen, are going to proceed on the assumption that the court will disallow Marat's claim."

"I will prepare papers under the Freedom of Information Act to obtain whatever documents the FDA has that pertain to Dulcian. And we will see what material the court will order Marat to hand over to us."

"They'll fight like hell," Larry interposed.

Mike gave Larry a stern disapproving look and jumped on the sideboard. By now his hair had become totally disheveled.

"Let them," he said. "I am going to have Maureen carry the ball, but I intend to keep a close eye on this, and we are going to chop those bastards to pieces. Any questions?"

There were no questions. As the meeting dissolved, Mike took Dan aside.

"How many cases have you got?"

"Eleven."

"Good. There should be more, and we'll help you find them." Then, seemingly as an afterthought, he added. "I'll walk you to the elevator."

They were outside the glass doors that separated the hallway from the offices of the firm and were waiting for the elevator.

"Maureen's a good woman," Mike said and pushed the down button. Without waiting for Dan to reply, he added. "If those guys ever find out that anything is going on between the two of you, all hell's going to break loose."

"What do you mean?"

"I'll tell you what I mean. They are going to say that you made up those cases in order to give some business to Cosgrove and Costello. That's why I think you better stop seeing her."

"That's unfair."

"Life's unfair, Dr. Lerner. In case you haven't found out by now."

The elevator arrived. Mike held open the door. "Think about it," he said. "We all have a lot to lose. And that includes Maureen."

\* \* \* \* \*

O<small>N</small> the plane that carried him from Chicago to Washington and the annual neurosciences meetings, Marty worked on his presentation—an overview of the role of neurotransmitters in the regulation of hypothalamic function. He had been assigned a prominent slot on the second plenary session: an hour, with the last ten minutes set aside for questions and discussion. He would start with a review of previous work on the subject performed at Harvard, Duke, and St. Barts, then present his own data, and finally, in the last ten minutes before question time, propose a new and revolutionary hypothesis. For this he had prepared three slides. They portrayed his hypothesis linking circadian rhythm and brain function with depressive disorders and episodic discontrol.

\* \* \*

It was the same hypothesis that he had presented to E.B. Wallace when the old man had visited his laboratory a week earlier trying to find an answer to why his son Franky, who was in jail for assault and battery, had always manifested a short temper and was prone to bouts of rage. While the sharp, angular face hunched across the desk from him, Marty had sketched on a sheet of

University of Chicago stationery the scheme that linked the circadian rhythm to disorders of mood and affect.

Marty could see that E.B. was puzzled.

"Let me take this back a few steps," he said. "You and I have a normal sleep-wake cycle. We sleep for eight hours and are awake for sixteen hours."

"I can do with five to six hours sleep."

"So can I. But that's not my point. There is a certain machinery in the brain that tells it when to wake up and when to go to sleep. And when we are asleep, our brain chemistry differs from what it is when we are awake. Hormone secretions go through a twenty-four-hour cycle, the electrical activity of the brain goes through a similar cycle, and all of this appears to be regulated by the hypothalamus."

"The hypothalamus."

"That's right. The hypothalamus, which acts as a relay station between the pituitary gland and the rest of the brain, has a large number of nerve cells that are on a twenty-four-hour cycle. If this cycle is disrupted by one means or another, we become liable to depression or various other mental disorders."

"Including episodic discontrol? That's what Franky has been diagnosed with."

"Including episodic discontrol."

"Am I right that this is only a theory of yours?"

"Don't worry. We are going to prove it," he said, and slammed his palm on the table.

"How long is it going to take?" E.B. asked, bending down for a second look at the sheet of paper. His white head was shaped by an anachronistic razor-top haircut.

"I am willing to bet we'll have a breakthrough before the year is over. No one outside this lab knows about it, but we've just set up this amazing study. . . ." Marty's voice dropped as he looked around as if to make sure the laboratory had not been bugged.

"Everything is so slow," E.B. complained.

"Slow, yes," Marty repeated, "but inexorable. Like the descent of a glacier."

E.B. nodded. Over the last few years he had become resigned to the fact that not even the infusion of the Wallace millions could accelerate the progress of science. What the old man did not know was that progress was much too slow for Marty's liking as well. Day after day his technicians and postdoctoral students accumulated countless data. He would pore over the results until long past dinnertime, restless and dissatisfied because the data necessary to support his theory continued to elude him. Sooner or later the breakthrough had to come. It could not be otherwise when a man was destined for success. All that was required was more time, more money, more personnel, and, of course, a bit of luck. Of these ingredients the most important were money and personnel.

Marty pulled out a fresh sheet of stationery from the top drawer of his desk and outlined his needs to E.B.—an additional grant of five hundred thousand dollars over the next five years for personnel. The old financier listened, looked down at the back of his dark hairy hands, and after a moment or two shook his head with a decisive movement that precluded any further discussion. There were limits to the amount of money he could funnel into Marty's project. Marty crumpled the sheet into a ball and with a careless gesture tossed it into the wastebasket.

A week earlier the university dean had been even less supportive, and his meeting with Marty had ended with nothing more substantial than a cordial handshake and a warm effusion of appreciation for Marty's contributions to the scientific reputation of the university. As for a request for additional money from the government, that would have to wait another two years. By then God knows what kind of funds the National Institutes of Health would have at their disposal. Come hell or high water he would have to dig up another source of support. The money was out there, that was for sure. It was solely a matter of finding it.

\* \* \*

As was his custom, Marty intended to read the first two or three sentences of his presentation directly from the manuscript. From that point on he would put aside the typed notes and talk extemporaneously, guided by the set of slides he had brought along. Over the years he found this to be the best way to deliver lectures. He despised people who got up in front of an audience, turned off the lights, and proceeded to read their papers while slides flashed across the screen like the northern lights. Such a presentation lacked spontaneity and precluded any interchange with the audience. For Marty spontaneity and simplicity were the key ingredients for the process of communicating the excitement of a new and unexplored concept.

He returned the folder with his lecture notes to the briefcase. Time to get up and stretch his legs.

He expected a good audience for his lecture. To be allowed an hour for his presentation was an indication that his work was beginning to be accepted. At thirty-five he was finally making waves.

* * *

"I want you to make waves, even after I'm gone. That's what I brought you to this country for."

Although the doctors had tried to hide it from the old socialist, he knew that he was dying, and in the manner of strong men who want their power to extend beyond the grave, he assigned tasks to each of his three children. Alice was all set. He approved of Gordon Miles, her Jewish stockbroker husband, even though at times he wished the man would make more money. After all, what use was a Jewish son-in-law if he was not immensely rich. John was a problem. At twenty he was still immersed in music and had his mind set on becoming a concert pianist. Whatever talent the young man possessed, he had not yet disclosed it to his father. Lacking talent and dedication, John would wind up teaching harmony at Western Massachusetts State College or some other equally undistinguished institution. The old man pulled himself to the side of the hospital bed, which had been moved into the heavily shuttered bedroom of the white clapboard DiChiro home, and took the hand of his younger son. He felt the fingers made strong by hours at the piano and made him promise to continue: practice, practice, practice, learn a respectable repertoire of concertos and start to perform in public. If he did not do so soon, he would have his father's thundering voice come down on him from beyond the grave.

As for Marty, there was nothing wrong with having a doctor and a scientist for a son, but there were too many doctors and very many scientists, and the old man wanted his older son to make a mark. Particularly because it had always been clear to him and to everyone else in the family that Marty was more than just smart or brilliant; he was a true genius, and the old DiChiro had greater expectations from a child who was a genius than from his other two.

\* \* \*

The fact was that one afternoon a few weeks after his third birthday Marty had been hailed as a genius. That notable event occurred when he astounded both family and parish priest by reciting the catechism by heart. To do so was amazing enough for a child of three, but when his father had questioned the boy, it turned out that Marty had taught himself to read on his own in order to be able to memorize questions and answers without having to turn to the grown-ups for help.

It was a remarkable scene. They were seated around the kitchen table in the gathering twilight—Guiseppe DiChiro, his beautiful but already ailing wife, seven-year-old Alice, and Marty.

"Tell me the truth," Guiseppe said, and his bushy eyebrows drew together, "you could not possibly have read it."

When Marty insisted that he had, his father made Alice bring one of her schoolbooks. He handed it to Marty. "Read!" he ordered him, and with a peeled slice of apple in his little fist, Marty started to read. His mother burst into tears and with hugs and kisses and sobs interrupted her son's rendition of "Our Wonderful Universe."

That also was the year the angel had first visited him. It was the night of November 11, the date of the feast of St. Martin and consequently his name day, when he was awakened by a strange rushing noise. He opened his eyes and was struck breathless by the brilliant phosphorescent beauty of immense white wings that hovered over the foot of the bed. The angel bent over him with folded wings and placed a finger across the child's lips, a sign that his visit must never be divulged.

"I know you," Marty said, sitting up and gazing into eyes of smaragdine green. "I have seen your picture. You are an angel and you have come to visit me."

At no time did he question why he had been selected by the angel, just as he did not question why he of all people had been selected to be able to memorize the entire catechism, and why at three he could read the little religious book without any help. He simply accepted his achievements; let the others be astonished.

"Will you be back?" he asked the angel.

The angel nodded and kept his word. As the years went by, Marty learned to count on his visits and on his occasional inter-cessions. Growing up is not easy, but with an angel to rely on, how could a child not become successful. What was even more impor-tant, Marty knew—long before the angel had disclosed it to him—that his mother loved him more than she loved Alice, or even John, who everyone in town said had a lovely sweet face and who sang in the front row of the choir before he was six years old.

And so as Marty grew up and the years went by, success fol-lowed success in a smoothly rising arc. First came a full scholar-ship to Harvard University, where he met, wooed, and married blonde and fair-skinned Jeanette Cobb, the only daughter of a suc-cessful Boston attorney; then the University of Chicago, the Wallace Foundation, and now his new hypothesis that would link mental illness to a disorder in hypothalamic circadian rhythm, a hypothesis that, if proven correct, could well garner him the Nobel Prize.

Yet as time passed and Marty's successes multiplied, the angel appeared to him less and less frequently; he reassured himself that adult eyes see only what reason allows.

What a pity that his parents were no longer around to admire him. Leaning against the bulkhead in the rear of the plane, he stretched his back and shoulders. By the end of the following week he would have to decide on Jack Brennan's offer. To stay on in Chicago or go West. One thing he knew: whatever path he select-ed it would be the right one. His mother and the angel had assured him of his infallibility.

He stepped into the galley and asked the stewardess for a cup of coffee. As she handed him the steaming hot paper cup, he caught a hint of her perfume—spice and lemon and something darkly alluring and indefinable. She was mahogany-skinned with slightly slanted Eurasian eyes and luminous black hair. Marty was overcome by a sense of instant exhilaration.

"Great coffee! You made it?" he asked.

"Of course." She smiled as he sipped.

"What lovely earrings," Marty said. Black onyx petaled flow-ers with red stamen centers.

"They are Brazilian."

"And so are you?"

"You guessed it."

"Not guessed it, I knew. What part of Brazil?"

"It's a small town. No one has ever heard of it. Maceio."

Marty closed his eyes. A map of Brazil appeared before him—vast expanses of green, shading into the light and dark brown of the Mato Grosso, and surrounded by the blue of the Atlantic.

"Maceio is not so small. It's on the coast, 200 kilometers south of Recife."

"You have been there?"

"No."

"Then how do you know?" After a pause, "Please tell me."

Marty smiled mysteriously, secure in the knowledge that he had won the game and that the rest was a mere formality, which he could play out as in college he would have played out a rook endgame with two pawns to his advantage.

Her name was Malvina and she was laying over for two nights at the Marriott before flying back to Chicago and San Francisco. Of course she would enjoy having dinner with him. The plane started its descent into National Airport.

"I'll be in the lobby at eight," Marty said briskly and returned to his seat. It didn't matter to him that the Committee on Developmental Neurosciences was to meet at seven. He would pop in, make a few remarks on how to go about encouraging new postdoctoral fellows to enter the area of spinal cord neurodevelopment, then leave and take a taxi to the Marriott.

\* \* \*

That is exactly what happened and when Marty arrived at the hotel shortly after eight, Malvina was waiting for him in the lobby. It was a balmy spring night, and she wore a long-sleeved sheer black dress with white, feather-like ruffles around her wrists. An exquisite ruby ring was on the finger of her right hand. With her legs crossed, she was sitting in an armchair; one arm rested on the glass ledge of a plant-filled terrarium, her hand draped downward in a posture of languid grace. As she rose and came forward, her long legs and the lightness of her posture reminded him of a ballerina in suspended flight.

Dinner was at the Melange, followed by drinks and dancing at the Band Box. She floated in his arms as if released from the bonds of gravity.

"I enjoy holding you," he said. "You seem weightless."

"I have always danced, my entire life."

After they sat down she ran her finger around the rim of her glass. "I know you are married, and I will try not to become jealous of her."

"Why should you be? No one and nothing can intrude on us tonight."

She smiled and took his hand as they got up to dance the next piece. The tempo was fast and she kicked off her shoes. The flight of her feet was faster than the eye.

"You are absolutely fabulous—bewitching," Marty said when they sat down again.

"Am I?"

"Perhaps I shouldn't have told you."

"Don't worry," she laughed. "I won't fall in love with you."

Over drinks Marty told her what brought him to Washington. He must have imparted to her some of his excitement about his new hypothesis.

"You are brilliant. But you already know that. What you don't know is that I have always enjoyed being with brilliant men. I think that is why I became a stewardess."

They finished their drinks.

"Shall we go to your hotel?" Marty asked.

"I have been waiting for you to ask."

\* \* \*

Using themselves and all that each had carried forward from their pasts, they created a few unmatched hours for one another. It was dawn when Marty woke up. Malvina was asleep; the curves of her back and buttocks were curled toward him, and dark arms encircled her pillow. As he moved closer to her, he inhaled the warm scent of lemon and spice. He put his hand on her shoulder; she turned and smiled without opening her eyes.

"I have to go," he murmured and pushed aside a new wave of desire. She nodded and kissed his hands.

Without turning on the lights, he slipped into his clothes and scribbled a note for her on the pad next to the telephone. "It was perfect. I'll call you tonight between 5 and 6."

The presentation went as well as Marty expected. The hall was crowded and the applause at its conclusion was more than perfunctory. As Marty stepped down from the podium, he was surrounded. Questions and yet more questions. He relished the excitement that his lecture had aroused.

He was about to leave the hall with the box of slides in his hand when he came face to face with an elderly man who had remained at the periphery of the swarm of young neuroscientists. He was dressed in a dark suit and an old-fashioned red and black regimental tie with a red presentation handkerchief protruding from his breast pocket. Neuroscientists are a casual crowd and Marty was surprised by the formality of the man's appearance.

"I am Albert Lessing." He offered Marty his card. He glanced at it.

"Marat International."

"That's right. I am medical director."

"I appreciate your coming to my presentation."

"An excellent lecture. Totally clear, with some very interesting data. May I take you to lunch?" Marty looked at his watch. Forty-five minutes before the seminar on the effects of neuroleptics on neurotransmitters.

"I will have to be back here by one-thirty."

"We can make this quick. I don't want to miss the opportunity of getting your input on one of our new projects."

The cafeteria was crowded, with long lines of people waiting to be seated. By contrast, the restaurant, which was considerably more expensive, was practically empty. The two men took a table and ordered quickly. Lessing wasted no time to start out.

"We have a new pharmaceutical that we believe will revolutionize the treatment of depression."

"What is it?"

"Obviously, it has not yet come on the market. We have just concluded our initial studies, what we call Phase I, and we are very encouraged by the results."

"And how does your drug differ from the two dozen other drugs that are being used to treat depression?"

"An excellent question. Let me enumerate the advantages of MI-37801—that's the in-house name for our new drug. First of all, it has a rapid onset of action. As you well know, all other antidepressants on the market have their onset anywhere from one to six weeks after the drug has been started." He raised his hand—elegantly curved fingers, manicured fingernails. "The next advantage of our drug is that it has a well-defined therapeutic level. This will permit physicians to adjust its dose to achieve optimal therapeutic effects. Finally, and most important, MI-37801 is safe. It has no side effects."

"None whatever?"

"I should not say none, but essentially none."

"Then how does your drug work?"

"We can talk about that some other time. Right now all I want to say is that its effectiveness is unrelated to a blockade of the reuptake of either serotonin, dopamine, or norepinephrine, and that as far as we know the drug does not block any known postsynaptic receptors."

Marty was astounded. Serotonin, dopamine, and norepinephrine are the major messengers within the brain whose levels are manipulated by every one of the scores of drugs that are currently used to treat depression.

"That is a surprise," he said. "Are you quite sure?"

"Yes. Absolutely sure. All these data will be presented in a symposium that we are organizing for next fall. I'll make sure that you receive an invitation."

"Fine. And what would you like me to do with this drug?"

"What I want you to consider doing is to examine the clinical reports that will come into our office from our preliminary drug trial studies, what we term the Phase II and III studies, go over them for completeness and accuracy, and alert our company if any major problems turn up, which I don't think will be the case. In short, we would like you to be our principal outside monitor for the trials that we must complete before we can submit our data to the FDA for approval."

"How much of my time will this involve?"

"I can assure you that the demands on your time will not be excessive. Four to five hours a month, at the very most."

"Fair enough."

"You do understand that Marat has selected you as a potential consultant because we recognize you to be an authority in the field of neurotransmitters and because you have truly impeccable scientific credentials."

"I see. And if I agree to help your company with these trials, what will be in it for me?" He stopped and smiled at his flippancy. "I can assure you, Dr. Lessing, if we had more time, I would be less blunt."

"I am certain you would be. But you are right: we should go into that as well." He paused and, using the back of his knife, drew an angular, five-pointed pattern across his napkin. "In consideration of your assistance Marat International is prepared to augment your research budget. We are in a position to provide your laboratory with discretionary funds that may be used by you as you see fit. All we will need from you is a signed agreement in principle so that we can count on your collaboration."

"And how much will these discretionary funds be?"

"That is open to negotiation. Marat International has a large but nevertheless finite budget. I would prefer that you first think about your needs, and when you get back to Chicago drop me a letter projecting a five-year budget. In the meantime, I would like you to sign this."

He took a sheet from his inside coat pocket and unfolded it.

"What is this?"

"It is an agreement not to divulge any information that our company might pass on to you. A mere formality, but absolutely necessary in order that we can keep sensitive in-house information from our competitors."

Marty scanned the sheet. By signing it, he undertook not to divulge confidential information to any person or persons not directly connected with Marat International. Dr. Lessing handed him his own pen, a heavy black Mont Blanc.

Pen in hand, Marty reflected on his position. For a relatively small amount of time, he would obtain funding for two additional laboratory technicians and two foreign-trained research fellows.

With that support in hand he would not have to depend on E.B., the dean, let alone on the National Institutes of Health.

"I feel like I am signing my soul away," he said with a laugh, as he signed. What he actually felt was that once again his angel had stepped in to provide for him.

"May I?" Dr. Lessing took the paper, dated it, and signed as witness. "That takes care of our paperwork. I intend to have Warren . . . Warren Berrich—he is our senior in-house counsel—countersign it when I return to the office. He will mail you a copy for your files." He pocketed the form. "I assure you, Dr. DiChiro, that we at Marat International are proud to have you associated with us. And, in turn, I am certain that you will find us totally committed to excellence in biological research."

The two men quickly finished lunch—for Marty that consisted of a small tuna salad and a cup of coffee—and parted ways. Marty agreed to send Marat International a budget and an up-to-date curriculum vitae by the end of the following week. In turn, he would begin receiving reports on the drug trials by the end of the month.

"By the way," Marty asked, "any idea what name you will use for the drug, what was it—MI-37801?"

"Not yet. Dulcian has been one of the suggestions."

"Dulcian, eh?" And he dashed off to the seminar on the effects of neuroleptics on neurotransmitters.

\* \* \*

The afternoon session was uninspiring. It dragged on with a procession of inept "me too" papers presented in a dark room, accompanied by an endless series of incomprehensible slides that added little to Marty's knowledge about neurotransmitters. Finally he could stand it no longer and left the conference room to phone the Marriott. To his surprise, Malvina had checked out earlier that afternoon and had left no forwarding address.

"Are you sure?"

The operator was sure and Marty hung up. At first he was incredulous and annoyed more than disappointed. He had left Malvina fully expecting to see her again. There had been no goodbye, no true parting of the ways. He had not obtained her last name or address and therefore had no ready means of reaching her.

He rejoined the seminar. As he stood in the rear of the auditorium, arms folded, his back against the dark formica-paneled wall, he tried to take in the ongoing presentation. Again and again his mind returned to Malvina and her unanticipated disappearance. He was confused, much as if he had put his hand into his rear pocket and suddenly found that his wallet had disappeared. That afternoon, possibly for the first time in his life, Marty felt exposed and unprotected, as if unforeseen currents were carrying him, an experienced swimmer, out of his depths.

* * *

Marat International was as good as its word. Within a matter of a few weeks its management approved the budget Marty had submitted to Dr. Lessing: five hundred and seventy-five thousand dollars over the next five years. In turn, drug experience reports started to pour into his office from all parts of the nation. Each set was in a bound folder, with the investigator's name and the patient code number on the left upper corner.

Marty scrutinized the first few reports with considerable care. The first page contained data on the daily dose of MI-37801, other medications taken concurrently, and some basic patient information: age, vital signs, and date of last clinic visit. A clinical summary was found on the second page, with an evaluation of mental status, current psychiatric symptoms, and any recent change in their severity. Routine laboratory data were recorded on the third page, together with a summary of the physician's impression on the effects of the drug had on the patient's depression. The last page was designed to record any adverse reactions, whether these were thought to be drug-related, their severity, and what actions if any the physician had taken to deal with them.

After reading and signing off on the first several dozen clinical reports it became clear to Marty that Dr. Lessing was indeed correct in claiming that with MI-37801 Marat had designed a drug that produced prompt and effective relief from depression.

Had negotiations with Jack Brennan not come to a head, and had Marty not agreed to take the professorship and move to the West Coast, with all the disruptions consequent to closing a laboratory, moving as many of his staff as wanted to go to California, and dealing with the turmoil in his home, he would probably have picked up on Patient Number 114 much earlier than he did.

As it was, he merely glanced at the case report and put it into a storage carton, together with those of Case Numbers 101 to 130, to be reviewed whenever he was resettled.

\* \* \*

And so it happened that the DiChiros and most of the staff of the Wallace Laboratories moved to California.

And so it also happened that one morning, not too many weeks later, Marty awoke to see sunlight throw bright trembling discs across the ceiling of his newly rented house in the Brentwood Hills section. He got up and slipped into a robe.

"The sun is out today," Jeanette said when he returned from the shower. She stood at the window and looked down into the terraced garden. Her blonde hair was lit up by the sun. "The weather is absolutely gorgeous."

"In California the sun is always out and the weather is always gorgeous."

As she turned away from the curtains her bare soles stepped into a patch of warm sunlight.

"Marty! Do come over and look! The garden is like a box of jewels—the hibiscus, the iris, the bougainvillea. In every imaginable color and shade. It's unbelievable!"

Marty was getting dressed but took the time to join her at the window.

"You are right, it is fantastic," he said.

"Such an extravaganza!"

"Extravaganza?"

"I wish I could find a better word for it."

"Don't you think you should put on some clothes? The children might run in any minute. I'll go down and make some coffee."

After a quick breakfast of coffee and half a toasted bagel, Marty packed his briefcase. It was his first departmental meeting, and it would never do to be late. As he left he caught a glimpse of Jeanette sitting in the breakfast room in her white linen robe, coffee cup in hand, marveling at the tropical foliage outside the window, and planning her day.

\* \* \*

There were thousands of things to do at work, and so it was that the storage box with case reports 101 to 130 was joined by a second storage box containing case reports for Patient Numbers 131 to 160, and a third box for Patient Numbers 161 to 195. Finally, nearly a month after he moved to California, Marty found the time to open the boxes and resume reading the clinical reports on MI-37801.

It was late, and it had been a long day. He was sitting in the office of his laboratory, the storage box at his feet, signing off on the reports when he came up to Patient Number 114. This was a 35-year-old woman, depressed and unable to sleep. She had been on MI-37801 for six weeks, receiving the usual dose—5 mg twice daily. The adverse reaction page had a note: "Change in personality over last two weeks, short-tempered, blows off." Under "Action Taken," the doctor has written "MI-37801 discontinued. To see me in 3 weeks." That had been over two months ago, so there should have been a follow-up report. He was about to look for it when there was a knock on the door.

"Come in."

Kyoshi entered and bowed. He was a small, thin man with eyes and hands that were constantly on the move.

"Thank you, Dr. DiChiro."

"What is it?

"I have a set of photos that I would be so pleased if you were to look at them." He placed a small tray on the table alongside Marty's desk.

"God damn it, Kyoshi! I don't have time to go over your photos. Not right now at least. Bring them back later."

"Yes, Dr. DiChir. . . ."

"And none of this Dr. DiChiro business. I told you in this lab I want to be called Marty. You understand?"

"Yes, Marty." With a reverential bow, Kyoshi backed out of DiChiro's office, the tray of autoradiographs held in both hands in front of him, much like an offering to one of the Shinto gods.

After Kyoshi left, Marty spent some time looking for the follow-up report on Patient 114. It had not been sent to him. He made a note to call Lessing's research administrator, and then turned to the next case report: Patient 115.

The following morning Marty called Lessing's office and talked to Eva, his administrator, a woman whose German accent had barely been softened by her years in the States. He asked her to get him the follow-up report on Patient 114. She promised she would see to it and matters were left at that.

* * *

In the meantime the newly transplanted Wallace Laboratories started to pick up work where it had been left off prior to the move. With four new pairs of hands, data were coming in faster than Marty could process them and write them up for his research papers.

"You are working harder than you did in Chicago," Jeanette complained one night after he returned home close to midnight. He was sitting in the kitchen munching a microwaved hamburger. Jeanette already was in her nightrobe. She pulled up a stool and watched her husband devour the hamburger. "Why do you work so hard?"

"I am trying to have my data fall into place. The guys in the lab are collecting more results than ever and still nothing is coherent. I know the results I should get but they won't come up."

"They will."

"Of course they will. But in the meantime I am like a Vegas gambler who keeps putting his chips on his favorite number waiting for it to come around." He tried a smile. Jeanette handed him a paper napkin, and he wiped his mouth. "Nothing has gone right for me since we came out here," he said.

"That's not true. You only feel that way because you are tired."

"I guess I am. "

"Don't worry. Tomorrow is another day. Are you coming to bed?"

"Not yet. I have a few more clinical reports to go over. They won't take more than half an hour."

But they did.

Patient 189 was a 44-year-old man with a disabling depression who had been placed on MI-37801 with good response. The initial reports stated that he had much more energy and had returned to full-time work. The page for side reactions only contained one statement: "Frequent outbursts of anger, change in personality." The investigator had scheduled a return visit but it had been canceled. No reason for the cancellation was given.

Marty made a note on his pad to get a follow-up on Patient 189 and went on. Ten minutes later, with the folder on Patient 194 in his lap, he was about to doze off. Another depressed middle-aged woman, another good response to the daily dose of 10 mg, and normal laboratory data. But when he came to the adverse response page he sat up with a start. "Frequent outbursts of anger. Husband states she has undergone a change in personality." The same adverse response, and once again there was no follow-up.

Marty went to his desk and after some searching pulled out the folder on Patient 114. "Change in personality over last two weeks, short-tempered, blows off."

Change in personality. All three patients had undergone a change in personality and all three had experienced outbursts of anger.

He put the three folders together. In the morning he had to speak with Lessing and find out why there had not been any follow-ups.

* * *

The following morning he got up an hour earlier than usual. It was about time that he resumed his morning jog. Two miles up and down the Brentwood Hills and a mile along San Vincente Boulevard. It was a good run and it made him feel as if once again all the strings for his life were in his hand.

The call to Lessing took top priority. He was quickly connected to him.

"Dr. DiChiro! So good to hear from you! How are things in southern California?"

"The place is an extravaganza. That's what Jeanette calls it."

"And the weather is perfect?"

"Absolutely perfect. Even though everyone complains of the smog."

"What can I do for you?"

"I need follow-ups on Patients 189 and 194. And some time ago Eva promised me the sheets on the follow-up visit of Patient 114."

"Let me have those numbers again so we can check on them."

"114, 189, and 194."

"I'll have Eva look for them when she comes back from lunch. Any problems with them?"

"All three of them seem to have had a similar adverse response."

"Is that right? What kind of adverse response are we looking at?"

"Some type of personality change."

"Aha. We will have to check that out, won't we?"

"Absolutely."

"By the way, did you get our invitation to the international symposium? It will be in White Sulfur Springs. I hope that you and your wife will be able to come as our guests."

"When will it be?"

"The last weekend in May. A perfect time. It will be both education and relaxation. Golf, long walks, a bit of tennis. In any case, we'll be talking long before then."

The next day Marty was on the phone with Eva.

"Any luck with the follow-up reports?"

"They haven't come in yet."

"Will you see what's holding them up? I can't sign off on these patients until I have reviewed them."

"I understand." There was a pause. If Eva expected Marty to hang up, she was wrong.

"Do me a favor," he said. "Look up the name of the doctor who was following Patient 114."

"I don't think I am allowed to divulge this information."

"What does that mean? I have been cleared for all confidential information. There is no reason I cannot have this doctor's name."

"I am sorry, but I have been told not to give out this information."

"I don't care what you have been told. I want that doctor's name."

They went back and forth a bit more before Eva agreed to get Dr. Lessing's permission to release the physician's name to Marty.

She must have received the necessary clearance, for when Marty picked up his messages the following morning, she had left the name for him. It was a Dr. Harry Levin in Morgantown, West Virginia.

Dr. Levin was not hard to find and before the day was over Marty had talked to him about Patient 114. Of course he remembered her. She had indeed undergone a change in personality after he had treated her with this new drug. She had become very short-tempered, with frequent and unprovoked outbursts of anger. After he stopped the drug she became even worse. At one time she had threatened her neighbor with a kitchen knife, and then, a few nights later, while her husband was asleep, she had jumped off the old B & O railroad bridge. Died instantly.

"She died?"

"I am afraid so."

"Was there an autopsy?"

"No. I signed her death certificate. I think I wrote her off as having committed suicide as a consequence of an endogenous depression."

"Of course. By the way, could you complete a follow-up report on her? It'll help us keep our records straight."

"I already did. Sent it in to your main office a month or so ago. You should have received it by now."

Marty thanked him and, after hanging up, put in a call to Eva, who swore she had never received Dr. Levin's follow-up report.

"What's happened to the other follow-up reports?" Marty asked. "I need them as soon as possible."

"We are working on it."

"Good."

Marty hung up with the same sense of incredulity and annoyance that he felt when the operator had told him that Malvina had checked out of the Marriott Hotel. He was confronting unpredictable events over which he had no control.

\* \* \*

The following Monday Marty was on the phone with Eva. There still were no follow-ups on Patient 189 or Patient 194.

"I must speak to Dr. Lessing," Marty said.

"I am sorry but he is out of town until Wednesday."

"You mean he cannot be reached?"

"He has left word that he must not be contacted unless there is an emergency. But he does check in with me every morning."

When Lessing phoned back the following morning, Marty was in the lab, looking over Takafumi's data. The man was as industrious as Kyoshi, but for some reason his experiments had up to this point not yielded as unequivocal results as those of his compatriot.

Having moved aside a couple of immunoassay kits, Marty picked up the phone on the lab table.

"Dr. DiChiro. I hear you have been looking for me."

"Yes. I am having quite a problem getting my follow-up reports."

"Is that right? Do we know who the physicians are who have been delinquent?"

"Eva does not want to provide me with that information. She tells me it is confidential."

"She is being overly careful. As soon as I return to the office I will see to it that you will have their names. Any other problems?"

"Not at present."

"Nice to hear from you, and have a good day."

After he had hung up, Marty wondered why he had not told Lessing about Dr. Levin's follow-up report. The one that had been sent in to the main office but had gone astray. Perhaps it had been a matter of not wanting once again to drift into an area over which he lacked control.

As it turned out, both Patients 189 and 194 had been under the care of Dr. Vernon Guthkelch, an internist who practiced in Akron, Ohio.

On the phone Dr. Guthkelch sounded like a young man with a hard, energetic voice. Of course he remembered Mr. Wright, who was Patient 189. He didn't know what had become of him after he had left town following a fight with his younger brother, during which he had attacked him with a 20-inch wrench. A week earlier Mr. Wright had a run-in with the toll collector on the Ohio Turnpike.

The police had to be summoned and Mr. Wright had spent a night in jail before being released on his own cognizance.

"What about his depression?" Marty asked.

"He didn't have any problems with that. He was like a new man. Energetic. For a time he even returned to his old job. Then he just became impossible."

Mrs. Wlzcek, who was Patient 194, was another story. According to Dr. Guthkelch, she did well on MI-37801, but then she too underwent a change in personality. In fact, one night the police picked her up dead drunk in a downtown bar. "Never done anything like it before," Dr. Guthkelch assured Marty. "Her husband called me up and was irate. I had turned his wife into a monster. Said he wouldn't let her take the damned drug any longer, and as far as he was concerned I could take those pills and . . . you know what. "

"How come there was no follow-up on her?"

"He wouldn't let her come to see me. I offered to go out to the house, but he wouldn't have any of it. In any case, I filled out forms for both of these patients and mailed them back to you people."

"I never got them."

"Is that so? Well, don't blame me. I did what you people told me to do."

Marty thanked Dr. Guthkelch for his cooperation and suggested that in a few weeks he might try to set up another appointment with Mrs. Wlzcek. Dr. Guthkelch promised to do so.

\* \* \*

"I don't like what's going on with these drug trials I got myself involved in," Marty said to Jeanette when he came home that night. He was a bit earlier than usual and found her on the balcony, drinking iced tea and looking down at the sloping garden. The sun had set and the light was violet and mauve. He bent down and kissed the top of her head: an aroma of chamomile. She must have shampooed her hair.

"It's getting chilly." She had not heard him come in. As daylight faded, her blonde hair became drained of color. Marty sat down next to her and took the glass from her hand. "Just iced tea," she said, as he took a sip. "Shall I make you some?"

"Sure." She went into the kitchen while he put up his feet on the redwood table. A nod of thanks awaited her upon her return.

"What I was trying to say is that I am not happy with the drug trial study. I know it's paying the salaries of my Japanese post-docs and a couple of technicians, but I still don't like what's going on."

"You know I won't understand any of this."

"I'll make it simple. . . ."

"Gee, thanks."

"You see, the long and short of it is that this drug, MI-37801—that's what it's called for the time being—is being used to treat people who have been down in the dumps, depressed, or whatever you want to call it. They are not the most stable folk, and some of them, when they get better, start acting up in the strangest way."

"What's that like?"

"I am not quite sure. They seem to undergo a total change in personality. . . ."

"Isn't that good? I mean if they had been depressed, a change in personality couldn't do them any harm."

"I am not so sure of that. It appears they get violent, get into fights, commit suicide. . . ."

"But you just said they had real problems before they were started on MI . . . what did you say that number was?"

"37801. I know. Maybe it's nothing, but I am not used to working in such a vague, uncertain field. Neurobiology is much more straightforward. Most of the time we can expect a yes or no answer."

"What are you going to do about it?"

"First, I am going to give Lessing a call. There are a couple of things he has to clear up for me."

"And then?"

"Then I'll talk to Jack Brennan."

"What on earth for?"

Instead of replying, Marty drank his tea. He swallowed a bit more than he intended and went into a coughing spasm that took a couple of minutes to subside.

"I think we should go inside," Jeanette said when he had recovered. She took both glasses and went to prepare dinner. Marty remained on the veranda looking down into the darkening canyon. The trees swayed as an unexpected gust of wind blew through them. Suddenly there was a quick movement in the undergrowth and a dark form materialized. Before he realized what had happened, he was staring into two gleaming eyes. He quickly got up.

"Guess what I saw," he said to Jeanette, who was bent over the stove.

"Tell me."

"A coyote."

"I don't like them. They are evil animals."

"As far I am concerned, they are survivors."

\* \* \*

"Have we been deluging you with our drug experience reports?" Dr. Lessing asked Marty the following morning.

"No problem so far. I think I am up to Patient 220."

"So what do you think? Do we or don't we have a winner?"

"I am a bit concerned."

"What about?"

"Those three adverse reactions I mentioned to you. I have been in touch with their treating doctors, and both of them relate a strange story. The patients underwent a change in personality."

"For the better, I assume."

"No."

"No? How so?"

"All three became violent, with unpredictable outbursts. One of them committed suicide."

"I assume this person who committed suicide had been depressed before he was started on our drug."

"Patient 114? She had a long history of depression."

"There you are."

"What I have been wondering is whether any of this came up during the Phase I trials?"

"No."

"How many subjects were enrolled in that phase?"

"Some forty or fifty. Mostly college students and other volunteers."

"Forty or fifty?"

"Something like that. If you want to have the exact number, I would have to ask Dr. McClellan."

"Up to now I have reviewed 220 case reports, and I have found three worrisome adverse reactions."

"Look, Dr. DiChiro. The world needs Dulcian, and we will have a very negative PR if we discontinue its development at this point in time. We have a tentative FDA approval and are scheduled to release the drug to some four thousand hospitals and medical centers by the end of the month."

"Are you sure you are not being premature?"

"I don't think so. This is a competitive business, and we have been led to believe that the Japanese are working on a similar drug and will probably be ready to release it by the middle of next year. We can't afford to have them beat us to the punch."

"Those three case reports worry me."

"That's three out of over two hundred, and I gather you are not at all convinced that they represent an adverse response."

"For me, three out of two hundred is unacceptable."

There was a pause on the other end of the phone. "I think the best way to resolve this is that we have you come out here and meet with our group. I will organize a small staff retreat after the holidays, and this will give you a chance to meet Marc Walton and Nick Cusworth. I know you'll feel better after you have talked to them. With any luck we can get R.J. to sit in on part of the meeting."

"R.J.?"

"R.J. Crowley. He is C.E.O. and chairman. What's your schedule like for the first weekend in February?"

"Looks clear to me."

"Good. I'd like us all to be sure where we stand."

\* \* \*

The retreat organized by Marat International was a class act. After a painless first-class transcontinental flight, Marty was met at Dulles Airport by a tall, cadaverous-looking uniformed chauffeur. The man's face was hollow; waxen skin was draped loosely across sunken temples and cheekbones.

"My name is Dumont," he said. "I trust you have had a good flight, sir." His voice was hoarse, as if he had not spoken for an immense length of time.

"Very pleasant."

Dumont picked up Marty's bag and led him to a black limousine. A few minutes later the lights of the airport were left behind, and Marty was on his way to Greensprings and the mountains of western Virginia.

Leaning back, eyes closed, his briefcase by his feet, Marty luxuriated in the scent of polished leather. Beyond the windows was a dark, ghostly blue, moonlit landscape. Hills blended into hills as the cone of lights raced ahead of the car, tunneling into the darkness as if descending a well.

"How much farther?" Marty asked as they swept around a series of unmarked curves cut into the mountainous country beyond Roanoke.

There was no reply. Marty became apprehensive. For an instant he again felt that something was going wrong in his life. Quickly, insistently, with a feeling akin to panic, he rapped on the window. Without taking his eyes off the road, the chauffeur reached back and slid open the pane.

"Do we have enough gas?"

"Enough to take us beyond Asheville, sir, if that's where you would prefer to go."

With a sense of relief, Marty dozed off. When he awoke, the car had come to a halt in the brightly lit driveway that curved in front of the Greensprings Hotel.

A young man in a green apron raced down the flight of marble steps to open the car door.

"Welcome to the Greensprings, sir."

Marty got out and stretched his legs. The air was clean and bitter cold. He followed the young man up to the hotel entrance. At the revolving door he turned to look back. The limousine had vanished.

\* \* \*

It was Albert Lessing in a white cotton jogging outfit who met Marty the following morning.

"I hope you slept well. I am afraid these cross-country trips must be exhausting for you."

"Not at all. The only drawback is that I lose out on my morning jog." A hot shower had refreshed Marty from a restless night, and he felt almost as fit as if he had managed a three-mile run.

"All of us at Marat appreciate the effort you are making on our behalf. R.J. should be here this morning. He knows what an important role you have in the development of Dulcian, and he is anxious to meet you."

Lessing led Marty to the Dogwood Room, where the retreat had been scheduled to take place. Tables covered with pink cloth had been arranged in the shape of a U, with about a dozen spaces marked by the presence of name cards, a water pitcher and glass, yellow pads and a pencil. In the back of the room a table had been laid out with an urn of coffee, cups, saucers and plates, and an assortment of Danish pastries. Marty accepted a cup of hot coffee from Lessing and joined some of the other participants who were standing in the back of the room, coffee and Danish in their hands.

"You must be Dr. DiChiro," said a tall man of indeterminate age in a green tweed jacket and dark linen pants. His eyes were hidden behind thick-lensed glasses.

"That's right."

"I am Warren Berrich, chief in-house counsel. May I pour you some more coffee?" Without waiting for a reply, he took Marty's cup to the urn and refilled it. "I suppose we have you to thank for this weekend at Greensprings."

Marty did not know how to construe the man's remark and grew uneasy under his relentless gaze. He felt as if he were about to be subjected to an interrogation. To prevent this from happening, he started on a fancifully revised version of his drive from the airport. All at once a hush fell over the room. A heavy-set man had entered. He was dressed in a gray turtleneck sweater, navy blue blazer, and charcoal gray slacks. With an energy that belied his heavy frame, he strode to the back of the room. Lessing came up to him.

"R.J., I would like you to meet Dr. DiChiro. He is our consultant for the Dulcian studies."

"Glad to have you with us, Dr. DiChiro. I have heard a lot about you. Word has it that you are an absolute genius. I expect you to provide us with some guidance."

Marty enjoyed the feeling of uniqueness that R.J. gave him but was unsure what type and how much guidance he was expected to provide.

"Shall we get started?" Lessing asked. He returned to his place and loudly tapped a spoon against the empty water glass in front of his yellow pad. Marty sat down between Lessing and a Dr.

Heinz Kleinwort, who had marshaled a dozen sharpened #2 pencils in front of him, aligned from the longest to the shortest.

R.J. went up to the lectern and laid out a few sheets.

"Ladies and gentlemen. On behalf of Marat International, I want to thank all of you for taking some of your precious weekend time with your families to come to Greensprings. We have a full agenda, and we therefore should start promptly and adhere to our schedule. First of all, I would like to make it official: MI-37801 is Dulcian. Dulcian is the name by which the entire world will know the drug. And I also want you to know that we are projecting sales figures of eight hundred million for the first year, and five billion—I did say billion—for the third year on the open market." He looked at his notes.

"It is timely that I now review with you Marat International's program for marketing and distribution of Dulcian. This will be a triple threat program. First, we intend to place adequate inventories in strategically located clinics and hospitals. Second, we will give these clinics and hospitals an incentive to sell Dulcian. And third, we will extend this same kind of a marketing plan to large pharmacies. These outlets will perform most of our sale and distribution functions."

R.J. stopped and looked around the room. "Above all, we must keep the commercial viability of this product in mind. HMOs, that is to say the numerous health maintenance organizations throughout the country, have greeted Dulcian with enthusiasm. The same goes for the major health insurance companies, who recognize that we have a drug that circumvents prolonged and expensive psychiatric care and gives the primary care physician an opportunity to treat the depressed patient without having to refer him or her to a specialist.

"But we must not be satisfied with these achievements. We must find new ways of researching the markets for Dulcian so that other potentials for this drug, which as yet have no current market, can better be defined. Gentlemen, remember: Dulcian is the new and more acceptable alternative to psychotherapy."

Marty scribbled a few perfunctory notes, the kind that would not make any sense to him two days hence, then listened to an interchange between R.J. and a red-faced young man with pudgy hands about the value of bringing out a long-acting form of

Dulcian. Someone from the other side of the room wanted to know what kind of product the Japanese were developing. R.J. admitted that he did not know. With a gesture of irritation, he folded the sheets and returned them to the inside pocket of his blazer.

"Frankly, it is maddening," he said. "The only information we have to date is that in their initial evaluations the Japanese drug appears to be quite effective not only in depression but also in a variety of other affective disorders."

"Do we know what type of chemical they are working on?"

This came from Melvin Walton, Vice President of Consumer Relations. He was a white-haired man with a pencil-thin white mustache that protruded beyond the edges of his mouth.

"No. The best guess we have at this point in time is that it is related to trazodone, which has been on the market in this country for several years."

Marty bent over to Lessing. "What's trazodone?" he asked.

"It's a complex heterocyclic compound that is thought to potentiate the actions of serotonin."

"Another kind of Prozac?"

"One might say so. Whatever it is, Dulcian is going to turn out to be much more effective."

Marty nodded and added a few more lines to his note pad.

\* \* \*

Lunch was served in the immense main dining room of the hotel. Lessing steered Marty toward R.J., and the three of them shared a cloth-covered table under windows that looked down on the circular driveway and, beyond it, on a large growth of conifers that rose into blue-gray hills. The sky was overcast—a portent of snow.

"Dr. DiChiro has some concern about what he thinks have been three adverse reactions to Dulcian," Lessing started out. Marty had the distinct impression that Lessing and R.J. had already spoken about them.

"Actually there now are four," Marty said. "Almost identical. People who experienced a dramatic change in personality."

"Dulcian is intended to induce a change in personality," R.J. said imperiously. "For the better."

"One of the subjects committed suicide. . . ."

R.J. turned to Lessing. "What is the incidence of suicide in chronically depressed patients?"

"Depends on whose study you look at. Among patients with recurrent depression, death by suicide occurs at a rate of about one percent per year. In long-term follow-ups, the death rate by suicide has been between 15 and 25 percent."

"I am not convinced that the explanation is that simple." Marty said, as he spread butter on his sourdough roll. The cold salmon filet was outstanding. "I have talked to the treating physicians and they are certain that these people have undergone a change in personality. They have become nasty, they are subject to outbursts of violence that they had never shown before."

R.J. smiled. A set of perfect white teeth appeared. "You see, Dr. DiChiro, your background of neurobiology leads you to expect perfection. There is no such thing as a perfect drug. Every drug has its risks, and we here at Marat International consider the risks that result from treatment with Dulcian to be acceptable. They certainly are less than those of the other drugs on the market."

"Are we sure?"

"We are, and if I were you, Dr. DiChiro, I would maintain an appropriate perspective on this subject. Always remember that we want you on our side." The force of the remarks preempted any further conversation.

The first couple of hours after lunch were set aside for free time. Marty elected to take a walk in the woods behind Greensprings. He was disturbed by his interchange with R.J. and Lessing and needed to be alone before returning to the afternoon session.

"You, too, are not one for a few holes of golf?" It was Dr. Kleinwort. Now that he had the opportunity to look at him deliberately, Marty saw him as a small, unattractive, thin-faced man with a chiseled accent and wandering eyes.

"No. The last couple of years I have had to watch my weight, so I prefer to jog or just take a brisk walk."

"I can believe it. These retreats are murder. Tonight we will have a six-course dinner with some incredible wines."

"So what do you do for Marat?" Marty asked as they strode around the back of the tennis courts in the direction of the golf course.

"I am their official statistician. I obtained my Ph.D. in mathematics from the University of Freiburg and after I left Germany I taught at M.I.T. for three years."

"So what made you leave Boston?"

"Money, my dear sir, money. M.I.T. pays $ 60,000 to their top ranked assistant professors, and Marat can triple that without even blinking an eye. And I have two aging parents to support."

The path started to climb and, to his annoyance, Marty found himself breathing heavily. He had not been jogging regularly and he was out of shape.

"I hear that you have been finding cases in which our drug has produced a marked personality disorder," Kleinwort said.

"It looks that way."

"What do you estimate is the incidence of this adverse response?"

"So far I have found four cases out of some 240 patients."

"That's seventeen per thousand."

"Yet you had no problems with your Phase I studies."

"That is what we are told. Of course, Ailesly is no longer around to report on them."

"I am confused."

"That does not surprise me. You see, at one time Ailesly was Director of Neuroleptic Drug Manufacturing. When he was removed from Marat International on half-pension, we lost the chance to make heads or tails of our mouse toxicity studies. Derek Osborne has tried to repeat them using Ailesly's methodology, but he is unable to get any meaningful data."

"That is worrisome. Any idea what's wrong?"

"Not really. Of course, I am not directly involved in these studies. I merely perform the statistics on whatever data are passed on to me. But from what I understand, we are now seeing toxic effects at doses that Ailesly had found to be nontoxic. At first we thought it was because we are using a different strain of mice, but Osborne doesn't think it is that simple, and he wants to start Phase I all over again."

"But aren't valid animal studies a prerequisite for any clinical trials?"

"Naturally. I have always maintained that the mouse toxicity tests we are using were inadequate to predict any adverse reactions in humans. That's why I wanted to have these tests performed on primates. Baboons, to be specific. A lot of people in the company thought that made sense, but R.J. was dead set against it and still is. He thinks that extended Phase I trials are not cost-effective and that to prolong them would delay the drug from coming on the market."

"So what's wrong with waiting a few months and getting these questions cleared up?"

"Can you imagine the adverse publicity Marat would get from such a delay? It would cut heavily into our market share of psychopharmaceuticals. And then, of course, the Japanese. . . ."

"What do you know about the Japanese drug?"

"Not any more than you heard this morning. That they well may have a safer and more broadly effective drug. That is why it is so important that Dulcian capture a large market share of the drugs that are effective in depression as quickly as possible. Consider that depression is the major illness of our society. Insurance companies would far prefer the depressed patient to be treated with two or three pills of Dulcian a day than have him undergo psychotherapy or, God forbid, psychoanalysis, which are immensely more costly. They want Dulcian to be safe and effective as much as we do. You heard what R.J. said. That we have found a drug that is the new acceptable alternative. Acceptable to whom? Alternative to what?"

"Why are you telling me all this?"

"Because, Dr. DiChiro, I have a conscience. Perhaps my conscience is too finely honed for my own good. But then quite a few Germans of my generation have developed a finely honed conscience. It's their response to Hitler and our extermination camps. My parents are still alive. They live in Cologne. Whenever I visit them I look at their friends and wonder what they did during the Nazi era. I have asked them. Almost all get angry at me for intruding into their past. The way I see it, for them there are only three alternatives. Either they knew about the camps and condoned them, which makes them criminals; or they didn't know about them, which makes them fools; or they knew about them and refused to speak up, which makes them cowards."

"What about your parents?"

"I knew you would ask. I am happy to say that they were the exception. They were part of a small underground. They set up a clandestine radio station, passed out leaflets, calling for the end of the war, the assassination of Hitler. Almost every one in their coterie was found out—betrayed by one of their members—and executed. By some miracle my parents escaped being picked up."

"I admire them for what they did."

"Not as much as I do. They were one of a select few. Many people dream of becoming heroes, but there always is a barrier between dreaming those dreams and acting on them when the moment presents itself. For most of us, that barrier proves insurmountable."

"Lack of courage?"

"Yes. But even more so an unwillingness to immerse oneself in an untested reality, of breathing the cold rarefied air of a zealot."

Marty nodded, and the two men walked on in silence. Puffs of steam danced in front of them.

"How were they to you?"

"Distant. I was like an orphan with two living parents. Both were quite young when they chose to dedicate themselves to their ideals. Once the war was over, they were unable to return to earth, to a love of simple things—their son, their family, the many warm prosaic moments. . . ."

He shrugged. "It doesn't matter any longer. I have learned to love my books, there is always a lot of work to be done . . . and I will forever idolize them for their bravery."

From somewhere in the gray distance they heard the cawing of crows. Like small floating feathers, snow started to come down slowly and spangled the golf course with white.

"I think we should go back," Marty said. He was shivering.

\* \* \*

During the afternoon session Derek Osborne presented the results of the mouse toxicity studies. Marty admired the eloquence with which the young man moved effortlessly between slides and his scant notes and made a mental memo to contact him when he got back to California to see whether he might be interested in an academic career. Dinner that evening was as predicted by Kleinwort—a melange of tastes and wines that started with fresh oysters and ended with baba au rhum. The following morning Marty had a breakfast meeting with Lessing.

"Before he left, R.J. wanted me to let you know that he appreciates the care that you have given to the clinical reports. But he also wants me to remind you to maintain objectivity and refrain from alerting other physicians about what you interpret to be adverse reactions."

Lessing went on to point out that whatever adverse reactions Marty had encountered in patients who were being treated with Dulcian, these were no worse than the neurologic side effects seen with most of the phenothiazines. It was a long list of often permanent disorders, which manifested themselves by an impairment in the control of normal body movements.

"What we have here is a much safer drug than any others that are being used in the treatment of disorders of mood," Lessing said. "This is going to remain our marketing strategy. We intend to tell professionals and patients that Dulcian is safe and effective, and that it comes down to weighing risks against benefits."

"I understand."

"Good. R.J. and I knew we could count on you."

\* \* \*

"Alice and Gordon are in town," Jeanette said after Marty had put his bag down in the hallway. "They're staying at the Peninsula Hotel. I've invited them over for dinner."

"Sounds great." Marty went into the bathroom to wash up and change. The mirrors and basins sparkled, and Jeanette had laid out fresh white towels and facecloths—a reassuring sense of warm intimacy. Even so, he remained ill at ease. He must have conveyed his discomfort to his sister, for after dinner she led him to the guest room. The curtains were pulled; bags and clothing were spread out over the bed.

"You look preoccupied," she said.

"I have to make some decisions."

"What about?"

"It's too complicated to explain."

"Something to do with Jeanette?"

"Don't be silly. We have a great marriage. Can't you tell?"

Alice sat down on the bed, leaned back, and stretched her legs as she waited for her brother to explain.

"It has to do with my work," he finally said.

"That's all right then. I know whatever you will do will be for the best. You are the smartest man I know."

"Is that a compliment?"

Alice leaned forward and ran her fingers through her brother's sparse hair. "What do you think?"

\* \* \*

When Marty got to the office the following morning, a Federal Express box from Marat containing twenty more case reports awaited him. There also were a dozen or more phone calls and a reminder from his secretary that he had to prepare a presentation for Tuesday's Grand Rounds. The topic was to be the Shy-Drager syndrome. Since Marty's work was not directly involved with this disease, the presentation required a quick trip to the library, looking up some recent references, and the computer-directed preparation of some two dozen slides.

The following morning Marty had a chance to open the box containing the case reports. He already had decided to defer making any decision unless he found further adverse responses. With the apprehension of a young woman awaiting the results of her pregnancy test, Marty went through the case reports. Everything was fine until he got to Patient 253.

This was a 35-year-old computer programmer who had become depressed after the breakup of his marriage. His internist had started him on MI-37801. Marty stared at the two lines on the adverse reactions page: "Feels as if he were programmed. Frequent violent outbursts. During one of them put his fist through the office window." The drug had been stopped, but once again there was no follow-up report. For quite some time Marty remained motionless, taking in the commonplace details of his office with a mechanical eye. If he waited for his angel to reappear, he waited in vain.

Finally he returned the file into the box and buzzed his secretary.

"Please call Dr. Brennan's office. Tell his A.A. I have to talk to him."

A couple of minutes later, Marty's secretary was back on the line. "Dr. Brennan said to see him after Grand Rounds."

\* \* \*

That evening Marty sat across the desk from Jack. With the five files in front of him, he gave his chairman a condensed presentation of the adverse reactions.

As it happened, it was the very evening that Dan was in the library of the neurology department poring over the statistics on "Risk factors in episodic discontrol: a case-control study."

"So what's your problem, Marty?" Jack asked, after Marty had concluded his presentation.

"I think the FDA has to be notified. This drug should be pulled off the market."

"What on earth for?"

"Marat has to clarify these toxic reactions. And until they do, Dulcian should not be on the open market."

"I understand where you are coming from, but I also want you to keep the whole picture in mind. You may not know it, but last week I met with some people from Marat, and they assured me they would fund our B floor imaging unit. In fact, I expect their written commitment any day now. So let's not rock the boat."

"I wouldn't want to do that. But at the same time I am their consultant and I have to do my job."

"I am well aware of your connection with Marat, but I don't want this to come out!" Jack had raised his voice. "Understand?"

"Do you expect me to let these adverse reactions go by?"

"Marty, you are being too simplistic about the whole issue. You have put in two years' work, first in Chicago and now here. You just can't throw everything over."

"But we are dealing with a serious side reaction. Some sort of encephalopathy."

"Never mind that. I think it is much more likely that you are dealing with a series of coincidences." Jack got up and paced the floor. "How about some coffee?"

"Sure. Why not?" Marty got up and helped himself to coffee.

"So what kind of a grant do you have from them?"

"Five hundred and seventy-five thousand over the next five years."

"And what do you think will happen to that grant if you call the FDA and tell them about your supposed adverse reactions?"

"I don't need their money. I can put together a supplemental grant application to the NIH. I've got more than enough data to back it up."

"I know you do." Jack drank his coffee reflectively and returned to his desk. "Do you see this piece of mine?" Jack pointed to the neuronal abstraction on the wall of the office. "I call it 'One for All and All for One.' Our department supports you, and we need your support. You agree?"

"I suppose so." The rushing noise of immense white wings did not materialize, and Marty was left to make his own decision.

"Good. So do you or don't you want to be a team player?"

"I guess I have no choice."

"Exactly. So let's sit down, and I'll tell you how we're going to manage this. First of all, it will be your opinion that these adverse responses are coincidental. Everyone knows that depression and anger are two faces of the same coin and that anger includes violent discontrol and even suicide."

"What about the incidence of these reactions? Any statistician. . . ."

"You know what Mark Twain said—'There are three kinds of lies: lies, damned lies, and statistics.' Keep that in mind."

Marty agreed to keep it in mind. He finished the coffee and got up to leave.

"By the way, Marty, I'm having some people over to the house next week. Do you think you and Jeanette can make it for dinner? Jan Olafssen is over here from Sweden, and I'm having the dean drop by for dessert. Nothing fancy, just a small group of us."

When Marty got home that night, he opened a fresh bottle of bourbon whiskey. There was nothing like good bourbon to dull one's conscience.

A few hours later, well past midnight, Jeanette tiptoed into the dining room. She found Marty staring at the dark window that looked down into the sloping garden. A glass was in his hand. The bottle was half empty.

"What are you doing?" she asked.

"What's it look like?"

"You're drinking. . . ."

"And thinking."

"What about?"

"Lots of things. There is a man named Kleinwort. He rubbed me the wrong way, although he shouldn't have. And then there is a black angel who comes and disappears, and a white angel who doesn't show up when I need him the most."

"You are drunk."

"Not drunk enough."

"Enough for me. Come to bed."

And Marty allowed himself to be led to bed.

* * *

The following morning Marty threw himself into his work with a blazing intensity. Over the next few weeks, he completed several papers and mechanically signed off on several more sets of case reports that were being shipped to him by Marat.

It was his signature, nothing more than his signature, he reassured himself. And it was much easier to sign those forms than risk a confrontation with Jack and everything that it entailed. What is conscience anyway, he reassured himself. A foreign plant that clings to us, like mistletoe clings to an oak.

Jeanette, who was a good mind reader, knew that something was amiss with her husband, that something had happened which deprived him of his usual verve and spontaneity.

"I worry about you," she said one night. Marty had come home late, the children had long since been put to bed, and she sat at the table with him as he washed down a hamburger with a bottle of beer. "I think you are in a turmoil."

"There is . . ." he started out and broke off. "Get off my case, will you?" he said coarsely.

"Please tell me. I feel so useless."

Marty shook his head. He did not want her to probe him; he was determined to maintain his facade. Jeanette detected new creases on his forehead and tried to smooth them with her hand.

"Would you like to make love to me?" she asked. Since Marty could not unburden himself, she saw her duty was to soothe and comfort him. It mattered little whether this called for her words or her body.

Marty nodded and downed his beer. Thanks to Jeanette's body he briefly became unmindful of his conscience. But when he awoke in the middle of the night, he had a vision of his life. It was no longer a smoothly rising arc but a jagged line that lacked direction.

* * *

In the morning Marty received a call from Tara, Jack's administrative assistant.

"Could you come to Dr. Brennan's office?"

"When?"

"Right now. He said it was a matter of considerable urgency." The A.A.'s English accent remained totally unruffled.

Sitting in Jack's office a few minutes later, Marty was reading the double-spaced manuscript by Dan Lerner and Peter Carter. "The Angry Puppet Syndrome: An Unusual Adverse Response to Dulcian."

"Did you have anything to do with this?" Jack asked after Marty had returned the paper to him.

"Certainly not."

"Good."

"They are writing about four cases. How many have you seen?"

"Eight, ten . . . I don't know. I have stopped keeping track. What are you going to do about this report?"

"I won't permit it to come out from our department. I can't let Marat down. There is too much at stake for us. And if Dan's a team player, he'll put that manuscript in a drawer and forget about it."

"I don't know whether he will. He is a strange man. Several years in the Peace Corps, and when he talks to you he never looks you straight in the face."

"I see no other alternative. I am going to be firm with him."

"That's what a chairman is for."

Jack smiled and gave Marty a playful tap on the arm. "For that, and for innumerable other trials and tribulations."

As Marty came out of Jack's office, he saw Dan waiting, a cup of coffee in his hand. He avoided Dan's glance for fear it would carry an indictment. Instead he gave Tara a quick nod and left the outer office.

* * *

Marty was in the lab a few hours later when he got a call from Dan.

"Listen, Marty, I've got to talk to you."

"I can't. I'm tied up."

"Don't give me that shit about being tied up. I want to know what's going on. I write a paper about these four patients we've seen who had a reaction to Dulcian, Jack has a fit about it, and you give me the cold shoulder. I've got a right to know what's it's all about."

"Look, I said I was busy."

"All right, so you're busy this afternoon. Then what about tomorrow morning or whatever time suits you? You've been working on Dulcian. You must know what I have stepped into."

"Come by my office tonight. Around seven."

Promptly at seven, Dan sat in front of Marty's lab table.

"I am going to give you a piece of advice," Marty said. "Don't publish those cases. At least not for the time being."

"Why shouldn't I?"

"Because if you do, it'll make more trouble for you than it's worth."

"Jack tells me these cases are mere medical anecdotes. In short, that they're crap and shouldn't see the light of day. You've looked through the manuscript. What do you think?"

"I don't know. I only know that if Jack tells you not to publish the paper, you're better off to stuff it into a drawer and forget you ever wrote it."

"I won't do that. I saw two of the patients and Peter Carter saw the other two in Boston, and I know that they represent four fundamentally important case histories. They bring up the question whether a drug such as Dulcian can induce permanent brain damage in a selected group of people."

"Have you contacted Marat about them?"

"Yes. I even talked to their medical director. What's his name?" He paused. Marty did not volunteer to fill in the blank. "Oh, it doesn't matter. He said I was dealing with a set of coincidences, but that he'd send a memo to their field representatives and tell them to be on the lookout for any similar cases."

"You should at least hold off with that paper until you hear from him."

"I don't think I ever will hear from him."

"I've got to ask you: what harm will it do to you if you don't publish this paper?"

"What harm?" Dan repeated and looked dissatisfied. He stared at the bound journals arranged on the shelf behind Marty's desk.

"We only live once, and at some time we will have to give an account of our life," Dan said. When Marty looked puzzled, he added: "I'm going to think about it. In the meantime, thanks for your advice."

"It's my pleasure. Let me know if there is anything else I can do for you."

"I will."

"By the way, Donna is a great girl. I am really glad that I was able to get her some funding."

After Dan had left the lab, he dialed the inside number of Jack's office. Jack picked it up.

"Just finished talking to Dan. If he listens to my advice, he will put that paper away."

"Excellent."

"If that happens, he'll need a bit of encouragement from your end."

"We can do. I'll think of something. He's a good clinician, and I hope he decides not to be a troublemaker."

"Me too. I should tell you though, my intuition tells me that he's going to publish these cases, no matter what you or I tell him."

"Let's hope your intuition is wrong."

After Marty had hung up, he turned off the lights in his office and took a quick walk through the lab. The animal room containing the rat cages was flooded in broad daylight; in the morning the room would be pitch black as part of the experiments manipulating the animals' circadian rhythm. The two Japanese post-docs must have gone out for dinner. The open lab books and the ticking timer indicated that they would be back before too long. They are hard workers, Marty thought. Before too long they will have accumulated enough data for a paper in *Nature*, the premier science journal. It would be a short paper, no longer than the one that Watson and Crick published in the same journal back in 1953. A paper that not only got them the Nobel Prize, but also opened a new era for medical science. With any luck his paper would be just as important.

Marty left the lab and drove home. Sunset Boulevard was nearly empty, and a strangely glowing full moon dominated the dark forms of trees and plants on either side of the street. Despite the late hour he was filled with energy. For the moment he had completely forgotten about Dulcian and the box of new case reports that had arrived that morning and were waiting for him in front of the door to his office.

\* \* \* \* \*

$\mathbf{M}$AX was gone. As Maureen was about to leave for the office she had called him and, contrary to his habit, he did not come into the service porch to check on the dish that she had put out for him. Still calling him, she looked on top of the kitchen cabinet, where he usually spent the night, and opened the door to the back stairs. There was no response. She went through the hallways of the apartment house and up and down the stairs. The cat was not to be found.

Annoyed with his disappearance, she took the elevator down to the basement garage. It was eight in the morning and since most tenants were late risers, the garage was deserted. Although there had never been any incidents in her apartment house, and despite the presence of several closed circuit TV cameras mounted on the massive cement support columns, Maureen felt vulnerable under the maze of black and steel gray pipes. She got into her car. As she was about to start the engine, she suddenly realized that the car door had been left unlocked. It was her habit to lock it, and she was quite certain she had done so when she came home the night before. Disturbed by what she first saw as a deviation from her routine, an unprecedented absentmindedness, she headed the Toyota out of the garage and into the hazy glare of Rossmore. At the first stoplight she reached for her sunglasses. They were not in the well next to her but were lying on the passenger seat. A shiver rose into the nape of her neck. Someone had entered her car during the night and had moved the sunglasses from their habitual place.

She turned on the radio in time for a recap of the news. Nothing out of the ordinary: an explosion at a Texas oil refinery, more skirmishes in the Balkans, and a cabinet reshuffle in Italy. The forecast was for early morning fog along the coast, clearing by midday, with a high in the seventies. Typical May weather.

As much as traffic on Wilshire Boulevard would permit, she glanced around the car. The maps in the side pockets, pencil and pen in the well, her cardigan in the rear seat, all appeared undisturbed.

After she had arrived at work and parked in her stall, she completed a check of the car. With a sense of outrage, she realized that her glove compartment had been pried open. Although its contents were in total disorder, car manual, insurance card, registration, and her small address book had not been removed.

With trembling hands, she locked the glove compartment and car and took the elevator to the office. Wishing her secretary a good morning with as casual a voice as she could muster, she entered the inner office, shut the door, and sat down behind the desk. Her first inclination was to phone Dan and tell him what had happened. She stopped herself. Dan was not an early riser, and for her to call him when he was still at breakfast would make her appear anxious and dependent. With carefully controlled movements she read through a brief that awaited her signature. After a few minutes she buzzed her secretary.

"Charlotte, can you see whether Mr. Cosgrove is available for a couple of minutes?"

\* \* \*

"You agree with me that this is connected to our litigation against Marat?" Maureen was sitting in Mike's ornate corner office. His offhand way of responding to the episode made her wonder whether she had not overreacted to it.

"Obviously they're up to some dirty trick or other," Mike said. "When you deal with these drug companies, anything can happen. I trust that none of this has upset you too much."

He leaned back and with hands interlocked behind his head gave his chair a full turn. Behind floor-to-ceiling picture windows the outlines of the Hollywood Hills were blurred by a scrim of dirty brown haze and smog.

"We just have to go on with what we are doing."

Maureen nodded. Mike came to the other side of the desk and sat down on the edge next to her. His feet swung back and forth. "Are you worried?"

"Just a bit. I live by myself, you know."

Mike smiled. "By choice, of course." He leaned back and lightly tapped Maureen's calf with his loafer. "I don't want to take you off the case. It'll be a cold day in hell when the two of us can't take care of the Brooks Brothers brigade."

Maureen nodded. Her hand rested on Mike's desk. Slender pale fingers stood out against the dark mahogany wood.

"Then again you have to make your own decision. We just took in a real good medical malpractice case. A brain damaged baby with absolutely horrendous obstetric care. I see it as straightforward and heading for a tidy settlement. I was going to assign it to Larry, but if you prefer that sort of thing, it's not too late."

"No."

"Good. I'd rather have you than Larry work on the Dulcian file by a long shot." As if imbued with a mind of its own his foot ascended to the hemline of her skirt. Maureen withdrew her hands and allowed them to fall into her lap as she pulled away from the advancing foot. Her movement did not escape Mike, who abruptly slid down from the desk and returned to his swivel chair, where he did two quick half turns. After a moment's reflection he jumped up. "Are you getting anywhere with discovery?"

"So far nothing more than I could have found in the Merck Manual or the PDR. They have refused to turn over any of their internal documents."

"Privileged information?"

"Right. According to them."

"Bullshit!"

"They asked the court for a blanket protective order. They claim that if any of their correspondence or any of their data concerning the development of Dulcian were leaked out, they would suffer at the hands of competitors. I have asked for a hearing on it."

"I don't have to tell you that without their internal documents we might as well forget about this case."

"Right. You've seen the statement I prepared? I asked Marat to produce any and all data and documents that a drug manufacturer customarily generates in the process of preparing an application to the FDA. I had Charlotte drop off a copy of my arguments. It should be somewhere on your desk."

Mike followed her glance and looked around the cluttered desk: files, folders, letters, a box with Polaroids, and inexplicably a book, *Ghosts in Irish Houses*. A cluttered desk, a cluttered life, a man who was perpetually driven and dissatisfied. He transmitted his annoyance with himself to Maureen.

"When did you have her drop it off?"

"Last night, before she left for the day."

"Why the hell didn't you just hand it to me?" His voice rose. "You couldn't have been that busy."

"No."

"Let me tell you right now: you are going to be on your own in front of that judge. I am not going to tag along as your nurse-maid." He stopped to gauge the effect of his remark on Maureen. She nodded without replying.

"When are you going before him?" He was calming down. His eyes were directed toward the row of old English maps on the far end of the office.

"Tuesday morning."

"Who'll be arguing for the defense?"

"Allan Handelsman."

"Handelsman." A smile came over Mike's face. The storm was over. "That'll be an experience for you, Maureen."

"What do you mean?"

"He is smart, and do I mean smart. Number one in his class at Harvard. He's been with his firm for less than ten years and he has just been made senior partner. Don't worry. You can run circles around him. If you are well prepared."

"I intend to be."

"Good girl. . . . By the way, he's an orthodox Jew."

Maureen looked puzzled. Mike explained. "Wears a skull cap, brings his own special kosher food to the office, and can't be reached from sundown Friday to sundown Saturday. Oh yes, I forgot to ask you. How are you coming on with the interrogatories?"

"I'm getting there. I think they want to inundate us with paperwork at every step of they way."

"Of course they do. I have run up against them before. Wyburn, Mason, Keene, and Handelsman are a bunch of clever Park Avenue lawyers who get paid by the hour. The more briefs they file, the more they can bill Marat. One more thing: I have some information on Judge Watson that you should stow away in your head. You never know when it might come in handy."

He rummaged through the jumble of folders on his desk, tossed aside the book on Irish ghosts, and finally pulled out a fax sheet. He was about to hand it to Maureen then changed his mind. Putting on a pair of glasses he read from it.

"Graduate of Stanford Law School, took his first job with Pratt, Tuttle and Willings. Environmental protection litigation."

He looked over the top of his glasses at Maureen; perhaps he wanted to make certain she was paying attention. "Became junior partner in four years, then moved to New York, where he became partner with. . . ." Mike paused and looked down at the fax sheet to refresh his memory. "Hobeson, Vogel, Whitehouse, and Shilling. Did a good deal of corporate law for them. To my knowledge he was never involved with Marat and did not get into any products liability litigation. Nixon appointed him to the bench. I hear he runs his court like a fast-food service." Mike snapped his fingers.

Maureen nodded. "Got it," she said.

Mike jumped up. "Now get back to your office and prepare your arguments. Impress Watson with citations, the more the better. In case you haven't figured it out by now, this case will be the most important thing you'll ever do."

Maureen did as Mike directed. On the way back to her office, she passed Tom Costello's office. The door was open, and Tom was sitting in his chair gazing at hills and high rises. The smog was too heavy to make out the ocean. He saw Maureen and gave her a smile and a wave.

"How you're doing, Maureen?"

"Working away."

"The Dulcian case?"

"Right."

He smiled again: an automated grimace more than a smile. "Those bastards sure screwed me up. I don't know how to describe my head. It expands and contracts like a supernova. Right now it's contracting, and that feels good. But when it expands . . . oh boy! I can't tell what might happen."

Maureen didn't know how to respond. "I've got to get back to my office." She tried to put as much sympathy into her voice as the words would allow.

"I know. Go get them. Let me know if there is anything I can do to help." But it sounded more like a request than an offer of help.

When Maureen returned to her office, she pushed Tom out of her mind and for the next several hours she prepared her case, going back and forth between her office and the firm's law library, where she looked up the cases most often cited by defendants in confidentiality hearings. She intended to argue that Marat's internal documents pertaining to Dulcian were not privileged information. Even if the court were to find them to be privileged, plaintiffs had a right to obtain them as an integral part of the discovery process, since plaintiffs could not prepare their clients' case without access to these materials.

It was past ten at night when she called it quits and drove home. Even though the garage at her apartment was well lit, she was still troubled. In this town one could take out a contract on just about anybody for a few thousand dollars. It would be far cheaper for Marat to do that than to hire Handelsman and a bevy of junior lawyers.

She locked the Toyota, made sure that none of the windows were open, and with brisk steps—she had read somewhere that women who walk briskly are less likely to be attacked—went to the elevator door and pushed the button. At last a soft whir. She opened the door. The elevator was empty; the air inside was filled with a musty smell compounded of mint, stale cigarettes, and something heavy and indefinable akin to engine oil.

When she unlocked her apartment there was still no sign of Max. She put down her briefcase, kicked off her shoes, and poured herself a drink. Glass in hand, she sat down at the dining room table and looked through the day's mail. Nothing of consequence, thank God. She wondered whether to start working on answers to the interrogatories, but then decided that enough was enough for one day.

She finished her first drink a bit too quickly and refilled the glass, adding ice cubes to dilute the alcohol. It had been over a week since Dan had phoned her to let her know that Mike had advised him against seeing her until the Dulcian case had been tried. Which could well take five years. She stirred the ice with her little finger. How typical of Mike Cosgrove to see nothing wrong with him wanting a quick fling with her, but object to her relationship with Dan on the grounds that he was a potentially important medical expert.

She picked up the phone to call Dan. No reason for Mike to find out. But what if he did? She saw herself being called into his office.

"Maureen! When I give you an order, I expect you to follow it. Is that clear?"

Mike's voice merged with that of her father, the man who had judged her at every step of her life and had always found her wanting. Was it because of her shortcomings or his? Dan's answering machine came on. She replaced the phone without leaving a message, tossed down the remainder of her drink, and went into the kitchen to prepare herself an omelet. Two eggs, whirled up with thyme, basil, oregano, and a few tablespoons of white wine. Before long the soothing fragrance of hot butter and wine filled the apartment. She laid out plate and cutlery in the breakfast nook and poured herself another scotch.

Tomorrow she would get up early and work on the interrogatories. It would be another fourteen-hour day. She winced at the thought. There must be an easier way to make a living. She thought of Judith tooling around Beverly Hills in her silver Rolls and chased away a moment of envy. She would never want to be a woman like Judith. Although she was quite certain of that, a few bothersome doubts continued to circle her. She downed the whiskey and refilled the glass.

\* \* \*

"So you think that you are no longer in charge of your life?" Bernice Feldstein repeated Maureen's complaint but her voice contained a hint of sarcasm. "Your statement is not only trite but also untrue. You are more in charge of your life than most women in this town, and that includes Judith." She bent forward; the palms of her small eloquent hands extended toward Maureen. Maureen leaned her head back and closed her eyes. Her hands cradled a cup of coffee, the staple for her early morning sessions with Bernice. For a brief time she succumbed to a luxurious feeling of being enveloped by the soft, dark green fabric-covered couch, of being totally accepted and taken care of. For the remainder of the hour she would not have to appear strong and resolute.

"I am overwhelmed," she said simply.

"By what?"

"This case has the potential of being absolutely enormous. I am up against some of the smartest lawyers in the country, and I don't know whether I'll be prepared for the hearing next Tuesday."

"So what is the worst that could happen to you?" Bernice's question echoed a question Maureen had put to Dan a few days ago. The tone was the same—solicitous and maternal.

"The worst? For the judge to deny our motion to obtain the in-house documents and grant them their motions for summary judgment and to dismiss our case for lack of evidence."

"Then what?"

"What do you mean?"

"Just what I said. Then what? Do you think Cosgrove and Costello are going to fire you?"

"They might. Particularly if I refuse to put out for Mike Cosgrove."

Bernice smiled. "Is that how you see it? Whatever value you have for the firm lies in your vagina?"

"I know that's what he wants from me. He did the same thing to Ingeborg. I have never mentioned her to you, but she worked with us for a couple of years. One day she was gone. Just like that. It was only much later that Larry found out that she and Mike had been having an affair and that she finally put a stop to it. According to Larry, she gave Mike an ultimatum: leave his wife or call it off. So Mike fired her. I tell you, that man can be incredibly vindictive."

"And you think the same thing could happen to you?"

"Right."

"I don't believe that for one second. But let's assume he did fire you—what does that have to do with the feeling you have that you are no longer in charge of your life?"

"It makes me think I am at his mercy. Like he can abuse me any which way he wants to and get away with it. You know that man told Dan that he couldn't see me as long as this case is in the courts."

"Did he give him any reason?"

"Sure. Dan is going to be our medical expert, and I suppose Mike is worried that the defense might find out about us and make a big stink. And, of course, Dan in his inimitable way just accepted it."

"What did you say to Dan when he told you?"

"Not much."

"Why not?"

"I don't know. I suppose I couldn't think of anything to say."

"How come? Lawyers are supposed to be able to think on their feet."

"I guess I waited for him to assure me he wouldn't listen to Mike, and when he didn't, I got mad at him for giving in instead of putting up a fight. Like I wasn't worth it."

Bernice nodded. "Precisely. He makes a decision about your relationship and expects you to accept it."

"You are so right." She emptied her cup and, straightening out, placed it on the table next to the couch. "I intend to call him and let him know."

\* \* \*

That evening when she connected with Dan she was irate with him, and it felt good to let out her anger.

"Do we have to talk about this over the phone?" Dan asked after she had finished saying what she had to say.

"Are you worried that my line is tapped?"

"No."

"Or that my apartment is being watched and that Mike might find out you came to see me?"

"I got you. I'll be right over."

"Sounds good to me."

Less than an hour later the two of them sat across from each other at Maureen's dining room table. She had opened a bottle of wine and after a glass each it was like old times. Then Max's form appeared on the other side of the frosted window that led from the butler's pantry to the back stairs. Maureen felt that for that evening, at least, her world was once again complete.

"How long has it been?" Dan asked. Maureen was impatient with his question.

"I don't keep track of things like that." She kicked off her shoes. "What's happening to that paper of yours?"

"I just found out this morning that Peter convinced the editor to arrange for an expedited publication. So it should be out in a couple of weeks."

"Good. And the dean?"

"I have not heard anything more from him. He probably assumes that I did what he told me to do. Withdraw the paper."

"How are you going to handle it when he finds out?"

"I am going to tell him that he cannot coerce me to withdraw a paper."

"You will need representation. I can tell."

"Will you handle it?"

"I wish I could. But this could be quite an involved matter."

"So who do you recommend?"

"I'll have to think about it. In the meantime, don't say anything to anyone. It'll just make matters worse."

"As if they aren't bad enough."

"Right. You'll probably be okay until your paper comes out. Then you better watch out. Those guys are playing for pretty high stakes. By the way, do you know of any more cases?"

"Three of them. Two in Fresno and one just outside. All of them are still around, although they had to lock up one of them in Porterville. You want their names? "

"Not right now. I first have to make sure that the judge doesn't dismiss our case for lack of evidence. Then we'll have to see how he is going to rule on the in-house documents."

"What do you mean?"

Maureen explained the points concerning confidentiality and privileged information in products liability cases. As she did so, Dan put his hand on her forearm. A firm gesture and with it a return of the old closeness. Nothing appeared insoluble. A gentle moment expanded to fill the night.

"Shall we adjourn?" she said.

"It'll be my pleasure."

"And mine."

Maureen blew out the candles on the dining room table. A soft light from the bedroom lit up two gray coils of smoke as they widened and rose to the ceiling.

* * *

Maureen woke up sometime during the night. She rolled on her stomach and, leaning on her elbows, kissed Dan: soft kisses on the forehead, cheeks, nose, and mouth that penetrated his sleep.

"Dearest," she murmured. He stirred and opened his eyes to the dark.

"Have you been awake?"

"What do you think? I am so happy to have you with me." She ran her hand down his chest. "Can we talk?"

"Why not."

"I've been fretting about Tuesday. I have worked so hard to get where I am, and I feel as if everything hinges on what happens at the hearing."

"You'll do fine. You are such an incredible person—smart, competent, and well-prepared. No one can beat that combination."

"Thanks." She rolled on her back and put her head into the curve of Dan's arm.

"I think I need you to do something for us," she said.

"What is that?"

"I want you to sign an affidavit stating that you have examined and read the medical records of the plaintiffs and that in your opinion these patients experienced an adverse reaction to Dulcian. I will submit this affidavit to the court together with your CV and the manuscript you wrote with Peter Carter. That ought to take care of their motion for summary judgment on grounds of lack of evidence."

"Sounds fine to me."

There was a quick, soft tug on the blanket. Max had joined them.

"What if I were to take off work on Tuesday and come to federal court?" Dan said.

"Would you do that?"

"If you want me to."

She wanted his presence but there was no way she could acknowledge it. Instead she closed her eyes and, with her limbs relaxed, listened to street noises being carried through the open windows. The night was unseasonably hot. With the rush of shifting gears a truck raced down Beverly Boulevard. From somewhere in the distance came the sound of a siren. It moved closer, then disappeared into the night.

* * *

At eight-thirty Tuesday morning Maureen was sitting behind the plaintiff's table in federal court. She had given much thought to her outfit: a black jacket and skirt, with a white blouse ringed by a lace collar. A statement that denoted both professionalism and femininity. At her feet were two boxes. One contained the medical records of Arnold Barton, Saul Marcus, Ella Dunmore, and the other eight cases that had been joined in the class action suit. The other box contained material on previous arguments concerning privileged information and confidentiality. As Maureen went over her notes, Betty sat down next to her. Mike had suggested that Maureen take Larry along with her to the hearing, but she considered Larry too scatterbrained to be of much help. Not that Betty was much better, but Maureen felt that she owed it to the young woman to let her attend the hearing.

"Anything else I can get you?" Betty asked.

"I don't think so. At least not right now."

"Are you nervous?"

"Don't ask, Betty. For God's sake."

"I keep thinking what if the judge. . . ."

"Be quiet. I must get myself organized."

Betty rose and moved away. Maureen looked up to see a tall figure stand in front of the table.

"I am Allan Handelsman." A slender, yet powerfully built man wearing a three-piece charcoal gray suit with a red and gray regimental tie. Surrounded by dense curly black hair, the small black skullcap was hardly evident. "I don't think we've met. I represent Marat International." His face was round and overpowered by intense dark eyes.

"Maureen Durrell," she said without extending her hand.

"We've heard a lot about you. Francis here went to Michigan. Graduated a couple of years ahead of you. I guess you two never crossed paths." His hands were constantly on the move.

"Not that I know of."

"I suppose this is your first big case." Said in a charming but condescending tone. Maureen bristled.

"Whether this is my first or my twentieth big case is hardly relevant at this moment."

Handelsman smiled and, pulling over a chair, sat down next to her. With a quick protective movement, she turned over the pages of her notes.

Three smartly dressed young men in grim faces and black suits, who looked for all the world as if they had come to a funeral, sat down at the table reserved for the defense and busied themselves with notes and files.

"I better get back to my crew," Handelsman said. "May the better man—" he paused and flashed a smile—"or woman win."

The bailiff stood up. With his hands behind his back, belly protruding over his belt, and obviously enjoying his moment of importance, he announced, "The United States Court, Central District of California is now in session."

Everyone rose and stood at attention as the judge entered the courtroom. It was exactly nine-thirty. Judge Armand Watson was a slight, white-haired man, with large, powerful hands and the restless eyes of an insomniac. He sat down, adjusted his chair, and looked down on the courtroom. The hearing had not received any publicity and the benches reserved for spectators were empty.

"You may be seated," the bailiff said, and sat down against the side wall of the courtroom.

The court clerk read from her files. "This is case number CV-10199 of Ella Dunmore and others against Marat International."

The judge opened the casebook and leafed through it. "I understand that this morning we are going to hear arguments on behalf of the plaintiff concerning a motion to deny a protective order requested by defense. I also am going to hear a motion by the defense to dismiss this case for lack of evidence. Are you ready, Ms. Durrell?"

"Yes, Your Honor."

"Are defendant attorneys ready?"

Handelsman got up. "Ready, Your Honor."

Maureen got up, gathered her notes, and went to stand behind the lectern.

"Your Honor. This is a negligence and a products liability case. Mrs. Ella Dunmore and the other plaintiffs whom we represent here this morning have been permanently injured by a drug called Dulcian, a drug that is manufactured and marketed by Marat International for the treatment of depression. It is our contention that Marat International failed to exercise reasonable and ordinary care in the preparation of this drug and in testing it for potential toxicity. The information sought from Marat International by plaintiffs in this case represents the kind of materials from which may be learned what precautions Marat has taken to ensure that Dulcian was a safe and nontoxic drug prior to seeking approval of the drug from the Food and Drug Administration.

"Marat argues that disclosure of information pertaining to the toxicity studies and to the generation of data required for submission of an application to the FDA would result in competitive harm to itself."

Although Maureen repeatedly referred to her notes, she no longer needed them. The essential issues of the hearing were engraved in her mind.

She went on to stress that plaintiffs would use the fruits of discovery for no other than legitimate legal proceedings and that examination of Marat's files was absolutely essential to pursue litigation.

"I would like to refer Your Honor to *Waelde v. Merck, Sharp & Dohme, Williams v. Johnson & Johnson*, and *Allen v. G.D. Searle & Co.*, which deal with almost identical issues, and which were resolved in favor of plaintiffs."

Judge Watson nodded and made some notes. "Anything else you would like to say, Miss Durrell?"

"Yes, Your Honor. At this time we would like to submit to the court an affidavit by Dr. Daniel Lerner, a neurologist at Southwestern University. Dr. Lerner states that the illness from which the plaintiffs are suffering represents an adverse reaction to Dulcian. I also am submitting to the court a manuscript by Dr. Lerner and his co-worker, Dr. Peter Carter, a professor at Boston

University. This manuscript will be published next week in the *Journal of Clinical Neuropsychology*, a highly respected international scientific journal. I also am submitting to the court résumés or curriculum vitae for Dr. Lerner and Dr. Carter."

"Thank you, Ms. Durrell. Any objections, Mr. Handelsman?"

Handelsman jumped up. "Most certainly. We have not been provided with a copy of this supposed manuscript. Nor have we had the opportunity of cross-examining these so-called medical experts."

"Mr. Handelsman, at this point it is premature for you to examine plaintiff's medical experts. Ms. Durrell, will you provide Mr. Handelsman with a copy of the manuscript you have referred to? And you might as well give the defense copies of the résumés of your experts."

"I will, Your Honor."

"Anything else you would like to say, Ms. Durrell?"

"No, Your Honor."

"You may be seated. Now, Mr. Handelsman, may we hear from you?"

As Maureen returned to plaintiff's table, she saw a lone figure in the last row of benches reserved for spectators. Despite her determination not to be distracted by Dan's presence, she missed the beginning of Handelsman's statements, the part that dealt with dismissing the case for lack of evidence. Now she heard him describe Dulcian as a remarkable drug that in its short time on the market had benefited thousands of suffering patients.

"I would like to make several additional points," Handelsman said. "First, production of documents is harassment. It is burdensome, and it is privileged work product. Marat has prepared a safe and effective drug, and plaintiffs are well aware of that. Nevertheless, plaintiffs seek to obtain what are valuable documents on the proposition that you never know what might turn up. In short, this is a classic fishing expedition being used by plaintiffs to harass and embarrass Marat International. Second, defendant considers that certain documents, which it may be called upon to produce, will contain trade secrets, proprietary or otherwise confidential information. For Marat to be compelled to divulge the manufacturing process for Dulcian and the procedures that have been used to determine its safety represents a clear revelation of such trade secrets, which should not and must not be disclosed to the public."

There was much more of the same. Judge Watson was taking notes, nodding when Handelsman made a particularly pertinent point.

"He is not going to find for us," Betty whispered to Maureen.

"Just keep quiet, will you?"

After some ten minutes, Handelsman finished and sat down.

"Anything else you might wish to say, Miss Durrell?"

Maureen rose and stood behind the table.

"Yes, Your Honor. Plaintiffs would like to submit that the documents at issue in this case do not come close to meeting the legal criteria for a trade secret. We also would like to make it clear to the court that plaintiffs do not now, nor will they ever, seek to disseminate the requested documents to the public in general or to the competitors of Marat International, and we are willing to agree to a protective order that forbids such disclosure to the public or to competitors of Marat International."

"Thank you, Miss Durrell."

"Anything from you, Mr. Handelsman?"

"No, Your Honor."

"Fine. The court will recess for thirty minutes." Judge Watson rose and, gathering up his robe, notes, and book, retired to his chambers. Maureen put her papers in order and went to the back of the courtroom.

* * *

"I don't know whether it was right for you to come to the hearing," she said to Dan as they sat over coffee at a food-stained corner table in the Federal Building cafeteria.

"What's wrong with my being here?"

"I don't trust Handelsman. What did you think of his presentation?"

"Very persuasive, but not in the same class as yours."

"Thanks. Of course, with Watson one never can tell. He's been known to make the most way-out decisions." She put down the coffee. "They are going to know about us."

"Does that matter?"

"I will have to talk to Mike. That is, assuming that the court denies their motions for summary judgment and to dismiss our case for lack of evidence." She looked at her watch and stood up. "I am going back. When Watson says thirty minutes, he means thirty minutes."

"I'll be sitting in the back."

"Up to you. Don't be surprised if someone goes through your car tonight."

\* \* \*

Fifteen minutes later Watson had made his decisions and Maureen was on the phone to Mike. She sat in the phone booth at the end of the second floor hallway with the door partly open so that Dan could listen in on the conversation.

"He went along with us," she said. "He found that the affidavits they submitted did not establish that the materials we want were confidential. And then he denied their motions for summary judgment and to dismiss our case."

"Good girl. When you get back to the office we'll decide how we're going to go about getting at all the material. There'll probably be tons of it."

\* \* \*

When Maureen returned to the office an hour or so later, she immediately saw that something was wrong. Two armed police officers stood in the waiting room talking with the receptionist. Larry was in the hallway with Edith, his paralegal, and Charlotte, who was wiping tears from her eyes with a crumpled handkerchief.

"Did you hear about Tom?" Larry asked. "He jumped through the window. About half an hour ago."

"I don't believe it!"

"It's horrible!" Charlotte sobbed. "Just horrible."

Maureen sat down in one of the waiting room chairs and buried her head between her hands. He was gone. Even though she had little contact with him over the last few months, she always knew he was in his office, available to her if and when she needed him. Before his illness—and she had no hesitation ascribing that episode of obscene behavior toward her to an illness—she could always rely on him; his affection for her was pure, without ulterior motives. She knew it to be a selfish thought, but now she had no one to replace him. Dan? She did not know where she stood with him, God knows when, if ever, she would. She was confronting the enormity of her loneliness when Larry came and stood over her.

"Val had just gone in to talk to him," he said, and his mouth sounded dry. "All at once he jumped up, screamed, and started to throw books at her. Out of nowhere. Before she could call for help, he turned around and went through the window, head first."

"Twenty-five floors," Edith said. "Twenty-five floors . . . twenty-five floors." It sounded like a prayer.

* * *

Later that day Maureen was in her office. It was after six, and the place had quieted down as the evening prepared itself for a glorious sunset. With only half a mind on her task, Maureen was reading through a brief when the intercom rang. The night secretary was on the line.

"A Mr. Handelsman for you, Maureen."

"Put him on."

A moment later, Maureen heard Handelsman's well-tuned voice.

"I want to get together with you."

"What about?"

"Our office has received some information that I would like to pass on to you. Sooner rather than later."

"What is it?"

"I prefer not to talk over the phone. Can we meet?"

"I suppose so."

"I think it should be on neutral grounds. Neither your office nor mine. How about the bar of the Peninsula Hotel?"

"The bar? That sounds more like my territory than neutral grounds."

Handelsman chuckled. "Don't be so sure."

"Good. Now that we've settled the where, what about the when?"

"How about at eight?"

"Not tonight."

"Dinner date?"

"Could be."

"After you hear what I have to tell you, you might want to cancel it."

"I have no intention of canceling it. Can we meet earlier, like in an hour?"

"Have it your way."

As it turned out, Maureen arrived before Allan Handelsman and was sipping a whiskey and soda when he came into the bar. Taking off a woolen muffler, which he had wrapped around his neck, he sat down across from her.

"Why don't you read this while I order a drink." He opened his briefcase and handed her a manila folder.

Maureen opened it. It contained a two-page letter on the stationery of the University of San Diego, addressed to Dean Roger Weigel with a copy to Dr. Jack Brennan. The light in the bar was poor, and Maureen had to put on her glasses. "It is with deep regret that I must inform you that the paper 'Neurotrophin-7 in cortex from Alzheimer disease patients,' by D.L. Lerner and Y. Eilat, which was published last year in the *Journal of Molecular Brain Research*, is fraudulent." The letter was signed by Bertram Crandall, M.S. Maureen read through it quickly, then more carefully.

After she had finished the letter, she made a mental outline of the allegations claimed by Crandall. First, that Dan had altered the clinical history of patients after Crandall had completed the laboratory assays for brain NT-7. The second allegation was that Dan had forged the results of the analyses so that the amount of NT-7 that he had reported in his paper was not that which was actually present in brain.

She closed the manila folder. By then Handelsman had been served his drink. The waitress brought them a plate with toothpicked cheese balls.

Maureen reopened the folder and looked at the date of the letter. It had been written April 29, a little over two weeks ago. She reread the letter.

"So, what do you think of your expert?" Handelsman asked.

"I want to know how you got that letter."

"Does it matter?"

"Very much so. An investigation of any potential scientific fraud has to be kept under wraps until it is completed. That letter had no business going to your office."

"These allegations would have come out anyway once we deposed Dr. Lerner. I only wanted to spare you the embarrassment."

"Thanks a lot." Two folds appeared between her eyes. "What if none of this is true?"

Handelsman extended a palm in her direction. "Come on, now, Maureen, be realistic. What's in it for Crandall?"

"A bit of change, just as a starter. I know that Dr. Lerner dismissed the man quite some time ago because he had caught him manipulating data."

The hand stopped in midair and fell to the table. It gripped the glass. "How do you know?" Handelsman asked. He no longer appeared self-assured.

"We have our ways," Maureen said mysteriously. She was encouraged by the fact that she had been able to disconcert Handelsman and dispel his omnipotence. "If you so much as bring up this investigation in your deposition of Dr. Lerner, I will object, and I will instruct the doctor not to answer unless he is ordered to do so by the court."

"You are a feisty lady." He picked up the manila folder and returned it to his briefcase.

"Anything else we need to talk about?" she asked.

"What do you have in mind?"

"I want to know what business a seemingly decent man like yourself has working for a company like Marat."

"Our firm handles their litigation, and I am one of the senior partners."

"And you are not weighed down by your conscience?"

"Wrong. My conscience is as strict as yours. But I also believe that every person, regardless of what he is being charged with, is entitled to be defended in court. Furthermore, I consider your litigation to be frivolous. In my opinion Dr. Lerner is one of those scientists who knows what results he wants to get and then sets out to get them by one means or another. Any physician will tell you that depression can take a million forms, and for Lerner to label one form of depression as the—what did he call it—the Angry

Puppet Syndrome, is not science. It is a grandstand play. Do I make myself clear?"

"Yes. Quite clear."

"You do know Dr. Lerner?"

"Yes."

"How well?"

Maureen sat motionless with both hands around her glass. Handelsman smiled. Not a cruel smile.

"You don't have to answer, Maureen. What does matter, though, is that Dr. Lerner in his eagerness to respond to what he considered an intellectual challenge decided to set logic aside and blame Dulcian for what probably was a somewhat unusual manifestation of the underlying disorder, namely, depression. Do you follow me?"

Maureen nodded. Her mind raced ahead. She would have to confront Crandall and find out what prompted him to make his accusations. "I have to get going," she said aloud and stood up.

"I'll take care of this," Handelsman said, motioning to the drinks.

"Over my dead body you will." She put down a ten-dollar bill and dashed off. At the door to the bar, she turned. Handelsman was still looking at her. He smiled and, without lifting his elbow from the table, waved his hand in her direction.

"What an asshole," she murmured to herself. But somehow she wasn't so sure. There was a wistfulness in Handelsman's gesture to which she could not help but respond.

\* \* \*

A few days later Maureen was back in Mike's office. It was early afternoon and the sun was pouring through the tinted glass windows. Mike pushed a bowl of nonpareils in Maureen's direction and got up to adjust the levelors.

"So, then, where are we?" He returned and sat down. With a quick movement he swung his feet on top of the desk.

"We have lost Tom," Maureen said.

"Yes. . . ." There was a lengthy pause. Maureen was the first to break it.

"We have two matters on our agenda," she said. "First, I am flying to New Jersey to go through Marat's in-house documents. And we are still waiting for some information on Bert Crandall."

"I have sent Bartlett down to San Diego. He is perfect for the job. Did you know that he was on their police force? Ten years. If he can't get us the lowdown on Crandall, no one can."

"Right."

"So when do you fly to New Jersey?"

"Next Tuesday." Seemingly as an afterthought, she quickly added, "I want to take Dr. Lerner with me." Her decision was not as impetuous as it sounded; she had amply reflected on it over the last few days. She wanted to spend some time with Dan in order to discover whether he could provide her with the affection she needed from a man and whether he was strong enough to replace Tom Costello. A few days earlier she had brought this up with Bernice, adding that she felt ashamed of her selfishness.

"There's nothing wrong with being selfish," Bernice had said. "With you, as soon as any relationship becomes close, you start to give and give until you grow angry from too much giving." It was comforting to have Bernice echo her thoughts; it made her ego sound louder and more important.

"You want Lerner to come with you. You must be kidding!" Mike said.

"I need someone with a medical background. I am going to be confronted with over twenty thousand documents, and there is no way I can tell what's important and what isn't. We have already disclosed him as our expert, so what more can be said?"

Mike shook his head. He pulled his feet off the desk and sat up straight. "This is serious between you and him?"

"Come off it, Mike. I told you I need a medical expert for this, and he is the obvious person."

"I can find you any number of medical experts."

"I am sure you can. What do you have against Dan Lerner?"

"Handelsman is going to find out about your relationship with him."

"I am sure he already knows. If he brings it up in deposition. . . ."

"He's too smart for that. He'll wait until trial and let the jury get an earful of it. And what about those allegations?"

"What about them? I don't believe a word of it."

"All right. But don't say I didn't warn you."

"Right."

"One more thing. Before you go I want you to remember that our clients cannot help us prove the case. After all, they were not hit by a truck. They are either dead or they don't know what happened to them. They only know that something has gone wrong. Our causation case has to be proved almost entirely from documents in Marat's files."

"I am well aware of that."

"And I'll have Bartlett call you when he checks back in."

\* \* \*

"There is something I want you to be absolutely straight about," Maureen said, putting down her menu.

After their cross-country flight she and Dan had checked into the May's Landing Holiday Inn—separate rooms—and they had just sat down for dinner in the Garden State Room. "Is there anything to what Bert Crandall says?"

"Of course not. The man is angry and vindictive."

"Good."

"I wonder who got hold of him?"

"Don't you think Jack Brennan is the most likely one?"

"But I fired Crandall before Brennan was appointed chairman."

"Are you sure?"

"Now that you ask, I am not."

"We don't need to talk about this any more. Let's wait to hear what Bartlett comes up with." She leaned forward and whispered, "I should have brought it up on the plane. Mike said that he wouldn't be surprised if our rooms were bugged."

"I hear you. Did he also tell you to check under the hood before you start your car?"

"Not yet. Although I have already thought about it."

"What good would it do them?"

"Right." She adjusted her glasses and returned to the menu. "Have you ever seen anything like it? Seared chicken breast with almonds, pineapples, and Chinese water chestnuts."

"What about this one—ravioli stuffed with turkey and almond paste?"

"And this—hamburgers with almonds and melted cheese. This menu is like a bad joke."

"The chef must have an almond fetish." Her nose wrinkled and she burst into laughter.

*  *  *

The next morning they drove their rented car to the North American headquarters of Marat International. It was early June, a dull and humid day, with only a faint ocean breeze to relieve a gathering and oppressive heat. The two- and three-story buildings of glass and steel flanked by dark poplars seemed to have grown out of the green rolling hills that surrounded them. Tinted glass walls reflected clouds and the distant ocean.

Dan parked the car in the visitors' parking lot in front of the administration building, and they walked up the curved ramp lined by boxwood that led to the entrance. The owl-like woman behind the oval information station in the lobby gave them a chilly stare.

"Can I help you?" Her mouth was fixed into two straight lines.

"I am Maureen Durrell of Cosgrove and Costello, and this is Dr. Dan Lerner. We are here on a court order."

The woman was unfazed. "I will have to see it." Maureen took the documents from her briefcase; the woman extended her hand. "May I?"

"No, you may not, but I can assure you they are in perfect order." The woman got up and went to a telephone at the far end of the information station. After some time and several phone calls she returned.

"Mr. Nesbitt will conduct you to the archives. You are required to sign in, and I must remind you that visitors have to leave the building by five o'clock."

"No exceptions?" Maureen asked playfully.

"None whatsoever."

Mr. Nesbitt was a uniformed private guard. His appearance was that of a retired boxer who spent most of his free time keeping in shape. He led Maureen and Dan across the travertine floors and down a staircase that appeared suspended in space. An elevator took them into the subbasement. Two corridors later Nesbitt unlocked a door.

"These are the archives. The files you want to examine are in here."

They entered a small, windowless, and poorly ventilated room filled nearly to the ceiling with numbered storage boxes. No chairs, no tables, no clock.

"I'll be back at five to five," Nesbitt said and slammed the door on them. To Maureen it seemed as if she and Dan had been locked in a jail cell. She took off her jacket and laid it on the nearest box.

"Where do we start?" Dan asked.

"Your guess is as good as mine. I suggest we sort the records into three piles—no, maybe, and yes. I'll empty out two cartons for the maybe's and yes's."

"I wish we had better light."

"Tomorrow we'll bring our own."

They began to go through the documents. Maureen glanced through each one first, then handed it to Dan.

"Anything?" she asked.

"No."

And she handed him the next document.

\* \* \*

When Nesbitt returned at five to five, they were hot, grimy, and exhausted. They had managed to go through fourteen boxes without finding anything of interest to them. The "yes" box was empty, the "maybe" box contained one document, a letter from a New England sales representative to the effect that two clinics had complained of reactions to Dulcian, and asking for guidance as to how he should answer these complaints and still retain sales.

"We'll be back tomorrow," Maureen said to Nesbitt, who acted as if he had not heard her. As they ascended to the lobby, the elevator filled with young men and women decked out with Lucite identification badges. Five o'clock was closing time, and the administration building was emptying rapidly.

"How was your day?" Maureen asked the owl, as they signed out at the oval information island. There was no reply.

It had cooled off considerably and the ocean wind carried a fine refreshing drizzle.

"Dinner at seven?" Dan asked as they parted in the lobby of the Holiday Inn.

"Sounds fine to me."

Back in her room, Maureen pulled the curtains, undressed, and filled the tub with hot water. The stopper leaked. She tried wrapping a facecloth around it, but when that didn't work, she had to keep the water running. As she hung up her skirt and jacket, she felt a paper in the pocket of her jacket. It had not been there that morning. She unfolded it.

"Box 28 contains some of what you are looking for."

Handwritten. No signature. She folded the note and put it into her purse.

* * *

"Let's take a walk," Maureen said. They had finished a dinner of spaghetti and meatballs, the only dish that had not been laced with almonds.

It was still overcast, but the ocean wind had picked up. They left the parking lot and headed in the direction of the surf. A sandy trail wound between clumps of shrub pine. After they had gone some distance, Maureen stopped and took the note from her purse.

"This was in my jacket tonight." She shone a flashlight on the paper.

"A man's handwriting," Dan said.

"Could well be. In any case, it's nice to know we have someone rooting for us at Marat."

* * *

The next morning they signed in at the information desk under the watchful eye of the owl, and with Nesbitt as their guide headed into the netherworld of the Marat archives. As soon as they were on their own they opened carton 28.

Wordlessly they went through the documents one by one.

The first sheet that had some significance was an interoffice memo from Nicholas P. Cusworth, Assistant to the C.E.O., Marat International, to R.J. Crowley, Chairman, President, and C.E.O. for Marat International. Subject: Minutes of the MI-37801 task force meeting of 3/17. In substance the memo stated that according to the most recent calculations, production costs for MI-37801 will be 15 percent of its market price, and that consequently there would be considerable room to lower the sales price should a competitive drug challenge Marat's position in the market.

"It's a 'maybe,'" Dan said.

"Right."

A few minutes and several documents later Maureen gave a sharp short breath and handed Dan an interoffice memo.

It was from Nicholas Cusworth and was addressed to R.J. Crowley. Subject: MI-37801 Toxicity Studies.

"Marvin Ailesly has become progressively more distressed with his toxicity analyses. In addition, he has a remarkable new finding that we must look into. I suggest that we discuss his problems in some detail before going further toward initiating Phase I and II studies."

The next document was dated some two weeks later. It, too, was from Nicholas Cusworth to R.J. Crowley.

"Marvin remains adamant about his results. He claims that he has always had difficulties with obtaining consistent data on his toxicity tests, and that with the new development that we discussed a couple of weeks ago, a more rigid toxicity test has to be devised before clinical studies on MI-37801 can be initiated. I am disappointed in him, and I think you will agree with me that we have invested far too heavily in terms of time and money to delay our production schedule with further toxicity tests instead of proceeding directly to clinical trials. I also think that Warren should be told about this in case there are other developments."

"What does it look like to you?" Dan asked.

Maureen laid a finger across her lips. "It's time we took a break." But they were locked in and, short of using the in-house telephone, there was no way for them to alert Nesbitt. So they went on sorting documents until he arrived at five to five and led them away.

"I think we've got our smoking gun," Dan said as they drove back to the Holiday Inn. "What perplexes me is that reference to a new finding of Ailesly's. I have no idea what it could be."

"Don't expect me to tell you."

"It must have been something very important or Cusworth would not have referred to it as remarkable."

"Right."

"By the way, who is Warren?"

"Probably Warren Berrich, their head in-house counsel."

"What would he have to do with this?"

"I wouldn't have the faintest idea. But I'm sure we'll find out sooner or later."

\* \* \*

A couple days later Maureen returned to an office littered with interrogatories prepared by the staff of Wyburn, Mason, Keene, and Handelsman. To be answered as soon as possible.

Maureen had just settled down to work on the interrogatories when Mike came into her office and established himself on the couch. Maureen looked up. As always, his bushy hair was in wild disarray. No doubt about it: despite his years, he was still a handsome bastard.

"How was Seattle?" she asked.

Mike had been looking into a potential litigation against the Seattle Transit Authority.

"Not worth talking about. More to the point, how was New Jersey?"

Maureen put down her pen.

"Interesting. I would say it was a good start."

"Fill me in," Mike said. And Maureen filled him in. Mike listened; his head was bent forward and rested on his hands.

"There must have been a top level staff meeting to deal with Marvin Ailesly's toxicity studies," he said.

"I am certain there was. If records of that meeting exist, I couldn't find them."

"Doesn't surprise me. Why don't you have Betty draft a motion to compel them to produce the minutes for that staff meeting? They'll probably tell us there was no such document. And, of course, we'll have to depose that man Ailesly. You said he left Marat."

"On half-pension."

"Interesting."

"By the way, do you know anything about Warren Berrich?"

"Like what? I know he is their in-house counsel."

"I think he was involved with this right from the start. Somehow that doesn't make any sense. Why would they call him in when they found out that Ailesly was having trouble with the toxicity studies?"

"Why?" Mike repeated. "I'll need to mull that one over."

When Mike left, Maureen returned to work on the responses to interrogatories. She worked through lunch and dinner. The night secretary brought her a tuna sandwich, which she ate absent-mindedly, washing it down with a diet Coke. It was past eight when the intercom buzzed.

"Can you take a call from Dr. Lerner?"

"Put him through."

"How are you doing?" Dan asked.

"Just working. Dull stuff, like answering their interrogatories."

"Our paper came out. I thought you should know."

"Congratulations."

"It should stir things up a bit."

"How do you think your boss will take it?"

"Who knows? I guess I'll find out before too long."

"Look, I am sorry I have to meet a deadline on these inter-rogatories. We'll get together as soon as I've sent off the replies."

"I understand."

A few minutes later the intercom buzzed again.

"A Mr. Bartlett wants to talk to you. Shall I tell him to call in the morning?"

"No. Set up a meeting with him, Mike, and myself."

And Maureen returned to her interrogatories.

\* \* \*

Bartlett had a weight problem. He was a balding man in his forties with a belt that struggled some six inches below what at one time had been a waistline. Mike and Maureen were with him in the small glass-enclosed conference room at Cosgrove and Costello.

"So what have you got?" Mike asked.

"Not much. No out-of-line bank deposits, no big purchases, no major credit card payments. Mr. Crandall leads a very colorless life." He laid out an assortment of computer printouts of bank statements, credit card charges, and telephone calls.

"What does he do for a living?"

"After he left the university he opened a small biochemical consulting firm. He has a courtesy appointment at the University of San Diego and a subcontract with Chemex-2000. He has been trying to get other subcontracts from drug houses, but so far he appears to have been unsuccessful. He attends St. Augustine by the Sea Episcopal Church and has a car phone that he hardly ever uses."

"What does he drive?"

"A Porsche 928. Has had it for six years."

"On a technician's salary?"

"He also gets a small monthly check from the R. and F. Crandall trust fund."

"I see. Any lady friends?"

"Nothing major."

"Gay?"

"Not that I could find out."

"So what does he do in his spare time?"

"Takes karate lessons and goes to the local police academy to perfect his handgun skills."

Mike became impatient. He stood up. "I am going to leave you two together. Why don't you go over those printouts and see if there is anything in them."

But there was nothing of note in the printouts.

"I still want to meet that man," Maureen said as Bartlett was packing up. "Do you have his phone number? And, by the way, can you get me some business cards with my name and the university logo? I may need them."

An hour later Maureen was on the phone with Bert Crandall.

"This is Maureen Durrell with the University Legal Services. I would like to make an appointment to meet with you."

\* \* \*

In the middle of the day, the drive from Los Angeles to San Diego can be relaxing. Maureen had the car radio on—soft music from the sixties.

She reflected on the Marat case. Handelsman was right when he had described Dan as a man who was eager to take up an intellectual challenge. She remembered that when Dan first encountered the Angry Puppet Syndrome he had told her that he felt as if his clock had suddenly been turned back, so that he once again was able to become excited by his work.

Perhaps there was something to what Handelsman said: Dan found the angry puppets because he needed to find them in order to maintain his self-esteem. And what did she, Maureen, need for her self-esteem? To take Marat to court and win a humdinger of a judgment against them? What would that achieve? Her father was dead, and as for her mother and brothers, nothing she could ever accomplish would make them respect her. With a shrug of her shoulders she turned up the music and sang along with the Beatles: "I want to hold your hand."

Coast Chemical Consultants was behind a storefront in a mini-mall off Interstate 5, just south of Mission Bay. A silver Porsche 928 and a green Nissan Sentra were parked in front of the one-story building. Maureen parked next to the Nissan and rang the bell. Through the glass window she saw a man in the front office get up to meet her. Bert Crandall was in his mid thirties, with blond hair and mustache and a pleasant but decidedly weak face. The pristine white lab coat appeared to have been selected for the meeting. He introduced himself.

"May I get you some coffee?"

"I'd love it." Bert went into the neon-lit laboratory. Through the open door, Maureen could see a small black woman in jeans and a somewhat frayed lab coat injecting something into a series of tubes. A shaker bath by her side went through its perpetual rotary motion. No other activity.

Bert returned with two cups of coffee.

"Cream and sugar?"

"Not for me."

He lowered the blinds, picked up a pencil, and sat down with his back to the computer.

"So . . . how can I help you?"

Maureen had already prepared her approach. The goals of her visit were to find out whether Crandall had contacted the university or vice versa, and how genuine Bert's allegations were. "In your letter to Dean Weigel you stated that Dr. Lerner altered the clinical history of patients after you completed the assay for neurotrophin-7."

"NT-7." Crandall nodded. "That's exactly what happened." He rolled the pencil back and forth between his fingers. "Do you know anything about the Alzheimer Disease Rating Scale?"

"You will have to fill me in."

"The rating scale we used consists of a series of five tests that measure attention, memory, conceptualization, and several other aspects of intelligence. It can be given to patients in less than an hour, and therefore is quite a useful means to assess the presence of dementia and its progression. For the purpose of our paper we correlated the last score that a patient received on this test prior to his death with the assay of the mRNA for NT-7."

"And?"

"And after I had completed my assays Dr. Lerner went back over the test results and changed the scores."

"On every patient?"

"On some."

"Up or down?"

"Either way. Whichever was necessary to improve the correlation."

"You saw him do this?"

"Not actually. But I do know for a fact that the results had been altered. I myself entered them into the computer, and I know that the database that contained the test scores was modified after I had completed my assays."

"Could anyone else have changed the scores?"

"Hardly. He and I were the only ones who knew the password that would allow us to call up the database."

Maureen stared at the coffee mug. A black and orange mug with the University of San Diego emblem. Bert Crandall's status symbol.

"You must have known for some time that these results had been changed."

"Indeed I did."

"So what took you so long to step forward and write that letter?"

Bert leaned back in his chair and rocked back and forth, tugging on his earlobe.

"Have you seen the paper? The one in the *Journal of Molecular Brain Research.* 'Neurotrophin-7 in cortex from Alzheimer disease patients.'"

"No."

"But you do know who authored it?"

"Tell me."

"D.L. Lerner and Y. Eilat. Shall I tell you who Eilat is? A neurologist who doesn't know the first thing about lab techniques. I had to teach him how to hold a micropipette, how to weigh out reagents without spilling them all over the floor, and how to clean up after himself. I'm certain that where he comes from no one cleans up after himself."

Without agreeing or disagreeing, Maureen waited for Crandall to go on.

"Dr. Lerner did not put my name on that paper because I was only a lab technician. Even though everyone knew I did most of the work. He had no problem putting Yaakov Eilat's name on it. That's because he was a doctor. You get what I mean?"

"I think so."

"When the proofs of that paper came back to us, I went into Dr. Lerner's office and asked him to add my name as co-author. I thought I deserved it more than that oily Eilat. He told me that it was inappropriate to have my name appear as co-author but that he would see to it that I got a raise. I got hot under the collar and told him that, in case he did not know it, a man like me could not be bought off. A couple days later he gave me notice."

"He did? Did he say why?"

"He said I had changed the results on the Northern blots."

Even though Maureen did not know what Northern blots were, she understood the gist of what Crandall had to say.

"If I had my name on that paper and maybe on one or two others," Crandall said, "I would be much better off now. I could get myself some more contracts, and who knows. . . ." Holding the pencil between thumb and forefinger, Crandall leaned forward. "In part I have only myself to blame. I never should have had anything to do with the likes of Dr. Lerner. You understand what I mean?"

Maureen nodded. She had the answer to her first question. As for her second question, it was quite obvious that Crandall would have used every possible means to pay Dan back for the slight he had received from him.

"Would you like to see my lab?"

"I'd love to, but I should be getting back to L.A. before the traffic gets bad."

"I understand. Let me just say a couple of words to Nancy and then I'll walk you to the car."

Maureen got up and moved to the door. On the way, she glanced at the wastebasket at the side of Crandall's desk. A torn envelope peered out over the edge. With a quick movement, she picked it up and slipped it into the pocket of her jacket.

Bert returned and, leaving open the door to the office, walked Maureen into the brilliant sunlight.

"Thanks for coming down and listening to me," he said.

"Thank you for the information. You should hear from our office before too long."

She revved the motor and backed out, leaving the blond young man standing in front of the storefront.

Before getting on the freeway, she stopped at a gas station. Time to fill up the tank and take a look at the fragment of that envelope. It was the top left quarter. "Marat International. Office of Legal Affairs."

Maureen could readily imagine Warren Berrich's letter to Bert Crandall. An appreciation for the man's assistance in an important matter.

\* \* \*

"Any news of Ailesly?" Maureen was sitting in Mike's office. She had just presented him with a capsule summary of her visit to Coast Chemical Consultants.

"Not much. The Personnel Division of Marat refuses to give out any information."

"They must be sending him monthly checks. Can't we trace those?"

"Not without their cooperation. We will have to get the court to order them to produce those records."

"I told you we have a mole at their headquarters. Do you think there is a way to find out who he is and perhaps get him to help us?"

Mike leaned back in his chair and closed his eyes.

"The profile of a mole: angry and dissatisfied. An outsider. The man who hears a different drummer." With a rapid movement he sat up straight. "Who said that?"

"Who said what?"

"The man who hears a different drummer. Thoreau."

The intercom rang. Mike picked up the phone. "She's here." He handed it to Maureen. "It's your boyfriend."

"Can you talk?" Dan said.

"I am in Mike Cosgrove's office."

"I just want you to know that my phone's been ringing off the hook with new cases. At least two dozen. I am going to see as many of them as can manage to come to L.A."

Mike was gazing at the collected volumes of California Appellate Decisions. He was an impatient man and a call to Maureen from Dan made him even more impatient. Maureen saw his movement.

"Why don't I phone you when I get through?" she asked.

\* \* \*

That night Maureen and Dan had dinner at La Torta Calda. It had been over a week since they had seen each other.

"I just heard who is on the committee to examine my data," Dan said. "Andy Walker, Colin Pearson, and Marty."

"Is that good for you?"

"Andy is an old-time clinical neurologist. I suppose he knows something about rating patients with dementia. Colin Pearson does PET scans on Alzheimer patients, and Marty . . . I've told you about Marty."

"He took over your lab and your technician."

"Donna. That's right."

There was a pause while they drank Chianti.

"I went to see Crandall," Maureen said. "That man would do anything and say anything to destroy you."

There was a long pause. Maureen proceeded to tell Dan about her meeting with Crandall.

"He hates me. Because I have a better education and get a better salary than he does. It's envy . . . pure envy," Dan said with a sigh. "It happens again and again. Just when I stop thinking about it, this sort of thing crops up, and I lose my trust in people. It was so much easier for me in the Peace Corps. I was the white doctor, and that was it, and no one seemed to care that I had a good watch and wore good clothes. But back in this country I keep running into people like Bert. They forget how hard I had to work to get where I am."

"I don't forget."

"You didn't have it that easy either. . . ."

"We're two of a kind. . . ."

Maureen sensed Dan's understanding. She put her hand on his.
"You and I, we must not lose our trust in each other."
"Never."
Maureen released Dan's hand and emptied her wineglass.
"Your place or mine?" she asked.
It was like old times.

\* \* \*

When Maureen arrived at the office the following morning
Betty met her with a downcast look.
"I don't think you'll like what I have to tell you."
Maureen sat down and prepared herself for the worst.
"Marat refused to release their personnel files. They asked for
a protective order and the judge has granted it to them."
"Did you tell Mike?"
"I didn't have a chance. He came in for a few hours and then
went out again."
Without the personnel files there was no way they could
locate Ailesly, and not knowing where he was, they could never
subpoena him.
"This is ridiculous," Maureen said. She picked up the phone
and told Chris Bartlett what her problem was.
"Wish I could help you. That man could be anywhere in the
world. From Alaska to Florida. Or overseas. I wouldn't even know
where to start looking for him."
"I'd hate to appeal Judge Watson's protective order," Maureen
told Betty when she got off the phone. "But I don't see any other
way to subpoena Ailesly."
"The judge won't like it. And we sure wouldn't want to antagonize him. Why don't we wait until Mike comes back. He might
have some ideas."
"Mike? Oh, God! I guess there isn't anything better for us to
do. In the meantime let's start to send out notices of intention to
take oral depositions."
"On whom?"
"On all of them—Dr. Albert Lessing, Medical Director, Marat
International, Melvin Walton, Vice President of Consumer
Relations, Marat International, Nicholas P. Cusworth, Assistant to
the C.E.O., Marat International, Derek Osborne, Director of

Neuroleptic Drug Manufacturing, and let's not forget R.J. Crowley, Chairman, President, and C.E.O. for Marat International. At least we know where to find those people."

"Will do. By the way, are you going to go out for lunch?"

"Lunch! You must be kidding! When have I had time for lunch?"

\* \* \*

Three days later when Maureen came home, a letter awaited her among the bundle of bills, catalogs, and mailers. It was postmarked Trenton, New Jersey.

"A. is Ashley Powell of Stinson Beach, California." Handwritten on good bond paper. She went to her desk and took out the note, which had advised her to look into box 28. As she had expected, it was in the same neat angular handwriting.

Even though it was late, she picked up the phone and called Dan. She read him the note.

"What does it mean?" he asked.

"It means that our mole has once again come to the rescue."

"And that Ailesly has changed his name to Ashley Powell. And that he lives in Stinson Beach."

"Right."

"But where on earth is Stinson Beach?"

"It's north of San Francisco. In Marin County. As it happens, I have an aunt who lives there. She must be in her seventies. I visited her, God knows how long ago. I am going to call her and ask her to put me up for a few days. And while I'm there I'll look up Mr. Powell."

\* \* \*

When Maureen got to the office the following morning, she buzzed Mike's secretary.

"Did Mike come in?"

"No. He went to Detroit on that General Motors case. He won't be back until next Monday."

"Anywhere I can reach him?"

"I can get you his number at the River Place Inn."

When Maureen called Detroit, Mike could not be reached. She left a message to the effect that she was off to San Francisco for a day or two to visit her aunt and that she would be back in the office the following Monday.

She buzzed Charlotte.

"Get me a round-trip ticket to San Francisco. I want to leave at around four this afternoon. And have a rental car waiting for me at the airport."

\* \* \*

Mrs. Edna Garrison lived in a wooden Victorian house that overlooked Stinson Beach. She had retired there some twenty years ago following her husband's sudden and premature death. Her days were spent tending a large rose garden that flourished in the temperate coastal climate, chairing the Stinson Beach Book Club, and conducting an extensive correspondence with her family in County Galway. Her niece's visit was more than welcome, and even though Maureen did not arrive until nine at night, roast beef, potatoes, and cauliflower dipped in bread crumbs awaited her.

"How is your mother?" Aunt Edna asked, as soon as Maureen had settled down to dinner.

"Quite well."

"She must be so proud of you."

Maureen did not reply. Instead she cast a longing eye at the sideboard, where there were a few bottles of wine. In spite of her years Aunt Edna was an astute lady.

"Would you like me to open a bottle of wine?"

Maureen said she would, and her aunt, like the perfect hostess she was, poured two glasses and did fair justice to her own.

The family coals were raked over a few times, and when they no longer gave forth any heat, Aunt Edna moved her chair up to Maureen.

"Tell my why you came here on such short notice? Not that I don't enjoy having you. But you must excuse my curiosity. Is it something to do with your work?"

"Right."

"I thought as much."

"Would you by chance know a Mr. Powell?"

"Powell? If you mean Ashley Powell, I certainly do. He comes to our book club every so often."

"Good. You wouldn't have his number?"

"Of course I have it. It's in my little book in the hallway."

* * *

The male voice on the telephone the following morning was brusque and unpleasant.

"I definitely do not want to see you or anyone else from Cosgrove and Costello." Maureen detected a Scottish burr, softened by many years on this side of the ocean.

"I should think you would prefer to talk to me on an informal basis rather than receive a subpoena to appear at a deposition."

"As far as I am concerned, all of you can go to hell. I am retired, and I want nothing more than to lead a quiet life and have you respect my wishes."

"If you can give me 15 minutes of your time this morning, I promise that our firm will henceforth respect your wishes."

"What do you want?"

"I would like to come to your house and chat with you."

"I prefer to do it over the telephone."

"We could be overheard."

"All right then. I'll hold off going into town until you get here."

"Thank you. I'll be by in five minutes."

The beach house owned by Marvin Ailesly, now known as Ashley Powell, was a small wooden bungalow of uncertain age hidden behind dense foliage. A curving flagstone path, flanked by crimson crepe myrtle bushes, led to the front door. The bell did not work, and even though the door was unlocked, Maureen used a rusty knocker to make her presence known. The door opened almost immediately. Marvin Ailesly was a tall, slender man in his fifties dressed in a tweed jacket and jeans. In his one hand was a pipe, in the other a newspaper with which he discouraged the approaches of an overly curious schnauzer.

"Let's sit down and get this over with," he said, as he directed Maureen to a dark green stuffed armchair, while he sat in an old cane-backed chair across from her.

"I will be brief. . . ."

"I shall appreciate that."

"You know about our class action suit?"

"Very little. To be frank, essentially nothing, and I prefer to keep it that way."

"That's fine with me. In any case, we have learned that a few years ago in the days when you were in charge of the toxicity studies on Dulcian—it was called MI-37801 when you were there. . . ."

"Yes, yes. Go on."

"You wrote a report to the effect that the results you had obtained were unreliable."

"Of course they were. For one, we used a variety of different strains of mice, and as a consequence we were getting LD-50s that were all over the chart."

"LD-50s. What are they?"

"You don't know what an LD-50 is? You come singularly unprepared."

"You will have to excuse me. I am only a lawyer."

Ailesly did not react. "LD-50 is the median lethal dose," he said. "That means it is the dose of Dulcian at which 50 percent of the mice who receive such a dose die from its effects."

"I understand."

"Good. Our problem was more complex than that. Not only were the LD-50s all over the place, but there was also something else that was of even greater concern to me."

"What was that?"

"The blood serotonin levels."

"Once again you are over my head." Maureen wished she had brought Dan along. She could have kept quiet, taken notes, and then after they had left Ailesly, she would have asked Dan to explain. "What is serotonin?"

"For your purposes it is a chemical that relays messages from one part of the brain to another. It appears to be important in connecting the oldest, that is to say the most primitive, portions of the brain with its highest structures. . . ."

"The cortex?"

"That's right. Now when I first looked at the chemical structure of MI-37801, it occurred to me that this is the type of a drug that might well have a profound effect on blood serotonin. So I set out to develop a very sensitive assay for it. A few drops of blood from the mouse's tail was all I needed."

Ailesly stopped and, taking a pouch from his pocket, set out to stuff his pipe. Wordlessly, he lit the pipe and took a series of puffs. His face contorted and he emptied the tobacco into a small blue enamel bowl at his side.

"And?" Maureen coaxed him.

"You must excuse me," he said, and got out of the chair. "It is so damp around here that my blend doesn't last long outside the canister." He went to the dining room. Through the archway, Maureen saw him at the sideboard, his head bent over an engraved brass canister as he restuffed his pipe. His movements were deliberate, perhaps it was a way by which he gained time to decide on what to disclose to her. The reception room was silent. Through the open window came the sound of breakers and the insistent shrieks of gulls. Somewhere in the distance a car started up. Ailesly closed the canister, returned to his chair, and, puffing contentedly, sat down.

"As you were saying . . ." Maureen resumed.

"What we found was that in about 25 percent of mice MI-37801 produced a dramatic drop in serum serotonin. The drop remained even after we took the animals off the drug."

"I see," said Maureen, although she didn't see.

"You are taking notes?"

"This is so far over my head, I will have to go home and digest it."

"And consult with your medical expert. Be my guest. In any case, I wrote up my findings and showed them to Cusworth. He organized a staff meeting and I presented my data. R.J. was there and he didn't think much of my results. He said for us to proceed to the clinical studies, that the Japanese were working on a similar drug, and that Marat would not want to be scooped by them. I admit I got hardheaded about it and told them they were making a mistake not to look into my findings and how these would affect human toxicity. When they wouldn't listen to me, I said I had enough of Marat and would like to take an early retirement. I think they were glad to get rid of me."

"I can imagine."

"So here I am. Stinson Beach is very quiet. Too quiet at times. That's when I go into town for a weekend."

"Town?"

"San Francisco. Where else? It has everything." He took a series of puffs. "Have I told you everything you wanted to know?"

"Not everything, but probably enough for a starter. We should get the rest when we depose Cusworth and the other people in top management."

"Unless they stonewall you."

She got up. "Sorry to have been such a bother."

"It's okay." He rose and, going to the back of the reception room, rummaged through the drawers of an old upright secretary. He came up with a dark-blue folder from which he removed a sheet of paper. "Here is something for you to take home. So you can prove to your boss you were here. Let me explain." He took the sheet into the dining room and, smoothing it down, placed it on the table. "Now these are two graphs. Mouse 22-B-819 is on the left graph, and mouse 22-B-822 is on the right. The blue bars represent the dosage of Dulcian. The red dots are the blood serotonin levels, as measured against the vertical line, with time on the horizontal line. The mouse plotted on the left did not experience any change in serotonin, but mouse 22-B-822, the one graphed on the right, had a profound drop within a week of our starting it on Dulcian. A very provocative observation, to put it conservatively. And these graphs are only a sample."

"What does a drop in serotonin mean?"

"Your consultant will explain it to you. That is if you have the right consultant."

He handed Maureen the sheet.

"I have much more I could show you. I have extensive data from the clinical part of the Phase I study, but this is enough for today."

"Can I make an appointment to come back?"

"Not right now. My life here has been very peaceful. I don't want you, or anyone else, to disrupt it."

Maureen folded the sheet and put it into her briefcase.

"In case you change your mind, here is my card. And this is my home number. Call me any time you feel like it."

Maureen handed Ailesly her card. He gave it a quick look, then put it on the table. After a few parting words she went to her car. The ocean fog had started to lift and a hazy sunshine was making its appearance. A blue heron soared overhead. But for the distant breakers all was silence.

She spent the rest of that day and all of the next in the company of her aunt. They walked along the beach, visited a nursery a few miles north on Highway 1, drank tea on the porch, and in the evening watched television. Aunt Edna insisted on cooking, so that Maureen felt incredibly pampered.

"I see you as being very happy," Maureen said after they had kissed good night.

"Happy at moments, contented most of the time."

"I wish I could be like you."

"You would have been if your father hadn't put a handful of burrs in your panties. They make you look at what isn't yours, instead of what is."

"That's too simple an explanation."

"Not in my book it isn't. What you need is to find yourself a kind and intelligent man who respects you. . . ."

"That's what Bernice says. She's my therapist. Perhaps when I am done with this case. . . ." She stopped. Would a jury verdict, a large award, a sizable bonus from Cosgrove and Costello be enough?

"Let's hope so, Maureen. The years go by so quickly."

Once more they wished each other good night and went to their bedrooms.

\* \* \*

L.A. was—as always—smoggy, noisy, and frenetic. Even though it was Sunday, Maureen went to the office, looked through her mail, and then called Dan. He was not at home. She left a message on his machine, then went down the hall to seek out Mike. He had not yet returned from Detroit. Annoyed and dissatisfied, she went to do her week's marketing. Chores and more chores. Every spare moment of her life was filled with them. By the time she returned to her apartment it was past five. Max was waiting for her. Without being ordered, he rolled on his back, paws in the air. Maureen rubbed his tummy.

"Would you like me to tell you a little story about some mice?"

Max purred but otherwise did not respond.

\* \* \* \* \*

"I scheduled a new patient for your clinic," Brenda told Dan as he came into his office. "You had an open slot at three, and the family wanted to see you as soon as possible. The husband is certain his wife has experienced a reaction to Dulcian. Her doctor wasn't so sure, so they want your opinion. And Dr. DiChiro would like to set up a meeting with you. Tonight or tomorrow night, whichever is more convenient."

"Is that what he said? Whichever is more convenient?"

"I am pretty sure he did. And you also have a call from Channel 4 News. It's a Joan Brierson. She would like to come by here and talk to you about Dulcian. And there is a Mrs. Sue Barton. She wondered whether you still remembered her husband. He was one of the patients who suffered brain damage after he was given Dulcian. She needs to talk to you as soon as possible. And . . . let's see. . . ." She ruffled through the telephone messages. "Oh yes, a Mr. Edward Norton called from St. Louis. He says he is a lawyer, and he would like to meet with you and talk to you about Dulcian. And . . . did I give you this one? Dr. Carter phoned. He said he has something important to tell you. And Miss Durrell called earlier. She is in court but she will phone again in a couple of hours."

She handed Dan the telephone slips.

"Anything else?"

"Isn't that enough?"

"I should think so."

The phone rang. Brenda picked it up. After a few moments she turned to Dan. "It's for you. A Dr. Sunika Patel from McLean State Hospital. She wants to talk to you about a patient. She is certain he had a reaction to Dulcian."

"Get her number. I'll call her back in half an hour."

Dan went into his office and started to sneeze. The morning mists had cleared and bright sunlight sifted through the dense olive green foliage of the eucalyptus trees in the Barrows Botanical Gardens across the street from his office. He pocketed the handkerchief and sat down behind his desk.

In the mail was an announcement of a two-day medical seminar to be held in Sun Valley: "New Treatment Strategies for Depressive Illnesses." The program was directed at primary care physicians and was sponsored by Marat International. It featured sessions on the benefits of Dulcian and the cost-effectiveness of treating depression with Dulcian as compared to psychiatric treatment. There also were two letters from physicians telling Dan that they too had seen cases of his syndrome in their patients. And a number of postcards asking for reprints of his paper as soon as they became available.

It was clear to him that his paper had aroused nationwide attention, and with some pride he told himself that he had uncovered what could well amount to an epidemic of his syndrome. What if by publishing his paper he had made a powerful enemy of a man who had at his fingertips a network of connections in academic medicine and science? He would not be deterred, regardless of what Jack, or for that matter the dean, could do to prevent him. With a determined movement of his head he picked up the phone and started on the calls. Marty took precedence.

"Marty. Dan here."

"Good. I want to get together with you. The sooner the better."

"Can you tell me what it's about?"

"Not right now. I've got an office full of medical students."

"Why don't I drop by your lab after clinic. Let's say five-thirty."

"Five-thirty is fine with me."

No question the call had to do with Marty's role on the committee that was charged to rule on the validity of Dan's lab data. A one-on-one meeting after-hours implied that anything said between the two would be unofficial. Dan played through a number of possible scenarios for the meeting but gave up. It was a waste of time.

Sue Barton was next.

"Thank you for calling me back, Doctor," she said. She reminded Dan that it had been six months since her husband died. "I have wanted to get in touch with you for quite some time and thank you for all you have done for us."

Dan was on the phone with her for nearly half an hour. Sue was anxious to organize the patients who had experienced an adverse reaction to Dulcian, and use them to pressure the government to force Marat International to withdraw the drug from the market. With her daughter's background in advertising she considered herself to be right person for this task. Last week she had flown to Washington to meet with her congressman.

"Any luck?"

"Not yet, although Gary Fowler was very interested and promised to put pressure on the FDA to review their approval of Dulcian. I don't know how long this would have gone on if it hadn't been for you and Dr. Carter."

No sooner had Dan gotten off the line than Brenda buzzed him.

"Dr. Carter would like to talk to you."

"Put him through."

Peter's smoothly polished voice came on the line. "What I wanted to let you know is that the APA is preparing a statement in support of Dulcian. They say it is highly effective and free of any side reactions."

"The APA? You mean the American Psychiatric Association?"

"That's right."

"How did you hear about that?"

"Through friends. I also heard that they are getting Maurice Templeton to write an editorial in the *American Annals of Psychiatry*. He will come down hard on us. Something to the effect that our data were entirely anecdotal and that it was irresponsible for us to publish it."

"What's in it for him?"

"The Marat Educational Fund. Over five hundred thousand a year. To be used by his department for the teaching of residents and junior faculty."

"We'll have to write a rebuttal."

"Don't waste your time. The *Annals* will never print it."

"You don't think so?"

"I know so. And did you get the announcement of next month's seminar on Dulcian? And they also are setting up a dozen or so satellite symposia touting the drug. John Wechsberg told me he was asked to speak on the one in Boston."

"Who is he?"

"He's head of psychiatry at the University of Massachusetts. Very much into drug therapy. He has been going around saying that general practitioners can treat most psychoses. That even his medical students can do as well with a depressed patient as a board certified psychiatrist. You can well imagine that the insurance companies love him for saying so."

A few other calls had to be taken care of before it was time for Dan to go to Grand Rounds. It was just as well that Dan attended rounds that day, for Jack Brennan was at his most brilliant and erudite.

The patient selected for this week's presentation was a Portuguese dockworker who had just been diagnosed as suffering from familial amyloidotic polyneuropathy, a strange and rare disease that had not been seen at the hospital for more than a decade. Striding back and forth in the front of the auditorium, Jack delivered what appeared to be a spontaneous lecture about this extremely rare hereditary disease, which affected all the nerves of the body. He reviewed the history of the condition, how it had been discovered in Portugal, and how since then it had been found in the various ports visited by Portuguese sailors. It was an incurable and inevitably progressive illness that resulted in loss of strength and feeling in arms and legs until patients reached the point where they became bedridden and died of heart failure.

With his chin jutting forward, Jack turned to the resident who had just finished presenting the medical history and the neurologic examination of Mr. Figueria.

"Now, John, what can you tell us about the basic cause of this man's illness?" He removed the pointer from his breast pocket and pointed it at the resident. The corners of his mouth turned up, the prelude to an automatic smile.

The resident was ready for the question. He had prepared several slides, the first of which he flashed on the screen: "Various defects in the gene for transthyretin." Dan tried to remember what transthyretin was. The second slide told him: it was a protein that was involved in the transport of thyroid hormones and vitamin A. It was not yet fully known how an abnormality in this protein produced such a devastating and ultimately fatal disease.

Dan sat at the end of the third row and on several occasions thought that Jack looked straight at him. He saw no recognition in the chairman's glance, only an overpowering, inarticulate malevolence. A picture of Maureen flashed through his mind. Pacing about his living room, a glass of whiskey in her hand, certain there was something in Dan's paper that threatened the man. What that was Dan did not know, but he hoped that time would tell.

\* \* \*

At three that afternoon Dan found Mr. and Mrs. Greenhall in the clinic waiting room. Mrs. Greenhall's medical history was pretty much like that of the other patients with the Angry Puppet Syndrome. Her physician had prescribed Dulcian for what appeared to have been a relatively mild depression. Initially there was some improvement, but about three weeks after she had been started on the medication she experienced a total change of personality. Dan already knew the questions to put to Mr. Greenhall, and the answers he received were those he had expected.

"What can you do about her, Doctor?" Mr. Greenhall was sitting in Dan's office while his wife was in the waiting room under the watchful eye of a clinic nurse who had been assigned to observe her and prevent any unexpected violence.

"Make sure she is under supervision at all times."

"That's impossible. I have a job, our children are at college, and there is no one to stay with her. Even if I could get a nurse or someone to watch her, I am sure our insurance won't pay for it." Then, after a pause, "She is not going to be like this for the rest of her life, is she?"

"I don't know."

"Dr. Williams said you had more experience with this condition than anyone in town."

Dan tried to explain. Since this was a new disease no one knew whether the symptoms were permanent or whether they ultimately would go away.

"What has happened to the other people who had this reaction?"

Dan was intentionally vague. There was no use talking about Mr. Barton or Mr. Marcus. Fortunately, Mr. Greenhall did not follow up on his question. By then it was four o'clock and at two minutes past the hour the clerk popped her head into the office.

"Will you be much longer, Dr. Lerner? There is another patient waiting for you."

Dan walked Mr. Greenhall out to the waiting room, shook hands with him and his wife, who at that moment looked no different from many other colorless and depressed middle-aged women forced to adjust to the passage of years and the departure of her children. Except for her smile. It was meaningless and appeared to have been painted on her face as an afterthought.

"One more patient for you," the nurse said, after the Greenhalls had left.

Jane Bentley was a dramatic teenager with what she described as "unbearable" headaches that were like a "pneumatic drill" pounding into her head. The way she talked about them they were not like migraine headaches and not quite like tension headaches, rather they resembled attention-getting symptoms. Jane, her mother, and Dan had a long talk about what caused headaches. Dan told them about family and school stresses and the different ways young people respond to them. It was a difficult talk for Dan to deliver being that it was the end of a long day and his mind was on his meeting with Marty.

\* \* \*

"You have some interesting findings," Marty said, pointing to Dan's notebooks, which were stacked on the laboratory table.

"What do you mean?"

"Did you notice what happens to NT-7 as Alzheimer's progresses? I found it fascinating. Really quite unexpected."

He removed a sheet of graph paper that was folded between the pages of the top notebook and flattened it on the table with his palms. He motioned Dan to sit down next to him.

"Let me show you the graph I prepared. It's pretty much off the cuff, but it'll serve its purpose."

"Now, right here I have plotted the values of NT-7 from the anterior temporal lobe with progression of Alzheimer's disease. They go down right from the very start of the illness. Compare this with the loss of NT-7 from the ipsilateral frontal lobe. There is hardly any change in its amount until the disease has reached its final stage. Then something happens, like this"—Marty snapped his fingers—"and there is a sharp drop-off."

"I never noticed that."

"I can tell you why you didn't. You are much too diffuse. You will have to learn how to focus on your work to the exclusion of everything and everyone else. You will have to do it like I do. When I review my lab results, I am alone with them. I don't think about my family, food, about Jack and his political shenanigans. I even forget to go to the toilet. I exist in a trance from which I wake up some hours later to rejoin the outside world. This is what you will have to do. Otherwise your work will never amount to beans. In any case, the data are all there in your books. These two curves are trying to tell you something about what's going on in Alzheimer's disease. Think about it. Whatever it is, it's a much more complex process than simply the deposition of beta amyloid protein."

"Of course."

"Rothstein doesn't think so. But we both know he is wrong. In any case, this is an observation that's worth pursuing."

"If I can ever get my grant funded."

Marty did not comment on the last remark. Instead he reached for the next black notebook, opened it, and quickly leafed through the pages. "As far as I am concerned, these are all in order. Of course, I cannot speak for Jack and Colin. But I venture to say they will come to the same conclusion." He shut the book with a sigh and rested his chin between thumb and fingers. "We all know Jack can be quite difficult, and I for one would not want to cross him. Frankly, I was surprised that you wrote that paper. It does not do you justice."

"It was a small clinical series describing what we consider to be a new syndrome. . . ."

Marty took a deep breath. "I know, I know, you forget I've read it. But then you went on to publish it in spite of my advice and over Jack's objections. I told you not to. Not only for your sake, but that sort of thing doesn't look good for our department."

"In whose eyes? Marat's?"

"You could at least have held off with it for a while. The way it is, you screwed yourself royally."

There was warmth in Marty's words, an unspoken connection as if he were empathic to Dan's dilemma.

"I think Jack overreacted to my paper," Dan said. "From the very beginning, when I sent it to him for what I thought would be his automatic approval."

"Could be."

"What do you think made him do it?"

That question made a partly open shutter close abruptly.

"I don't know," Marty said, "and I certainly wouldn't want to guess."

"So what are you going to say in your report?"

"That our committee failed to find the evidence necessary to demonstrate that data had been altered."

"Guilty until proven otherwise?"

Marty smiled. "If you want to put it that way. The Scottish courts have a better word for it—unproven. That's the best we will be able to do without falling out of Jack's good graces. There is a lot of work I want to get done in the next year or so, and I don't want anybody to interfere with it."

"What kind of work?"

"Whatever I am destined to accomplish."

Destined was hardly a term that befitted a bustling neuroscience laboratory. It belonged in an alchemist's vocabulary along with phlogiston, vitriol, and the elixir of life. Dan said as much.

"Precisely," Marty said, with an energetic nod. "You see, there are myriad facts in the universe. Immutable facts that have been and always will be. In our lifetime we scientists select a handful of them and direct ourselves to find them and turn them over. What facts we select and how we interpret them once we have turned them over depends to a great extent on what kind of a person we are. It is like dialing a telephone number. There are millions of them, from Alaska to Zanzibar, and we never dial randomly, but only Aunt Millie's number, or that of Walt Penrose in Oxford. I am a neuroscientist and I work on the primate hypothalamus because of my genes, my upbringing, and my environment. Do I make myself clear?"

"I think so."

"Now as for you," Marty said, "I don't know how I can be of help. If Jack has it in for you, it'll be hard to get him off your back. Perhaps if you were to move out to La Virgenes. . . ."

"And do what there?"

"Carry your patient load and keep a low profile."

"Right now that's pretty hard for me to do. I get a dozen or so phone calls a day about Dulcian and the letters have started to pour in. I am supposed to be interviewed for the 'News Today' program. . . ."

"Tell them you're not available. At least not until this whole thing blows over."

But Dan was on a high and did not want the matter to blow over.

* * *

The following night over dinner at their little Italian restaurant, Dan brought Maureen up to date. She had flown back from Boston a couple hours earlier and her face was lifeless, with a pattern of fine creases around her eyes that Dan had not seen before.

"You look tired," Dan said.

"Tired and harassed. I didn't tell you but the Dunmores want to pull out of the litigation."

"What makes them do that?"

"That son of a bitch Handelsman called Mr. Dunmore and offered him a settlement. Four hundred thousand if they will drop their litigation against Marat and withdraw from the class action suit. He knows goddamned well he is supposed to go through us and not speak to him directly."

"How is Ella Dunmore?"

"About the same, as far as I could tell. She's got a nurse-companion who is built like a lady wrestler and who, I was told, can control her outbursts. So you see, I don't blame her husband. He needs every penny he can get right now to take care of the medical expenses. I spent four hours this morning talking to the two of them. I appealed to their conscience, told them to think about all the other people who were damaged by taking Dulcian. Thank God they're not too badly off, so they weren't panting for the money. I still consider her to be our best plaintiff."

"Do you think they will stay in?"

"I hope they will. As long as I can keep Handelsman from putting pressure on them. Right now, I don't care. I just want to get into bed with you and forget everything. At least for the time being."

Despite the closeness of their bodies they both felt as if there were an unseen presence between them, a force that prevented their free expression and reduced lovemaking to its mechanical minimum. The following morning, as they sat over breakfast under the watchful eyes of Max, Maureen turned to Dan.

"Tell me about serotonin." She must have been thinking about Ailesly's data all night.

"What would you like to know?" For Dan it was much easier to discourse about serotonin than reflect on his relationship with Maureen and his feelings about last night's lovemaking.

"When I was up to see Ailesly he gave me a graph that he said showed how in some mice Dulcian produces a sharp drop in the amount of serotonin in blood. He told me he wanted to look into this finding some more, because he considered it to be of considerable importance, but the management at Marat wouldn't let him. That's one reason why he resigned."

"So. . . . Dulcian lowers blood serotonin."

"In some mice, not in all of them. And when it happens it occurs abruptly." Maureen refilled their cups. "Why is that so important?"

"Let me explain it to you."

And Dan set out to clarify the role of serotonin in brain function, at least as much of it as is known. Serotonin, he explained, is one of many neurotransmitters, that is, one of the many chemicals, that send messages from one nerve cell to another. This particular chemical was made in cells located in the very depths of the brain, in those areas that are called "old" because they can be found in the simplest animal brains and have changed very little in the course of evolution.

Cells that manufacture serotonin have extensions that reach out into almost every part of the brain, even those parts of the brain that are unique to humans and are involved with intelligence and reasoning. Was it not strange, Dan reflected, that the highest centers of the brain are continuously exposed to a chemical signal from one of its most primitive portions? It was as if even the most abstract thoughts could be influenced by dark primitive processes.

Maureen nodded and opened her briefcase. Taking out a fresh pad of paper—her briefcase always had several fresh virginal pads—she took a few notes.

Dan went on to tell her that there was much recent research to show that there was an abnormal output of serotonin—either too much or too little—in people who suffered from hallucinations or anxiety attacks or who were depressed to the point of being suicidal.

"I get it," Maureen said when Dan had finished. "At least I think I do. Having too much or too little serotonin in your brain can throw you off your rocker. I wonder if Ailesly's mice acted crazy."

"I wonder."

Maureen closed her pen and returned the pad to her briefcase. "God, that man would make a fantastic witness for us. Maybe Mike can talk him into agreeing to be deposed."

They each had one more refill of coffee, then Maureen got up to clear the dishes.

"I hope you won't mind if we don't have dinner tomorrow night. I have to prepare myself for Lessing's deposition."

"Didn't you say Mike was going to take it?"

"He is, but I am the one who is drawing up the questions for him. He has been so involved in his General Motors case, he hasn't had a moment to think about Dulcian."

"I understand."

"Good."

"I wish you wouldn't work so hard."

"I don't have any other choices, do I?"

\* \* \*

It was late Friday afternoon, and Maureen had finished briefing Mike on everything she knew concerning the actions of

Dulcian and the various other antidepressants on the market. Before going home she packed away Lessing's depositions in the Breathelite cases. To be read, indexed, and annotated over the weekend. Then all at once she remembered the rise and fall of the breakers at Stinson Beach, the beckoning she heard from Aunt Edna's rose garden, from Ailesly's bungalow. If not a shared life, then at least a tranquil one. According to Bernice, she was not ready for either.

"But I have promises to keep, and miles to go before I sleep. . . ."

On an impulse she picked up the phone and dialed the Los Angeles office of Wyburn, Mason, Keene, and Handelsman. The night secretary answered.

"I would like to speak to Mr. Handelsman."

"Who shall I say is calling?"

"Mrs. Ella Dunmore from Boston."

"Just a minute. I will see if he's in."

A few moments later Handelsman came on the line. A soft, well-polished voice.

"Ella. So good to hear from you."

"This is not Ella. This is Maureen Durrell, and you are a fucking bastard." There was a long silence on the other end.

"I am very sorry you feel this way."

"Goddamn right I feel this way. You have no business talking to our plaintiffs behind my back. You know this sort of thing is unethical and that we could have you disbarred for it."

"Why don't you calm down. I was just about to leave my office. I have to be home before sundown. . . ."

"I have had my say. I won't keep you."

"Of course you won't. But I would like to talk this over with you."

"I don't."

"I must insist that we talk. How is Sunday?"

"Sunday will suit me fine."

"Good. I'll see you at six in the bar at the Peninsula. That'll leave you enough time for your dinner date."

"I won't have a dinner date."

"Is that right?" There was a significant pause. "See you Sunday."

Maureen hung up and shut her briefcase. Time to go home. Max was waiting for her.

\* \* \*

"Tell me, Dan, what do you make of that business with the serotonin?" David asked. It was Friday night and they were having dinner at La Torta Calda. Only a handful of tables were occupied, and the posters of Florence, Tuscany, and Lake Como looked more dilapidated than ever. The Chianti, however, had a surprising vitality.

"It's not an area I am well versed in. I would love to talk to Ailesly about it."

"But I gather he won't talk to you. He prefers to keep a low profile. If I were you, I would get in touch with Charles Forbes. He might well be able to help you."

"Did you say Forbes? I don't know him."

"I don't either, at least not personally, but he has been doing some good work on serotonin. Just had a review come out in the *Annual Review of Neuroscience*. He's in Cleveland. I can give you his number."

"Thanks. . . ."

For the remainder of the evening they talked about books they had read, a noncommittal topic that allowed each of them to keep the other at arm's length.

As they were ready to leave, David rubbed the back of his neck. "I worry about you," he said. "Jack's the wrong person to antagonize. He is out for power. And he won't have small fry like you or me stand in his way."

"What do you think he'll do?"

"Who knows? That man is capable of anything."

When Dan came home that night, he called Maureen.

"I hope it's not too late."

"No. I'm working. Going over Lessing's depositions in the Breathelite cases. Is he slippery! Mike's not going to be able to get one thing out of him."

"I missed you tonight. Dave and I had dinner at our favorite restaurant, and it wasn't the same without you."

There was a pointed pause on the other end of the line.

"When will I see you?" Dan asked.

"When do you want to see me?"

"How is Sunday night dinner for you?"

"I may well be too busy. You don't realize the pile of paper-work I have left to do before Mike and I go back East for Lessing's deposition." Then after a pause, "I'll see how things work out and I'll call you."

"Okay."

"Something just occurred to me." She paused, then pushed ahead. "I think you are more comfortable talking to me over the phone than person to person."

"What makes you say that?"

"I don't know. It's just a feeling I get."

\* \* \*

The bar at the Peninsula Hotel was crowded. Handelsman arrived early. He took off his scarf, stuffed it into the pocket of his jacket, and sat down at the first free table. When the waitress came up to him, he ordered a single malt whiskey and a glass of water. Leaning his head back, he closed his eyes and waited for Maureen or the whiskey, whichsoever might arrive first.

Maureen was on time. As she entered the lounge she peered into a mirror and saw a woman no longer young with a hard face and a tense mouth. The Dulcian case was exacting its toll. A second look at herself was less disturbing. Her outfit was perfect for the occasion: she was wearing her favorite lightweight gray tailored jacket with broad lapels and a matching skirt. It made her look professional and assertive.

"So be it," she muttered to herself and entered the bar with a determined stride. She spotted Handelsman and quickly sat down across from him.

"What would you like me to order for you?" he asked.

"I am perfectly capable of ordering for myself." She signaled for the waitress and asked for a glass of white wine. "You know very well you had no business contacting the Dunmores. There is no excuse for that sort of behavior."

"Yes, there is. I have been retained by Marat International to defend them according to the best of my abilities. And it is my opin-ion that settling with the Dunmores not only will help my client but also will help them. If they accept our offer they will get more money from us than they will ever get from you. You know very well your chances to win this case are nil. You have nothing—a case that no jury will believe in and two off-the-wall experts. We are going to call to the stand the luminaries of American neurology and psychiatry. They are going to testify for us and make mincemeat of your doctors. And, finally, permit me to remind you that we are the largest drug house in the world and that we have the money to drag this case through the courts until your firm is broke." He took a deep breath. Maureen knew he had played every one of his cards.

"A very good summary, Mr. Handelsman, clear and concise."

He ignored her remark. "What kind of settlement do you people want to get you off our backs?" he asked and smiled.

"What are you willing to offer?"

"It will probably cost us over half a million to defend this case."

"Is that all?"

"Perhaps a bit more. Whatever it will be, our client is prepared to offer you a settlement of four hundred thousand."

"I see. Don't you think that's somewhat of a pittance?"

"Hardly. I view it as generous."

"Do you?" She paused. "Did you know that since the publication of Dr. Lerner's paper he has been swamped with calls. He must have heard of several dozen new patients. It is practically an epidemic."

Handelsman was unimpressed. "I would prefer to call it mass hysteria."

"And what do you think a jury will call it? You forget this is going to be a jury trial."

"You drive a hard bargain. My clients have given me permission to make you an offer in any amount up to half a million to settle this case. Does half a million sound any better?"

"Not much. I am certain Mike would never accept that sort of offer."

"You are very confident about what he will or will not accept."

The time had come for her to bluff. She took a deliberate sip from her glass and fixed Handelsman.

"I should be. We have obtained some interesting information. When it comes out in court it will make this case worth a lot more than half a million."

"What are you talking about?"

"You will find out—in due time."

Handelsman did not reply. Instead he drained the last bit of whiskey and washed it down with water.

"You and I must learn to think of each other as people, not as characters in our respective roles." His voice had become soft. In her mind Maureen preferred to term it unctuous; she wanted to continue to disapprove of him, to dislike him, because of what he stood for. Yet as she saw him slumped forward with hands encircling the glass of water and the plaid scarf protruding from his coat pocket, he appeared needy and vulnerable.

"How do you want me to think of you?" she asked.

"As a man who has worked hard to get where he is—full partner in a very waspy firm. I would like you to respect that."

"No problem. In case you are not aware of it, in most law firms women are considered second-class citizens. In fact, I didn't see any women on the letterhead of Wyburn, Mason, Keene, and Handelsman."

"We just hired Ann Townsend, but you have made your point. We two have much in common."

"Right."

"So remember me in your prayers. If and when you pray."

"What does that mean?"

"Some day you might find out. That is, if you are still interested."

And he left it at that.

* * *

The glass-enclosed conference room of the New York office of Wyburn, Mason, Keene, and Handelsman had a dizzying view of the Manhattan skyline. It was a steamy July morning, the kind that made one long for the cool breezes of Martha's Vineyard or the eastern tip of Long Island. Maureen and Mike had flown in the previous night, with Maureen feeding questions to her senior partner as she sat next to him on the plane.

The deposition was scheduled for ten o'clock. They arrived early and took their seats at an immense rosewood-veneered table, waiting for Lessing to make his appearance. With the court reporter at the other end of the table listening to their conversation, they had to fill in time with meaningless chitchat. Mike became restless. He got up and paced about.

"This is some high-class painting," he said, pointing to a black and red abstraction. "What do you make of it?"

"I don't know," Maureen said. "I never was one for contemporary art."

"Neither was I. I nearly flunked my high school class in art appreciation."

Ten minutes after the appointed time, Lessing arrived. He was accompanied by Handelsman and two junior attorneys, including a grim and prim young woman, who Maureen knew had to be the newly hired Ann Townsend. Introductions and greetings were restrained. Handelsman avoided looking at Maureen. Instead he opened a fresh yellow pad and headed it with the date and "Dr. Albert Lessing."

"I trust we are ready," Mike said. The deposition had not even started and his hair was already in disarray.

"We are," Handelsman responded.

"Good." Mike turned to the court reporter. "Swear in the witness."

This was done, and Mike started out.

"Good morning, Dr. Lessing."

"Good morning." Lessing's face was motionless. Maureen thought he would make a good poker player.

"Please state your name for the record."

"Albert T. Lessing."

"You are an employee of Marat International?"

"I am."

"What is your current position with Marat International?"

"I am medical director."

"I understand you have given a deposition before. Is that correct?"

"It is."

"Would that have been in the Breathelite matter?"

"It was."

"Would you then agree that I can dispense with the usual admonitions?"

"You can."

Maureen barely listened to the questions that dealt with Lessing's education and background. Undergraduate work at Lehigh University, then Indiana University School of Medicine, followed by an internship and residency in internal medicine. A good but not brilliant background. He had been with Marat for fifteen years, in his present position for eight years.

"Did you have occasion today to meet with any lawyers?"

"I did."

"Who did you meet with?"

"Mr. Allan Handelsman, Miss Ann Townsend, Mr. . . ." Lessing paused and looked at the other junior attorney.

"Mr. Bruce Crawford," the young man filled in.

"Mr. Crawford," Dr. Lessing repeated.

"For how long did you meet?"

"About two hours."

"And have you met with anyone else from the firm of Wyburn, Mason, Keene, and Handelsman on any previous occasion?"

"I have."

"On more than one occasion?"

"Yes."

"And what was the purpose of the meeting that you had this morning?"

"Objection," Handelsman interrupted. "I will object and instruct the witness not to answer on the grounds of this being attorney work product."

Maureen knew that there was not a chance in the world that they would learn what Lessing and Handelsman talked about prior to the deposition or at any other time. Of course, it didn't hurt to try to find out. It was already evident to her that Dr. Lessing was a well-instructed witness.

Mike followed up with a series of routine questions designed to delineate Lessing's professional duties, the person he reported to, and the staff under his direction. Lessing remained precise; his face did not betray an ounce of emotion.

"Dr. Lessing, as medical director of Marat International, were you made aware of any adverse reactions to the drug Dulcian?"

"Objection!" Handelsman said. "Made aware by whom, and under what circumstances?"

"Dr. Lessing, are you the person at Marat who would receive any adverse reaction reports on Dulcian?"

"I am."

"From whom would you receive such reports?"

"From physicians or other health care professionals."

"Have you at any time heard of the Angry Puppet Syndrome?"

"No."

"Have you read a paper by Lerner and Carter describing this syndrome and attributing it to Dulcian?"

"No."

"Dr. Lessing, in your capacity as medical director of Marat International do you know of any side reactions to Dulcian?"

Handelsman stepped in. "Other than those that are listed in the PDR or in the package insert?"

"Other than those listed in the PDR or in the package insert."

"No."

"No one has ever informed you that some patients who receive Dulcian undergo a remarkable change in personality."

"Objection. Vague and ambiguous. Mr. Cosgrove should define what he means by the word 'remarkable.'"

"Dr. Lessing, do you know what I mean by 'remarkable'?"

"No."

"By 'remarkable' I mean a dramatic change in personality."

Handelsman objected to the word "dramatic" and to every other word that Mike could come up with. Finally Lessing said that as far as he knew, patients on Dulcian had undergone changes in their personality, but that physicians prescribe the medication in the hope that they would. After all, getting out of a depression represented a change in personality. At the end of the first hour of his deposition, Lessing had not provided any information that was not readily available in the PDR, the package insert to Dulcian, or any standard textbook of pharmacology.

They took a break. "That man lies," Maureen whispered to Mike as they stood in the hallway. "Ask him about his conversations with Dr. Lerner."

"Will do."

They returned to the conference room. One of the secretaries refilled coffee cups for anyone who wanted them refilled. Maureen noted that Handelsman declined coffee. She was certain that he considered the cups unclean.

"Dr. Lessing," Mike started out, "do you know a Dr. Dan Lerner?"

"Not at this point in time."

"I see. Have you ever spoken with Dr. Dan Lerner? In person or over the telephone?"

"Not that I can remember."

"If Dr. Lerner were to testify that he spoke to you on at least one occasion, would you say he was lying?"

"I would not. I receive innumerable phone calls from physicians, and there is no way I can remember the name of everyone who calls me."

"Dr. Lessing, you do keep records of telephone conversations?"

"We do, but only for one month. They are then destroyed."

"Why are they destroyed?"

"Because they take up valuable space."

"So it is your testimony that you never spoke with Dr. Daniel Lerner?"

"That is not what he testified to," Handelsman interrupted. "He said he does not remember such a conversation."

Dr. Lessing also did not remember conversations with any regional sales representatives, in particular with Frank Duffy.

Mike bent down and opened his briefcase. He took out a copy of the letter from a New England sales representative in which the representative reported that several clinics in his area had complained of reactions to Dulcian and had asked for guidance. Handelsman wanted to see the letter.

"I don't see what this letter has to do with your litigation," he said. "But I will allow you to show it to the doctor." The letter was duly marked as plaintiff's exhibit.

Mike gave the letter to Dr. Lessing, who read it and then placed it on the conference table in front of him.

"Now, Dr. Lessing. You have read this letter?"

"I have."

"Have you seen this letter before?"

"I have not. It is not addressed to me. It is addressed to Marat International, May's Landing, New Jersey."

"And you have never seen it?"

"No."

"Can you tell me why this letter was not forwarded to you?"

"I would have to speculate."

"The doctor is not allowed to speculate," Handelsman rapped out. And that was the end of this line of questioning.

By the time the next recess had come around, Mike was seething and Maureen had to cool him down.

"See what he does with the serotonin," she said.

When the deposition resumed, Mike turned to a new page on his yellow pad.

"Dr. Lessing, do you know what Phase I studies are?"

"I do." Lessing then went on to a detailed description of the initial evaluation of any new drug such as Dulcian.

"Do you know the results of the Phase I studies on Dulcian?"

"No."

"Why not?"

"Conducting and evaluating the Phase I studies was not my responsibility."

"Whose responsibility was it?"

"I don't know."

"You don't know? Who then does?"

"R.J. Crowley." Maureen felt as if another door had shut in their face. A door for which they did not have a key.

"Dr. Lessing, do you know a Dr. Marvin Ailesly?"

"No."

"Do you know that at one time he worked for Marat?"

"We have forty thousand employees. There is no way I can keep track of every one of them."

"Do you know Dr. Derek Osborne?"

"I believe I do."

"Would it surprise you if I told you that when Dr. Ailesly retired he was replaced by Dr. Osborne?"

"It would not. As I said to you before, I do not recall the name Ailesly, and I do not keep track of the personnel at Marat. To do so is not one of my responsibilities."

"Did you know that Dr. Ailesly performed the initial toxicity studies on Dulcian?"

"I did not."

"Dr. Lessing, do you know what serotonin is?"

"Yes. It is a neurotransmitter. A chemical that transmits messages from one nerve cell to another."

"Do you know what effect Dulcian has on blood serotonin levels?"

"Objection," Handelsman rapped out. "Vague and ambiguous. Blood serotonin levels in whom, under what circumstances, at what dosages?"

Once again Mike was confronted by a locked door. Each time he reworded the question, Handelsman found another objection.

"Dr. Lessing, do you know of any Marat memos or in-house communications that deal with or have dealt with the effect of Dulcian on serotonin levels?"

"No."

"Did you and Mr. Handelsman discuss serotonin at any time prior to this deposition?"

"Objection." Handelsman smiled. This was too obvious. "Attorney work product. I will instruct the witness not to answer."

"Dr. Lessing, I will show you a memo, and I will ask you whether the signature under this memo is in your handwriting."

"Could I see this first?" Handelsman asked. Mike handed him a copy of the in-house memo that Maureen had given him, and which asked Melvin Walton to provide Jack with support for the PET scan unit. He read through the memo. "This memo has nothing to do with Dulcian."

"MI-37801 is Dulcian," Mike said.

"I am well aware of that. This memo deals with support for a research unit and has nothing to do with the claims in this case. I will instruct the doctor not to read the memo and not to answer any questions concerning it."

Dr. Lessing's deposition was over before lunchtime.

"They are stonewalling us," Mike said to Maureen as they stood outside the building waiting for a cab to take them back to their hotel.

"Right."

"I wish you would come up with something smarter than just 'right.' You are supposed to be brilliant. At least that's what Tom used to say about you."

"I don't think we will do any better with Walton or any of the others."

This was indeed the case. When Melvin Walton was deposed the following morning, he would not answer any questions concerning side reactions to Dulcian. His position was Vice President of Consumer Relations, and reports concerning side reactions to Dulcian were routinely turned over to Dr. Albert Lessing.

"I am not a clinician, I have no medical training, and therefore I am not in the position to evaluate side reactions to any drugs that are marketed by Marat."

"Did you at any time receive reports about side reactions to Dulcian?"

"I don't remember. Whatever reports my office received were funneled over to Dr. Lessing."

That remained his position, and Mike was unable to get around it.

He did no better with Nicholas Cusworth, who also stated that he was unaware of any side reactions to Dulcian and was certain that had there been any such side reactions, Dr. Lessing would be the person who would have kept track of them.

"Mr. Cusworth, let me show you this memo."

"May I see it first?" Mike handed the memo to Handelsman, who read it, frowned, then tapped his pen across it. "You may show it to the witness, although I don't see what it has to do with your case. It has to do with marketing of Dulcian and determining its price structure."

Cusworth read the memo. When Mike questioned him he did not recall writing it. An administrative assistant might have written it and as a matter of routine he would have signed it.

"Let's try this one then," Mike said. From his briefcase he took out the two memos Cusworth had written to Crowley in which he stated that Ailesly was becoming unhappy with his toxicity studies. These two memos were his trump cards. They were read by Handelsman, admitted as plaintiff exhibits, and then read by Cusworth.

"Mr. Cusworth, did you write these memos?"

"I did."

"Prior to writing them, did you have any discussions with Dr. Ailesly about his toxicity studies?"

"I don't remember."

"In your memo you state, and I quote, 'Marvin Ailesly has become progressively more distressed with his toxicity analyses.' What did you mean by 'more distressed'?"

"I don't remember."

"You don't remember?"

"The document speaks for itself," Handelsman interposed.

"You also state, and I quote, 'He has a remarkable new finding that we must look into.' What was that remarkable new finding?"

"I don't remember."

Mike did no better with the second memo. Cusworth's memory was as poor as before. He did not recall any conversations with Ailesly or with R.J. Crowley concerning the subject of the toxicity studies.

"Perhaps, then, you can explain the last sentence to me: 'I also think that Warren should be told about this in case there are other developments.' Who is Warren?"

"Warren Berrich, chief in-house counsel for Marat."

"Thank you. I am glad you remembered. And why did you think Mr. Berrich should be told about Dr. Ailesly's toxicity tests?"

"I don't remember."

"You don't? Then perhaps you will remember what other developments you were expecting?"

"I don't."

"You don't remember anything?"

"Objection. Please don't argue with the witness."

"I am not arguing with him. I am simply amazed that this man, who does not appear to be suffering from Alzheimer's disease, does not remember anything about this memo. Mr. Cusworth, is there a reason you don't remember any portion of this memo?"

"Don't answer that question," Handelsman snapped. For a moment Maureen thought that Mike was on the verge of obtaining some important information. Handelsman made sure he didn't, and the best Mike could do was to submit the memo as the next plaintiff's exhibit.

That night Mike and Maureen were sitting in Mike's hotel suite planning Derek Osborne's deposition. The room was strewn with medical records, ring-bound folders containing the documents that Maureen and Dan had obtained from the New Jersey headquarters of Marat, and copies of the various depositions given by Marat employees in the Breathelite case. Osborne was their last chance to get any information as to what Marat knew about adverse reactions to Dulcian before marketing the drug. The key to the deposition lay in finding out how much if anything Ailesly had told Osborne about his Dulcian toxicity data before he retired from Marat. If Osborne's memory turned out to be as deficient as Cusworth's, plaintiffs would be confronted with a summary judgment against them. Although Maureen knew that such was in store, she did not mention it to Mike. The man would fly off the handle and God knows what might happen.

The phone rang.

"Why don't you get it," Mike said. He had just torn up a series of questions and was in the process of rewriting them.

Maureen picked up. "Hello."

"Is this Maureen Durrell?" A male voice—angular, distorted, with a hint of an accent.

"Yes."

"Ask Osborne about his statistics." And the line went dead.

"Who was that?" Mike asked.

"I don't know. A man with a carefully disguised voice who said for us to ask Osborne about his statistics."

"What about his statistics?"

"Your guess is as good as mine. I think our secret ally has struck again."

* * *

The following morning it was the same scene in the same setting with the same actors except for Dr. Derek Osborne. Since R.J. Crowley was out of the country and would not become available until fall, Osborne's deposition completed the first round of witnesses called by plaintiffs' attorneys.

Osborne looked handsome but uncomfortable in a navy blue blazer and light gray pants with a gray and red regimental tie. Maureen was certain he was far more accustomed to working in a denim shirt and Levis. He was extremely articulate and spoke rapidly, so rapidly that at times the court reporter asked him to slow down. His answers were precise, and when he described his research work, it was evident that he was an intelligent, if not brilliant, man.

By training Osborne was a neuropharmacologist. He had received a bachelor's degree at Cal Tech and a Ph.D. at Yale. His thesis dealt with opiate receptors in the brain. Opiate receptors are natural constituents of brain cells that have the property of recognizing opium or drugs like opium and allowing these drugs to bind to the cell. After two years of postgraduate work, Osborne had joined Marat. When asked what prompted the switch from academic research to industry, he made it plain that the reasons were financial. He had one child at the time, with another one on the way, and Marat offered him a salary that was at least three times that which he received from Michigan.

"Dr. Osborne, what is your current position with Marat?"

"I am director of psychotropic drug manufacturing."

"In this capacity are you presently in charge of the toxicity studies on Dulcian?"

"I am."

"You replaced Dr. Marvin Ailesly when he left Marat?"

"I replaced Dr. Ailesly when he retired."

"When was that?"

"About two years ago."

"Two years ago, when you took over Dr. Ailesly's position, did you and he have any discussions with respect to any toxicity studies performed on Dulcian?"

"I did not. I never met Dr. Ailesly. He had left the company by the time I came on board."

"Did Dr. Ailesly leave behind any data, notes, or memoranda concerning his toxicity studies?"

"Not that I know of."

"Do you know anyone who has seen such data, notes, or memoranda?"

"No."

Osborne sounded so truthful that it appeared unlikely he was hiding any information. So far, everything had gone as Maureen expected. Handelsman sat across from her, his eyes closed.

Obviously Osborne had been well coached by him. Ann Townsend and Bruce Crawford were taking notes.

"Dr. Osborne, are you at the present time conducting any pharmacologic or toxicity studies on Dulcian?"

"I am."

"Can you tell me about them."

Osborne proceeded to elaborate. His group was in the process of evaluating a long-acting form of Dulcian, which could be given to depressed patients on a once-a-day basis, and there also was an ultra-long-acting form in the pipeline, which could be administered once a week. When Mike questioned him further, he provided considerable detail on these studies, most of which was far over his head or that of Maureen.

"You must have accumulated a large amount of data in the course of these studies?"

"I have."

"Do you have anyone who evaluates these data from a statistical point of view?"

"You mean a statistician?"

"Yes. Do you have a statistician who works with you?"

Handelsman opened his eyes. He had not expected this question.

"Yes," Osborne said.

"And who is this person?"

"Dr. Heinz Kleinwort."

"What is Dr. Kleinwort's position?"

"I don't know his exact title. All I know is that he is in charge of medical statistics."

"How long has he been with Marat?"

"Five years, or perhaps even longer than that."

"We're going to have to depose this man, Kleinwort," Mike said to Maureen after they had finished with Osborne's deposition. They were standing outside the offices of Wyburn, Mason, Keene, and Handelsman, waiting for the elevator.

"Right. As soon as we get back to L.A. I will send out a notice."

As it turned out, deposing Kleinwort was easier said than done.

\* \* \* \* \*

SEVERAL weeks passed. Dan had just returned from seeing a patient at the hospital one night when Judith phoned.

"Dan, I must see you. Can I come over?" Having lived with her for several years, Dan knew that when Judith asked for his permission, something serious had happened. He quickly considered the alternatives—death, illness, financial ruin, cancellation of her Neiman Marcus charge account.

"What's wrong?" he asked.

"I don't want to talk about it over the phone. It might be tapped."

"You're kidding." Judith might have been neurotic, but she had never exhibited signs of paranoia.

"She is not there, is she?" she asked.

"No, she isn't."

"I'll be over in fifteen minutes. Would you put on some coffee?"

The coffee was ready by the time Judith rang the bell.

"You've moved the chairs, haven't you?" she asked as soon as she came in. "And that blue and yellow shag rug is new."

"Is that why you came over? To talk about my shag rug? Next you'll tell me I've gained weight."

"You have." She sank into the sofa and sighed. "I can smell the coffee."

"Mug or cup?"

"I don't care." She chose the mug. "Are you up to date on the mortgage payments for our house?"

"You mean your house."

"Whatever. Have you been paying them?"

"Of course. Why do you ask?"

"This man called tonight and insisted on coming over. He wanted to know where you lived, and what you were doing, and whether you had been sending me my allowance. And did I know about your affair with this patient of yours."

"What affair with what patient?"

"I don't know, and frankly I couldn't care less how many women you are screwing these days. But he said she was a minor and he wanted to know whether you had been having affairs with young girls while we were living together."

"A minor? He said I was having an affair with a minor. . . ."

"Who was your patient."

"That is an absolute lie. Who was this man?"

"Frank Johnson was his name."

"Did he give you his card?"

"Yes. He was some sort of private investigator."

"And you talked to him. How stupid can you get?"

"He seemed to know everything about you."

A light came on. Dan gave Judith an outline of the Angry Puppet patients, the paper describing the syndrome that had just come out, and Jack's response to it.

"You really think that this is all happening because of your paper? I have never heard such a thing. At least not this side of the TV screen. Couldn't there be a mistake?"

"I don't see how."

"It's unreal. I mean it. Are you quite sure you are not having an affair with one of your teen-aged patients?"

"I told you no. Absolutely not."

"You are having an affair, though. I know that. You had one while we were still living together."

"Do you want more coffee?"

"That's no answer. I wish you'd come home with me instead of staying in this horrible little apartment. If you hadn't left me, you wouldn't be in the mess you are in now."

"I don't see why not."

By the time Judith left, it was too late to phone Maureen. The following morning when he told her of his conversation with Judith, carefully omitting the fact that she had been over to his apartment, Maureen was furious.

"I can't believe it. I am sure your chairman is behind this. He is such a bastard! What are you going to do?"

"Nothing right now. What if Judith had not told me about the investigator?"

"Right. I suppose it can't hurt to wait and see what he is up to next."

Dan soon found out what Jack was up to next, for on coming to his office the following day, Brenda handed him a message asking him to see Dr. Brewster Lawson, Director of the University Hospitals and Clinics. A matter of considerable urgency.

He put on a fresh white coat, adjusted his tie, took along some Kleenex in case his nasal allergies acted up under the stress of the interview, and marched over to the director's office. After two cups of coffee and a twenty-minute wait in the outer office, he was ushered into Dr. Lawson's presence. Brewster Lawson was a red-faced, paunchy man in his early forties with manicured fingernails. He was seated behind an immense, angular, glass and aluminum framed desk, flanked by two large potted rubber plants that tried bravely, but unsuccessfully, to soften the ultramodern ambience of the office.

"Dr. Lerner," Dr. Lawson said without any introductory chitchat. "I would like you to comment on a matter that has just come across my desk."

He handed Dan a memorandum from Jack.

"This is the letter I spoke to you about," the note read.

"You will agree with me that it is of some urgency."

Stapled to the memorandum was a two-page, home-typed note addressed to the Head of the Neurology Clinics, University Hospital.

Dear Doctor:
This is to inform you of a most disturbing occurrence affecting Dr. Daniel Lerner and our daughter, Jane Bentley, aged six-

teen. For the past seven years Jane has suffered from the most intense headaches. We have been to see several physicians without luck. Finally, out of desperation we went to the University Hospital. Dr. Lerner saw Jane in the clinic and examined her on June 30.

We are aware that Dr. Lerner is a well-known and respected physician. However, the matter that has come up is of such gravity that we ask you to investigate it at once, for the only other alternative we have is to file a complaint with the office of the District Attorney.

From what Jane told me on the way home from the hospital, it was clear to me that Dr. Lerner attempted to engage her in sexual intimacy. The extent of Dr. Lerner's irresponsibility and perversion is appalling to us. To allow a man such as he to practice medicine and continue to be in contact with young women is extremely disturbing.

We therefore request that you look into this matter at once and undertake all necessary disciplinary steps. Let us assure you that we are neither hysterical nor crazy parents. We only wish that this letter had not been necessary.

Very truly yours,

Mr. and Mrs. Andrew Bentley

Dan put down the letter. He sensed that his face was flushed and that there was perspiration on his forehead.

"Jane Bentley," he said, as if to himself. Then he recalled the dramatic teenager with pneumatic drill headaches whom he had seen in clinic the day the Greenhalls had consulted him.

"This is preposterous."

"I see," Dr. Lawson said and rubbed the tip of his nose. "You mean you have never seen this patient?"

"Of course I have. But for her parents to claim that I attempted to. . . ."

"This letter is quite explicit."

"But I am telling you nothing happened, absolutely nothing."

"The one thing this hospital does not want is a confrontation, the doctor's word against that of the patient. The publicity in such instances is absolutely intolerable. Do you understand?"

"Yes."

"I don't want to be the one to take final responsibility in this case and neither does Jack Brennan. What I therefore propose to do is to refer this letter to our Professional Standards and Ethics Committee. They will deal with it at their next meeting and will prepare a report for the State Board of Quality Assurance. It will then be up to the Board to handle the question of your continued licensure in the state."

"You mean my medical license?"

"I am afraid so. You do understand that this is a serious matter should our investigation substantiate the charges."

"Will I be able to attend the committee meeting?"

"No. That would be against hospital policy. If you wish, you may, however, prepare a statement or whatever material you choose and submit it in advance of the meeting."

"Tell me, Dr. Lawson, do you believe me or this letter?"

"At this point in time I have no opinion. My role in such instances is to obtain the facts, all the facts, examine them, and do whatever needs to be done to preserve the reputation of our hospital."

Dan felt like he was floating in a vivid dreamscape. Unaccountably, he took note of the small garden outside the windows of the administrator's office. It was enclosed by a trellised redwood fence and there were ferns in it, a couple of miniature palms, a jacaranda, some bright orange birds of paradise, and several clusters of broad-leaved plants.

"Dr. Lawson, this letter is a put-up job."

"I consider your remark totally inappropriate."

"I am sure you would."

"If you have no further comments or questions, Dr. Lerner, I will ask you to excuse me."

On his way back Dan felt naked and exposed, the victim of an unreal conspiracy. All at once, while still waiting for the elevator, he became engulfed by a feeling that was utterly foreign to him, one that he could scarcely recognize as being his own—an intense rage, a passionate fury, a compulsion to return to Lawson's office and destroy the man by whatever means he could. He started to retrace his steps and got as far as the outer door of the administrative suite when he stopped. With arms crossed, he stood outside the door. A minute or two passed. No one noticed him and no one came in or out of the office.

"Shit," Dan said at last. "Fucking shit." He said it loud enough for two nurses who walked by at that moment to turn and look at him with distinct disapproval.

Brenda must have noticed the change in his appearance.

"Everything all right?" she asked.

"Sure."

He got on the phone to Maureen. Her secretary said she was out of the office, but she would see to it that Ms. Durrell returned the call when she phoned in for messages.

He tried to dictate his consult notes but was unable to concentrate. In an attempt to keep his thoughts off the interview, he spent the next few hours with mindless tasks—sorting and filing reprints, organizing his desk drawers—all the time wondering whether Mrs. Bentley's letter was a forgery. If it was genuine, what could he have said or done that Jane Bentley and her mother interpreted as attempted sexual intimacy.

For a while he sat at his desk and looked at the patches of dusty green eucalyptus in the Barrows Botanical Gardens. Above them cotton wisps floated in a murky blue. The view had never looked as tranquil and inviting as it did that August afternoon.

"I have a serious problem," he said to Maureen when she finally returned his call. He tried to keep his voice as calm as possible. "But I can't talk about it on the phone."

"Then come over for dinner. I'll pick up some food on the way home. And don't bother bringing any wine. We can use up some of the bottles I keep under the sideboard."

A few hours later, after having downed a preliminary drink, Dan told Maureen about his meeting with Lawson and the letter from the Bentleys. Her face turned thoughtful, and her green eyes started to shimmer.

"How do you know this letter is genuine?"

"I don't. I never had a chance to look closely at it."

"Here is the situation the way I see it. You have published a paper that, for reasons we don't yet know, seriously threatens your boss. What can he do? He ordered you not to publish it but you decided to go over his head. So the best thing he can come up with now is to discredit you as effectively as possible."

"You do know I saw this girl."

"Of course you did. All this man had to do was to have someone go over the list of patients you have seen during the past month or two, find out which of them were teen-aged girls, and then get out that letter."

"That was my first reaction, and that's what I told Lawson."

"Good."

"And?"

"What have you got to lose by phoning the Bentleys? If they are a nutty family, they would call you a few names and hang up on you."

"And if they are not?"

"Then you've got your proof."

"I don't remember them as being nutty enough to make up such a story."

"There you are. So give them a call first thing in the morning."

"I could ask about Jane and how she was getting along with her headaches."

"Right."

"By the way, you never even questioned me as to whether there was any truth to that letter."

"Why should I? I know you prefer older women."

\* \* \*

The following morning Dan obtained the Bentley's home phone number from his office file and dialed their number.

"Hello," answered a female voice. "This is 752-8901."

"This is Dr. Lerner." The moment of truth.

"Yes?"

"I was just calling to find out how Jane was."

"Oh, thank you for thinking of her. She is so much better. That talk you had with us must have set her straight. It's been weeks since she last complained about her head. Why, this weekend she was able to go to choir practice, and, would you believe it, she came home. . . ."

Dan listened to a lot more of this with an escalating feeling of elation, much like when one is dealt an unbeatable poker hand. This feeling was quickly replaced by anger.

"Those bastards!" he muttered to himself after saying good-bye to Mrs. Bentley. The next question was how to play the unbeatable hand he had been dealt. He called Maureen.

"Do you want to hear about the Bentleys?"

"Of course I do."

"They're playing hardball," she said after Dan had finished telling her. "We have to figure out how to respond to them. Do you think Lawson is in on this?"

"Probably not. He just took Jack Brennan's word. No reason for him not to."

\* \* \*

Allan Handelsman was working late. Seated with Ann Townsend at the conference table in his office, he was in shirt-sleeves with a glass of club soda at his elbow. The blue and white fringed tzitzis around his waist that usually were hidden under his jacket were evident and caught Ann's attention. Never having seen anything even remotely similar, she was unable to take her eyes off them.

"The first thing I want us to do," he said, ignoring her fascination with his attire, "is to prepare a motion for summary judgment. I want it ready to go to Judge Watson after they have finished deposing Kleinwort. For your information, we are contending that the evidence given by our key employees is so overwhelmingly in our favor that a jury trial is totally unnecessary. You undoubtedly will want to know what evidence I am talking about. First, that Dulcian did not produce any untoward effects in any of the plaintiffs, and second, even had any untoward effects been produced by Dulcian, Marat had no prior evidence of any toxic effects of the drug."

Handelsman paused and looked at Ann's gray eyes—tense and anxious, as if she herself had been put on the stand. Being the first woman in his firm, she was trying extremely hard to make a good impression.

"You understand, of course, that we must, at all costs, avoid a jury trial. Juries are unpredictable, and there is a current groundswell of popular antagonism against drug firms, to which I must not expose our clients."

"I understand."

"Good."

"I will start working on this tomorrow morning."

"Another thing. I also want you to prepare deposition notices on all the plaintiffs. Just in case the judge does not go along with us." He handed Ann a list. "Then I want you to get out deposition notices on Dr. Lerner and Dr. Carter. They are the plaintiffs' experts. Don't forget to get some background information on both of them. The more the better. One never knows what we might dig up."

"I will get to work on that as well."

"Great. You know that they noticed Dr. Kleinwort's deposition. I objected but the court considered him another key employee. I wish I knew what they want to ask him."

"I can't help you in this matter."

"Of course you can't. I am just thinking out loud. I suppose I should have a chat with him. Let's get him on the phone the first thing in the morning and let him know I would like to meet with him. The sooner the better."

"I will have my secretary do that." A little assertion of her status with the firm.

"Of course." Then after a pause. "I am sorry. It must be quite difficult to be a woman attorney in a firm where the only other women are secretaries or paralegals."

"It is." Said without any apparent emotion. After Ann left, Handelsman remained in his office and reflected on the Dulcian matter. The careful preparation of the Marat employees had paid off, and he now was on the threshold of getting rid of this case, the biggest one he had ever been involved in. "Life consists of one failure after another through which runs the thread of success." Where had he read that?

"Let's see if she is still at work," he muttered.

He picked up the phone and dialed Cosgrove and Costello. The night secretary answered.

"This is Allan Handelsman. Could I speak to Maureen Durrell?"

"I will see if she is still in." She was in, and moments later she came on the line.

"I am preparing a motion for summary judgment. Based on the lack of evidence. . . ."

"So go ahead. Why tell me about it?"

"My offer of five hundred thousand still stands. Have you discussed it with Cosgrove?"

"Of course I haven't. He'd have a stroke, or maybe worse."

"What's worse than a stroke?"

Maureen laughed. A surprising laugh.

"Try to break it to him gently. He's a man with a lot of experience and savvy, and he should know by now that it's the best offer he is going to get from us."

"I'll see what I can do." There was a pause.

"By the way, why are you deposing Dr. Kleinwort?"

"I don't consider that an appropriate question."

"I suppose it wasn't. I hope you didn't mind my trying to find out."

"Anything else we should talk about?"

"You are working late."

"So are you."

"A lot needs to be done."

"Right."

"We'll be in touch."

"I am sure we will be."

\* \* \*

Since it was the only game in town, Allan Handelsman and Bruce Crawford checked into the May's Landing Holiday Inn when they flew to New Jersey for a predeposition meeting with Dr. Kleinwort.

The menu in the Garden State Room was unchanged from the one that had confronted Dan and Maureen. Handelsman had brought along his special food. Having ordered a glass of mineral water, he unwrapped knife, fork, and a paper plate on which he placed a portion of cold boiled chicken accompanied by a few slices of corn rye bread.

Kleinwort arrived promptly. He was in an open-necked denim shirt, light tan slacks, and white canvas shoes.

"Do sit down, Doctor," Handelsman said. "May we get you a drink?"

"I would prefer to wait. Perhaps I'll have some wine with my meal."

"You will have slim pickings." Handelsman handed Kleinwort the menu. "There is house red wine and something white and probably sweet from upstate New York."

Kleinwort decided on a whiskey, and both he and Crawford ordered the seared chicken breast with almonds, pineapples, and Chinese water chestnuts.

"You know that Marat is being sued with respect to Dulcian?" Handelsman said.

"I am aware of that."

"I expect that by now you have received a notice for deposition."

"Yes. I have gone over it, and I gather that my deposition has been scheduled for next week in New York. The notice also instructs me to bring to the deposition all documents, memoranda, and correspondence that pertain to Dulcian and which are in my possession."

"Such a demand is customary. I don't suppose you have too much material."

"Actually I do. There are the notes I took at the retreat."

"What retreat?" For an instant Handelsman lost his composure. His hands moved quickly to encircle the glass of mineral water.

"The one R.J. organized at Greensprings last February after he heard about the side reactions."

"What kind of side reactions?"

"Dramatic changes in personality with outbreaks of violence. I think there was even a suicide or two."

"Who did you say reported those side reactions?"

"Dr. DiChiro. He is our university monitor. That is why Lessing put together a top level staff meeting."

A sense of unreality enveloped Handelsman. He looked at Crawford. In the dim light of the Garden State Room the young attorney appeared pale and frightened. His fork was held suspended over the seared chicken breast as if the animal had suddenly writhed and come back to life. Handelsman felt depleted. For a moment he thought Kleinwort was playing a practical joke on him. But there was not a hint of a smile in the man's unpleasantly gaunt face.

"You see we never have been able to make heads or tails of Ailesly's toxicity studies," Kleinwort continued. His words had a guttural quality, a German accent that Handelsman found exceptionally unpleasant. "I have some of his data, but in their present form they don't make any sense. When Osborne tried to repeat the work he found that when he used Ailesly's methodology he was unable to obtain any consistent data. What worries him even more is that he now is seeing toxic effects at dosages that we were told were not toxic. I suggested to him that it was because we were using a different strain of mice, but Osborne didn't think it was that simple. Of course, we should never have used mice in the first instance. Monkeys, baboons, or some other primate species more closely related to humans would have been far better. Everyone knew that, but R.J. wouldn't let us. He said the studies would take too long and be far too costly."

All Handelsman could think at this point was that if Mike or Maureen were to hear any of this it would blow his case sky-high.

"Is that what the retreat was about?"

"That was one of the topics."

"What were some of the others?"

"Oh, let's see. . . . I didn't bring my notes along, but I remember one of them had to do with how Marat was to increase its share of the antidepressant market and how the company should respond to the new Japanese product that is supposed to come on the market early next year."

"Anything else?"

"What we could do to downplay reports of adverse reactions and avoid any adverse publicity."

"Was that it?"

"As far as I remember. As I said, I have all my notes at home."

"Good."

Handelsman leaned back in his chair. The cold boiled chicken remained untouched. He was in no mood to eat. The first thing he would have to do was to call off Kleinwort's deposition. That would give him an opportunity to meet with Lessing and confront him with the information Kleinwort had just given him. For the time being it was crucial not to appear surprised or concerned.

"May I buy you a drink?" he asked Crawford after Kleinwort had left them. Putting his hand on the young man's shoulder, he steered him into the bar.

"So what are you going to do?" Bruce asked, after both had downed a whiskey.

"At this point in time we will have to review our options. You must understand that I was never told any of this. When our firm was asked to handle this litigation, I met with Lessing, R.J., and Warren Berrich, Marat's in-house counsel. They all assured me that plaintiffs' case had no merit whatever. But now. . . ." He looked into the empty glass. "So now, tell me, Bruce, how would a young man like yourself handle this?" For Handelsman, questioning Crawford was an intellectual exercise.

"I would try to restrict plaintiff's questions to the area of Dr. Kleinwort's expertise."

"Statistics."

"Yes. And instruct him not to digress into any other areas."

"Excellent. Do you think Kleinwort will cooperate?"

"I think he will. He could be made to understand that this is a matter of loyalty to Marat and that his job is on the line."

"And you would suggest that approach to Marat management?"

"I certainly would. Needless to say, this has to be a top echelon decision."

"And what would you do in the event that Kleinwort insists on telling plaintiffs' counsels everything he has told us—and more."

"I would try to circumvent Kleinwort's deposition."

"And how would you go about doing that?"

"Make him unavailable to plaintiffs."

"Like presenting him with a one-way ticket to Pago Pago?"

"Perhaps. Plus a large enough bonus for him to retire there and never be heard from again."

Handelsman nodded, then turned to the younger man.

"Do you have any moral compunctions about any of this?"

"Not at all. Our first duty is to our clients."

"Very well put, Bruce. You will go far in our profession." Said with a trace of sarcasm. He lifted his glass. "Now let's have one more each and then hit the sack."

Handelsman found sleep not easy to come by. After saying his nightly prayers, he lay awake with his eyes open. The room had a heavy antiseptic odor. He got out of bed and opened the sliding glass doors. Traffic noises invaded the room, a confusion of strange sounds. He turned on the light and opened the Bible.

"But wisdom, where shall it be found?
And where is the place of understanding?"

* * *

At ten o'clock the following morning Handelsman and Crawford were in Dr. Albert Lessing's office. The floor-to-ceiling tinted glass made the room look transparent. Cedarwood walls were hung with diplomas and formal or informal photos of an assortment of luminaries of international medicine.

Lessing's secretary entered and placed two pots of coffee— one decaf and one regular—and a set of cups on the conference table.

"Please help yourselves, gentlemen," Lessing said.

Handelsman declined and instead asked for a glass of water.

"So now, tell me, to what do I owe your presence?" Dr. Lessing asked.

Handelsman gave a concise presentation of his meeting with Dr. Kleinwort. Lessing started to take notes, then stopped and tore up the sheet.

"I think we should have Nick and Warren join us." He buzzed his secretary and asked her to see if Mr. Cusworth and Mr. Berrich were available. Having learned that they were, he instructed her to hold all calls.

When the two men arrived, Lessing asked Handelsman to report on his conversation with Kleinwort.

"I think the whole matter can be handled quite simply," Cusworth said. "This is what I would propose to do, that is if we all are in agreement. We will have Heinz come over and we will explain our problem to him. I am certain he will understand."

Cusworth got on the telephone and dialed Kleinwort's number.

"Heinz . . . are you free? Good. Why don't you come by here for a few minutes? A few of us are in Al Lessing's office."

When Kleinwort came in he was in Levis, sneakers, and his usual open-necked denim shirt. He accepted the coffee, which Lessing quickly offered him, and sat down.

"How can I help you?" he asked, crossing his legs. Evidently he was not overwhelmed by the awesomeness of the gathering.

"Allan, will you explain to Heinz the ground rules for his deposition."

"They are quite straightforward," Handelsman said. "Whatever question you are asked, you will restrict yourself to answering it in the most direct manner. All of us here will be most appreciative if you were not to digress, and we certainly do not want you to go into matters that were discussed at the February retreat. The one you told me about last night."

"And my notes? What would you want me to do with them."

"Destroy them."

There was a long pause. Kleinwort uncrossed his legs, leaned back, and, reaching for the coffeepot, refilled his cup. Sunlight was pouring into the room through the tinted glass windows. Lessing got up to draw the shades.

"I don't think I can do that," Kleinwort said. He appeared to be completely composed. Lessing turned abruptly. He looked as if he were about to explode.

"And may I ask why not?" He hacked out the words.

"Because it would be wrong."

"Wrong!" In an instant Lessing stood over Kleinwort. "I instruct you not to make your notes available at the time of your deposition! You will shred them! Shred them! Do you hear? Right now! And that's all there is to it." His face had become flushed.

"I want to second that order," Cusworth said. He was more composed. "There is no other alternative. Warren, I expect you will agree with me."

"Absolutely."

Kleinwort closed his eyes, as if by doing so he could escape the intensity of the confrontation.

"All my life I have been proud of my parents because at the risk of their lives they did what they knew was right. Unlike the rest of their generation." His voice had become so soft that Handelsman thought he was speaking to himself. "As I sit here this moment, I am glad that I have been given a small opportunity to prove to myself that I am nearly as strong as they were, that a bit of the iron that flows in my parents' veins and made them join the German underground flows in mine as well."

The assemblage ignored Kleinwort's overly dramatic remark.

"What on earth do your parents have to do with this matter?" Lessing asked. Handelsman rubbed the side of his nose. For him the answer was all too apparent.

"You see, I don't care what happens to me," Kleinwort said. "All I know is that if at my deposition I do not produce whatever I am asked to produce, and not tell everything I know, and do so truthfully, I shall not be able to live with myself."

"Heinz!" Cusworth's arm stretched out in Kleinwort's direction like a club. "If you betray us, you no longer have a job."

"A very small price to pay." As Kleinwort raised his voice, his German accent became more evident. "Pitifully small."

Handelsman realized that a point had been reached at which he would have to intervene.

"I think this impasse can be resolved if I could have a few minutes with Dr. Kleinwort. In private."

After the three men had withdrawn, Handelsman refilled his glass of water and leaned back in an apparent show of relaxation.

"From your résumé I gather that you were born and educated in Germany. Is that true?" He heard himself, and it was as if he were questioning Kleinwort in court.

"Yes. That is my burden."

Handelsman had not expected the remark. Up to now he had lived with the knowledge that it was a burden to be a Jew. A burden and a challenge. Now he heard the same feelings from Kleinwort.

"I understand. And because of this burden you propose to betray your company and your fellow workers."

"I don't consider it a betrayal."

"That is how you see it." He bent forward; the tips of his index fingers rested on his upper lip. "When you signed your contract with Marat both you and your company undertook certain obligations. Your company has adhered to its obligations. You must do likewise."

"Not if my obligations force me to . . . to lie. I can never do that."

"Aha. Even if I were to tell you that what you see as truth is a totally destructive act? Destructive as well as self-destructive."

"Even so."

"You see, Dr. Kleinwort, for me dishonesty is to deviate from the path that God has set us out to follow. For you it must be otherwise."

"It is."

"Well, then, we have nothing more to discuss. For your sake, though, I hope that you will reflect on your decision. As someone said before me, 'I beseech you, in your heart of heart, think it possible you may be mistaken.'"

* * *

"Well, gentlemen," Handelsman said after Kleinwort had left and the three men had returned to Lessing's office, "we will have to come up with another plan of action. Dr. Kleinwort doesn't care about his job or about his company. He insists that once he takes an oath to tell the truth and nothing but, he will disclose everything he knows about Dulcian."

"That is quite a predicament," Lessing said. He leaned forward and refilled his coffee cup.

"Where do we go from here?" Nick Cusworth asked.

"We can always postpone his deposition," Handelsman said.

"Sounds like a good idea."

"Of course, this would be merely a delaying tactic. If we keep on pushing back the date, plaintiffs will suspect that we are trying to hide the witness, and they will go to court and obtain an order for us to produce him."

Warren Berrich was rubbing his eyes and forehead with both hands out of sheer irritation. After some time he looked up.

"If we consider our alternatives I am certain something can be worked out." He looked at his watch. "It isn't too late. I'll put in a call to R.J. and bring him up to date."

A few minutes later he was on the private line in his office. His secretary buzzed him. "I have Mr. Crowley on the other end."

"Good to hear your voice, R.J. How are things in Brussels?"

"The weather has been absolutely splendid." R.J.'s voice was as clear as if he were speaking from across town.

"That's great."

"So what's going on at the store?"

"I thought I should call you and bring you up to date on that Dulcian matter."

"Haven't we settled that yet? I had our management committee approve an offer of half a million."

"Plaintiffs won't accept it. They want more."

"How much more?"

"I don't know." And Berrich started to tell R.J. about the stale-mate with Kleinwort. "I need your okay to follow up on an idea I have."

When he had hung up, he buzzed his secretary.

"Call up personnel and have them bring me the complete file on Kleinwort, Heinz Kleinwort. Be sure to specify that I want the complete file."

\* \* \*

A couple of hours later, as they were flying back to Los Angeles, Handelsman told Crawford about his inability to obtain Kleinwort's promise to keep silent.

"No Pago Pago for him," he said. "That man insists on coming out with everything he knows."

"What makes him do that?"

"I leave that question to the psychoanalysts. So, then, what would you propose to do next?"

Bruce looked thoughtful. He had an intelligent face. Handelsman remembered looking through his dossier. Phi Beta Kappa, second in his class at Rutgers Law School. The prestige of Wyburn, Mason, Keene, and Handelsman permitted them to hire the cream of law school graduates.

"So then," Handelsman prompted, "any suggestions?"

"We could declare Dr. Kleinwort as being unfit to be deposed. Of course, not physically unfit, but mentally unfit. We could say that he has suffered a serious nervous breakdown, or maybe that he has lapsed into a depression and is under the care of a psychiatrist."

"Or under the care of his family practitioner being treated with high doses of Dulcian?" Handelsman laughed.

"Why not? It's the best drug on the market for depression."

"Bruce, my boy, you are right, absolutely right! That is exactly what I shall suggest. I will let plaintiffs know that the deposition is off. For a long time, if not for good."

Bruce nodded and gave Handelsman a look of admiration and homage.

What neither of them knew was that by then Warren Berrich had obtained R.J.'s approval to proceed with an even better plan.

\* \* \*

The following morning Allan Handelsman gathered with Bruce Crawford and Ann Townsend in the small conference room of the Los Angeles office of Wyburn, Mason, Keene, and Handelsman. The topic was preparing for the forthcoming deposition of Dr. Daniel Lerner.

To get the ball rolling, Bruce read from the plaintiff's designation of expert witnesses, which Maureen had prepared and submitted to Judge Watson.

"Here is what she says about what Dr. Daniel Lerner is going to testify to: 'Dr. Daniel Lerner is board certified in neurology and has been provided with the pertinent medical records of the plaintiffs. He is expected to testify that Dulcian was responsible for the neurologic and behavioral abnormalities of the plaintiffs, and that these abnormalities have resulted in death or permanent and irreversible incapacity of all plaintiffs. He also is expected to testify that the neurologic and behavioral abnormalities include alterations in personality, predisposition to violence, and uncontrollable self-destructiveness.'"

Handelsman nodded. "Nothing unexpected there, that's for sure." He placed his hands flat on the conference table. "Our first aim is to impeach Dr. Lerner's credibility. We can always deal with his medical testimony at trial. Let's hear from you, Ann. What do we have on him?"

Ann shuffled through the stack of documents and folders in front of her.

"To start with, we have a copy of a letter that was written to the dean of the medical school by his former laboratory technician. It accuses Dr. Lerner. . . ."

Handelsman interrupted her. "We all have seen that letter, and there is no need for you to read it to us. Do we have any follow-up on that matter? I understand that he was investigated by a committee appointed by the dean and the chairman of his department."

"Is that Dr. Brennan?" Bruce asked.

"You are right on top of it," Handelsman said with an ironic smile.

"I have prepared copies of the committee's final report," Ann continued. "In essence, the three members concluded that they failed to find the evidence necessary to demonstrate that data had been altered or that there was scientific fraud."

Handelsman scribbled on his pad and nodded. "Sounds like a half-hearted acquittal."

Ann did not comment, and without changing expression returned to her notes.

"There is a second item. I have obtained a copy of a letter that was recently sent to his department chairman by the mother of one of his teen-aged patients."

"Let's look at that." Ann handed Handelsman a copy of Mrs. Bentley's complaint. He carefully read through the letter and handed it to Bruce.

"Pretty impressive, eh?"

"These are serious charges," Ann said. "It is the intention of the hospital to have them considered at a hearing before the Professional Standards and Ethics Committee."

"When will that be?"

"I can find out."

Ann scribbled a reminder on her pad. "We also have learned that the National Institutes of Health has refused to support his research project and that he has been unable to get any significant funding for his work from any other source."

"Good."

"I have obtained the criticisms of his research proposal which were compiled by the scientists working as consultants for the National Institutes of Health. Do you want to look at them?"

Handelsman took the sheet that Ann handed him and read portions aloud.

"Unimaginative proposal . . . derivative . . . incomplete review of other scientific work in the field. . . . Looks like something we might want to use. What else do we have?"

"His laboratory has now been taken over by a Dr. DiChiro."

"That is Dr. Martin DiChiro," Bruce amplified.

Handelsman scribbled down the name.

"Go on."

"We also have a lot of adverse information concerning Dr. Lerner's personal life. He and his wife separated several years ago and he spent three years in the African bush. . . ."

"Doing what?"

"Working in a hospital."

"And clearing out the cobwebs in his head. Go on."

"That's pretty much it. Except for one matter. He and Miss Durrell may be having an intimate relationship."

"I suspected as much. How long has that been going on?"

"I wasn't able to find out."

"What I would like to know is whether this syndrome of Dr. Lerner's was not a means of bringing some business to Miss Durrell's law firm. What do you think, Bruce, any ideas?"

"Seems logical. I also was thinking that this information will be quite useful to us for our deposition of Dr. Carter."

"Forget about Dr. Carter. We may never need to get to him. If we make mincemeat out of Dr. Lerner, we can go back to the court and make another motion for summary judgment. If our deposition of Dr. Lerner goes off as well as I think it will, I am confident Judge Watson will grant it to us. Now then, let's start outlining the questions we intend to ask the doctor. I don't want to leave anything to chance."

* * *

At about the same time, Maureen and Dan were closeted with Mike.

"Let me give you a couple of pointers," Mike told Dan. Hands behind his head, he was leaning back in his chair, gazing at the distant, smog-veiled Hollywood Hills. "We want you to be honest, and we want you to be objective. Is that clear? We don't need you as our advocate. Maureen is enough of an advocate. And remember: your credibility is crucial. Without your credibility you are no use to us." He frowned and turned to Maureen. "What about you two? Are you still seeing each other?"

Dan and Maureen exchanged glances. Dan was the first to speak. "Yes."

Mike exploded. "God damn it! I told you to lay off until we have this case settled."

"For a time Dan was ready to," Maureen said.

"Then we reconsidered and decided that neither of us was. "

Mike jumped up and paced his office. "You two are really fucked up. You'll see. When Handelsman finds out about this, shit will hit the fan."

"Why should he find out?" Dan asked.

"Because that's his job." Mike sat down and shuffled through his notes. "Maureen you're on your own with this. If it comes up during the doctor's deposition, you handle it any way you see fit. Now go leave me alone. I need to think."

* * *

Dan's deposition was held the following Monday morning in the small conference room at the Los Angeles office of Wyburn, Mason, Keene, and Handelsman. Handelsman was interrogating Dan, with Ann Townsend and Bruce Crawford sitting in attendance at the other end of the table. The court reporter was on Dan's left, and Maureen was on his right. After he took the oath, Handelsman started out.

"Dr. Lerner, have you had your deposition taken before?"

"Yes."

"On how many occasions?"

"Once."

"What type of situation was that?"

"My wife brought a suit against me for spousal support."

"How long ago was that?"

"More than five years ago."

"Are you presently divorced?"

"No."

"Do you intend to file for divorce?"

"Objection," Maureen interposed. "Whether or not Dr. Lerner intends to file for divorce has nothing to do with his role as our expert witness."

"It certainly does. This is a question that is designed to bring out information with respect to this witness's character and credibility."

"I don't see how."

"You will, as the morning goes on."

"I will instruct the witness not to answer."

"That is your choice, Miss Durrell, but remember that you are not representing the doctor. I am certain the court will agree with me on that point. Now, Doctor, will you please answer my question. Do you still remember it, or do you want the court reporter to read it you?"

"I remember it. At this time, I do not intend to file for divorce."

Maureen stared before her; her face remained impassive.

"Thank you, Doctor."

With Dan's professional curriculum vitae in his hand, Handelsman proceeded to go over Dan's education, professional training, and background. They were routine questions, and Dan was fully prepared for them.

"Dr. Lerner, have you ever been sued for malpractice?"

"No."

"Have restrictions or limitations been placed on your hospital privileges?"

"No."

"Have complaints ever been lodged about your ethical conduct toward patients?"

Dan hesitated and gave Maureen a questioning look.

"Doctor, I would like a yes or no answer."

"Yes, but. . . ."

"Just a minute, Dr. Lerner. Your answer was 'yes.' That is all I want."

"Dr. Lerner should be given a chance to explain his answer."

"That is your opinion, Miss Durrell. Now, Doctor, I will hand you a document." He handed Dan a copy of Mrs. Bentley's letter to Jack Brennan. "Have you seen this letter before?"

"Yes, but this letter was not written. . . ."

"You have. Good. Then I want the court reporter to attach this letter to the doctor's deposition as defendant's exhibit A. Now, Dr. Lerner, as of today, are you still licensed to practice medicine in the state of California?"

"This is like asking him if he has stopped beating his wife," Maureen interposed.

"I shall object to your remark, and I will request the court to strike it from the record as argumentative. Now, Dr. Lerner, I understand that you are employed by the university. Is that correct?"

"Yes."

"Can you outline for me your current duties."

Dan went into some detail about his clinics, his patients, and his position at Las Virgenes.

"I understand that in the past you have been engaged in some research. Is that correct?"

"Yes."

"Could you be so kind as to explain to us the nature of your research work."

Dan complied, and before long he was forced to admit that his work was no longer being supported by the National Institutes of Health. Handelsman then read him portions of the criticisms of his work that the consultants had prepared, and had the document attached to the deposition as Exhibit B.

"I presume that your work has been well received?"

"Yes."

"By everyone?"

"I think so."

"You have never been informed that allegations of scientific fraud have been brought up against you?"

Once again, Dan was on the spot.

"You will have to answer," Maureen whispered to him.

"Miss Durrell, are you trying to help the doctor with his testimony?"

"No."

"I believe that you are sufficiently experienced in this matter to know that you can't."

Before long, a copy of Crandall's letter was marked for identification and attached to the deposition as the next exhibit.

At the first break, Maureen took Dan into the next available empty office.

"He is trying to impeach you."

"What do you mean?"

"It's a legal term to indicate that he is trying to discredit you to the point where your testimony can no longer be trusted or accepted by the court . . . would you like some coffee?"

"I could use some."

"I bet." She whisked out and soon returned with two cups. "You better have some. This is going to be a long deposition."

She was wrong.

When everyone had reconvened, Handelsman turned a few pages of his notes.

"Dr. Lerner, what did you and Miss Durrell talk about during the break?"

"Nothing much."

"Nothing?"

"I will instruct the witness not to answer," Maureen said.

"Miss Durrell! I once again must remind you that you are not here to represent Dr. Lerner."

"I am not, but your question has nothing to do with the substance of the doctor's testimony."

"We will leave the court to decide on that point. In the meantime, Doctor, I would like you to answer my question. Otherwise you will risk being barred as a witness, and you could also be cited for contempt of court. You are aware of that, are you not, Miss Durrell?"

"Dan, you will have to answer him." No sooner had she spoken than Maureen wished she had kept her mouth shut.

"Doctor, I gather that you and Miss Durrell are on first name basis. Is that correct?"

"Yes. At times we are."

"For how long has that been the case?"

"I object," Maureen interrupted.

"On what grounds?"

"This question is not designed to lead to any admissible evidence."

"I would like the court to be the judge of that. Dr. Lerner, what is the exact nature of your relationship with Miss Durrell?"

Dan's face flushed. Reminding himself to remain calm, he rubbed fingers against thumb.

"I am an expert witness for the plaintiffs in this litigation."

"Is that all?"

"Yes."

"Are you sure that your relationship with Miss Durrell has not extended far beyond the scope of your being an expert witness?"

"I am sure."

"Thank you, Doctor. And are you equally sure that you and Miss Durrell are not lovers?"

Dan had expected this question, and his response was prompt.

"I don't have to answer that."

"I didn't think you would, Doctor. Your refusal to answer is sufficient for me."

Handelsman turned to Ann. "Anything I have forgotten?" She shook her head.

"You haven't asked the doctor anything about his profession-al opinion on the causation of the plaintiffs' neurologic damage," Maureen said.

"I don't need to. I have his statement and I will leave it up to the court and the jury to determine its credibility. I have nothing further. Thank you, Doctor." He rose and went to the court reporter to make the necessary arrangements for transcription of the deposition.

"I have never heard anything like this in my life," Maureen said to Dan. They were in the parking garage, waiting for their cars to be brought around.

"I am sorry."

"Why should you be sorry? There is nothing you did that brought this on. I blame myself for giving that jerk the opportuni-ty. . . . Mike is going to kill me when he finds out."

"So what are you going to do?"

"Right now, I don't know, but one thing I do know is that I am going to do a lot of heavy thinking tonight. We have to counterat-tack. For starters we will depose Kleinwort, then we will bring in Crandall and Mrs. Bentley."

"Why Crandall?"

"The man is such a bigot, he's going to antagonize every member of the jury."

"The best defense is an offense."

"Right."

Their cars were driven up.

"Let's have dinner tonight," Dan suggested.

"If that's what you want."

"See you at seven."

"Right."

They each got into their cars and for the time being went their respective ways.

\* \* \* \* \*

M<small>ARTY</small> did not see Malvina on his flight to Boston until he took his first stretch promenade around the plane. He was on his way to New Hampshire and the Labor Day Weekend Gordon Conference on circadian rhythms, for which he had been designated one of the discussion leaders.

"Hello, there," he said. She was in the galley with two other stewardesses and they were setting up lunch.

She looked up. A smile of instant recognition. "Hello."

"It's been a long time."

"How have you been?"

"So-so."

"I am sorry I had to leave abruptly. It was a matter of considerable urgency . . . business."

"I see. . . ." He felt weary. Too weary to ask any further.

Indeed for the past few weeks things had not gone well with him.

At first it had been no more than a series of small annoyances. His paper, jointly authored with Kyoshi, had been returned by the editors of the *Journal of Neuroscience* with a request for amplification of some of the data that had been submitted with it. Under normal circumstances it would have been no more than a weekend's work for the Japanese post-doc to provide the editors with the information they requested. This was not to be. For some inexplicable reason, Kyoshi hit a snag. Marty had to send a fax to the editors of the journal to inform them that he had elected to conduct a few additional experiments, and that at their conclusion Kyoshi and he would promptly resubmit the manuscript.

In order to expedite the research, he asked Takafumi to stop his own work and assist Kyoshi. Until the two Japanese postdoctoral students had solved this apparently simple problem, all further experiments in Marty's laboratory would have to stop.

One night when Marty returned home from the laboratory, frustrated and exhausted by additional, unavoidable delays, he found Jeanette lying face down on the bed, fully clothed.

"What's wrong?" he asked.

"Everything." She was drunk and had been crying.

"Tell me."

She sat up and put her hands over her face.

"I want to leave you." She sounded distraught.

"What would make you do that?"

"Because there is something horribly wrong with you."

"There is nothing wrong with me. I just have a lot on my mind." There was no way he could elaborate. He would have to start by telling her about his angel, and he had not shared this knowledge with anyone.

With a sudden movement she balled her hands into fists and screamed at him, "I won't have you distance me! I can't stand it! I'd rather be on my own!" This was followed by a howl, which gradually transformed itself into a series of heart-rending sobs. When Marty tried to put his arms around her, she pushed him away.

"I don't need you. You're so conceited you'd like to think I do, but I really don't. I just want to go home."

That night, even though tired to the point of exhaustion, Marty could not drop off to sleep. What had happened to his life? Where had it gone wrong? Ever since moving to California he felt abandoned by his guardian angel, and without his guidance, he sensed himself to be unprotected and as liable to experience misfortune as any ordinary human being. With a shock he realized that the imperturbable confidence he had treasured, and that had sustained him for his entire life, had evaporated under the hot California sunshine.

The implications of Marty's "so-so" did not escape Malvina.

"I am staying overnight in Boston," she said to him after lunch had been served and cleared. The plane was crowded and she had no time to exchange more than a few words. "What about you?"

"Me, too." Marty said. The truth was that he had planned to rent a car on arrival at Logan Airport and drive to New Hampshire. "Shall we have dinner?"

"I would love it."

They arranged to meet in the lobby of the Ritz Carlton, where the airline was putting her up, and have dinner in the upstairs restaurant. With a feeling of solace for having found a friend to whom he could at last unburden himself, Marty set out on another circumambulation of the plane.

* * *

Ever since their last encounter Marty suspected that Malvina had the gift of second sight. Over dinner that night his suspicions were confirmed.

"When I first saw you on the plane I could tell you were pre-occupied," she said, as she broke off a small piece of bread and spread it with butter. As on the occasion of their last dinner, Malvina was in black. This time she was in a simple form-fitting dress slit at the sides to disclose her legs and highlighted by an ebullient white lace collar. In the presence of her familiar perfume, lemon and spice, Marty felt as if he were on the verge of being drawn into Malvina's landscape, a land where time ceased to exist and where he could find a new identity.

"My work has been piling up on me," he said.

"That's not it. Whatever it is, don't hide it from me."

"I am not sure what is going on in my life."

"Then I will help you find out. Let me look at your hand. I must see what worries you."

Marty extended his hand. She took it, and with two fingers lightly stroked his palm.

"You are concerned about your wife," she said after a minute or two. She closed her eyes. "Her name is Jean, isn't it?"

"You are amazing! Actually she calls herself Jeanette."

"You are worried about Jeanette because she is unhappy with you. You are afraid she may leave you."

"She says that ever since we came to California I have been distancing myself from her. That may be part of her unhappiness, but I also think she has been unable to put down roots."

"I would not expect her to. Not with her background . . . she is from New England, isn't she?"

"You are absolutely right."

"But there is more," Malvina continued, ignoring his compliment. "Your work is not going well."

"You can see that?"

"Yes . . . but there is something else that disturbs you even more. Something that keeps you awake at night." She bent her head over Marty's hand and carefully traced the lines in his palm. "Wait," she said and concentrated.

"Wait," she repeated, then suddenly she called out, "I have it! You are worried about your soul. You have bartered it for a mandrake root."

"A mandrake root?"

"Yes. For ambition. Without your soul there is a void within you." She smiled. "Isn't that true?"

Marty reflected. "Perhaps. Is anyone else aware of it?"

"Jean . . . Jeanette suspects it, but she is afraid to say anything to you."

"What about the people at work? The other members of my department?"

"They don't have enough time to notice. And even if they did, they don't care." She released his hand. "So then . . . that's enough for one night."

"You think I have bartered away my soul," Marty reflected. "That sounds serious. I will have to consider the implications."

"I can tell you don't believe me . . . even though you know quite well that is exactly what you have done."

"How and when did it happen?"

"I am not certain. My aunt, from whom I have inherited my gift, would have been able to tell you everything."

"Since you are not certain, I shall tell you." He ordered a second bottle of champagne and, after it had been brought to the table, proceeded to relate his experience with Dr. Albert Lessing, his contract with Marat International, and the case reports to which he had signed his name against his better judgment.

"What do you honestly think about this drug . . . this . . . what is it called . . . Dulcian?"

"That it may be good for depression but that the incidence and the type of side reactions that it produces deprive it of all value."

She gave him an odd look. "Is that what you really believe?"

"Yes. And that it should be taken off the market. The sooner the better." He refilled their glasses.

"And what are you going to do about it?"

"I don't know. At this point I don't see a way out. Every door has become bolted on me. . . . I know what I would like to do."

"What is that?"

"Leave everything and everybody and escape to Brazil with you. To Maceio." She smiled and held up her hand. The ruby sparkled in the candlelight.

"You would not like Maceio. It is a horribly boring town, little more than a village. The only reason Maceio looks good to you tonight is that you have no answer to your dilemma and you have had a lot of champagne."

"What about you?"

"I am ready to go upstairs."

"What a good idea!" They drained their glasses and left the table. As they were waiting for the elevator, Malvina said with a smile, "I would not want to be in Maceio with you. But Rio, now there is a real possibility."

"Do you really mean that?"

"Perhaps I do. But first I would like you to find your conscience. Think of where you lost it and retrace your steps." She burst into laughter. "And that's enough about that subject. At least for tonight."

"You are right," Marty said lightly. By giving him a task, Malvina restored his sense of purpose.

\* \* \*

With fingers and hands interlocked, they slept through the night. Marty was the first to wake up. He put his arms around Malvina. Luxuriating in the warmth of her soft dark body, he reflected on the events of the previous evening. Even though both had become drunk toward the end, the image, albeit a trifle faded in the morning light, of leaving with Malvina for Brazil persisted. An object gazed at uninterruptedly in bright light remains imprinted on the retina.

Malvina stirred and opened her eyes. "Good morning, darling."

"Good morning." He kissed her tenderly.

"What time is it?"

"Seven."

"I don't have to be back at Logan until noon. Would you mind terribly if I stayed in bed?"

"Not at all. But I have to drive to New Hampshire."

"Is it a long drive?"

"Not too bad. I will have time to think."

He kissed her again and got up to shower.

"How will I be able to find you?" he asked when he returned to the bedroom, fully dressed and ready to leave. "I don't want us to lose each other like we did the last time."

"I don't either. I promise to get in touch with you as soon as I know that you have regained your conscience."

"How will you know?"

"I have my ways, Marty. Different from your American CIA, but equally efficient."

"Explain yourself."

"Not this morning. Some other time."

It was a three-hour drive from downtown Boston to Andover, New Hampshire, the site of the Gordon Conference. Traffic was light, and there indeed was enough time for Marty to ponder on how best to go about retrieving his conscience. The alternatives that presented themselves were at best inadequate; at worst they were self-destructive and threatened to bring about the end of everything he had so diligently and persistently worked for.

He knew he had arrived at a crossroads.

There was a time—before his angel had abandoned him—when he could have made the right decision instinctively. This was no longer the case.

He drove into Andover and quickly saw the signpost to Colby College. He followed the road, which wound up the hill between rows of maple trees in their full September foliage, and before long he was at his destination.

* * * * *

T HE idea came to Maureen in the middle of the night. She thought of picking up the phone on the spot and calling Dan but decided against it. The call could wait until morning.

"Didn't you tell me that there was a man at Tufts who had a case of the syndrome?" Maureen was sitting over breakfast—coffee and a toasted bagel. Without butter.

"That's what Peter said. He had heard about this case before I called him with mine. The neurologist's name is John Rose."

"How reliable is he?"

"He's reputed to be a solid clinician."

"I am going to get in touch with him and see if he will agree to serve as our expert witness. We may need him as your backup in case Judge Watson strikes you off the list."

"Do you think that's what'll happen?"

"I hope not . . . but with him one never can tell."

\* \* \*

"This is preposterous," Mike thundered as he stormed into Maureen's office, handing her a fax. "They are refusing to let us depose Kleinwort."

"I know." Maureen had been working on the affidavits for Jane Bentley and her mother. They had to be ready and notarized in time for Dan's hearing before the hospital's Professional Standards and Ethics Committee. Half an hour earlier, as she was finishing the first draft of Mrs. Bentley's affidavit, Handelsman had phoned her with the news that Dr. Kleinwort's current mental instability precluded the deposition.

"Why didn't you tell me as soon as you found out?" Mike stormed.

"I was too busy."

"You are always too busy! You know goddamn well this means the end of our case. First your boyfriend's deposition . . . and now this. It's the one-two punch!"

Mike threw himself across the sofa.

"I don't believe them for one minute," Maureen said.

"What good does that do? Read this." Mike waved the fax at her. "Kleinwort has signed a notarized affidavit in which he declares that his current mental status precludes him from testifying at this time and in the foreseeable future. Ann Townsend has handed the original to Judge Watson, together with supporting letters from two qualified psychiatrists."

"I bet he knows something they don't want us to find out."

"I am sure of that."

"What puzzles me is why he agreed to signing that affidavit. That runs counter to his being our secret friend at Marat."

"What makes you so sure that he is our secret friend?"

"The person who called us in New York had a German accent."

Mike sat up and thoughtfully folded the fax.

"There is no way they could have forged his signature."

"I didn't say they did," Maureen said, "but they must have something on him that made him go along with them."

"Like what?"

"I wouldn't have the faintest idea."

"And you're supposed to be smart. Tom used to brag about you, said you were the smartest woman lawyer in all of L.A. So why can't you come up with something clever?"

"Whenever you tell me that, you sound positively stupid."

Maureen was indignant, and she didn't mind letting Mike know. What was the worst he could do to her? She looked at him as he slouched on her couch. He was angry with the world because the case was going against him, and angry with her for preferring to go to bed with Dan. For an instant she felt sorry for Mike—another married man in a long series of needy and dissatisfied married men who wanted to have an affair with her. She pushed aside these thoughts and concentrated on Kleinwort.

"My intuition tells me that despite his affidavit we are going to hear from him before too long. In one way or another."

"Let's hope you are right," Mike grunted. Without another word he got up from the couch. Slightly bent forward—his back had been giving him trouble lately—he left Maureen's office.

* * *

When Maureen returned to her apartment much later that day and checked her answering machine, there was a call from Ailesly. Without even taking off her shoes or jacket, she quickly dialed his number.

"It's Maureen Durrell returning your call. How have you been?"

"Quite well."

"How are things in Stinson Beach?"

"I want to be brief. I have reconsidered matters and I am ready to testify for you. That is, if you still need me."

"Of course we need you." Maureen could feel the excitement rise into her throat.

"For the record, my legal name is still Marvin Ailesly, and I know you have my address."

"I will have a subpoena drawn up first thing in the morning. You should receive it in a few days."

After she hung up she phoned Mike. He was at home and his wife answered.

"This is Maureen Durrell. May I talk to Mike?"

There was a moment of hesitation. Maureen had the distinct impression that Ilona was about to ask her what it was about.

"Just a minute. I will try to find him." Ilona's sexy Hungarian accent made Maureen wonder why Mike was trying to cheat on her. Men are such enigmas, she thought as she waited for him to come on the line.

"I have great news," she said, and told him about Ailesly. Her exuberance was contagious.

"We'll cream those bastards," Mike said when she had finished.

"I am going to get together with Handelsman and let him know that we've lined up Ailesly."

"At this point he'll be unimpressed. He thinks he has two strikes against us."

"So what! It can't hurt us, and it might make him insecure."

"Fine with me. Just remember: a threat is always better than its execution."

Her next call was to the office of Wyburn, Mason, Keene, and Handelsman. The night secretary answered.

"This is Ms. Durrell. Could I speak to Mr. Handelsman?"

"Let me see if he is still in. This is Friday evening and he leaves early."

A few moments later, Handelsman came on the line. "I was just on my way out."

"I am glad I caught you. We have to talk."

"Not now. It's too late."

"I understand. How about Sunday at six?"

"That's fine with me. Same place?"

"Right."

\* \* \*

That Sunday evening the cocktail bar at the Peninsula Hotel was crowded, and Maureen and Handelsman had to make do with a small table by the entrance.

"So what's on your mind?" Handelsman started out.

"A simple question. How much is Marat willing to offer us to settle this litigation?"

"Nothing, my dear lady, not one penny. You missed your chance. Next week I am going to ask Judge Watson for a summary judgment. Before you know it, your case is going to get thrown out of court. "

"We have some more witnesses the judge and you might want to hear from."

"If you are thinking of Dr. Carter, I am not going to waste my time and my client's money by deposing him."

"I wasn't thinking of him."

"I am certain you don't want to hear from our experts. Like Dr. Charles Forbes. Or Maurice Templeton. Dr. Templeton will have a few interesting things to say about Dr. Carter and his reputation in professional circles."

Maureen remembered that Dan had mentioned both names to her. Forbes was the world's expert on serotonin. Templeton was one of the most respected American neuropsychiatrists.

She took a sip of wine.

"For one, Dr. Marvin Ailesly has agreed to testify for us."

"Ailesly?" For an instant Handelsman was genuinely surprised. His prominent lips drew into a pout and he appeared worried.

"In case you don't remember, he worked on the Dulcian toxicity studies before he resigned from Marat."

"Yes, of course. His name did come up a few weeks ago." Handelsman was once again in control of his emotions.

"Right. We intend to notice his deposition."

"Ailesly knows nothing about Dulcian. He ran a few experiments, and by playing around with some of his data managed to delay Marat's Phase II and III studies."

"If that is what you wish us to believe, I would like to remind you of another matter. When Judge Watson granted our motion to compel Marat to produce all the records in the company library, you agreed to it. Right?"

Handelsman did not reply.

"So if this case comes to trial I intend to prove to the jury that you did not comply with the order and that you failed to produce a number of important documents. Ailesly will provide us with copies of those documents."

"You are bluffing."

"Then call my bluff. Just remember what happened in the Dalkon Shield litigation when it came out that some of the evidence had gone missing. Punitive damages. And the company attorneys didn't look too good either."

Handelsman nodded and slowly ran his forefinger around the edge of his glass.

"Do you think I should have another one?" His lower lip drooped slightly.

"Another what?" She did not expect him to ask her a question like that. For an instant she saw him as a child turning to his mother for advice.

She chose not to respond to his question. "There also is a new expert witness you will find of some interest. A Dr. John Rose."

"John Rose?" The name meant nothing to Handelsman and he was truly puzzled.

"He is Clinical Professor of Neurology at Tufts and he has independent experience with the Angry Puppet Syndrome. Dr. Rose has agreed to be our expert, in case the court disqualifies Dr. Lerner, or in case we need a rebuttal witness."

The fact that she had not even spoken to John Rose did not deter her. She would have made a great poker player.

"What does he know about this litigation?"

"A lot . . . as you will find out. I would advise you to go back to your clients and tell them that unless they make us a meaningful offer, we will produce several startling and unpleasant witnesses."

Handelsman nodded. Maureen could tell that he was forcing himself into a composure that did not come readily.

"You can be sure that I will relay this information to Marat management."

"I will hear from you then."

"You will."

\* \* \*

Maureen called John Rose's office the first thing next morning. The departmental secretary who answered said that Dr. Rose was in clinic and would not be back in his office until late that afternoon.

"I would like to set up an appointment with him."

"For you or for a relative?"

"Neither, but it is a very important matter."

"Are you a lawyer?"

"Yes."

"Dr. Rose does not see lawyers."

"Never? This is extremely important, and it involves someone he knows well . . . a Dr. Carter, Peter Carter."

"Oh yes . . . Dr. Carter." There was a pause while the woman did a quick mental review of the protocol appropriate to this particular circumstance. "I cannot make an appointment for you until I speak with the doctor."

"That's fine. Tell him I would really appreciate a few minutes with him. Assure him that he will be compensated for his time."

"Dr. Rose does not accept compensation for legal consultations. If your firm wishes to make a donation to the neurology department. . . ."

By now the secretary's prissiness and her New England patrician airs had become more than Maureen could tolerate.

"Just let him know I would like to meet with him," she said and hung up.

A few days later a message awaited her that Dr. Rose would see her in his office Saturday morning at eight. Both date and time were unalterable. When she told Mike that she was taking the Friday night red-eye to Boston to see John Rose, he shook his head.

"You're going on a wild goose chase. I know his type. You'll be lucky if you get that man to give you the time of day."

"I'll charm him."

"I am sure you can. Let's just hope it works."

\* \* \*

Dr. John Rose's office was in the old part of the medical school. It was a tiny and cluttered room, stuffed to the ceiling with books, medical journals, and patient charts in what appeared to be total disarray. A human brain sitting on the windowsill in a pickle jar filled with liquid formalin yellowed by age seemed to gaze blindly into the room. When Maureen was shown in by the secretary, the doctor was on the telephone.

"Clear those off," he said with one hand on the mouthpiece, and waved her to a chair on which there was a stack of library books. Maureen did as she was ordered. She moved the books, sat down, and, having placed her briefcase between her legs—there was hardly any room elsewhere—waited for the doctor to finish his conversation.

Rose had a narrow bony face highlighted by a pair of small steel-rimmed glasses, which gave him an arid owlish look. A tuft of black hair that he must have overlooked while shaving that morning protruded from the left corner of his jaw. His white coat hung loosely across his shoulders, and even when he was seated it was evident to Maureen that he was an exceptionally tall lanky man.

"So Peter Carter sent you?" Rose started out.

"In a way he did."

"What do you want to know?"

"You are seeing a patient with a neurologic illness that resembles episodic discontrol. Dr. Carter said that you discussed this woman. . . ."

"It's a young man."

"You discussed this young man with him several months ago, and he was as puzzled about the diagnosis as you were." At this point she chose not to mention that the man had been taking Dulcian. To bring that out might increase the doctor's reluctance to talk to her.

"How do you think this man contracted his illness?" she asked.

"I don't know."

"Any ideas?"

"Miss," John Rose glanced at the card which his secretary had given him—"Miss Durrell, please don't fence with me. You and I both know that this man had been given Dulcian and that you would like me to say that his condition is the result of his having received the medication."

"Is it?"

"No."

"No?"

If he says "no" again Maureen told herself, it will be the end of my interview with him, and my trip to Boston will have been the wild goose chase that Mike predicted it would be.

"That is my opinion. The reason I can say this so categorically is that the man was actually enrolled in the Phase I studies of Dulcian."

"You mean he was one of the paid volunteers who offered to take the drug?"

"He was. What was not known at the time he was entered into the study is that he had been a chronic abuser of yohimbine."

"What is yohimbine?"

"It is a drug derived from the bark of the yohimbe tree. It has been used to treat sexual impotence for centuries, if not millennia. If you are interested in the topic I can refer you to several important papers."

"And your patient had been taking this drug before he was given Dulcian."

"For many months, if not years. That is what he admitted to his physician after he had developed his symptoms."

"Is that so?"

"That is what I was told. Of course, by now the man denies ever having taken yohimbine."

"Why would he do that?"

"Who knows? A sense of guilt. . . ."

"Could you give me the man's name?"

"Absolutely not."

"It would be very important to me if I could speak with him."

"I said I would not provide you with his name."

"But you still see him, don't you?"

"I do. He is severely incapacitated by his symptoms. But I assure you there is no way I will disclose his name to you."

"No?"

"No!"

Maureen saw she had come to an impasse. She offered to take the doctor to dinner, which he refused. She offered to take him to lunch, which he also refused on the grounds that he was too far behind in his dictation to take time off to have lunch with her even on a Saturday. Seeing that she had gone as far as she could, she stood up and retrieved her briefcase.

"By the way, can you tell me who the physician was who first saw this man of yours?" Her hand was already on the door handle, and John Rose was about to start the morning's dictation of patient reports. He looked up.

"Jack Brennan. I took over some of his patients when he left Tufts. You might have heard of him. He is out in your part of the world."

* * *

After returning from Boston that night Maureen checked her answering machine. Only two messages. One from Dan, saying that according to the arrangements they had made before her quick trip to Boston, he'd be over at nine for a late supper. The second message was from Aunt Edna. Having washed up and changed into more comfortable clothes, Maureen returned it.

"Aunt Edna," she said as soon as the old lady answered. "I have been so busy I haven't had a chance to tell you what a wonderful time I had with you. Thank you ever so much. . . ."

"Maureen." There was a dark tone to her aunt's voice. "Your friend, Mr. Powell, was hit by a car this morning. He was walking along Highway 1. Killed instantly."

"What!"

"He was coming back from breakfast at the Sea Air Café. A hit-and-run driver. No one got his license number. What a terrible accident!"

"That was no accident."

"You don't think so? They said he was walking with his back to the traffic."

"Believe me, it wasn't an accident. And maybe you should start locking your door."

As soon as Maureen got off the phone, she placed a call to Mike and told him about Ailesly.

"I'll be damned!" And for a time that was Mike's only response.

"Now what?"

"Why don't you give Bartlett a call and see whether he can do better than the Stinson Beach police. Tell him to get himself up there. Tonight. We'll pay all expenses."

Maureen's next call was to Bartlett. In a few sentences she told him the circumstances of Ailesly's death.

"You think he was murdered?" Bartlett asked.

"I don't know, but it certainly is a good likelihood. If he had testified for us, he would have made a very strong witness."

"I know some people with the Marin County Police Department. I'll let them know what you said about this being no accident."

"Thanks. And keep in touch."

"Let's hope there won't be any more surprises."

When Dan arrived, Maureen made no attempt to hide from him how upset she was.

"I thought we were back in the ball game," she said. "With a good chance for a nice settlement. But now. . . ."

They were standing in the kitchen and Maureen looked wistfully at the porterhouse steak in the broiler.

"I've opened a nice cabernet . . . ," Dan said.

"Not even that will help."

"You still have Kleinwort."

"You don't understand," she said in an uncharacteristically loud voice. "We don't have Kleinwort. We don't have him as long as he claims he is mentally unfit to give his deposition."

"I could fly out and talk to him."

"I've thought of that. I've tried to reach him, but he's not at home and he doesn't return my messages."

"What if you were to get me the rest of Ailesly's data. I bet I could make some sense out of it."

"Not a bad idea. I know exactly where he kept it. I'll get Bartlett to copy it. When we sit down at the table, I'm going to tell you what I found out from John Rose."

Over steak and baked potatoes, Maureen related what little information she had gleaned on her trip to Boston.

"So Jack saw this man while he was still at Tufts. I wonder what his diagnosis was."

"Yohimbine addiction. That's what John Rose said."

"Rose worries me. He is as much of an organization man as Jack. I am surprised he even agreed to talk to you."

"He doesn't know that I am going to name him as a witness."

"Be careful with him."

"Mike told me to charm him. I tried my best. But he kept looking at the pickled brain that sits in his window."

"It always works with me."

"Thanks. . . ."

She smiled at Dan, who pierced the steak with his fork.

"This steak is perfect," he said, "just perfect. Lots of people don't like porterhouse steak. They consider it to lack the flavor of the more expensive cuts. . . ."

Maureen closed her eyes. "Keep on talking. Otherwise I'll fall asleep over the table."

* * *

It was Monday morning. Maureen had no sooner settled down to go through her mail when she was buzzed by Charlotte.

"Mr. Bartlett's on the line. Can you speak to him?"

Chris Bartlett was calling from Stinson Beach.

"This is some crazy business with that man Powell, or Ailesly, or what have you! The police are quite sure that someone entered his house the morning he was run over. One of the neighbors says she heard a car drive up and the door open and close. She didn't think much of it until she found out that Ailesly had been run over a couple of hours earlier."

"Anything missing?"

"Not that the police could tell."

"When he and I talked at the end of June, he gave me some old data that he fished out from the secretary in the front room. He also said that he still had extensive data from the clinical part of the Phase I study. I wonder if any of that is still around."

"I'll find out."

"If you do, ask the police to let you copy everything, I mean everything, and bring it back to L.A."

"I don't know if anyone of us will know what you are talking about."

"Of course . . . if I fly up tonight, do you think you can get me into the house in the morning?"

"Don't see why not. The police are real relaxed around here."

"All right then. See you outside Ailesly's place tomorrow morning."

Having made all the arrangements with Bartlett, Maureen went to see Mike and inform him of her decision to fly up to Stinson Beach.

"I hope you won't take what I'm going to tell you too personally." He leaned back in his chair and closed his eyes. "The way I see it, you are going to need a lot of help with this case. My help." He sat up straight, and a moment later jumped out of his chair. He did a few steps around the office then whirled around.

"Any idea how much we have put into this thing so far?"

"About fifty thousand. . . ."

"We're going to spend a hell of a lot more before we get through with it. That's why I don't want this to be your sole responsibility. Understand?"

"Right."

"Okay, you're flying up to Stinson Beach this evening. And I can expect you back in here on Wednesday morning."

"Barring the unforeseen."

"God damn it! I don't want any unforeseens, Maureen. Keep that in mind. I've had enough unforeseens in this case to last me a lifetime. The other thing I want you to do is make me a summary of everything you have done or intend to do on this case. I don't want to sound ghoulish, but if these people knocked off Ailesly. . . ."

"I got it. I will dictate everything this morning. You will have it on your desk before I fly up."

"Good girl."

"And I am sending a copy to Dr. Lerner."

"Be my guest."

\* \* \*

Aunt Edna was delighted to have Maureen return so soon after her previous visit. To her annoyance, advance notice had been too short this time to prepare an elaborate dinner.

"I'll make up for it at breakfast, Maureen."

"Please don't bother. I intend to have breakfast at the Sea Air Café." The old lady frowned and gazed into the creamy depths of her celery soup.

"I won't permit you to walk up there."

"Don't worry, I'll drive. And later on the police and I will look through Ailesly's house. That's the man you knew as Mr. Powell. I want to see whether his data are still around."

For a makeshift affair, Aunt Edna's dinner was first class. Soup was followed by stewed beef with boiled new potatoes and a raspberry crumble, which admittedly had come from the freezer. Soft sounds of the radio and casual chitchat, at which Aunt Edna was a master, brought the evening to a close.

\* \* \*

Coffee at the Sea Air Café was plentiful; useful information on the late Ashley Powell, alias Ailesly, was sparse. The waitress knew him as a regular, but aside from the fact that his table was closest to the kitchen to allow him to smoke his pipe while reading the *Chronicle*, she had little to offer Maureen but her sympathies. She had heard that there was a nephew who would be coming over from Scotland, and people thought he would put the bungalow up for sale.

"I suppose you were a friend of his."

"Not really. . . ." Although the waitress was anxious to hear more, Maureen did not elaborate.

After breakfast Maureen drove back to Stinson Beach. The drive was just over two miles—it would have been a pleasant walk alongside a fairly quiet highway. She parked her rental car outside Ailesly's bungalow and rolled down the window. From forty yards away came the sound of the breakers as they rose and subsided. Their sound evoked a poignant feeling in her—a rhythm of energy and endless time—past, present, and future merging into each other.

At ten-fifteen—the meeting had been arranged for ten— Bartlett and Sergeant Colin Schweiger of the Stinson Beach Police drove up in a squad car. Schweiger unfastened a plastic yellow tape that had been stretched across the front door and led the way into the bungalow. The front rooms appeared unchanged. The dark green stuffed armchair in which Maureen had sat on her visit to Ailesly and the old cane-backed chair that Ailesly had used were in their original places with an impassivity that reminded Maureen of a stage set after final curtain. For the first time she had a chance to look closely at the titles in the bookcase: a biography of John Knox, The Reformation in Scotland, *History of Mary Queen of Scots* by Adam Blackwood. Ailesly had been well-read in Scottish history.

"He took the graph that he gave me from in there." Maureen pointed to the bottom drawer of the secretary. Schweiger opened it. "It was in a dark-blue folder." Maureen added.

"This?"

"Right."

"Let's see what else is in it." Slipping on plastic gloves, he took the folder to the dining room table and opened it. There was little of interest—a home owner's insurance policy, a car insurance policy, a bill from the local nursery, and a few other odds and ends; all appeared to have been undisturbed.

Sergeant Schweiger was visibly disappointed. "Anything else you might want to see before we leave this place?"

"No," Maureen said. And then she noticed the sideboard. When she had watched Ailesly restuff his pipe, there had been three tobacco canisters: one of ornamented brass and, flanking it, two old-fashioned tin boxes decorated with castle scenes and probably brought over from Scotland. Now there were only two canisters: the brass one and a tin canister picturing Fotheringay Castle. The other tin box—the one that had a picture of Carlisle Castle—had disappeared.

She quickly explained this to Sergeant Schweiger. He took out his notepad.

"Are you sure?"

"Absolutely."

"Isn't that something! I wonder what he kept in it."

"Your guess is as good as mine," Maureen said. "But I wouldn't be surprised if that's where he kept the data he was talking about."

"Don't touch those boxes! I'll get Mark to come by and check them for fingerprints."

"There also was a schnauzer," Maureen said. "Do you know what happened to him?"

"Sure. One of the neighbors took him in," the sergeant said. "I hear he is pretty disconsolate and off his feed."

"That's dogs for you," Bartlett said. A reflection on the faithfulness of animals.

Once they were outside the bungalow, Sergeant Schweiger replaced the plastic ribbon. "Wanna bet we'll never get to the bottom of this," he said. "Not in a million years." He looked rather pleased with the idea. Maureen saw him as a man who delighted in unsolved mysteries.

\* \* \*

"I suppose there is no way they can ever find out who ran down Ailesly," Dan said. He and David were having dinner at La Torta Calda.

"What makes you say that?" With a thoughtful movement of the hand, David brushed several locks of graying hair from his temples. "Do you remember that book by Ronald Innes? He has a somewhat similar situation. Except that the man who was killed was the only witness to a murder. 'A Lady in the Lake.' It's set in a fishing lodge on Lake Louise. Of course, that detail is irrelevant." David was a voracious reader of detective novels and, helped by his prodigious memory, retained the plot of each and every one of them.

"The first question you must ask yourself is whether the car was rented or not. What do you think?"

"Rented."

"I fully agree. There is no reason for anyone in Stinson Beach or its neighborhood to wish this man out of the way. Unless he had been annoying the ladies at the book club with anecdotes about Mary Queen of Scots."

"Someone could have driven up from San Francisco."

"Not too likely. If we assume that this assassination was directed from New Jersey, you will have to concede that it is far easier to find a hit man on the East Coast and fly him out to San Francisco than to find such a person in a town three thousand miles away."

"Why didn't they kill him before Maureen went up to see him?"

"I don't think they expected anyone on the plaintiff's side to track him down. They couldn't have foreseen that Kleinwort—if that's who it was—would reveal Ailesly's whereabouts. Now then, what the police should do is check the Bay Area car rental agencies for any damaged car that was turned in last Saturday or maybe Sunday morning. That's what Frank Emmett did in 'A Lady in the Lake.' You can be sure that you don't run someone down at full speed without at least producing a slight dent."

"There is a Sergeant Schweiger in Stinson Beach. Maureen says he is in charge of the investigation. You might want to talk to him."

"Maureen should call him. He knows her, and he doesn't know me from beans. By the way, I am sorry she wasn't able to be here tonight. I was looking forward to meeting her." He stared into the wineglass and drained it with a quick movement.

"What's happening with your hearing in front of the Ethics Committee?"

"It's been postponed until some time in November. Maureen says that once they received the affidavits from Mrs. Bentley and Jane, they were thrown into confusion, and now they need time to regroup."

"I bet they do."

"Maureen also thinks that postponing the hearing was Jack Brennan's idea. Marat has promised him money to develop the B floor. That's where the new PET scanner and the functional MR imaging unit is supposed to go."

"And he wants to curry favor with Marat by ruining your qualifications as an expert witness."

"Something like that. What do you think?"

"She's got a good point. But then, she always has, according to what you tell me about her."

\* \* \*

When Dan got home, he phoned Maureen. She was still at the office.

"Dave and I had dinner tonight. He says you should call Schweiger and tell him to check the Bay Area car rental agencies for a damaged car that was turned in last Saturday or Sunday."

"Is that right?" Maureen seemed preoccupied.

"You don't seem interested."

"I am much more interested in the missing tobacco tin. I want to know what was in it."

"Copies of his toxicity studies."

"Is that all? I was trying to think of something more spectacular."

"Like what?"

"I wish I knew. If I get any bright ideas, I'll pass them on to you."

\* \* \*

When Maureen arrived at work the following day, she was told by Charlotte that Mike wanted to see her immediately. She stepped into his office.

"Say, girl! Do you look great this morning! I don't know how you manage it, day in and day out. Despite all the hassle."

"Thanks."

"Did we hear anything from Bartlett?"

"Not a word. For all I know he went back to San Diego."

"Give him a call. Maybe that'll stir him into action."

As it turned out, Bartlett called her before she did.

"We were just talking about you, Mike and I."

"Mental telepathy. Let me give you the latest from Stinson Beach. The police managed to trace a car that had been returned Sunday morning with a dent in the right front fender. Actually it was more than a dent—it had traces of blood on it. And it matched Ailesly's."

"Go on."

"The car had been checked out Friday night from San Francisco International Airport and was returned there on Sunday morning."

"Do you know who checked it out?"

"Some man from New Jersey."

"Do you have his name?"

"Certainly. I wrote it down. Just give me a second." There was a pause on the phone while Maureen drew interlocking circles on the pad of yellow paper in front of her. "Here we are. It's a Dr. . . . I'll spell the name: K-L-E-I -N-W-O-R-T."

"Kleinwort!"

"That's right. The first name is Heinz."

"Heinz," Maureen repeated mechanically.

"Do you know the man?"

"Very well."

"No kidding. The police were going to pull him in for questioning, but the address on the driver's license was wrong or something."

"I know where to find him. Or at least I think I do. He works for Marat. He's their statistician."

"Their what?"

"Statistician." Maureen thought she'd be damned if she was going to spell the word for Bartlett and define it for him. "We were all set to depose him, but he was declared mentally unfit."

"Maybe he is."

"Maybe."

\* \* \*

That night over dinner at their favorite little Italian restaurant, Maureen gave Dan the news that Bartlett had relayed to her.

"This makes absolutely no sense whatever," Dan said, then added, almost as an afterthought, "I have to tell you—you look terrific." She was wearing a black skirt and a clinging lightweight emerald green sweater, a perfect match for her auburn hair.

"Thanks," she said, then quickly changed the subject. "That still doesn't explain why Handelsman won't let me depose Kleinwort."

"Why should he? Kleinwort could have been Marat's hit man as well as their statistician."

"Right."

"Now if Handelsman knew that Kleinwort had been assigned by Marat to run down Ailesly and didn't report it to the police, he would be an accessory to the murder."

"Right."

"From what you tell me about him, he doesn't appear to be that type of person."

"He doesn't, but one never knows." A sudden thought came to her. "He might even wear lace panties under his trousers." She laughed, a free and clear laughter, one that Dan had not heard for a long time.

"So what d'you think is going to happen?" he asked.

"Sooner or later the police are going to pick up Kleinwort and question him. We should know a lot more in a few days."

A silence rose up between them. Maureen drained her glass.

"How is Judith?" she asked.

"She might as well be out of my life."

"But she isn't."

"She phoned a couple of weeks ago and told me she had joined the Beverly Hills Kabbalah Center. She said she is searching for a new perspective on life."

"What is the Kabbalah Center?"

"You don't know?"

"If I knew, I wouldn't have to ask you." Maureen sounded annoyed.

Dan set out to explain the role of the Kabbalah in Jewish thinking. "I have not had any firsthand experience with it, but I gather that through a study of the writings of the Kabbalah man can achieve the means for a mystical union with God."

Maureen listened and nodded. When Dad had finished his exposition, silence once again hovered over them. A few sessions ago Bernice had warned her that once a relationship starts to move apart, it is doomed to failure. Maureen put down her reading glasses and looked into the distance. "As soon as this case is over, one way or another, I am going to do something for myself. I don't know what I have been waiting for all these years. All I know is that I can't go on much longer in this business. I don't think any woman can. It's a man's world."

"I couldn't do your kind of work either."

"What I mean to say is that you men have the stamina, the . . . hormones for confrontations. We women don't do so well at that, and when we try it takes a lot out of us. As the years go by, time turns all of us into caricatures."

Another silence. It grew hard and dense.

"I didn't think I'd find you here." David stood at their table. "And you must be Maureen. I've heard a lot about you."

"Please sit down," Dan said quickly. Maureen too was relieved. She had become despondent about herself and angry with Dan for not fulfilling her expectations. Would any man, ever? She reminded herself to bring up that question in her next session with Bernice.

With a few sentences Dan filled David in about Kleinwort.

"Strange . . . very strange," David muttered, and looked thoughtful. When the waiter came to their table, he offhandedly ordered some antipasto, and Dan asked for another bottle of Chianti and an extra glass.

When the antipasto arrived David paid little attention to it.

"Let's try to analyze the situation," he said, without even picking up his fork. "Either Heinz ran down Ailesly or he didn't. Are you with me?"

"I guess so," Maureen said. "Even though I am just a dumb lady lawyer." She gave a short but honest laugh.

"Now if Heinz ran down Ailesly, then something or someone made him do a sudden and complete about-face."

"Please explain," Dan said.

"From what you two tell me, Heinz is probably your secret informer. In that case he was ready to provide you with information that Handelsman didn't want you to obtain, and therefore made him unavailable for deposition."

"That makes sense," Maureen said.

"For Kleinwort to run down a potential star witness of yours means that he has switched sides, so to speak. Or. . . ."

"Or that he didn't run down Ailesly," Maureen interposed, "and his wallet was stolen."

"I think that is highly unlikely. Not without his knowledge." Dan said.

"I would agree with you," David said, and turned to Maureen. "What is the first thing you would do if your wallet were stolen?"

"I would call the Motor Vehicles Bureau and the various credit card companies."

"I assume that did not happen."

"So . . . what do you think did happen?" Dan asked.

"Right now, I don't know. One thing I do know is that time will provide us with an answer." Having said that, he at last turned his attention to the antipasto.

\* \* \*

David was right. Time did provide an answer and it came four days later.

Maureen had been working late trying to clear the most urgent items from her desk. First there was the matter of finishing the final draft of a statement to the court as to why the deposition of Dr. Heinz Kleinwort should proceed as originally requested—if and when the man could be found. She had also obtained copies of successful arguments against summary judgments, which she wanted to study before the forthcoming hearing in front of Judge Watson. There also was the matter of educating herself on the neurologic and behavioral effects of yohimbine. She had Betty go to the university library and copy a series of articles, which she planned to struggle through before going home.

It was past eight o'clock when the night secretary buzzed her.

"A call for you."

Knowing it was Dan, she took her time picking up the telephone. She was still angry and dissatisfied with him. When she finally answered, there was no one on the other line.

She was surprised, and a quick chill ran down her neck and across her back.

"Nerves," she muttered to herself, and decided to call it quits for the night. She stuffed the yohimbine papers into her briefcase to be studied at home, turned off the reading light on her desk, and left.

Traffic on Wilshire Boulevard was light and fifteen minutes later she drove into the garage of her apartment house. As usual it was deserted. She took her briefcase out of the back seat, locked the car, and went to the elevator. After a few steps she sensed that she was not alone in the garage. Acting against her better judgment, she stopped and looked around. There was no one in sight. As she buzzed for the elevator the feeling that she was being watched resurfaced. She turned and, with her back to the elevator door, surveyed the garage. There was no movement and no sound but the hum of the compressor and the whir of the descending elevator. The elevator arrived, and she heard the door open behind her. Before she had time to turn, her wrist was grabbed from behind, and she was pulled into the elevator.

"Be quiet and you'll be all right."

The doors closed on her.

"What the hell!"

"I told you to be quiet!"

With a sudden movement, she wrenched herself free and wheeled around to face her attacker. He was a rather small, pock-marked man with a bony face and intense eyes. He was hardly muscular and without the element of surprise there would have been no way that she could have been overpowered by him.

The elevator stopped at her floor and the door opened.

"Get out," the man ordered.

"What do you want?"

"I said get out."

"Who are you?"

"First open the apartment and let me in."

By then it was clear to Maureen that the man was unarmed, and since she felt more than a physical match to him, she opened the door of her apartment and let herself in. The man followed her inside.

"We have to talk," he said.

"You bet we do. I am a nervous wreck. Look what you did to my jacket. And I left my briefcase down in the garage."

"It can wait there. Let's sit down."

"What if I don't feel like sitting down?"

"That is your choice, Miss Durrell."

All at once Maureen knew who her attacker was.

"You are Dr. Kleinwort? Dr. Heinz Kleinwort."

"Correct. And you and Mr. Cosgrove have been anxious to talk to me."

"We have been. But that was no reason for you to give me the fright of my life." She rubbed her wrists, more as an expression of resentment than because Kleinwort had bruised them.

"I am sorry."

There was an airiness to Kleinwort's apology that infuriated her.

"Oh, for God's sake! Why didn't you simply call my office and make an appointment?"

"You know quite well that the way things are right now I can't reveal my whereabouts either to my employers or to the police."

"You didn't have to use force on me," Maureen said tersely.

"You're right. I was being overly dramatic. But you will agree that an occasion such as this does call for some drama."

"If that's how you see it." Maureen sighed and sank into the couch. Kleinwort was like no man she had ever met. She waved him to a chair. He followed her direction.

"I want to go through with my deposition," he said. "I will feel safer once I am done with it."

Maureen linked her fingers and reflected on how best to deal with the man who was sitting across from her. A deposition cannot be arranged on the spur of the moment. Particularly when the other side is unwilling to have the witness come forward.

"First, let's talk about Ailesly," she said. "Why did you run him down?"

"Who said I did?"

"The Stinson Beach police. They traced the rental car and found that you had used your driver's license to check it out."

"And to you that means that I killed him?"

"Unless you can provide me with a better explanation." She thought of the two alternatives presented by David.

"I can. And you must try to believe me."

"First, let's hear what it is."

"Let's see now. What day is today? I have lost all track of time."

"Tuesday, the twenty-second."

"Then it was three weeks ago that Berrich called me into his office. I don't know whether you are aware that I had told Al Lessing and all the other people in Marat management that at my forthcoming deposition I did not intend to confine myself to statistics, which is what they wanted me to do, but that I would disclose everything I knew about Dulcian."

"I bet they didn't go for that."

"They didn't."

* * *

Kleinwort was telling the truth. Three weeks ago he had been called into the office of Warren Berrich. His personnel file was on the desk.

"A few days ago, when we met with Mr. Handelsman," Berrich started out, "you told us that all your life you have been proud of your parents. That they serve as an example to you."

"They do. I want to follow in their footsteps. They always did what they knew was right."

"Does that include betraying their comrades to the Gestapo?"

"What do you mean?"

"Did they ever tell you about a resistance group called 'White Rose'?"

"That was the group they belonged to. My father was one of its organizers and leaders."

"Then I would like you to take a look at these documents."

Berrich opened the file in front of him and handed several sheets to Heinz. "This is a notarized English translation of the original document. If you prefer to read it in its German version, I can provide you with that as well."

Heinz started to read. "As you will see," Berrich said, "the former East German police took out an arrest warrant for a Dieter Kleinwort—he is your father, is he not?"

"Yes."

"And for Else Stroop Kleinwort. . . ."

"My mother. . . ."

"On the charges of having betrayed to the Nazi Gestapo the group called White Rose. . . ," Berrich started to read from the copy in front of him. "The leaders of the group included Professor Kurt

Huber, Father Franz Gruber, and Hans and Sophie Scholl, all of them prominent in the German underground. As a consequence of the information provided to the Gestapo by Dieter and Else Kleinwort, every member of White Rose was apprehended and summarily executed."

"My parents. . . ."

"I thought this information would be of interest to you."

"How did you get these papers?"

"We at Marat are fortunate to have had contacts in East Germany who provided them to us at the time you applied for a position with our company. As you well know, we are very thorough in our investigations of high-level personnel."

Kleinwort was dazed. "I can't believe this. . . ."

"Please feel free to look at the originals. Your German is far better than mine."

With an automatic movement Heinz reached for the papers and sifted through them, turning the pages back and forth in complete silence.

"You may wonder why the German police did not act on these documents after unification," Berrich said. "We have good contacts at the German Ministry of Justice, and as you can well imagine there was no need to cause embarrassment or pain to someone who up to recently has been of considerable value to our company. Now, however, that the situation has changed. . . ." Berrich chose to leave the rest unsaid.

"What can I do?"

"I was certain you would understand your position." Berrich's smile made his mouth look like a scar. "We have prepared an affidavit that we want you to sign. Once you have done so, these documents will return to your file. They will not be transmitted to the German police . . . is that clear?"

"They are old people."

"And they will live out their remaining years in freedom. Thanks to their son."

Heinz nodded. A few minutes later his affidavit was signed and notarized.

* * *

When Kleinwort had finished relating these events, Maureen got up and went into the dining room.

"Can I get you a drink? Some scotch? A sandwich?"

"A glass of wine will do."

She poured herself a glass of whiskey and brought an open bottle of white wine from the refrigerator.

"Help yourself," she said as she set down the bottle and a glass in front of Kleinwort.

"These have been the worst weeks of my life."

"I can imagine. To say the least, those people are playing hardball. Now then, what about Ailesly? Did they make you run him down?"

"No."

"You gave the rental agency your driver's license."

"I haven't been to San Francisco in months. . . . I am not a killer . . . but then, I don't know what I am anymore. Everything has become. . . ."

One hand clung to the stem of his wineglass. With the other hand he groped the air as if he were trying to reach for the appropriate phrase with which to finish his sentence. "A copy of my driver's license is in my file as well. They keep one for every employee. It doesn't take much technology to apply a transposed photo to it."

"I am sure it doesn't. Why didn't you go to the police and give yourself up?"

"I don't know. When I heard from a neighbor at the apartment house where I used to live that the police were looking for me and that I was wanted for murder, I must have gone out of my mind. It reminded me of the stories I heard about Nazi Germany. Innocent people being picked up in the middle of the night, never to be seen again. I packed a few things, threw them into the trunk of my car, and drove out West. I didn't know what I was doing except that I had to escape."

Maureen got up and, glass in hand, paced up and down the living room.

"So why have you come to see me?"

Kleinwort drank slowly and thoughtfully. "As I said to you, I am ready to testify. I have decided that my parents will have to fend for themselves."

"Is that what you really want to do?"

"Yes. Two wrongs don't make a right. Look, I have spent many sleepless nights in a series of depressing motels thinking this over, and I just want to go ahead and get everything behind me. I want to start a new life. Somehow . . . somewhere."

He fingered the buttons of his shirt.

"A number of people at Marat have the data on the Phase II studies," he said. "There would have been no reason to go to such lengths to prevent Ailesly from testifying about them."

"So what did he know that worried Marat?"

"He probably had some data from the Phase I studies. Which I have as well. Would you like to hear about them?"

"Sure. But first I'm going to call Mike. I want him to be in on this."

"I knew it was you, girl," Mike said when he got on the line. "What's up?"

"A lot." She filled him in. "I want him to come over to our office the first thing in the morning."

"What time?"

"Let's make it at eight. The three of us can decide where to go from here. And we'll have to get him a good lawyer. He'll need one when he goes to the police."

"Right."

"Thanks for everything," Kleinwort said when Maureen returned. "In case you want to get in touch with me, I have checked in at the Cahuenga Motel under the name of Erich Winkler. It's not a place I would recommend to my friends. I have already seen three cockroaches in my bathroom, and the night is still young."

He tossed down his wine and left.

\* \* \*

It was Betty who brought Maureen the news.

Maureen came in early and was waiting for Kleinwort to arrive when Betty rushed into her office.

"Did you see it on TV this morning?"

"What?"

"They killed Dr. Kleinwort. The police cornered him in a mini-mall and shot him dead before he had a chance to surrender to them."

"You mean our Dr. Kleinwort?"

"That's right. They came to his motel to arrest him and apparently he slipped away from them. A short time later they tracked him down to a mini-mall a couple of blocks away. That's where they shot him."

"He was unarmed."

"That's what they said on TV. Apparently the police were real upset about that. They claimed they had received an anonymous phone call warning them that the man was armed and that he was crazy and dangerous."

"Oh, Betty . . . he was over to my apartment last night . . . he is . . . was strange, but not crazy. I'll vouch for that. In fact, I was beginning to like him."

Mike took the news badly. At first he cursed the L.A. police in words that echoed his Irish boyhood on the streets of Boston, then he turned on Maureen.

"Why the hell didn't you tell me last night? If I had known that the cops were tracking him down, I could have put him up at my place."

"How should I have known?"

"Come on, girl, don't you ever have any foresight?" Then all at once he became despondent and sank into himself.

"Okay," he said. "We've lost it. There is no way we can ever put our case together. I am ready to call it quits and go to St. Columba."

St. Columba was Mike's country home in Connemara, in the West of Ireland. He had purchased it several years ago, with a view of having it as his second home or a place to retire; these days he barely managed to spend more than one week a year there.

"I disagree," Maureen said.

"Listen, girl, I've been in this business much longer than you have. When I get dealt a bad set of cards, I fold. The sooner the better."

"I am going to contest defense motion for summary judgment, with or without your help." Maureen was determined to make a brave show of it.

"You are not going any further with this. Not with my money."

"Then I'll use mine. I know we still have a good case. . . ."

"With no living witnesses. For God's sake, Maureen, you don't know when to give up."

"I don't. It's something I've learned from you and Tom."

She was rewarded with a weak smile.

"For starters, I am going to depose Dr. Rose."

"He won't give you the time of day."

"He will have to. I am going to call him as a percipient witness." That meant that he would be asked to testify as to the facts of the case without being expected to render an opinion.

"You can't, you don't know his patient's name. Without knowing that, you can't prove that he has seen him."

"I'll get his name."

"How?"

"Don't worry. I'll figure it out." Although at that moment she did not have the slightest idea how to go about it.

"You better do it fast. Before the court grants defense their new motion for summary judgment."

"The hearing isn't for another two weeks. It was going to be this Monday, but, thank God, Handelsman can't make it because of the Jewish New Year."

"And you are going to depose Rose within the next two weeks?"

"No reason I can't. And if Cosgrove and Costello won't pay my fare to Boston, I'll pay for it myself."

"Boy, are you getting to be a feisty lady! I wouldn't want to be married to you."

"Likewise."

For the next few days, Maureen read as much about the Kleinwort shooting as she could find in the papers. The full investigation called for by the Police Commissioner had uncovered little more than what was known immediately following the incident. Dr. Kleinwort had been struck by six bullets fired by officers from two of the three squad cars, which had surrounded him in the mini-mall. Based on a phone call received at headquarters earlier that night, the police who had been sent to the Cahuenga Motel to arrest Kleinwort had cause to believe that they were dealing with a man who was armed and dangerous.

Despite a fair bit of investigation, no one could trace the source of this anonymous call.

\* \* \* \* \*

THREE weeks had elapsed since Marty had returned from the Gordon Conference, three weeks that seemed like a lifetime to him, for during that brief period he had undergone a complete transformation.

"Anything wrong?" Colin Pearson asked him after Tuesday morning Grand Rounds. The two of them were walking down the hill from the hospital for a quick lunch at a Mexican restaurant.

"I've been fretting about my research."

"From what I've heard, it's going well."

"Not really. We've been having problems with purifying our antibodies."

Actually this was no longer the case. After a considerable amount of labor-intensive work, his two Japanese post-docs had managed to once again obtain reproducible data. In a week or so the revised version of his paper would be ready for resubmission to the *Journal of Neuroscience*.

"I think I am entering my midlife crisis." Marty tried to speak lightly.

"A bit early for you, isn't it?"

A picture of Malvina flashed through Marty's mind. He managed to push it aside, only to have the business with Dulcian reassert itself in all its permutations.

"Shit," Marty said aloud, and shook his head as if a fly had settled on his temple. Colin gave him a puzzled look.

"What did you think of Grand Rounds?" he asked.

"It's the third one this year we've had on Alzheimer's. I am getting bored with the topic."

"Me too, but the more I get to know Jack, the more impressed I am with him. At first I thought he was just another neuro-politi-cian. . . ."

"He is not," Marty snapped.

"That's just what I was going to say."

"Then say it! Don't beat around the bush!"

"What is the matter with you, Marty? You are not your old self."

Marty remained silent. For much of the remainder of their lunch—chicken fajitas washed down with iced tea—the conversation revolved around Colin's PET scanner, his need to recruit a junior faculty member who was an expert in functional MR imaging, and the fact that Jack had at long last managed to secure the necessary funds for renovating the B floor and moving the PET scanner from radiology to neurology.

When at one point the talk returned to midlife crisis and impotence, Marty commented that he had read that a number of psychiatrists who were prescribing Dulcian for depression had noted that impotence also was improved.

"Don't you think that this was because their depression was lifted?" Colin asked.

"That's too facile an explanation," Marty said. "I think that Dulcian has other, less well explored properties. They could well open up a whole new market for the drug."

"Such as?"

"I don't think this is an appropriate time to talk about it," Marty said, and sunk into deep thought.

While they were waiting for their separate checks, an idea, which had hovered within Marty for quite some time, materialized and came out into the open.

"The miraculous comes for those who await it," he said aloud.

Colin was taken aback. No one he knew talked like that. Uncertain how to respond, he ignored the remark.

\* \* \*

Later, however, after the ensuing events had taken their course, Colin would say, to whomever cared to listen, that the last time he had lunch with Marty he appeared preoccupied and stressed out.

"He would say things that made no sense." When asked for an example, he tried to repeat Marty's statement about waiting for the miraculous, but the intervening time had made him forget its exact wording.

\* \* \*

The secretary's voice came through on the intercom.

"There is a Mr. Toru Shimizu who wants to have a word with you." Marty picked up the telephone. He was just about to go to his laboratory, and a phone call from an unknown Japanese was the last thing he wanted to deal with this afternoon.

"Dr. DiChiro here," he snapped.

"I am profoundly sorry to be bothering you, Dr. DiChiro, but I would like to take a few minutes of your precious time in order to meet with you."

"Not now."

"Of course not. That would be most presumptuous of me. Would tomorrow be better?"

"Oh, God," Marty mumbled, and standing at his desk, he turned the page of his calendar. "I can meet with you at seven-thirty in the morning. In my office. For no longer than twenty minutes."

"It will be my pleasure."

"Can you tell me what this is all about?"

"Not over the telephone."

When Marty arrived at his office the following morning, he found a small Japanese man already waiting for him in the hall outside. The man was dressed in a navy blue pin-striped suit with a tie dotted in pink and silver. He was wearing rimless glasses, and his dark hair was streaked with gray. At his feet was an expensive looking black leather attaché case.

"I am sorry to make demands on your time," the man said, and having bowed, handed Marty his card. Marty looked at it.

"Toru Shimizu. Director of Operations. Nitansha Pharmaceuticals." The back of the card was in Japanese.

He motioned Shimizu into his office. A chair by the side of his desk was waiting for the visitor.

"What a lovely family, Dr. DiChiro." He motioned to the silver-framed family photo on Marty's desk.

Marty nodded his thanks.

"So, Mr. Shimizu. What brings you to America?"

"A matter of business."

"That is usually the case."

"Can we speak without being disturbed?"

"Yes. My secretary does not arrive until eight."

"Good. I have been told that you have an interest in drugs that are used to treat depression." The visitor's English was nearly perfect.

"Yes."

"Specifically, that you have been working on Dulcian. I also have been informed that you are concerned about the drug's side reactions. That you have found many patients in whom it has induced a dramatic and irreversible change in personality."

"Who told you that?"

"Reliable sources."

"That means nothing to me. Can you be more specific?"

"Not this morning. If I may beg your indulgence, I would first like to finish what I have come here to tell you."

"Go on, then."

"Those same reliable sources also have informed me that you are in a predicament as to how to best respond to these side reactions, which you consider to be so severe as to be unacceptable. You also recognize that Marat International is a rich and powerful organization and you are unwilling to risk antagonizing them."

"You are indeed well informed."

"Thank you. In fact, this has become a serious moral issue with you."

"Now wait a minute," Marty broke in, "how did you hear about that? I have told no one."

"No, Dr. DiChiro. You have told someone. . . ."

"Malvina. . . ."

The visitor nodded. "One of our . . . consultants. Our company has found that we are able to obtain a considerable amount of information about our competitors through a worldwide network of informants—strategically placed and loyal. You see, an alert stewardess is invaluable . . . and inconspicuous."

Marty had wondered about the origin of Malvina's ruby ring and had attributed it to a generous boyfriend. Now he knew where it came from. He glanced at the card that his visitor had handed him. "This is your company?"

"Nitansha Pharmaceuticals. We are the second largest producer of psychotropic drugs in the world. Second only to Marat International."

"Ah, yes. You are the people who are working on a new drug that is related to trazodone."

"You, too, are well informed, Dr. DiChiro. But I must come to the main reason of why I am here to see you. Nitansha Pharmaceuticals is prepared to offer you a position on the board of their senior management. The actual title would be Vice President of Discovery Research, and you would be in charge of our American Research Laboratories. Since our company is in the process of opening American headquarters in Petropolis—that is a few miles outside of Rio de Janeiro—we would like you to be based there. I expect that you would prefer such an assignment to a similar one in Tokyo."

"I am astounded."

"I am not surprised. You are confronted by a big decision, Dr. DiChiro, and Nitansha Pharmaceuticals does not expect an immediate response. May I assure you that your future salary and working conditions would be far superior to current ones."

Marty felt as he did one night many years earlier, when he was awakened by a rushing noise and found an angel with phosphorescent wings hovering over the foot of his bed. A dream had become transmuted into reality. Not to be questioned, but accepted as his due.

"What about my research on circadian rhythms?"

"Our company will be honored to have a man of your caliber continue his work under our auspices. Nitansha Pharmaceuticals believes that the creation of fine science depends on giving the greatest scientific minds an arena in which to express themselves."

"I shall keep that in mind and give your proposal considerable thought."

"Thank you, Dr. DiChiro. That is all we can ask from you at this moment. I shall be at the Peninsula Hotel until Friday. Should you come to a decision before then, please contact me there. If not, my card has the telephone number of the Tokyo office. Our board meeting is scheduled to be held in two weeks, on October 7, and we would appreciate hearing from you by then, one way or another."

* * *

For the next several days Marty kept the job offer to himself. Until he had time to fully dispel the air of unreality that it had for him, he saw no reason to discuss it with Jeanette, who would undoubtedly become frantic at the prospect of once more moving the family, this time to South America, to a country whose language and customs were totally foreign to her. At various times of the day, he would take out from his wallet the card Shimizu had given him, look at it, and run his finger along its edges. If the card was real, the offer he received had to be as well.

As he had been scheduled to participate in the meeting of the Advanced Studies Institute on Circadian Rhythms, Marty flew into Tucson for the weekend. There he was expected to give a presentation in which he reviewed the cellular mechanisms of circadian clocks.

It was a small meeting, with no more than fifty participants, and since Marty had prepared a similar lecture for a different gathering some three months earlier, he had little work to do and considerable time for reflection.

By the time he boarded the plane for his return flight to Los Angeles, he had arrived at a decision. If Jeanette proved to be even minimally amenable to living in Brazil, he would accept the offer and move family and as many of his laboratory personnel as possible down there. Since his two Japanese post-docs, who carried the major weight of his research effort, would undoubtedly be eager to accept a position with a highly respected firm such as Nitansha, he was certain his work would be interrupted for only a short time.

What if Jeanette would not even consider such a move? Although this was a likely scenario, Marty put it aside for the time being. He had sufficient faith in his angel, now that he had reappeared to him, to postpone thinking about that possibility until it actually had presented itself.

Marty retrieved his car from the airport parking lot and drove home. As soon as he opened the door, he realized that the house appeared strangely silent. His first thought was that Jeanette had taken the children to the Brentwood Country Fair, or some similar event, and would bring them back in time for dinner.

He set down the bag in the hallway and climbed the stairs to the bedroom. The bed had been neatly made, and there was a letter addressed to him pinned to the bedspread.

He opened the envelope and unfolded the paper inside.

"Dear Marty," he read. "I know it reflects on my own shortcomings, but I can no longer live with you. Ever since we came to Los Angeles I felt as if I were in a foreign country. I have tried to reach out to you on ever so many occasions, but you were always absent—physically or emotionally.

"I have therefore decided to take the children and myself back to Boston, and we will stay with my parents for the time being.

"I know this is not the right way to solve the problems that have arisen between us, but it is the only way I am capable of.

"Jeanette."

Marty put down the letter and stared at the closet. Only now did he realize that the door was open and that Jeanette's clothes were gone.

He sat down on the bed. As he unlaced his shoes, his emotions oscillated between outrage at Jeanette's desertion and confusion as to what to do.

\* \* \* \* \*

THE letter arrived Monday morning. It was addressed to Maureen in neat, angular handwriting and was marked "Personal and Confidential," twice underlined in red pencil. Charlotte brought it into Maureen's office unopened and handed it to her.

"It feels bulky," she said. "What do you think is in it?"

"A letter bomb . . . from Marat."

"For God's sake, don't open it! I'll call the police."

"You don't need to. It's from Dr. Kleinwort. I can tell from the handwriting."

"But he was killed."

"Obviously he mailed it before he died."

Despite her reassurance to Charlotte, Maureen opened the letter a bit more gingerly than she would under normal circumstances and removed a sheet of notepaper and a 3-inch floppy disk. With Charlotte standing over her, the two women read the note.

"Dear Miss Durrell.

"I can see that the police have started to stake out the motel. I must therefore mail this disk before I am picked up by them. It contains all the material on the Phase I study that I was privy to. Tell your friend Mike that I am innocent and would appreciate his help.

273

"Thank you, H.K."

Since Mike was in Chicago addressing a meeting of the Illinois Trial Lawyers Association, an unavoidable commitment he had made several months earlier, Maureen picked up the phone to call Dan. She reached him at his clinic in Los Virgenes. In a few words she told him about Kleinwort's letter.

"I am dying to see what's on the disk," she said.

"So am I."

"Your computer or mine?" she laughed.

"Yours," Dan said. "I would hate to have Marty walk in on us while we are looking at the data."

"Come on over here as soon as you are finished."

"It'll be late."

"Don't worry. I'll be here."

* * *

The disk contained a database file into which had been entered the report forms of all subjects—59 of them—who had been enrolled in the Phase I studies for MI-37801, later known as Dulcian.

The database was fairly standard. Basic information had been entered on the subjects, who were identified only by code number. The information included age, height, weight, blood pressure, and previous medical history, which usually was none, for these were intended to be healthy controls. There also were fields for the dosage of MI-37801, the duration over which the drug had been given, and other concurrently taken medications. Finally, three fields had been set aside for adverse responses: immediate, medium-term, and long-term, which in this instance meant adverse responses that developed after more than two months from when the drug was first given to the subjects.

The pair scrutinized the data slowly and methodically.

Two hours later they were forced to conclude that they had found nothing out of the ordinary.

"So what's all the fuss about?" Maureen asked.

"I don't know. Let's print out everything. Perhaps we can see something we missed."

When they did print out the data they found to their surprise that there were no records for subject I-16.

"One record has been deleted from the database," Dan said.

"What do you think happened to it?"

"Maybe it is somewhere else on the disk."

But the directory listed only one file. The one that contained the records of 58 out of 59 subjects who had been enrolled in the Phase I study.

"What would happen if someone had separated the record of subject I-16 and then had erased it?" Maureen asked. "Would it be gone permanently?"

"Not necessarily. There are a number of unerase programs. I am certain I could borrow one from David."

He phoned David, who indeed had such a program and was happy to lend it to Dan.

"Maureen and I will be right over," Dan said.

"Now? It's ten o'clock. Can't it wait until tomorrow?"

"No. This is far too important."

An hour later, after a quick drive to David's apartment in Santa Monica, the two of them were back at the computer, installing David's unerase program. Before too long the disk, which up to then showed only one file in its directory, now had three files—the original file and two new ones—which the directory now listed as #-16, and #emo.

"Number 16 must be the record we are looking for," Maureen said.

Indeed it was.

The subject was male, aged 22. He had a negative past medical history and no concurrent or past drug intake. The daily dosages of MI-37801 that he had taken were 5, 10, and 15 mg over three successive two-week periods. There were no immediate side reactions, but under medium-term and long-term reactions, both fields read: "Outbursts of unprovoked anger. Has become violent for no apparent reason. Feels that he has lost control over himself."

"Wow!" Maureen said. "Exactly like your angry puppet patients."

"This has to be the same man who is being followed by John Rose. . . ."

"And who was seen by Jack Brennan before him. Except that Brennan said that the man had been a long-term abuser of yohimbine."

"The records say nothing about yohimbine. They specifically state that there was no prior drug intake."

"Right."

"What must have happened is that this man's adverse reaction was noted in his file, but then someone removed his record before submitting the Phase I studies to the FDA with subjects renumbered as I-1 to I-58."

"So instead of submitting the records on 59 subjects, there were only 58 subjects in the Phase I study. I can have Betty check this in the morning. We have been provided with all the documents submitted by Marat to the FDA as a backup for their new drug application."

"I wonder what's in the other file," Dan said. "Let's look at it."

Dan closed file #-16 and opened #emo.

As they had both suspected, it contained a memo:

From: Dr. Albert Lessing

To: R.J. Crowley

Subject: FDA application, MI-37801.

Jack Brennan has asked for $500,000 to implement departmental improvements at Tufts. I think we should give it to him. We have already motivated him to obtain favorable results, and, thanks to his input, we have been able to close out our Phase I studies on MI-37801 on schedule, and can now start to enroll subjects into our Phase II and III studies, which should be completed within 18 months.

Let me have your response as soon as you can arrive at a decision.

"Wow!" Maureen said. "What do you think the connection is between this memo and the records on subject I-16?"

"I think we can both guess."

"I wish we could get I-16's name. Once we have that we can depose his treating physicians. And that would include Jack Brennan."

"I'd love to see you or Mike depose that man."

"I bet you would. From what you have told me about him, he sounds slimy."

"He is driven by the lust for power."

"Right."

"Are you hungry?"

"A bit," Maureen said. "I'm much too tired to cook. It's nearly midnight. How about going down to Clifton's for a hamburger?"

"Sounds fine to me."

The two of them were the only customers in the white-tiled, brightly lit coffee shop around the corner from Maureen's office. They settled themselves into a booth facing Wilshire Boulevard and placed their orders. Traffic was sparse by then, and at first they both were too emotionally drained to talk.

The waitress brought out two plates with hamburgers and French fries. "Ketchup or brown sauce?"

They opted for ketchup and a diet Pepsi, which they shared.

After a few bites, Dan looked up at Maureen and pointed to the trickle of ketchup on her upper lip.

"I must be a mess," she said, licking her lip.

"Not a bit—just lovable." He smiled and, feeling his closeness, she relaxed.

"What a pair of night owls we are," she said.

After they finished the hamburgers, they felt better.

"I wonder whether the FDA has the code for the patients who were enrolled in the Phase I study," Dan said. "You could get it from them under the Freedom of Information Act."

"Sure I could. In a year or two. Except that we need to notice the deposition of the treating physicians before we go before Judge Watson. If we don't, we're finished with our discovery phase."

"Shall we call it quits?" Dan suggested.

"About time," she said and took his hand.

"Let's get our cars."

"Your place or mine?"

"Your place is much closer."

"Okay, but I won't promise anything."

"Neither will I."

A few minutes later as Dan and Maureen were driving down Wilshire Boulevard in their separate cars, each of them was wondering how to obtain the name of subject I-16. It turned out to be a simpler task than they had expected.

\* \* \*

A couple days later Dan received a phone call from Sue Barton.

"Do you remember me, Dr. Lerner?"

"Of course I do. How are you doing with your organization?"

"Very well. We decided to call ourselves FAD, that stands for Families Against Dulcian. Last week we received approval of our nonprofit status. Now we can start to raise money to lobby in Washington and get the FDA to withdraw Dulcian from the market. I wanted to tell you that we saw you on the Channel 4 News, and you looked terrific. We got quite a lot of calls from families and doctors all over the country as a result of that program."

"Sounds as if you are moving ahead."

"I know we are. Some of us started to compile a list of people who were damaged by taking Dulcian. If you saw the number of names on it, you would be impressed. We have become a force. We are no longer powerless victims who are battling the two most powerful segments of our society, the pharmaceutical industry and the insurance companies."

"Why the insurance companies?"

"Don't you know? They think Dulcian is the best thing that happened to their profits. They see it as the least expensive way to treat a depressed patient. Primary care physicians can administer the drug, which makes it much cheaper than having him being treated by a psychiatrist. By the way, while I think of it, there is a doctor who called me about a patient she thinks was damaged by Dulcian that I wasn't sure about. Would you have time to speak to her?"

"Of course. What's her name?"

"It's a Dr. Sunika Patel and she works at McLean State Hospital."

"Sunika Patel. The name is familiar."

"She called you a few months ago, but you never returned her call."

"How unlike me."

"She says that she is taking care of a young man who has had the same condition that you described in your paper. But he has had it for more than two years."

"That is much longer than any of the other cases we have run into."

"I know. That's why I wanted you to talk to her. Arnold didn't begin to show his strange behavior until the end of last year, and you said he was the first case you saw."

"I will call Dr. Patel. Do you have her number?"

Sue Barton gave Dr. Patel's number to Dan, and after a few more minutes—it was always difficult to get Sue off the telephone—Dan phoned McLean State Hospital and asked for Dr. Patel.

When the doctor came on the line, Dan apologized for not having returned her call.

"I can readily understand, Dr. Lerner. You have become a very famous person." Her voice was like that of a chipmunk. "We here at McLean have a young man who has all the signs of your syndrome. He was brought in by his family because they no longer could manage his outbursts. But between his attacks he is very nice and cooperative, and very unhappy that he cannot control his behavior. Now, Dr. Lerner, you will be interested in this. He says that three years ago he volunteered for a research program to try out a new drug that was going to be used against depression. At that time he was an undergraduate student at Tufts."

"Tufts!" Dan could not believe that he had heard correctly.

"Yes. In his second year. He told me what he was majoring in, but I have forgotten."

"What's his name?"

"Todd Schafer. He has been with us since April. His parents were afraid he might kill himself or become violent in some other way, so they persuaded him to sign himself in on a voluntary basis. He has very good insight into his behavior, but when these episodes come on, there is nothing he can do to stop them."

"I would like to fly out and see him."

"We would love to have you. I will speak to our director and see if he can arrange for you to give us a noon seminar. You can talk about the Angry Puppet Syndrome. I know you will have a large audience."

\* \* \*

"If you will wait here, I will see if I can bring Todd down from his crafts activities."

A male nurse in faded blue jeans and a white shirt with sleeves rolled up to the elbows showed Dan into the third floor day room at McLean Hospital.

In spite of the effort that must have gone into making the room appear as cheerful as possible, the outcome was a forlorn appearance. Everything had an undusted, desolate look. This included the books and magazines that lay scattered about, an upright piano that sat neglected in a dark corner, and the television set topped by a vase that held a bouquet of crimson plastic tulips. The pictures that hung on the pastel peach walls, although undoubtedly intended to induce a tranquilizing effect, appeared to have been crucified into their positions. Only the view through the dirty windows, across sunlit rolling hills in their early autumn amber and olive foliage, had anything to recommend it.

From down the corridor a man's voice sounded, rising and falling. The words were indistinguishable to Dan, but their sound frightened him; they held an irrational, uncontrollable anger.

Before long the attendant returned, escorting Todd Schafer.

"This is Todd." Todd was in his mid-twenties, with a pale oval face and a day's stubble of beard. "This is the doctor from California who wants to talk to you."

As Todd sank into a chair, a smile came over his face. It was an expression that Dan knew well by now, having seen the same expression on Mr. Arnold Barton, Mrs. Greenhall, and the several other patients with the Angry Puppet Syndrome whom he had encountered over the intervening months.

"I've been told about you," Todd said. "You're interested in whatever it is that has hit me. Let me tell you, man, it's shitty." He went on to describe his symptoms. They were identical to those Dan had already heard many times. What interested him more was whether Todd had been on yohimbine, as John Rose had claimed. He questioned Todd, who denied ever taking any drugs, except a bit of pot off and on during his freshman year. Finally Dan asked him specifically.

"Yohimbine? What on earth is that?"

"It is a drug that's supposed to turn you on, give you a great erection."

"Was I supposed to have taken that? That's a joke. Or better yet . . . it's an insult. Now, of course, it's another matter. They've got me so sedated I couldn't care less if Sharon Stone walked in stark naked."

He stared at the floor. "What's going to happen to me, Dr. Lerner? Is this the way I am going to be the rest of my life?"

"I don't know."

"If you don't know, who the hell does? The way I feel now I can't leave here. I am scared to. When I was home, I nearly killed my girlfriend. Banged her head against the wall . . . they had to take her to the hospital. We were great pals, but when that thing came over me . . . I couldn't help myself. It's a bitch!"

"I know." It was the best Dan could come up with.

When the nurse came to pick Todd up for his afternoon group therapy session, Dan took out a pad and made some notes. They were to help Maureen with her deposition of John Rose.

\* \* \*

John Rose's deposition turned out to be brief and scarcely worth Maureen's flight to Boston. As it was, Handelsman had delegated Bruce Crawford to attend, an indication that he did not attach much importance to the proceedings. Since the doctor's office was far too cramped to allow the presence of two attorneys and the court reporter, the deposition was held in the George A. Kellogg Conference Room.

After the doctor had been sworn in, Maureen quickly established that following his examination of Todd, he had prepared a report to the referring physician at the Student Health Clinic. In this report he summarized the young man's medical history—including the fact that he had been a chronic abuser of yohimbine—and described his current neurologic symptoms, which he labeled as episodic discontrol–like behavior. In the report there was no mention of Todd having been given MI-37801.

After Dr. Rose had finished reading the letter and his original medical notes into the record, and Maureen had asked him to clarify a few terms that a potential jury might not understand, she turned to the question of the yohimbine intake.

"Doctor, in your letter to the referring physician you did not make note that Todd Schafer was one of the subjects enrolled in the Phase I study for Dulcian, a drug that in those days went by the name MI-37801. Why is that?"

"Because I did not consider it to be of significance."

"I see. And when you say 'significance,' do you mean significance as to causing the young man's neuropsychological problems, specifically his attacks that you have termed episodic discontrol–like behavior?"

"Yes."

"And why did you not consider this man's intake of MI-37801 to be of significance?"

"Because of the known neurologic effects of chronic yohimbine intake, which I believe fully explained this young man's condition."

"Now, Doctor, you tell me, and you so stated in your letter to the referring physician, that Todd Schafer was a chronic abuser of the drug yohimbine. Is that correct?"

"Yes."

"Did you obtain this information from Mr. Schafer?"

"No."

"From where or from whom did you obtain this information?"

"From the neurologist who had evaluated Mr. Schafer on one previous occasion."

"Who was this neurologist?"

"Dr. Jack Brennan."

"Is this the same Dr. Jack Brennan who is currently chairman of neurology in California?"

"The same."

"And from where or from whom did Dr. Brennan obtain that information?"

"You will have to ask him."

"You mean to say that you simply accepted Dr. Brennan's insinuation that. . . ."

Crawford raised his hand. Up to then he had sat quietly at the far end of the conference table.

"I object. The word 'insinuation' is argumentative."

"I will rephrase my question. Dr. Rose, do you mean to tell me that you accepted Dr. Brennan's history of Todd Schafer's yohimbine intake without further questioning Dr. Brennan?"

"Yes."

"Did you at least question Todd Schafer about his yohimbine intake?"

"I did."

"And what did Mr. Schafer tell you?"

"He denied it."

"He denied it?"

"Yes."

"And you chose to disbelieve him. . . ."

"Objection."

"I shall withdraw my question." Maureen rummaged through her legal pads, turned a few pages back and forth, and looked at Bruce Crawford. He was evidently uncomfortable with Dr. Rose's responses to her last few questions, and it gave her a small sense of accomplishment for having put him into that state.

As the two lawyers walked to their rented cars in the south parking lot of Tufts University School of Medicine, Maureen turned to Crawford.

"We're going to have to depose Dr. Brennan."

"You won't be able to. Allan has already prepared a motion for summary judgment, which he will present to the judge this Thursday."

"You know we are going to fight it."

"Be my guest."

\* \* \*

The intervening six months had not done much to change federal court. If anything, the bailiff's belly was even more prominent than it had been, and the court reporter was wearing the same faded gray suit and paisley tie that he had worn on the previous occasion.

"Mr. Handelsman," Judge Watson started out, after going through the usual preliminaries, "I have read your brief in support of a summary judgment. Anything you would like to add to it?"

"Yes, Your Honor. Plaintiffs have deposed all of Marat's key personnel. Even though these depositions have been conducted at considerable cost to the defense and have disrupted the normal working conditions at Marat, plaintiffs have come up with absolutely no evidence to show that Dulcian was not subjected to the strictest testing procedures ever devised and that these procedures were not monitored carefully at every step before submitting the necessary documents to the FDA. Plaintiffs also have failed to show that Dulcian is responsible for what they so poetically call the Angry Puppet Syndrome; in fact, they even have failed to show that such a syndrome exists. At this point any further depositions are a total waste of time, and we respectfully move for summary judgment."

"Thank you, Mr. Handelsman. As always, you are clear and succinct. Can I now hear from you, Mr. Cosgrove?"

Mike got up and, after a quick movement of his hand through locks of already unruly hair, started out.

"As Your Honor already knows, our case has been seriously hampered by the unexpected loss of two of our key witnesses. . . ."

"I have read your brief, Mr. Cosgrove. Is there anything you care to add to it?"

"It is plaintiffs' position that discovery has not been completed, and we therefore would like permission of the court to depose at least one more witness."

Handelsman jumped forward. "Your Honor, Dr. Jack Brennan, the witness whom plaintiffs would like to depose, was never listed by them. It is clear to me that they are on a fishing expedition and are desperately hoping to find some lapse in our testing procedure, something on which they could hang their hat in order to piece a case together at a point when it has become clear that their evidence is too paltry for the court to allow their litigation to proceed."

Judge Watson turned to Mike. "I understand that you had noticed Dr. Kleinwort's deposition prior to his death. Would you consider Dr. Brennan to be a satisfactory substitute for Dr. Kleinwort?"

Mike quickly knew which way the wind was blowing, and that by allowing plaintiffs to depose Jack Brennan, Judge Watson was precluding any chance for them to appeal his pending decision for summary judgment.

"Yes, I would, Your Honor," he said without taking a breath.

"Your Honor, Dr. Brennan's expertise is in neurology; Dr. Kleinwort's was in statistics. There is no way that Dr. Brennan could be a substitute for Dr. Kleinwort."

"Well, I don't want them to start looking around for a substitute at this late date. I want this case to be over as soon as possible. If it has as little merit as you are trying to make me understand it has, then I want this case closed. Mr. Cosgrove, I will allow you to depose Dr. Brennan, and then unless plaintiffs uncover any new and significant evidence, I will allow you, Mr. Handelsman, to renew your motion for summary judgment."

Handelsman nodded in agreement.

"What about you, Mr. Cosgrove? Is this acceptable to you?"

"I suppose it will have to be."

Mike stepped back from the bench and sat down behind the plaintiffs' table. A few moments later, he slumped forward. He remained motionless in that position long enough for Maureen, who had stood next to him through the entire hearing, to realize something was wrong. Handelsman, Crawford, and the defense entourage were packing up when she bent down over him.

"Mike . . . are you all right?"

"No."

"What's wrong?"

"I feel horrible. Like there is a weight on my chest. Not pain though . . . not pain . . . I think I am having a heart attack."

He was right, and an hour or so later he was resting fairly comfortably in the coronary care unit of University Hospital.

\* \* \*

Maureen went there to visit Mike three days before Jack Brennan's deposition. By then Mike had been transferred out of the coronary care unit into a semiprivate room and was free of much of the array of plastic tubings and monitors, which Maureen had always found intimidating. When she came in, she found Mike in bed. He looked pale and ill and considerably older than she had remembered him. Ilona got up from a chair by the window. She too appeared to have aged since Maureen had last met her at Cosgrove and Costello's Christmas party.

"Would you like me to leave?" Ilona asked Mike.

"Hell, no."

But she left nevertheless, announcing that she would go down to the cafeteria and be back in fifteen minutes.

"Say, girl," Mike said, after Ilona had gone, "thanks for stopping by to see me. Pull up a chair and tell me what's been happening at the office." The words were there all right, but the voice had lost its glitter.

Maureen related a bit of gossip—Betty's new boyfriend, Larry's planning to go to the South of France for Christmas. Mike interrupted her.

"What's going on with the Dulcian case?"

"I'm getting ready to depose Dr. Brennan. Dan's been a great help to me with some of the questions. And so has his friend Dr. Carter. Remember him. He is back in Boston. I sent Chris Bartlett out there to work with him." She was reluctant to go into any details for fear of upsetting Mike.

"I feel like I have abandoned everyone. I worry that Handelsman will be too much for you."

"Gee, thanks."

"Sorry to be so blunt. But when one is where I am, it becomes presumptuous not to speak the truth." He sighed and adjusted his pillows. "Well, girl, you are on your own. If you make it, you get all the glory, and if you don't . . . don't fret. We'll have other fish to fry." He laughed.

A laugh that hovered on the brink of tears.

\* \* \*

The Bruce and Wilma Harper Conference Room on the first floor of the medical school was sufficiently large to accommodate the four lawyers involved in Dr. Brennan's deposition. Although quite new, having been renovated with a recent grant to the department of neurology from Marat International, the oakwood shelves, filled with old books and journals, conveyed the look of permanence and learning that had always been the image of the university.

Maureen arrived early. She took out several ring binders from her case and sorted out the yellow legal pads that contained the various pathways along which she intended to question the doctor.

At precisely ten o'clock, Jack Brennan arrived in the company of Handelsman, Crawford, and Townsend. They each took their places.

Jack was in his sparkling white, lightly starched Grand Rounds coat, with his reflex hammer protruding from the side pocket.

"Good morning," he nodded graciously, and the thin-lipped, automatic smile crept across his face.

Maureen responded to his nod and turned to the court reporter.

"Please swear in the witness."

This was duly accomplished. The smile remained on Jack's face.

Maureen felt the tips of her fingers turning cold. Clearing her throat, she told herself to relax and, hearing Bernice's voice, asked herself what the worst thing was that could happen to her.

After a few preliminary questions, she came to the central point of the deposition.

"Dr. Brennan, did you at any time see in consultation a Todd Schafer?"

"I am afraid I don't remember."

"Then I would like to show you a note."

"May I see this first," Handelsman interrupted. He looked at the note and returned it to Maureen.

"I would like to make this plaintiff's exhibit 1," Maureen said. "This is a note on stationery of the outpatient clinic of the Tufts University Hospital. Please look at it, Dr. Brennan, and tell me if this note is in your handwriting."

Jack gave the note a cursory look and returned it to Maureen. "It is."

"Good. This then is your note on a Mr. Todd Schafer. Is that right?"

"It is a copy of my note." Said with a return of the smile.

"I am sorry. You are right. It is a copy of the note. I would like you to read your note into the record."

Jack started out, "This is a 22-year-old student who is referred for a neurologic evaluation. . . ."

"May I stop you at this point. Who referred Mr. Schafer to you?"

"I don't know. I assume Mr. Schafer was referred by the Student Health Service."

"Are you sure?"

"Yes."

"Then I would like to show you Mr. Schafer's medical notes from the Student Health Service."

"Just a minute!" Handelsman held out his hand, and without hesitating Maureen handed him two sheets of medical notes, each entry stamped with its date and "Tufts University Student Health Service." Wordlessly, Handelsman returned the sheets to Maureen.

"I would like to make this plaintiff's exhibit 2," Maureen resumed, "Now, Dr. Brennan, may I ask you to look at these sheets and tell me whether you see any indication that Mr. Schafer was referred to you for a neurologic evaluation."

"No." Said after an extensive pause.

"In fact, these notes do not reflect any illness that could be construed to be neurologic. Is that correct?"

"Yes."

"Then who did refer Mr. Schafer to you?"

"I don't know."

"You don't?"

"Objection," Handelsman jumped in. "Miss Durrell, I do not want you to argue with this witness."

Maureen ignored the interruption.

"Dr. Brennan, do you know a Dr. Lee Choi?"

"Objection. This question is irrelevant. It has nothing to do with the medical history of Todd Schafer. And that is the sole topic of Dr. Brennan's deposition."

"As you will see shortly, it has everything to do with Todd Schafer." Maureen responded. "Would you like me to repeat my question, Doctor?"

Jack hesitated.

"Dr. Choi's title was research neurologist, Tufts University School of Medicine," Maureen continued. "Does that refresh your memory?"

"Dr. Choi worked for a time in my laboratory."

"Who provided Dr. Choi's salary?"

"The university."

"All of it?"

"No."

"What percentage of Dr. Choi's salary was provided by Tufts University? If you know."

"I don't know."

"If I told you that it was only five percent, would that be grossly incorrect?"

"Probably not."

"Then from what source did you obtain the other 95 percent of Dr. Choi's salary?"

"I don't remember."

Maureen had expected this remark. She flipped through her notebook and produced a sheet.

"I would like this to be marked as plaintiff's exhibit 3. Would you agree with me that $40,000, or 95 percent of Dr. Choi's salary, came out of a grant to you from Marat International, and that Tufts University only provided you with Dr. Choi's medical insurance and various other minor benefits."

"Wait a minute!" Handelsman shouted. "What are you reading from?"

"Tufts University Form 34-271. Record of Extramural Grants."

"Let's see it."

"It'll be my pleasure." She handed Handelsman a copy of the form. He glanced at it.

"I would like to take a break," he said. "Dr. Brennan and I will need to confer."

"As long as you wish."

Handelsman and his entourage left the room with Jack Brennan. The court reporter leaned back, closed her eyes, and massaged her hands. So far, so good, Maureen thought. Peter Carter and Chris Bartlett had done a good job and had done it quickly. But the hard part was still to come.

A few minutes later everyone returned to the conference room and resumed their places. Maureen turned to the court reporter.

"Will you read the pending question?" The court reporter did as directed, and Jack agreed that 95 percent of Dr. Choi's salary came from a grant from Marat International.

"Now, Dr. Brennan, what were Dr. Choi's duties in return for this salary?"

Jack hesitated and looked at Handelsman, whose face remained impassive. Bruce Crawford and Ann Townsend were taking notes. Jack took the small nickel-plated pointer from the breast pocket of his white coat, briefly extended it to about ten inches, and then with a quick movement of both hands returned it to its original size.

"He worked on the Phase I studies of MI-37801."

"Was this under your direction?"

"Yes."

"Would you please explain to us what are Phase I studies?"

With an abrupt movement of his hands, Jack placed the pointer diagonally on the table in front of him, then proceeded to explain the nature and intent of the Phase I studies.

"Then I gather these studies were intended to ensure the safety of the drug subsequently called Dulcian?"

"Yes."

"And this drug was tested on healthy volunteers?"

"Yes."

"All right, then I will direct you to read the rest of your note on Todd Schafer into the record."

Jack proceeded to read a description of the young man's outbursts and erratic behavior.

"Is it not true that Dr. Choi referred this young man to you because he was concerned with these symptoms and wanted you, as his supervisor, to examine him?"

"I don't remember."

"I see. Now let's look at the last few lines of your medical note. What was your final diagnosis on Mr. Schafer?"

"I did not have a final diagnosis. I wrote down a differential diagnosis."

"And what was your differential diagnosis?"

"It was epileptic disorder, atypical episodic discontrol, or drug reaction."

"And because you suspected an epileptic disorder, you obtained an electroencephalogram?"

"I did."

"And that subsequently was found to be normal?"

"It was."

"And that excluded an epileptic disorder?"

"Not completely."

"But for all intents and purposes?"

"Yes."

"That left you with the diagnoses of atypical episodic discontrol and a drug reaction. What drug reaction did you have in mind?"

"A reaction to a chronic intake of yohimbine."

"And where in your notes do you see anything about a chronic intake of yohimbine?"

"In my follow-up note. I will read it: 'Patient admits to a chronic intake of yohimbine.' I obtained this information on Mr. Schafer's return visit."

"But that was two weeks after you had already made a differential diagnosis of a drug reaction. Correct?"

Jack once again extended the pointer and returned it to its original size. There was savagery in the movements of his hands and wrists.

"I am waiting for your answer," Maureen said carefully.

"You will have to answer," Handelsman said.

"Yes."

"So then. When you put down 'drug reaction' on the list of diagnoses at the time Mr. Schafer saw you for the first time, what drug did you have in mind?"

"Yohimbine."

"But at that time you had not obtained any history of yohimbine intake. Correct?"

"This is absolutely ridiculous," Jack exploded. "You are trying to make me out to be a liar."

"I am simply trying to obtain an answer to my question. What drug did you have in mind when you wrote 'drug reaction' in your list of differential diagnoses?"

"I suppose you want me to say it was Dulcian."

"Was it?"

"No. Of course not. We encountered no adverse reactions on any of the subjects in our Phase I study."

"Are you certain?"

"Absolutely."

"How many subjects did you include in the Phase I study of MI-37801, later known as Dulcian?"

"I don't remember."

"I will be happy to refresh your memory, Doctor." Maureen pulled out a copy of the material that Marat had submitted in support of their application to the Food and Drug Administration. Jack quickly took the sheet from her, too quickly for Handelsman to ask to see it. From the fact that Jack's hands were quivering, Maureen knew she was on the right track.

"There were 58 subjects who were reported to the FDA as being included in the Phase I study. Is that correct?"

"Yes."

"Thank you. And these subjects were identified by you as I-1 to I-58. Right?"

"Right."

"I now would like to show you a printout from a database that contained the information subsequently submitted to the Food and Drug Administration."

"Wait a minute," Handelsman said. "Not so fast. Where did you get this printout?"

"From a disk given to me by the late Dr. Kleinwort. Another copy of this database was kept in Dr. Ailesly's tobacco tin—the one with a picture of Carlisle Castle, and the one his murderer removed at your behest."

Handelsman jumped up. "Are you accusing me of murder?"

"Of course not. Not even of obstruction of justice or spoliation for hiding crucial evidence. Now, Dr. Brennan, if I may ask you to look at this printout. How many cases are in this database?"

"Fifty-nine."

"Thank you. Now I would like you to look at some of the subjects in this printout. Can you show me subject number I-15?"

"Here."

"And where is subject I-17?"

"Here."

"Thank you. And where is subject I-16?"

"This is totally preposterous!" Jack slammed the pointer against the table. "I refuse to let this woman insult me! I am going back to my office!"

Handelsman placed his hand on Jack's wrist. "You cannot terminate this deposition. It is being held under court order."

"Fuck court order!"

Maureen acted as if she had not heard. "Now, Dr. Brennan, I will show you the printout of I-16. This contains the data of the subject whom you removed from the study because he developed an adverse event to Dulcian. Would you like to look at it?"

"No."

"Then I will present you with the pertinent data. Subject identification Number: I-16. Male. Aged 22. No history of prior drug intake. At the time you saw him, Mr. Schafer was a male, aged 22. With no history of prior drug intake. Correct?"

"I refuse to answer." Jack's face was flushed, and there was perspiration on his forehead and temples.

"Are you pleading the Fifth Amendment, Doctor?"

There was no response. Maureen repeated her question. There was no reply.

"You will have to answer, yes or no," Maureen said. When Jack continued to remain silent, she added, "You may wish to confer with counsel. Shall we go off the record?"

"Come on outside," Handelsman told Jack. He turned to Bruce and Ann. "You two stay here."

Several minutes passed in total silence. Bruce got up and stretched. Ann stared blankly at the yellow lined pad in front of her. Finally Jack Brennan and Handelsman returned.

"I am going to put in a call to Judge Watson," Handelsman said. "Ask him to terminate the deposition at the request of the deponent. I suppose you will object."

"Not at all," Maureen said sweetly. "However, I would like to append one more document to the deposition. What exhibit will this be?"

"Plaintiff's exhibit 4," the court reporter said.

"This is a copy of a memorandum from Dr. Albert Lessing to R.J. Crowley. Subject: FDA application, MI-37801." She handed the printout to Handelsman. He read through it.

"Where on earth did you get this from?"

"Certainly not from Marat. Even though you were under court order to produce all documents pertinent to this case."

"How did you get this?"

"I have my ways."

"You are unbelievable!" Said with a touch of admiration.

"Thanks."

Handelsman put through a call to Judge Watson, and a few minutes later Jack Brennan's deposition was terminated at the request of the deponent.

"I'll give you a call," Handelsman said, as everyone filed out of the Harper Conference Room.

"Be my guest. You have my number."

* * *

"I can't believe how well it went." A drink in her hand, Maureen was stretched out on the couch in Dan's apartment. She had just finished relating the outcome of Jack's deposition. "That man fell apart in front of my very eyes."

"I'll drink to that."

With her eyes closed, Maureen sipped from her glass.

"Now what?" Dan asked.

"I imagine I'll hear from Handelsman. Sooner or later."

"By the way, I read in the paper that the police decided that Kleinwort did kill Ailesly."

"Not a chance."

"Do you think Handelsman knows who did?"

"I doubt it."

The phone rang. "That wouldn't be him, would it?"

When Dan picked up the phone, it was not Handelsman, but Marty.

"I must talk to you!"

"What's wrong? You sound upset."

"There are lots of things you should know about. Can we get together first thing in the morning?"

Marty gave a quick laugh. "For you I'll make it at ten. I'll come to your office."

"Fine with me."

"What do you think this is all about?" Maureen asked.

"I don't have the faintest idea. I've heard that he has been acting quite strange lately. How about dinner?"

"Sounds great to me, but I want it to be someplace special."

"How about La Toque?"

"Why not? If you think you can afford it." She smiled, and her smile, the first genuine one in many weeks, prompted Dan to give her a long hug.

\* \* \*

While Dan and Maureen were sitting over dinner at La Toque, Handelsman was in his office trying to reach Warren Berrich. He finally succeeded in tracking him down to his beach house on Long Island. In a few well-chosen sentences—Handelsman had the gift of quickly summarizing the most complex information—he brought the Marat in-house counsel up to date on the outcome of Jack's deposition.

"We have problems," Berrich said simply.

"Quite a few."

"Why don't you fly out and I'll arrange for all of us to meet with R.J."

The following morning, after a twice delayed and bumpy cross-country flight, Allan Handelsman sat slumped in a red leather chair in R.J. Crowley's office. He was bleary-eyed—a quick shower at the May's Landing Holiday Inn had done little to wake him up—but his mind was quite intact. R.J.'s office was sumptuous and remarkable for its collection of French Impressionist paintings, a late eighteenth century ormolu clock, and an immense antique Kirman carpet. The view from the windows was of a misty morning, with the coastline lost in heavy overcast. As they awaited R.J.'s appearance, Al Lessing, Warren Berrich, and Melvin Walton were sipping coffee; Handelsman had asked the secretary to bring him a glass of water.

A few minutes after the appointed time, the president and C.E.O. of Marat International strode into the room, sat down, and poured himself a cup of decaf coffee.

"So where are we?" he started out.

Handelsman filled him in with the details of Jack Brennan's deposition and its various legal implications.

"We have a problem," Berrich said. "Even if it is our position that Dr. Brennan bore sole responsibility for the Phase I studies. The memo. . . ."

"I am aware of the memo," R.J. interrupted. "So, then, Allan, what do you see as our options?"

"I would suggest settling the case. I would not like to see it go any further. Dr. Brennan's testimony would be quite damaging to us."

"We could make Dr. Brennan unavailable," Berrich suggested.

"I don't want to take that chance. He is much too high profile to even consider such an idea." R.J. turned to Handelsman. "What would it take to get these people off our backs?"

Allan did some quick mental calculations. "About eighty-five million."

"Marat could declare bankruptcy," Berrich said. "Like Johns Manville did after the judgment in the asbestos cases."

"I refuse to even consider this alternative. Marat is not Johns Manville," R.J. rapped out. "I am prepared to accept your figure, Allan. Eighty-five million is about seven cents per share. It will mean that we will have a profit of three dollars and ten cents for the first quarter of next year instead of the projected three dollars and seventeen cents. We should be able to compensate for that easily by the end of the second quarter."

Dr. Lessing nodded in agreement. R.J. turned to him. "Now then, Al, what do you suggest we do with Dulcian?"

"Derek Osborne tells me that it looks as if these reactions are not due to Dulcian itself but are the result of a contaminant that crept into the synthetic process."

"How easy will it be to remove that contaminant?"

"Derek does not know yet. It might take months."

"Should we have him join us? He could fill us in on the details," Berrich said.

"I would prefer not to. It is best that we remain a small group," R.J. responded. "There'll be less chance for any leaks. So what do you propose we do in the meantime?" When R.J. did not obtain an immediate answer, he continued, "Anyone have any idea what the incidence of this adverse reaction is?"

"Plaintiffs claim that there are now some two hundred litigants in their class action suit," Handelsman said.

"No more?"

"I won't vouch for the exact figure."

"Two hundred out of one million who have taken Dulcian is one in five thousand. Right?"

The group nodded.

"I consider this an acceptable figure. At least for the time being. But how do we make sure there won't be any more?"

"There probably will be," Handelsman said. "Unless Dulcian is taken off the market."

"We would have to do this in such a way as to not impair Marat's image in the eye of the public," Melvin Walton said. He had been staring into his coffee. R.J. leaned back.

"Earlier this morning I had an extensive conversation with Dennis Wilson."

"Who is he?" Handelsman whispered to Melvin, who was sitting next to him.

"C.E.O. of Delta Health and Property Insurance," Melvin returned the whisper.

"Dennis is extremely supportive of us in our aim to develop a safe and easily administered drug for the treatment of depression. He already has noted that Dulcian has had a significant impact on his company's efforts to curtail medical payouts." He turned to Al Lessing. "Do we have anything in the pipelines to replace Dulcian?"

"The Japanese are just about ready with a drug that is related to trazodone."

"I don't give a hoot about the Japanese! I am asking you whether there's anything of ours that's on the horizon."

Al Lessing went into some detail about a new drug, MI-54912, which had shown considerable promise as an antidepressant. R.J. listened with hands tented in front of his mouth.

"When do you think this drug will be ready?"

"We should start our Phase I studies by the beginning of next year."

"Good, good. Allan, I would like you to negotiate a settlement. I want to have you get the judge to seal all records, evidence, depositions, and details of the settlement, and make plaintiffs' agreement to that condition a prerequisite for the settlement. Is that clear?"

"Yes," Handelsman said.

"In the meantime I want you, Melvin, to initiate a campaign to educate both the public and physicians on the merits of Dulcian. Minimize its side effects and stress its benefits—prevention of suicides, prompt return to family and workplace . . . you understand."

"Yes. A risks versus benefits campaign."

"Then I can leave this in your hands. There is another avenue I have started to work on," R.J. continued. "I have had preliminary discussions with Senator Derkin. He has agreed to sponsor a bill that should help us avoid any future problems. The way he has drafted it, it calls for the following." Using his fingers, R.J. enumerated the points of the bill. "First, we will be allowed to use compliance with FDA standards as a defense for future lawsuits. Next, we will be allowed to name the scientists who are going to review for the FDA the safety and effectiveness of our new drugs. Finally, the bill is intended to put a cap, that is to say a maximum, on the amount of damages a jury may award in any similar cases. I am quite certain that all of the major pharmaceutical companies will support this legislation, and Dennis has assured me that not only Delta but also all the other health insurance carriers will lobby for it. Once that bill is signed into law, it should preclude our having to confront a similar situation with Dulcian or with any of our other products."

There was a general murmur of approval.

"I think we have dealt with the most pressing issues. Any other business?" When there was no response, R.J. rose from his chair.

"Thanks for flying out on such short notice," he said to Handelsman.

"I am sorry we could not do any better."

"You did your best," R.J. said, and patted him on the shoulder. "That's all we can expect from anyone." He looked around. "Right?"

Everyone agreed. End of meeting.

\* \* \*

When Dan arrived at his office shortly after ten, Marty was already waiting for him.

"Did Brenda offer you some coffee?"

"She did, but I am off coffee for the time being. It makes me short-winded."

"You are getting old," Dan said lightly.

"Don't remind me."

Dan sat down and gave a quick glance at the telephone slips, which Brenda had set out on his desk.

"So what's on your mind?" he asked.

"I want you to look at a copy of a letter I have just sent to Al Lessing at Marat." He handed Dan two sheets of paper, which had been stapled together. Dan started to look at it.

"You can read it later," Marty said. "In essence I am telling them that I have reported to the FDA a number—five to be exact—of major adverse reactions to Dulcian and that I no longer can function as their university monitor."

"Wow!" Dan heard himself and thought he sounded like Maureen.

"This letter also describes the nature of these adverse reactions, and they are, as you might guess, quite similar to those that you and Carter described in your paper in the *Journal of Clinical Neuropsychology*."

"What are you going to do?"

"I have accepted an exciting offer from Nitansha Pharmaceuticals. Vice President of Discovery Research. I will be based in Brazil. I will have the opportunity to design my own laboratories with three times the space and three times the support I have here."

"Congratulations."

"It'll be a lot of hard work, but I feel certain that I was destined for this position. If ever you feel like a change of scenery, drop me a line. I can probably find you something interesting." He paused and looked around Dan's office as if he were comparing it with the office that he would receive from Nitansha.

"What about Jeanette?"

"I am going to work on her to join me down there. If she won't. . . ."

With a quick movement he got up. "I've got to get going. There are a million things left to do."

"Have you told Jack?"

"I've left a message with his administrative assistant. He hasn't been in for a few days. Probably out of town for one thing or another."

Dan did not enlighten him. It would have been too complicated.

"By the way," Marty said, as he was about to leave, "I got a letter from Harry yesterday. He's my youngest. He hates Boston—it's much too cold—and he wants to come and live with me in Brazil. What do you think of that?"

Dan thought of the scowling rebel in the happy family photo in Marty's office.

"He's a rebel," he said.

"He always was."

* * *

For several days following his return from New Jersey, Handelsman had been despondent. As if he were on automatic pilot, he had met with Maureen, and the two had made the necessary arrangements to settle the class action suit. Even though Mike had been discharged from University Hospital, he had absented himself from the meeting on the advice of his doctors.

"Eighty-five million is a nice figure," he said when Maureen came to his house to report to him. He was sitting in the TV room, wearing a dark red paisley robe. "You've done a great job, girl, and I'll make sure your Christmas bonus will reflect that."

"Thanks." Mike would probably keep on calling her "girl," even after she had become full partner in the firm.

She went off to the Federal Building to tie up various loose ends.

For his part, Handelsman took himself to the library of the Kabbalah Center. For several years he had been working on a book, which he had tentatively entitled "Ethical Aspects of the Kabbalah," and he had frequented the library whenever he had managed to set aside an hour or two.

That evening he was reading a passage from one of the medieval rabbis: "When the people of Israel are worthy, which they obtain by performance of the commandments, they add to the divine power and glory; when they transgress they weaken it."

He paused and, having placed his finger inside it, closed the book. He asked himself whether he had transgressed the commandments. If so, when and how?

As he considered the question, Allan saw a woman two tables away from him. She was reading and at times making notes in a spiral notebook. She was fair-haired, slender, and graceful, with a good figure and strong, vital eyes. Allan was unable to take his eyes off her. Finally he got up and went to the librarian.

"Do you know the woman by the window?" He was embarrassed by the directness of his question.

"No. But she has been coming in quite frequently."

Finally, there was nothing left but for him but to take the bull by the horns. He went up to her table.

"I sorry to disturb you, but would you like to have a cup of coffee with me?"

The woman looked at him. After a few seconds' hesitation, she nodded.

"I was just about ready to take a break." She closed book and notebook, pushed back her chair, and got up.

"I am Allan Handelsman."

"Good to meet you. I am Judith Lerner. Shall we go down to the cafeteria?" As Allan followed her down the stairway, he admired her shapely legs.

A few days later, Dan received a call from Judith.

"I am getting a divorce. I've decided it's about time I drew a line under my past."

"Really?"

"I knew you would be surprised. You see, I have met a man . . . quite a prominent attorney. . . ."

"I don't want to hear. . . ."

* * *

"So what are you going to do with yourself?" Maureen asked Dan. They had just left Cosgrove and Costello's Christmas party at the Century Club and were having a late snack in the Ambassador Grille. The evening had been upbeat. Mike had returned to work, and even though details of the Marat settlement could not be released, everyone at the firm knew that they had been extremely favorable.

"I don't think I am cut out to do research. I am getting quite used to going out to Las Virgenes. And with Jack having gone on an extended sabbatical and Colin Pearson taking over the department, things are settling down for me."

"That's great."

"What about you?"

"Mike has offered me a partnership. . . ."

"Cosgrove, Costello, and Durrell. . . ."

"Right. But I don't think I want to accept his offer. At least not for the time being."

"No?"

"I've decided to have a baby. It's an experience I don't want to forego. And I would like you to be its father." She paused and smiled. Her eyes were twinkling and she looked beautiful. "Mind you, I am not asking you to marry me."

"I understand. I still feel I am on the verge of a commitment."

"It's about time you made a commitment. . . ."

Dan reflected. He looked at the remnants of his hamburger and the half-empty glass of diet Pepsi. Hope lay elsewhere.

"I want us to stay together," he said. "You are too important to me."

"So?"

"I'll accept your offer."

"Good. I thought you would. I've gone off the pill. From tonight on it'll be for real."

"Your place or mine?"

"Whatever," Maureen said.

We shall let her have the last word.

\* \* \* \* \*